WHEN WILL YOU RAGE?

Edited by Stewart Wieck

D1598384

Table of Illustrations

Moon Claw by SCAR (Antoinet Ryder and Steve Carter) 4

Female Ahroun by Ron Spenser 20

Brawl by Ron Spenser 34

Glass Walker by Jeff Rebner 56

Wendigo Galliard by John Bridges 100

Honor by Dan Smith 122

Rage by Matt Korteling 148

Crinos Shadow Lord by Dan Smith 162

On the Hunt by Dan Smith 186

Cub by Ron Spensser 210

Black Fury Crinos by Ron Spenser 232

Gaia's Warrior by Dan Smith 244

Banes by SCAR 262

City Hunter by John Bridges 280

Skinner by Jeff Rebner 296

Growl by SCAR 330

Challenge by Ron Spenser 358

Fighting the Wyrm by SCAR 384

Mixed Heritage by Dan Smith 422

Contents

The Waters of Lethe by Bill Bridges   5

Coyote Full Moon by Sam Chupp   21

A Sheep in Wolf's Clothing by Vincent Courtney   35

Transitions by Nigel D. Findley   57

Fang of the Wolf by Owl Goingback   101

Hunter's Blues by Scott Ciencin   123

The Bye-Bye Club by Ray Winninger   149

Wolf Trap by Richard Lee Byers   163

Predator and Prey by David Chart   187

Lone Werewolf by Lois Tilton   211

Shards by Phil Brucato   233

A Day Off by Thomas Kane   245

Little Flea by Scott Urban   263

A Wolf in Shepherd's Clothing by Edo van Belkom   281

For Auld Lang Syne by James A. Moore   297

A Third World by Graham Watkins   331

A Useless Death by Don Bassingthwaite   359

Calley's Story by Alara Rogers   385

Trickster Moon by J. S. Banks   423

Lexicon   438

The Waters of Lethe

by Bill Bridges

Doctor Murry F. Bruckner scribbled more notes onto his pad, put his pen down, and looked over at his patient. The man was lying on the couch looking uncomfortable and nervous. It was only the patient's second therapy, and he was still unsure of the process. Doctor Bruckner cleared his throat.

"Ahem. Are you ready, Mr. Barnes?" he asked.

Mr. Barnes breathed deeply. "Yes. Go ahead. We might as well start now."

"All right. It really is for the best, Mr. Barnes. I'm sorry: Charles."

"That's not my real name, you know. I just pulled it from a phone book."

"Yes, I know. But let's use it for now, as if it had meaning. All right?"

Mr. Barnes was silent for a moment, then responded in a low voice. "Okay."

"Charles, have you thought more about your dream from last time?"

"Yes. But I've had another, stranger, dream."

"Oh? Does this one seem more important to you than the last one?"

"Yeah. I guess so."

"Then let's talk about it. What happened in this dream?"

"I — I was standing on the street, outside the hospital. The hospital was dark, evil. There was no light. I. . . knew that. . . *things* moved in there. I had to get away. So I ran. I ran all the way here, to your office. But this building was dark also. I was worried. Something was behind the door. I didn't want to go in."

"Something? What kind of thing?"

"I don't know. It was evil."

"Was it an animal? A lizard or mammal? A person?"

"It was all three, I don't know."

"Did any of it seem familiar to you?"

"Yes. The *things*. I've met them before."

"In other dreams? You remember these dreams?"

"No, not in dreams. In real life."

"Hmm. I think perhaps your memories of dreams and actual events is somewhat confused. But it's a good sign. At least some memories are coming back."

"No. I'm sure it was real. It wasn't a dream before."

"Charles, dreams can have an amazing pull on our psyches, especially upon a wounded psyche such as yours. You're suffering an advanced case of amnesia. You are desperate to have your memories — your life, your identity — back. In such an instance, I'm not surprised fantastic dreams seem so real, as if they actually happened."

"Then how do you explain the weird shit in every dream I've had for the past three weeks?!"

"Calm down. As I said before, it's either a reaction to whatever caused your traumatic amnesia, the psyche's attempt to make you deal with it by veiling it in symbols and mythic images, or perhaps you were a science fiction writer, and these images are things from your stories."

"Wait — that seems close. I almost remembered something when you said stories. Maybe that's it. Maybe I do write stories."

"You see. No cause for alarm. Our session is almost over. I want to see you again this Friday. Realize that our task in these sessions is to awaken the memory. You've drunk from the waters of Lethe, to use a classical metaphor for amnesia. But nothing is ever really forgotten; it's all in there somewhere." Bruckner tapped his head as he said this. "In the meantime, I recommend you go to the library or bookstore, to see if anything seems familiar. Who knows? Maybe you'll find a book or two you wrote."

Charles tried to fake a smile, but Bruckner wasn't fooled.

• • •

"Now," said the psychologist. "Tell me what happened in your dream last night."

Charles stared up at the ceiling as he spoke. "They're killing me: the dreams. I wake up every night sweating and shaking. I swear they're real — or at least they seem to be."

"Have you seen the 'things' yet, or do they still lurk outside your vision?"

"No. I haven't seen them. But I heard something new: a bark — a dog barking somewhere in the distance."

"From what direction?"

"Huh? I don't know. It was just far off."

Bruckner wrote something down on his pad. "Anything else?"

"No, just the same dream for a week now — except for the bark."

"Yes, the bark. Interesting. Do you recall ever owning a dog?"

"I don't remember. Maybe I did. I do like dogs."

"Oh? How do you know?"

"Well, I pet them when I see them. They seem to like me too."

"Good. Good. I like them too. I have a few myself. A setter and a beagle. What about the fiction? Have you looked in any stores to see if you recognize any books?"

"Yes. But I don't recognize anything. I don't think I've read anything in those stores."

"Really? Not even Huck Finn?"

"What?"

"*The Adventures of Huckleberry Finn* by Mark Twain. Ring any bells?"

"No. Is it a bestseller?"

"Sort off. Just about all American schoolboys are required to read it sometime in their education. So, either you did not have conventional schooling or your memory loss is still chronic."

"I guess so. I still don't remember anything."

"Well, just try those exercises I gave you; the memory tests. Perhaps by next week we'll have seen some progress."

"Okay. Thanks." Charles rose from the couch and headed for the door.

"Goodbye, Mr. Barnes," Bruckner said.

• • •

"Oh, God. I don't know what's going on anymore!" Charles cried.

"Get ahold of yourself," Bruckner said, sitting Charles on the couch. "Let me get you some water. Just sit down and tell me what happened."

Charles buried his head in his hands as Bruckner poured some water from a decanter into a glass and brought it over to him. He looked up and accepted the water. "Thanks."

"All right. From the beginning," Bruckner said, sitting in his chair and arranging his notebook.

"One of those things attacked me. And it wasn't a dream."

"What?! When was this? Where?"

"Outside the hospital. Last night. I was walking to the market when it jumped out of the bushes. God, it had huge teeth and claws, like a bear's. It was dripping pus and screaming at me! Oh, God, I—"

"Stop it! Don't let yourself get carried away by this. It was obviously a hallucination. Brought on, perhaps, by the stress of your situation. Maybe you shouldn't go near the hospital any—"

"Doctor, it wasn't a hallucination! Look. . ." Charles pulled back his right sleeve, revealing three huge, closely spaced gashes across his arm. They appeared to be infected.

"Good God! Have you seen a doctor about this?"

"No. I was afraid. I just ran. I couldn't go back there. It's waiting for me."

Bruckner got out of his chair, moving over to look at the arm more closely. The injury appeared to be claw marks from some animal. The wound was too jagged, too irregular for a knife injury.

"I've got to get you some help," Bruckner said.

"Doctor, it's not my arm I need help with. It's my sanity. What's happening to me? You said the thing was just a dream, but it attacked me."

"Nonsense! Don't fall into that pit! You've been attacked by a wild animal, perhaps escaped from the zoo. Certainly not by a creature from your dreams!"

"But, it was so real."

"Of course it was. Your in the grip of an archetypal image, perhaps even your shadow. We must change our tactics somewhat. I hadn't thought your condition was so severe. I think we should try hypnotism."

"Will that work? I thought that was just hocus pocus."

"It can be a very effective tool when used with skill and understanding. It is a tool of discovery, not control. May we try it?"

"I've got nothing to lose. Why not? When should we start?"

"Right away. I see no reason to delay. If it can help calm you and release you from the grip of whatever unconscious content holds you in its sway, it can only help us now. Now, lie back and breath deeply."

Charles did as Bruckner told him and immediately calmed down. Bruckner pulled his watch and chain from his vest — an old, but effective standard in hypnotism. "All right. Stare closely at the watch. As it swings, you will be getting very sleepy."

Bruckner went through the whole routine. In minutes, Charles was in a deep, hypnotic state. "Now, Charles, when I snap my fingers, you will awaken. You will remember only what is good from our talk, not what is bad. Only what is good, what you want to remember, not what is bad, not what hurts to remember. Nod if you understand."

Charles nodded.

"Good. Now, let's go into your memories, your deep memories, the ones you have not been able to access recently. Can you do that? Nod if you can."

Charles nodded.

"Good. Now, Charles, what is your real name?"

Charles thrashed on the couch, but then calmed down. "Holds-Their-Songs," he replied.

"Holds-Their-Songs? Is that your name, Charles, or what you were told to do?"

"My name," Charles said. "And what I was told to do."

Bruckner looked perplexed and wrote some things down on his pad.

"Let's go farther back, to your childhood. Do you remember your name then?"

"Yes."

"What was it?"

"Daniel."

"Daniel? Was that your full name? Did you have a last name also?"

"Robertson."

"Did you have a happy childhood, Daniel?"

"No."

"Oh? Why not? What was bad about it?"

Daniel began to thrash about on the couch again, still hypnotized. He began to growl low and menacing.

"Why are you growling, Daniel?"

"Angry! Like a dog!"

"Why like a dog, Daniel?"

"I am a dog!"

"I thought you were a boy?"

Charles wrinkled his brow in confusion and squirmed on the couch.

"Aren't you a boy, Daniel, not a dog, but a boy?"

Silence for a moment. "Yes."

"What made you angry?"

"Hurt. Pain. Nobody understands."

"How old are you now, Daniel, when you feel this pain?"

"Thirteen."

"Don't the other kids feel the same, Daniel? Why is your pain special?"

"They don't! They don't understand! They hate me!"

"Why? Why do they hate you? Tell me why, Daniel."

Charles began swinging his arms about, contorting his face into a mask of animal menace. He growled loud and angrily.

"Stop! You are no longer Daniel but Charles, who does not remember the pain."

Charles was immediately still.

"All right, Charles. When did you get the name Holds-Their-Songs? How old were you then?"

"Twenty."

"Who gave you this name?"

"Celeste."

"Who is she? Your girlfriend?"

Charles growled threateningly.

"Stop. Be calm. Who was she?"

"Leader. Sept leader."

"Sept? What is that?"

"All of us."

"Who do you mean by us?"

"The other wolves."

"Wolves? Are you a wolf now?"

"Yes. No."

Bruckner scribbled more notes. "Why did Celeste give you this name?"

"So I would remember."

Bruckner was silent for a moment. "But you didn't remember. You don't remember their songs."

A tear ran down Charles's face, and he began crying.

"Why not? Why did you forget?" Bruckner asked.

"They are dead! All of them dead!"

"Who? Who are dead?"

"My pack. My pack."

"Your fellow wolves?"

"My fellow Garou."

"Garou? What does that mean?"

"The People."

"What kind of people?"

"Werewolves."

Bruckner didn't say anything for awhile. He looked down at his notes and over at his patient. He snapped his fingers. Charles blinked and looked around, as if coming out of a nap. He craned his neck around to look at the psychologist.

"Well? Did you find out anything?" Charles asked.

"Yes," Bruckner replied, looking out the window, not meeting Charles' eyes. "But. . . I need to think about it. Would you please come back at your usual time?"

"All right. Thank you, doctor," Charles said and headed for the door.

"Oh, Charles?" Bruckner said, not looking away from the window.

"Yes?"

"Get that wound looked at, will you? It's very bad. You never know what type of infection could get into it."

• • •

"Charles, I want to hypnotize you again. Is that all right?" Bruckner said.

"If you feel it's best, all right. But what did I say last time?" Charles asked, sitting in the couch again.

"Why don't we talk about that at the end of the session? I still have some unanswered questions."

Charles shrugged.

"Let's begin then." In a few minutes, Bruckner had Charles in a deep trance. He sat back in his chair and reached into his pocket, pulling out a small tape recorder. He pushed the record button and set it down with the microphone facing Charles.

"You are not Charles now, but Holds-Their-Songs. Who am I speaking to?"

"Holds-Their-Songs," Charles replied woodenly.

"Good. You said your pack was dead. How did they die?"

"The Wyrm killed them."

"Wyrm? What is that?"

"Dragon. Corruption."

Bruckner smiled and wrote something down on his pad.

"What do you mean by corruption? Have you done something corrupt?"

"No. The Wyrm is corrupt. I fight the corruption. Protect Gaia."

"Who is Gaia?"

"The Mother."

Bruckner smiled again. He wrote a small note in his pad. "This Wyrm. It tries to harm the Mother?"

"Yes. It tries to destroy Her."

"And you stand against it? You alone?"

"No. All Garou fight. My pack fought."

"They died in the fight. Where did they die?"

"Near oil factory. Gasoline smell. Foulness."

Bruckner wrinkled his brow. "When did they die?"

"One moon ago."

"One moon? One month?"

"Yes."

"Why didn't you die also?"

"Last standing. Escaped to spirit."

"What do you mean, 'escaped to spirit?'"

"Reached. Step sideways into spirit world."

Bruckner smiled once more. "So you retreated to a spirit world where they couldn't get you?"

"No. Retreated and ran. They are there also. Blights."

"So the corruption is in the spirit world also?"

"Yes."

"I want you to go back farther in your memories, to your childhood. I'm speaking to Daniel now. Daniel?"

"Yes?" Charles said, in a childish voice.

"When did your mother die, Daniel?"

"She's not dead."

"What about your father?"

"He's not dead."

"Daniel, did your father ever hit your mother?"

"No."

"Are your sure?"

"Yes. Why?"

Bruckner looked a bit annoyed. "Never mind. Daniel, have you ever done anything bad? Anything you wanted to forget and never remember?"

"Yes."

"What is that? Can you tell me?"

"I let my pack die," Charles said, in a deeper voice.

Bruckner looked annoyed again. "Is this Holds-Their-Songs now? Can you think of anything else? Any other bad things?"

"No."

"Tell me about the spirit world. Have you been there recently?"

"Yes, in my dreams."

"What about now, under hypnosis?"

"Yes. I'm here now. You are too."

"I am? Where am I? Where are we?"

"In a Chimera. A dream realm."

"Why? Why are we here? Why am I here with you?"

"You created it. The hypnosis."

"But I thought you went here in your dreams? They happened before I hypnotized you."

"Those were different places."

"Is there anything else here with us?"

Charles was quiet for a moment, as if thinking. Then he let out a low growl. "Yes — *it's* here. It followed me."

"Here? In the dream realm with us? Can you see it?"

"No. Sense it. Smell of Wyrm." Charles' voice was deeper, more menacing.

Bruckner squinted and stared at the couch and reached over to the lamp on his desk, which he pivoted and pointed toward Charles. Bruckner's eyes widened; Charles had grown larger. He was bulking his muscles up, stretching out, his feet hanging over the edge of the couch. Bruckner had seen contortionists before, but never this convincing. Charles was growling and thrashing his head about.

Bruckner began writing notes. He stopped for a moment, confused when a shadow moved across the wall. A shadow cast from behind him. He turned around and barely suppressed a scream.

Shuffling across the room on all fours, toward the couch, was a hideous beast, a slimy thing with spiked fur and huge fangs. Its fingers were razor sharp talons and it eyes gleamed with a greenish light. It ignored Bruckner and appeared to be sneaking up on Charles.

Bruckner stared in shock and dismay. As it got closer to Charles it drew back, about to strike. Bruckner shook his head, trying to clear it, and snapped his fingers.

Instantly, Charles woke up — but the thing was still there. It leapt at him, screaming. Bruckner yelled in horror as it landed on Charles and began to claw chunks of flesh from his torso. Charles screamed — and the scream became an animal howl of rage as his body instantly grew to almost twice its size, now covered in fur. His head was that of a wolf.

Bruckner sunk low in his chair, trying not to be noticed.

The werewolf and the shambling thing tore into each other. The thing seemed at a disadvantage now, no match for the towering werewolf and its jaws. In seconds, it screamed and disappeared, like wisps of smoke in a breezy room.

Charles — Holds-Their-Songs — stood panting and catching his breath. He turned to look at Bruckner; the psychologist was whimpering in the chair, curled up in a fetal position. Holds-Their-Songs shifted back into human form and walked over to him. Bruckner didn't seem to notice him; he just stared at the wall.

"I'm sorry," Holds-Their-Songs said. "But thank you. I know who I am now. I had forgotten. The pain of my loss drove me to forsake my birthright. But I am a Galliard, and it is my duty to remember the songs of those who fall in the battle against the Wyrm. You have helped me remember them today."

Bruckner showed no response whatsoever.

"Don't worry; I know you won't remember this yourself. The Chimera is gone now. It was only a temporary creation. The Banes won't bother you anymore. It was me they wanted."

Bruckner began to slowly rocking back and forth in the chair, still not responding.

Holds-Their-Songs took the tape recorder and removed the tape, putting it into his pocket. He took the doctor's notepad and tore out the pages with the session's notes. He looked at them for a moment and shook his head.

"Possible Oedipus Complex? Is that all the Wyrm is? I'm afraid not, doctor." He crumpled the notes, putting them in his pocket, then walked out the door, closing it quietly behind him.

Five hours passed, and it was dark before Bruckner finally came to his senses. He looked about, confused, stood up and stretched. He looked at his notepad for a clue as to why he fell asleep so early, but there were no notes for today; only the last notes he had taken when his patient, Charles, had claimed to be a werewolf. Bruckner couldn't suppress a strange shudder. He shook his head and walked over to his desk.

He should probably go ahead and file commitment papers for Charles, just in case. His problem was obviously deeper than amnesia. Any fool who thought he was a werewolf certainly had bigger troubles than a small-time psychoanalyst like Murry Bruckner could fix. Perhaps Edward Gorrel, over in Utah, could handle this. Bruckner recalled he had mentioned a case with a supposed "wolfman" once.

Christ, Bruckner thought, what if this was becoming a common psychosis? What could possibly trigger such a wide-scale derangement in modern society? It doesn't matter, Bruckner decided. That's for the experts to determine. I'll just take the small cases, thank you.

He walked over to the window and looked out. On the street below, a man was walking a large dog, which began barking as it passed the building. Bruckner shuddered again. He hated dogs.

Damned smelly, dangerous brutes. ///

Coyote Full Moon

by Sam Chupp

The howl echoed through Muir Woods, caught and dampened in tone and volume by the cloaking, surrounding fog. It was high, pure-voiced, and true, filled with hope and tinged with sadness. In the center of the caern, around young redwoods, a small, carefully tended fire blazed, and the moot of the Sept of the Western Eye was in progress.

"This is a good time, a time when the veil between worlds are thin, when our dead come to us and whisper secrets, when we honor those who have passed in the year past." Celeste Snowtop said quietly, her strong alto voice piercing the darkness. She was dressed as a Shining One, as the fog-totem Aeolus, having Opened the Sky to the four winds and the totem of the caern. She shook her braids. "For our Uktena friends, it is a time for change, for among them is a long-lost kin. I welcome Andraste Deathshadow, Ahroun, to our sept."

Able Heart, guardian of the sept, smiled as he looked at his charge. As he stood next to the tall, yellow-haired Andraste, her skin pale white and her eyes piercingly blue, he could hardly believe that just four weeks ago she had come to the sept claiming to be a lost cub of the Uktena. She was clearly not a Native American (she was Germanic in face and form), but she was heartily accepted by the Uktena at the caern, especially Silent Fist-that-Wins, the Master of the Challenge, and Sharon, who was the Keeper of the Land. It was amazing to him how easily she had learned the Ahroun Gifts he had taught her, how hungry for wisdom she was. She saw things from a spiritual perspective, which was not at all strange for the Uktena, but was very strange for an Ahroun.

The Howl of Welcome surrounded Andraste. Normally quiet and totally controlled in her emotions, Andraste bowed her head at this to accept the accord. She did not let them see her private tears. She wet the ground with them.

Suddenly, a brilliant, blue-white light filled the glade, shining through the young redwoods. Able Heart moved to the caern's center and stood in Crinos form next to Hot Eye, the Gatekeeper of the sept. Hot Eye said aloud, "I did not open this moon bridge. It is a Rite of Luna's Spear. They are breaking through uninvited."

At this, Able Heart directed the other Ahrouns to quickly take up their weapons and stand at the ready. There was silence in the glade as the moon Bridge formed its exit arch.

Hot Eye stood with his staff resting in both hands, contemplating the newcomers as the pale azure light from the bridge died away. Able Heart stood next to the Gatekeeper with his hand resting on the hilt of his great klaive.

Andraste stood in the rear with the other Ahrouns and watched the caern center. Standing in the clearing were three Garou wearing armor, chains, and leather. Two of them seemed identical even in the half-light of the fire: both of them carried huge battle-axes slung across their shoulders. The third was either in Glabro form, or was immense as a human, though shorter than the towering Crinos. He wore a large leather robe with a single, iron chain belt. The figure was bald with thick, immense arms, legs, and fingers. Andraste's breath caught as she saw the huge raven on the smaller one's shoulder and new, immediately, who they were: Tyr's Garou. The Patriarchy had found her.

The huge man spoke, his voice booming through the clearing. "*Guten nacht.* I am Jarg, Claw of Maug, Forseti of the Hand of Tyr, servant of the Get of Fenris. These are my honor guards Jeti and Geti. I apologize for our haste, but we have urgent business here. If you'll give us leave, we'll be off with no further interruption."

"Your business will await the Cracking of the Bone. We have opened the sky, and welcome you to revel in it with us," Celeste said, her no-nonsense tone clear and plain, even to Andraste's ears. Andraste smiled to herself as she realized the Sept Warder's attitude toward the Get: she was not pleased with their interruption. With no further words, the immense Philodox bowed and indicated to his guard to join the circle. They did so with a clanking of armor and chains, and stood silent as well with their master.

Andraste was filled with both fear and curiosity. She wanted to run far, away from the ironclad figures, for she knew what their presence here would mean. And yet, she needed to know for sure. She stood quietly, hoping that her traditional dress and the large full-moon symbol on her forehead would provide some camouflage.

Andraste watched as the raven was released from the Jarg's shoulder. It flapped up to a nearby redwood and stood, peering down at her. She fought the urge to growl at it.

Celeste finished the Opening of the Sky, holding her gourd rattle high in the air, closing her eyes and praying to Gaia for peace and strength. Then she brought the rattle down with a crack, and the entire moot changed suddenly. She was all business. She held the rattle up and in her sharp clear voice said, "The Cracking of the Bone! Now we come to the business at hand in our sept. We have visitors from far away. What do you wish of the Garou gathered here?"

"We have come seeking a fugitive from our justice. Her name is Andraste, also called Deathshadow. She has befouled her name, the honor of her tribe, and her pack has disowned her. Do you have her among your sept?" Jarg's voice was as harsh as rusted metal wind chimes.

There was a general commotion among the Garou assembled, until Celeste said, "Silence! We have that one among us. She stands there with her Uktena kin, among the other Ahrouns."

Jarg smiled quietly, showing tombstone teeth, and turned with the rest of the gathering toward Andraste. "You have blasphemed Fenris' ways! You have broken with the Sacred Path! You will be taken with us back to the Patriarchy and dealt with most severely, Theurge!" he said, an accusing finger pointing at her.

Jarg's guards moved two steps and positioned themselves in front of him, growling. They held silver shackles in their claws. Sharon, her Ragabash friend, had moved to her side, silently lending her strength. Andraste's eyes narrowed, and her rage boiled within her. She could not help but speak the truth to all those assembled.

"You are the ones who dishonored me! First lie to me about my birth, lead me to believe that I am something I'm not, then you — my fine Tribe — you repudiate me for trying to learn the secrets of my true moon!"

Jarg turned to Celeste briefly, in explanation. "She was a failure as a Theurge, Leader. The spirits would not come to her call, for they were frightened of her. She never meditated, never spent time with the wise elders. It is her own fault that she has failed. She was born under the crescent moon, but there are those among us who lied to her grievously, and this caused her to believe other than the truth."

Celeste put our her hand. "Wait! I am Truthcatcher here. This is going too fast for me. I call for a formal trial, here and now. I wish to know the root of this problem. Both of you, come over here and stand — and be still. Andraste, calm yourself, or I shall do it for you. On this full moon night, we cannot afford war in our own sept. Jarg, put your bodyguards over there with the rest of the Ahrouns. This is no time for fighting, nor is it time for chains. Our Master of the Challenge will see to your security."

With that, Silent Fist-that-Wins and two of his Ahrouns escorted the visiting Get to their warrior's circle, where they began to grumble and discuss the situation among themselves. Andraste stood to the side of them, quietly defying their claims even now.

The whole gathering relaxed a little as the trial was arranged in traditional formal style: the Truthcatcher in the center, the Defender, Andraste, to the left, and the Accuser, Jarg, to the right.

"Now, then, the trial is arranged. I'd like to ask Andraste a few questions. Realize that Gaia's truth is evident to me and I will know if you lie."

"Wait, *Madrone!* I have a request. I am asking that I be allowed to stand up for Andraste. She is my wolf-sister and I wish to speak for her. " Sharon turned to Jarg, by way of introduction: "I am Sharon Morning Cloud, the Keeper of the Land and a Ragabash."

Celeste turned to Andraste. "Do you wish her representation?" Andraste took a long look at Sharon, then looked back to Celeste. "Yes, she is my friend and knows my story."

Jarg shook his head slowly. "This is a strange trial, madam Leader. A Ragabash Advocate? Certainly you understand the authority of the Get in this instance. Their needn't be any trial."

Celeste turned sharply to Jarg. "We have not yet established that she is a Get, Jarg. She claims Uktena. Please be silent and let me ask the questions. Now, Andraste, when you came to us you claimed the Uktena as your tribe. Is this your true tribe?"

Sharon looked briefly at Andraste, nodding that she should answer. "No, Snowtop-rhya. I had hoped to become accepted by them eventually, but—"

"—but she chose to hide her true tribe. Did she also tell you she was Ahroun? That too, is a lie."

"Silence, Jarg! I will speak. You will listen. If you speak again, I will have to silence you."

Jarg bowed slowly.

"So, child, what is your true tribe? The tribe you were born in."

"I am a Valkyrie of Freya, of the Get."

Jarg growled low under his breath, but said nothing.

"So, you lied to us. Very well, that is for your own soul to deal with. What's this business about your auspice? Are you a Theurge? Or are you Ahroun, as you say?" Celeste asked, her irritation beginning to show.

Sharon spoke up. "I will speak for her. Snowtop-rhya, I believe firmly that Andraste is an Ahroun. Although she has been taught many of the Theurge Gifts, the crescent moon holds nothing for her."

Jarg's eyes got large. He spoke quietly, however. "Leader. Truthcatcher. I request that I be allowed to speak on this."

Celeste looked first to Sharon and then to Andraste and finally to Jarg. Quietly, she said, "You may speak, but speak to me. I catch the Truth. Confine your comments to peaceful words, if you can manage such."

Jarg strained visibly as he spoke. "One thing that many Garou do not know about the Get of Fenris is our ways concerning births. Although we have many Ahrouns, Fenris who is our Father does not see fit to make the bitches of the tribe warriors. This is part of the natural order — they must breed future Sons of Fenris. Our mothers cannot make war in this manner, or so Fenris has decreed. It is impossible that this one was born under the full moon, for Fenris does not allow that to occur. As we have said, she was born under the crescent moon, and there are elders who will swear to this fact."

Celeste nodded slowly. "Andraste has served as Ahroun to this sept, learning the Ahroun's Gifts. She seems well suited to it. Like you Sharon, I sense there is a deeper Rage within her. However, it is known that Theurges among the Get seem to have a greater Rage than most of their kind. It is their way, being war-shamans." Celeste looked again to Jarg. "You said that some among the Get lied to her about her auspice. Who were these?"

Jarg growled low. "These Valkyries that Deathshadow-yuf spoke of. They convinced her that she was Ahroun, and she grew discontent with her true Auspice. When she was not allowed to learn the Gifts of the Ahroun from our tribe, she fled. We have traced her here, and request that we be allowed to take her back to our sept for judgment. Only the Wyrm loves a coward, and the Get do not tolerate cowardice, for whatever reason."

"Pardon me, gentle warriors all. I speak to you as Theurge, for that is what I am. My name is March Lion. You talk as if Auspice is what you can change. But a wolf, she is born under the moon and it is only in one phase, not two. This human idea, that you can change your moon, it is foolishness."

Jarg smiled and bowed. "Indeed."

"So, then, it should be no trouble to ask Grandfather Wolf what moon shone in the sky of her birth, and thereby prove her to be Theurge or Ahroun. I will summon him, if the sept asks it," March Lion said, smiling a ragged smile.

Jarg looked uncomfortable. "I would not ask that of you, great Theurge. The Get merely wish to have our own returned to us. This is nothing to involve the Uktena with."

Able Heart spoke up, his low rumble echoing through the clearing. "The Uktena were involved when Andraste claimed to be of them. Now they will aid in resolving this question. I say let March Lion summon Wolf."

Celeste looked around the clearing, then back to the Get. "You will accept the judgment of the spirit of Grandfather Wolf?"

Jarg looked to his brothers and sketched a bow. "Yes. Fenris is our Father. How could we not?" He nodded briefly to Jeti, who put his hand over an iron mandala he wore. Still, sweat beaded on Jarg's brow and his teeth were clenched together in frustration.

March Lion closed his eyes and began to chant, and tossed a handful of dried herbs and special incense in the fire. The flames crackled and sparks spit up into the air. A tendril of smoke rose like a great snake into the night air. March Lion chanted in his native tongue and held up a single wolf's tooth to the moonlight. With a howl of

28 _When Will You Rage?_

his own he threw the wolf's tooth into the fire and brought his staff down with a crack.

There was silence amongst the fog. Then, as if in answer, another wolf howl was heard. The sound made all gathered there startle, and instantly want to answer back. The clearing rang with howls, the Get and even Andraste joining in. In respect many of those gathered took on Lupus form, silently waiting for the approaching spirit.

Then, without warning, a huge wolf sprang into the clearing. A huge beast, it slammed into Jarg and slammed him into the ground, despite the Get's immense bulk. The wolf's fangs were all at once around Jarg's neck, biting down.

"Who summons me?" The wolf demanded, not moving from its position atop Jarg. The two Get guards refused to move against their totem.

"I do, great Grandfather Wolf," March Lion spoke calmly. "There is a question concerning this Garou, here; the one they call Deathshadow, the one humans call Andraste."

Fenris' immense eyes and head swiveled over to look upon Andraste for the first time. "What of this one, who is most-favored of my children?" Fenris spoke in low, growling tones.

Celeste spoke up. "What moon shone in the sky when she was born, great Wolf? We must know."

Slaver dripped onto Jarg's face as the giant dire beast peered into Andraste's eyes. Terribly afraid, but unwilling to look away, Andraste met the beast's eyes and stood her ground, feeling her heartbeat pound against her chest.

Fenris turned aside and looked down at Jarg again. After a few seconds, he spoke. "She is of the full moon, one of the first of the Coyote moon pack, born to my Get." The huge spirit looked up at Geti and growled.

"Now, can you all leave this wolf alone? There is sleeping to do, and hunting. I will not be bothered again, or I will Rage!"

March Lion spoke up. "Then go to your rest, Grandfather Wolf. We thank you for your wisdom."

The great beast turned, slaver drooling from its mouth, and loped from the clearing like a dream stalking a nightmare. When his spectral form had vanished, Jarg slowly got to his feet.

"Jarg, I believe the judgment of Fenris is clear. Congratulations, you have a new Ahroun for your tribe. I'm sure you will accept Fenris' judgment if no one else's," Celeste said, her voice registering some of the humor she saw in the situation.

Jarg put out his hand. "No."

Andraste's voice was inhuman as her Rage took her over: "What do you mean, no? You just heard it straight from Fenris!" Her body shifted into Crinos much faster than Jarg had thought possible, and she sprang.

Geti leapt in front of his elder and grappled with Andraste, watching as her rage boiled within her. Andraste gnarled Geti's fur in her talons and ripped a hole in the guard. Geti brought a huge chain to bear and wrapped it across her shoulders, but Andraste did not feel the pain. Her talons were a hundred blurring knives as she applied attack after attack to weaken the warrior. Her Rage was tantamount, and he could not block the blows. Jeti made a few moves here and there to join the combat, but was stopped by stern looks from Able Heart and some of the other Ahrouns from the sept. This was a challenge, to their eyes.

Geti gambled on a high attack, trying to use his height in Crinos to an advantage, then discovered that Andraste had learned much already from some Ahroun. She had learned the trick of using her inner Rage to speed her shifting and suddenly took Lupus form as Geti towered down on her from above. She went into a roll that slammed into Geti's Crinos shins, and he fell face-forward onto the ground. With a single change into Hispo, she planted her talons on his back and bent to bite Geti firmly on the neck, threatening to tear out his throat.

Jarg crossed his arms. "Theurge Andraste. Let go of your brother's neck and come with us. I trust not Uktena sorceries or this sept any longer. You will come with us and accept the judgment of the tribe."

"Not so fast, you fat-assed, son of a bitch. You're not taking her anywhere she don't wanna go." Celeste was livid. This Get was everything she hated about the Garou. "I'm Sept Leader. You have no authority here. We have done your testing. She has even defeated one of your warriors. If you still do not accept her as an Ahroun, I cannot help you further. As far as this sept is concerned, she is of the full moon, and she will remain that way. This is my judgment, and so it shall be howled to every Garou in this land." Celeste's voice did not for once waver, even though it was clear that both Get were near their breaking point.

Jarg shook his head to his guard. "Release him!" he said to Andraste, who growled once, bit deep, and released Geti. Andraste scrambled off of him and once again took on human form, the scraps of her Uktena traditional garb hanging tattered and torn on her lean form. She suddenly felt the weight of a terrible force, words rising up inside of Jarg that would spell fate for her.

Jarg's face darkened. His demeanor became formal, cold. Jarg put his left hand on his right shoulder, his right hand on his left shoulder. "Then, though Ahroun you may be, Andraste Deathshadow, let that be your only comfort, for you will not be Get. I cast you out." Jarg turned on his feet, his back facing Andraste, his face away from her. The two other Get, Geti still bleeding, repeated the action, saying, "I cast you out."

Andraste felt the discommodation like a glass dagger broken off in her gut. "What? You can't — you can't do that to me! I was born a Get! You can't!" Sharon stepped to Andraste's side, took her hand, looked her in the eye. The Get stalked past them. Hot Eye had already opened the moon Bridge out of the caern by the time they got there and not a single other word was heard whispered among the assembled Garou.

As they vanished, Celeste said, "Thank you, Hot Eye."

"*No problema, Madrone*. I think they will have a good time in Los Angeles, no?" Hot Eye said with sarcasm in his voice. "Teach them to spear my caern."

Smiling, Celeste addressed the sept. "Now, my Garou, speak. Is there other business?"

March Lion nodded, bowed, and spoke. "I would like to tell a thing and ask a thing. First, the tale: I have moved among the Get before, and I know some of their secrets. I have seen a Get mother hide away their girlchild, so that she is not found to be born on the full moon. Many of these become their Galliards, or Philodoxes, or in some cases Theurges, for it is thought fitting that a woman be a Theurge among the Get. So you are not dishonored, Andraste, for you were not in control of what your mother did. Now, I would like to ask a formal thing. We, the Uktena, wish to say this: We would have Andraste, called Deathshadow, among us. We will adopt her as one of us. She is outcast, as we are so often, and she is great of spirit as well as Rage. We would ask her to come to us as an Ahroun. What say the sept?"

The howls of agreement echoed through the fog. Celeste said, "Thus ends the Cracking of the Bone for this night. And you, Hot Eye, will tell us a tale of the

Coyote moon pack that Fenris spoke of. What is this pack, Galliard? A pack not yet formed, but spoken of in legend?"

Hot Eye smiled and sang to them the verses of the Silver Record:

> "And the Last Days will see
> Coyote full moon pack: strong, wise,
> but strange in the ways of Gaia.
> Dare you trust them?
> Full moon reclaimed,
> half moon reborn,
> crescent returned,
> no moon revealed,
> they walk a new path
> and follow the old ways.
> They bring a new road
> and call up the old ones
> What will they do?
> Who can say?
> Wise they are, but hard is their road.
> Coyote's children are strange." ////

A Sheep in Wolf's Clothing

by Vincent Courtney

April 12, 1943

Sitting on the muddy ground, the little boy watched the man in the gray uniform gently place the blond-haired boy on the hood of his staff car. The man flipped the snap on his holster and pulled his Luger. He sauntered over to where a woman, the little boy's mother, stood waiting. He pointed the pistol at her. The man smiled, a death's-head grin, and pulled the trigger. It clicked once.

The boy's mother flinched and whispered a prayer.

It clicked twice.

She twitched. The man with the gun chuckled as he pulled the trigger a third time.

The barrel flashed smoke and fire. A red blossom bloomed on the mother's bare breast. She fell, a slow motion dance with death, and hit the ground by the edge of the pit.

The man laughed and sauntered over to her. She looked up at him and whispered, "Dieter."

The man in the uniform, still smiling, aimed a jackbooted kick into her face. Her head snapped back and she tumbled into the pit. He motioned to several of the stick men standing nearby to fetch her. They staggered into the pit and pulled her from the tangle of arms and legs. The man directed them to take the woman and place her in his staff car. He said she would make a fine jacket.

The man turned and stared at the little boy sitting on the ground. His eyes narrowed. He aimed the pistol and fired. The little boy felt a kick in his side and tumbled into the pit. The sound of the staff car speeding away was the last thing he heard before darkness overwhelmed him.

• • •

October 31, 1994

The white skull of an Ahroun moon peered from between slices in the mist. The fog bled across the San Francisco streets. Rivulets of murk spurted into alleys and surrounded the deserted buildings. Klaus Hurst stepped out into the street and took a deep bite of the damp, night air. He was pleased with how well the second moot had gone. Since his arrival in San Francisco from South America, a few new members had joined the new camp eager to fight the corruption of the Wyrm so strong in the city. One of them, a brash, young blonde named Dolph, challenged his leadership. The whelp said they needed a Jarl who was young and strong. Klaus changed his mind by spilling his guts onto the meeting room floor, and by doing so, the Garou named Sheep-Shredder reasserted his hold on the group.

Klaus heard footsteps rapidly approaching. Perhaps one of Dolph's friends was seeking vengeance. He turned, unsheathed his knife, ready to fight.

"Hold your blade, Shredder. It's me."

It was Axel Haamer, his closest friend. Axel was built like a powder keg, with a temper to match. His thick chest was scarred from battles with the Wyrm, as was his craggy face. A jagged slash started at his hairline, paused to pluck an eye, then continued down his cheek, ending in a hook on his cash register chin. With his flat nose and jutting lower jaw, he resembled a swine when in Crinos form, hence the Garou name of Boar-Tusker.

Klaus tucked his weapon back into the sheath. "What is it, Axel?"

"I just got word from Jurgi Hatchet-Thrower."

"What is it?"

"Bad news."

Klaus's gut cinched. "Father?"

Axel nodded. "Someone shot him through the head. A silver bullet. He never knew what hit him."

Klaus felt the anger rise. He slammed his fist into the door of a pawnshop. The wood splintered and several jagged slivers stabbed the meat of his hand. He didn't notice.

"Father didn't deserve to die like that. A warrior should die in battle. The Wyrm will lose many for this. I will gather the Sword and we'll find the nearest pit. The night of a Modi moon is a good one on which to die."

"Yes, it is," Axel said, unsheathing a wicked-looking knife. "There was a witness, a boy from the village. He was in the woods hunting when he came upon your father and a man."

"Did he see the bastard that did it?"

Axel nodded as his features slowly began to alter. His voice transformed into a growl. "There's something we have to settle. Disturbing news."

"What do you mean?"

Klaus heard a sharp crack. A wet spray hit his face. He turned and saw his friend slump and fall against the brick wall, a red hole drilled neatly in his chest. He dropped to the ground and sniffed the air.

Axel coughed bloody words. "Must die . . . boy said . . . you de—"

Another shot split the silence of the murky night. Axel's head exploded, spattering the wall with blood, brain, and bone. He fell to the ground, dead before he slapped pavement.

Klaus looked up in the direction of the gunfire and growled at the fog for obscuring his vision. He wondered how the sniper could see in the mist and darkness when he, a Garou, had trouble doing so.

It didn't matter. Whoever was suicidal enough to fire on the Get of Fenris had to be in the deserted building across the street. For speed and agility, he assumed the form of a large gray wolf. He snarled and ran onto the pavement, veering to his left, then his right to make himself a difficult target.

Before the man could get a bead on him and fire another shot, Klaus leapt for the sidewalk under a cement awning. A stone gargoyle, perched on a ledge above him, watched the scene with lifeless eyes.

Klaus jumped through a broken window and checked out his surroundings. The interior of the building was a black and blue bruise of shadows. Desks and toppled chairs were joined by intricate spider webs. Several ceiling tiles, cracked and dusty, testified to last Friday's earthquake. The air was plump with menace.

Klaus snatched the odor of dust, mildew, and death in his flaring nostrils. A low growl rumbled from deep within his throat. He took a few padded steps toward a room to his right and saw what remained of a human. The man was dressed in a black suit and tie. A notebook with the name Penco Real Estate lay by his side. A heavy brass statue had fallen and crushed his skull during the quake. Rats chewed on the carcass.

Klaus cocked a pointed ear toward the second floor and perceived faint footsteps. Sneaky. The steps of a hunter.

We shall see who hunts whom, Klaus thought as he narrowed his eyes and bounded toward the stairway. He slammed through the door and took the steps by fours, climbing., saliva dripping, blood lust rising.

When he reached the second floor, he stopped in his tracks, shocked by the smell coming from the stairwell above him; a scent he had known his whole life: the scent of his father!

At the same time his heart soared, Klaus's mind swirled with conflict. How could this be? Hatchet-Thrower told Axel that his father was dead, and a Jarl wouldn't lie about such a thing. Then how could he be alive?

Klaus considered that perhaps Father had faked his death to gain some advantage over his enemies, but quickly dismissed the notion. Such a Machiavellian plan was the way of a Shadow Lord, not one of the Get. Father always met his foes face to face, tooth and claw.

He heard a click and looked up expecting to see his father, but instead saw a bizarre figure standing in the shadowy doorway. He had never seen anything like him. He was a big man about Klaus's size when in human form: 6' 4", close to 260 pounds. His head looked to be that of an insect, bulging green eyes, small antennae. Some mutated blend of man and bug created by the Wyrm no doubt. The insect monkey set the heavy caliber rifle he was carrying against the wall and slipped a strange looking pistol from the holster next to the sheath on his belt. The explanation of his father's scent hung from the man's shoulders; a gray pelt with a patch of white fur on the head.

The bastard had skinned his father! That must have been the news that Axel was about to tell him before he was killed.

"Hello, Klaus," the insect monkey said. The pistol hissed with a sound like a stabbed tire.

Klaus lurched to his left to avoid the round, but he was too late. The poisoned dart nicked his right shoulder, spun, and stabbed the wall. Its toxic coating quickly took effect. Klaus's right leg collapsed causing him to tumble down the stairs. When he stopped rolling, he sprang to three paws, his right leg useless.

"Stand still, Klaus," the insect monkey said as he stepped onto the stairway and aimed again. "We have things to settle."

Klaus roared and, in a cloud of bloodlust, almost sprang. Instead, he dropped into a crouch when the pistol spat and a singing dart traced a path in his fur. He turned and, with a three-legged gait, loped to the window. He looked back once, saw the insect monkey coming down the steps then pounced into the fog.

Klaus knew that the strange being would follow him and die by his fangs and talons. He darted across the street and crashed through a window to gain entrance into the building.

The *drip drip* of a broken water main was the only sound in the big room. Dusty computer monitors and keyboards littered the rows of desks that lined one wall. Most of the room dividers had tumbled under the power of the quake. The rubble in the room was ideal cover for a trap. He found a strategically sound position and waited for the insect monkey to show his misshapen head so that he could tear it from its shoulders.

Already his tremendous recuperative powers were beginning to combat the effects of the poison. He felt the nerves in his leg coming back to life. Soon he would be ready to strike with full force.

Just then, he heard stealthy footsteps shuffling across the carpeted floor. In the shadows, he saw the insect monkey standing 15 feet away. A thin smile sliced into his hairy jawline. He watched the creature pass him, then silently sprinted across the carpet and sprang at his father's killer. His growl shredded the musty air.

The creature spun and fired the dart pistol, hitting Klaus in the teeth. The dart chipped a canine, but didn't penetrate flesh.

As he struck the insect monkey with his front paws, the steel jaws of the werewolf tore off the creature's face. Their tangled bodies hit the floor. The dart gun skittered across the floor and landed under a desk.

Klaus clenched the man's face in his jaws and shook it. The skin tasted bitter in his mouth. He spit it out and saw green plastic lenses, metal parts, leather, computer chips.

What the hell was this?

His query was sliced by the sound of a knife being unsheathed. He looked up and caught the glint of the klaive, a silver fetish blade, his father's klaive! This bastard had not only skinned his father, but dishonored him by taking his sacred knife!

The creature, now revealed to be a human about Klaus's age, slashed the air with the klaive. Although the shadows obscured his features, something about the man was familiar.

"You have the advantage, Klaus," the man said, backing away toward the pistol. "No more infrared to help old Max see in the dark and fog."

Klaus paused trying to get a better look at the man, then realized there was no point in recognizing a dead man. He let the Rage well up inside him like lava in a volcano. A searing frenzy of anger over his father's dishonor released.

Let this human feel the terror of the Delirium before he dies.

His gray fur rippled in waves of growth. As the Garou's frame enlarged, the room filled with the sound of bones knitting. His front paws lengthened into fingers tipped with razor-sharp talons. Lupine jaws shortened into a short, powerful snout filled with sharp daggers. Klaus grew to his full height and filled his broad chest with air. He seethed hatred.

Now he would remove this tumor from Gaia's body.

Klaus's bloodshot eyes pierced the darkness and stabbed the human's face. Klaus saw no fear, no unbridled terror — just a thin smile as Max tried to reach the dart pistol under the desk.

Klaus realized he had made a mistake. This man, Max, was kinfolk, immune to the Delirium. He needed to act fast before Max retrieved the gun. Klaus charged, springing into the air, jaws agape, talons slashing.

Max didn't have time to get the gun. At the last moment, he rolled out of the way, slashing with the silver klaive. Klaus landed on the desk shattering it. The werewolf rose quickly. His ankle was on fire where the knife had severed his Achilles tendon. The window panes trembled at his howl of Rage. He took a hobbled step toward the big man, his left foot flapping.

"I knew you'd be this way," Max said, flipping the knife from hand to hand. "That's why I used the tranq darts."

Klaus roared and charged, but his damaged ankle gave way, and he stumbled. While falling, he managed to catch Max across the chest with a swipe of his talons.

The four grooves in the human's flesh oozed blood.

Klaus looked in his hand and snarled. He had torn a necklace from around the man's neck. A gold star hung from the chain.

"*Jude*," Klaus said, spitting out the German word as if it was a piece of Wyrm flesh. He tossed the necklace into the man's face.

"That's right," Max said. "A Jew."

Klaus stopped. His blood dripped in a steady patter onto the dusty, worn carpet. He stared at the man. A glimmer of recognition lit on his brain and then danced off like a bat. It didn't matter. He would figure out who the man was after he was dead at his feet.

"You die for kill father, coward," Klaus said, the words difficult to form in the Crinos state. "Great warrior of Get should not die in sneak attack."

"Great warrior," Max laughed, a bitter indictment of the claim. "A killer of women and children and helpless men."

Klaus growled. "Enough monkey babble. Time you die, Jew."

"I doubt that," Max said, as he pulled out a small, round object. He pulled a pin and tossed it at Klaus's feet. The gas grenade popped and green smoke hissed from it.

A black blade sliced into Klaus's head. He felt funny. He had encountered this gas before when a witch hunter had tried to take him. Clamping his paw over his mouth, he charged the man. They collided, their momentum carrying them into a bay window. The glass offered little resistance. The two tumbled into the street in a hail of shards. The klaive clattered across the asphalt and teetered on the edge of a sewer grate.

Klaus wobbled to his feet, the gas working on his brain. He gulped fresh air in an effort to ratchet the black blade from his mind.

Max rolled and jumped to his feet, his eyes darting for the location of his weapon. They lit upon the klaive and he started to run for it.

Klaus saw him, then the klaive. He lurched forward, rubbing his temples, driving out the darkness in his head. He had to stop the man from possessing so dangerous a weapon again. He cut Max off, but the black blade carved the street from his vision. He staggered, digging his knuckles into his eyes, and the world winked on again. Max was past him grabbing the weapon. Klaus snarled then loosed a bone-chilling howl.

The human disappeared into an alley and the shadows cast by the massive buildings.

Klaus paused to clear his head. After he was OK, he would wrap his damaged ankle and the hunt would begin again. Only this time he would be the hunter, not the prey.

● ● ●

Max Feingold darted into the alley. He cursed the loss of the dart pistol and the one gas grenade he had managed to acquire. Now he might have to use the klaive to kill Klaus, and at 49 years old, even with his martial arts training, he was in no condition to be fighting werewolves at close quarters. His bones ached from the collision with Klaus. He needed time to recover from their encounter. He hurried deeper into the darkness afforded by the corridor.

Klaus had called him "Jude". The word awakened the memories of his past, the corpses he kept buried in a crypt in the darkest corner of his mind. They clawed their way into his consciousness, strong and nasty, unrelenting in their horror. He recalled the stench of the dead so strong it hurt your eyes. The moaning, a constant chorus in the background. Muzak of the damned. The sound of gunfire and bodies dropping. The smiling arrogant faces.

The shuffling of feet snapped Max from his reverie. His muscles coiled. He clenched the klaive in his fist. He crouched and peered between the toppled trash cans and saw an aged Garou. His face was more jackal than wolf. His body, a blotchy wasteland of chapped pink skin and havens of hair overpopulated with fleas. He was arranging a brass lamp on top of a huge pile of assorted junk. Max saw TV trays, an aluminum baseball bat, miscellaneous costume jewelry, a model of Lon Chaney as the Wolfman, and other trinkets of little value, but a treasure to one of the Bone Gnawers.

Max moved closer.

The Bone Gnawer sniffed the air, once, twice, three times, as if trying to jumpstart his olfactory system. He caught a scent and turned to stare into the eyes of Max Feingold.

"You 'bout got scared me to death," he said, his accent all grits and gravy. "Don't tell me Taco-Gobbler hired himself a mercenary to steal my treasure — and a damn ape to boot. I know I'm old, but no human with a big toothpick is about to take me out less'n he wants to see his heart for he dies."

"I'm not here for your treasure."

"Then why you got that pig-sticker?"

Max looked at the blade in his hand and lowered it to his side. "I don't want any trouble. Got enough of my own."

Pea Eye reached out and grabbed Max by the elbow. He raised his arm until he could see the knife.

"Hoowee," the Bone Gnawer's eyes widened in amazement. "That's a goddamned klaive." Pea Eye licked his lips then scratched his chin with a broken nail. "Where'd you get it?"

"Look, I haven't got time to talk."

"That sure would make me king of the pack," Pea eye said more to himself than Max.

His gaze slowly shifted to one of beady-eyed menace. Max felt the Garou's grip tighten on his arm.

"Yes, sir. King of the pack."

A growl shredded the dank air of the alley. The Bone Gnawer's fangs nicked Max's throat as his head flew past him and *thunked* against the cement wall. The decapitated body crumpled into Max's lap and began to revert to human form. A red asterisk on the wall marked the spot of Pea Eye's death.

Max looked up into the glowering gaze of Klaus Hurst Sheep-Shredder. The werewolf's claws were black with the blood of the Bone Gnawer whose head he had just removed with a powerful swipe of his claws.

"Now, Jew, you die," Klaus said, thrusting his claws downward to rip out Max's guts.

Max grabbed the body of the dead werewolf and lifted it.

Klaus's claws buried into the changing body. The human flesh shrunk and clung to his hand like a leech. He lifted the corpse over his head and shook it trying to lose the parasitic flesh.

Max scrambled backward on his hands and feet putting as much distance between him and the werewolf as he could.

Klaus's hand came out of the corpse with a sluicy pop. The headless body twirled in the hair and thumped against a door. A woman opened it onto the scene in the alley, gasped and ducked back into her apartment.

"You only delay the inevitable," Klaus said, still struggling with the human tongue.

"This is the way you like it. A fight with a weaker opponent."

Klaus laughed, a deep rumble that shook Max's guts, before willing himself to human form.

"You like this better." He grinned and pulled the knife from his sheath. "I'm still gonna throat you for dishonoring my father!"

Max shook his head. "He lost his honor 50 years ago when he was running the concentration camps."

Klaus nodded as it all became clear to him. So this is what this was about; the so-called Holocaust. Father preferred to call it a return to the Impergium, a way to weed out the inferior breeds of human. He and other members of the Sword of Heimdall joined the Nazi party who had ranking officers that were kinfolk and respected the Garou. It was easy for Father to plant the idea of a purge of the mongrel races, the Nazis were looking for scapegoats on which to blame the country's troubles.

"The Sword culled millions who sought to dilute the perfection of the Get of Fenris." Klaus smiled. "All without drawing suspicion on the Garou."

"Millions of innocent people."

"They weren't innocent. The Wyrm's corruption burned deep within them. The Jews were sick with its poison; money-grubbers, destroyers of the land. They had to die. Father was saving Gaia from the Wyrm."

"You're the one who's polluted. You're closer to the Wyrm than any human. Your hate works into its plans perfectly."

"We despise Jormungandr. Many of the Sword have died in battle with the agents of the Wyrm. Just as you will die now!"

Klaus lunged with the blade. Max parried and backed away.

"Do you remember when you and your father left the compound?" Max asked.

Klaus narrowed one eye. "Compound? I was only a pup—"

Max cut him off. "I remember. He shot a woman that day."

"Father did what he had to."

"A woman with dark brown hair and eyes that caressed with their tenderness and love. Do you remember her? He shot her in the chest and then kicked her into that . . . that pit of death."

"I saw many humans die. They had to be culled."

"A beautiful, loving woman." Tears glistened in Max's eyes. "He ordered her removed from the mass grave. Said her skin would make a fine jacket." Max ground his teeth when he recalled the smug grin on Dieter Hurst's face. The superior stride as he walked to the staff car and hugged his little boy while the woman bled to death. His anger burned away the ache in his bones. His muscles felt like steel. He clutched the silver blade and coiled his body preparing to strike. "Then he shot a boy, her son. He fell into the pit with all those dead people, those bloated, rotting corpses."

"A friend of yours no doubt," Klaus said. "Another Jew. They had to die for the good of Gaia. The inferior races must be culled."

"Then take this blade and plunge it into your black heart."

"You dare to call me inferior? I'm Klaus Hurst Sheep-Shredder, son of Dieter Hurst Man-Killer, Modi of the Get of Fenris. I am the purest of Garou."

"Did you know your mother?"

"My mother died in childbirth."

"Is that what Dieter Man-Killer, the great Modi, the honorable Garou, told you?"

"I saw her picture. A good German woman. He showed me."

Max laughed. "Showed you."

"Yes," Klaus said. "Now I'm tired of your babbling. Father killed your friend and his mother and you have come to avenge them after all these years. Your story is so trite."

"I was her son."

"To avenge your family then. I cannot say I'm sorry they died."

"You don't get it. I was the boy he shot. An American GI pulled me out of that deathtrap and raised me."

"So you killed my father to avenge your mother's death and now you seek my life as well?"

"He made a fucking coat out of mother's skin so I did the same to him. It took decades, but I finally tracked him to Argentina. I found him in that little Nazi town that the Get control. After I told him who I was, I put a silver bullet in his head and skinned him. It's a nice fit, don't you think?" he said bitterly. "Like we were cut from the same cloth."

Klaus bit his lip and tried not to Rage into Crinos form. He wanted to kill the man on his terms.

"Don't I look familiar to you, Klaus?" Max said stepping into the glare of a street lamp. "Look closely."

For the first time, Klaus was able to get a good look at the man. The blue eyes looked familiar, the broad chin, firm and resolute. His nose was straight. Who did he resemble?

Recognition hit Klaus with the power of a Fomori body-barb. By the great Fenris, this man, Max — he looked like him!

"You see, Dieter Hurst and I *were* cut from the same cloth. He was my father, *our* father. We are brothers, Klaus. Fraternal twins. Dieter Hurst was our father and the woman he mated, the woman he shot, was a Jew. Our mother. You have so-called mongrel blood running through your veins."

Klaus was stunned. "Father would never—"

"—but he did. Mother was a beautiful woman. Stunning when she arrived at the camp. Dieter was visiting the camp that day to see how the operation was running. He saw mother and ordered her into his quarters. He used her for his pleasure then cast her out into the prisoner population."

"But I saw the pictures of my mother."

"A lie."

Klaus's head spun. All of this was too much to absorb at one time.

Max continued. "After we were born, mother protected us. She traded sex with the guards for our lives. For three years, she sacrificed that way and grew old before her time. Then Dieter Hurst returned. With the war nearing an end, he had come to eliminate the entire prisoner population of the camp. It was then he discovered that you were Garou."

"I cannot believe you," Klaus said, his words dwindled into wisps of air.

"He knew that you had Jewish blood, but couldn't bear to kill you. He decided to keep it a secret. He shot Mother and me to silence us forever. The bastard shot *your* mother and brother to preserve his honor among the *honorable* Sword of Heimdall. He knew if any members of the Sword found out that his son had tainted blood in his veins, they would have shredded you both."

"I am a Jarl. They wouldn't dare question my heritage." Klaus tried to sound convincing, but his voice had lost its power.

Max ignored his blustering comment and went on, "One of the boys in the village was in the woods and learned your secret when I confronted Dieter. He must have told someone in the Sword. Earlier tonight, your pigfaced friend was about to attack you when I shot him."

Axel's words came to him. "Must die. . . boy said. . . you de—"

Jude! It was German for Jew. He had been accusing him of being a Jew!

Max looked into his eyes. "You are my brother. We share Mother's Jewish blood."

"No," Klaus whispered.

"*Das ist richtig, Klaus,*" a guttural voice said in German from behind them.

The two men turned and saw the silhouettes of three figures blocking the alleyway. One of the them stepped into the dim light. Klaus recognized Jurgi Hatchet-Thrower, the Jarl of the Argentinean camp of the Sword of Heimdall, the camp formed by his father. The other two with him were from Klaus's San Francisco camp. They were Conrad Weiss, his second-in-command, a tall, lanky Garou with a penchant for collecting ears and Fat Lars Boomhowl, whose long nose looked like a carrot stuck in his wad of dough face. He carried a club studded with nails.

"You must die," Jurgi said, switching to English, then back to German. "*Und das Jude.*"

"This Jew lies," Klaus said stabbing a finger at Max. "He's trying to discredit me and Father because his mother died in the camp."

"No, he's not. Your father admitted it," Conrad said biting off the words. "The boy heard him."

Klaus's mind reeled from the barrage of information. Could it be true? Could his life have been a lie for all these years?

Suddenly, the irony struck him with the force of a sledgehammer. In one fell swoop, because of the blood running through his veins, he had gone from a respected Jarl to a hated enemy. If no one had discovered the truth, he probably would've died a great warrior, perhaps a legend, had he succeeded in defeating the Wyrm. But now, because his mother turned out to be a Jew, everything had changed. All the years of service to the Sword of Heimdall were cast into ruin. In the eyes of his peers, he was now a mongrel, a cur to be wiped from the face of Gaia. And all because of something in his past, something over which he had no control. It wasn't fair.

Another hammer-blow fell upon him when he realized that such naked prejudice was the foundation upon which the Sword of Heimdall based their whole ideology; the belief that the way to Wyrm corruption came from the mingling of bloods, the tainting of racial purity. And now the revelation of his true bloodlines shoved those beliefs down Klaus's throat. He had lived the life of a fierce warrior, fought Fomori and Black Spiral Dancers, reveled with his peers, and, despite the Jewish blood in his veins, had never been in danger of the Wyrm's corruption. He suddenly realized that it was the courage inside his heart, not the makeup of the blood coursing through it, that had made him immune to the corruption of Jormungandr. It was the tenets of the Sword of the Heimdall that were the lie, not his life.

Conrad broke in upon his thoughts. "To think we had a fucking Jew, an inferior cur, as our Jarl. It sickens my guts."

Klaus's eyes became glowing red slits. "Then allow me to remove them," he said before his flesh began to ripple with waves of hair. His bones crackled with growth. Meaty muscles bulged. He charged the threesome while they were starting to change to Crinos form.

Klaus's first blow tore out Conrad's throat. The geyser of blood sprayed the streetlight casting the alley in a murky red glow. The second blow ripped his arm from his shoulder. He fell to the ground in anguish.

Suddenly, powerful arms grabbed Klaus from behind, locking his arms to his sides. Klaus struggled to break free, but Jurgi was a mighty fighter, the longest reigning Jarl among the Get of Fenris and his grasp wasn't easily broken.

"Kill him!" Jurgi shouted.

Fat Lars raised the spiked club to brain Klaus and screamed. He clutched at the back of his head while spinning in a circle. Klaus saw the klaive buried in his skull. Max stood behind the shrieking werewolf, his eyes glaring with the heat of battle, and then disappeared under a mountain of bloodstained gray fur. Conrad wasn't dead yet.

Klaus shoved backward with his legs and slammed Jurgi against the concrete wall. The werewolf's grip loosened for a moment, but a moment was all Klaus needed. He drove the back of his head into Jurgi's chin and then shifted his weight flipping Jurgi hard onto the corpse of Fat Lars.

Klaus looked over at Max and saw that Conrad was on top of him. Gouts of blood from the werewolf's stump sprayed Max as Conrad prepared to strike with his good hand. Klaus lunged forward, yanked the klaive from Fat

Lars's head, rolled, and threw it in one continuous motion.

The blade struck Conrad in the side. He howled with pain then slashed Max across the face exposing the man's teeth. Max tried to grab the hilt of the klaive, but his fingers were slippery with the werewolf's blood and his own. Conrad slapped his hand away and yanked the blade from his side. Max screamed as Conrad stabbed him in the chest with the klaive.

"No!" Klaus howled charging Conrad. He kicked him in the face with such force that the werewolf's head snapped backward touching his spine. Conrad collapsed like a hairy rag doll. The klaive clattered on the ground next to Max.

Klaus heard a roar from behind him and spun around to face Jurgi's charge. The werewolf's talons tore across Klaus's chest spraying blood into the fog.

Again, Jurgi slashed and his steely claws found meat.

He did it again.

And again.

The air rained red.

Klaus growled and tried to mount an attack, but another powerful swipe ripped him open. Blood coursed down his body. He was weakening and he knew it.

Max, his life ebbing from the sucking wound in his chest, watched his brother fall to his knees.

"You die now, Klaus," Jurgi said with the same smug smile on his face that Dieter Hurst had worn when he had killed Jews. The arrogant smile forever burned in Max's brain.

Max screamed, a howl worthy of the mightiest warrior.

Klaus turned and saw his brother slicing the air with his arm. A glint of metal flashed past the corner of his eye. He heard a growling gasp from Jurgi and turned to face him. He saw the klaive sticking out of the werewolf's chest, a direct hit to his heart. Jurgi tottered forward and fell, driving the blade up to the hilt. He growled once, then was still.

Klaus looked over at Max and saw his head collapse onto his outstretched arm. He staggered to his feet and stumbled to his brother's side.

He looked into Max's staring blue eyes and saw emptiness. There would be no last minute absolution. No meaningful family reunion.

There was only the silence of death.

Klaus heard a dripping sound and realized it was coming from his wounds. He looked down at the crimson puddles around him as his blood mingled with Max's. He bent over and smeared his palm in the red pool.

Klaus stepped over to the body of Jurgi Hatchet-Thrower, a pure-blooded Get of Fenris. He dipped his other hand into the Garou's blood then stood and thrust both hands into the light. He stared at his scarlet palms, examining the blood.

There was no difference. ////

Transitions

by Nigel D. Findley

Tired. Very tired.

Jim Laurence shook his head.

Not physically tired — well, that too, but he could handle that. *Had* handled that. On the job, when a project had to be finished, and to hell with late hours. Or on the hunt.

No, it was a different kind of tiredness he felt now. Not of the body, or even of the mind.

Of the soul?

He shook his head again.

He drew a deep breath, felt the air-yet-not-air of the Penumbra fill his lungs. Waited for the rejuvenation he usually felt — sighed when it didn't come.

He looked around him. The small cove where he stood was empty. The cold, black ocean — infinite, it looked here — lapped against the shore. In the physical world, he knew that the Pelican Beach Inn — a small Tudor building where he'd often stopped to tip an ale or two before a moot — would be to his right, with a wind-swept headland — steep enough to make for a tough hike, but definitely climbable — to his right. In the Penumbra, the pub looked like a small stone hut — only the shimmering Weaver-patterns of its ESPN feed, big-screen TV and stereo system showing it for a 20th-century structure — and the headland had become a vertical mountain face, a thousand feet high and as sheer as if the rock had been sliced with a knife. The trees of Muir Woods, those ancient redwoods, were unchanged, though. He couldn't see them through the fog that always seemed to cloak this part of the Penumbra, and he could not smell them, not quite. But *feel* them, know they were there.

The full moon was just touching the mathematically straight horizon, its light already starting to fade. In the physical world, he knew, the eastern sky would be tinged with pink: "The harbingers of dawn." The quote bubbled up from the depths of his memory. Here, though, it was darkness that was starting to spread in the east, the dark "light" of Helios, the Penumbra's analog of the sun.

He sighed again. The moot was over for another month, the Run completed. Under the full moon, he'd listened to the Theurges speak the ancient words, howled with his brothers and sisters. The primeval woods had rung with their voices, while in the distance he'd still been able to hear the firecrackers as the humans had held their own celebration: Halloween.

Jim smiled faintly, wryly. The ironic parallel wasn't lost on him. Halloween — All Hallows Eve — was an ancient ritual. Some Philodoxes claimed its antecedent — pagan, before the Christian systematizers tried to reframe it in a form congruent with the inflexible dogma of their religion — dated back to the days soon after the Wyrm turned and the realms of flesh and spirit separated. How many of the humans — "monkeys," many of his brothers and sisters would call them — knew just what it was they celebrated? How many felt the touch of the powers their revels once propitiated? How many felt the old truths touch their soul?

The parallel was bitter. Tonight he'd gone through the forms of the moot, he'd offered the correct responses as the Master of the Rite had recited the words her ancestors had remembered across the centuries. But somehow nothing had touched him. He'd felt isolated, alone even though he was surrounded by his own kind. More alone, somehow, than he felt when he walked alone through Golden Gate Park.

Where's the justice?

He smiled again at the question, a smile that felt more like a grimace. He knew the answer many of the Galliards would give him — there *is* no justice for one who doesn't know himself, and isn't honest with himself. For one who doesn't accept the world as it *is*, not as he'd like it to be. Before tonight, he'd never have put himself in that category. He'd prided himself on his engineer's view of the world; engineers *always* dealt with the world as it was, that was their job. But now?

He'd *needed* this moot, he just hadn't known how much he'd needed it. He'd got the news on Friday — Black Friday, his few co-workers who'd been kept on called it. It had hit him hard. (Not that he hadn't been expecting it for some time. But there was a big difference between abstract and reality, between the thought, and the way the actuality seemed to kick him in the gut.) He'd drifted through Saturday and Sunday almost in a daze, hardly aware of what was going on around him. On Sunday night, as the sun had sunk toward the horizon, he'd climbed into his car, eager to head for Muir Woods and the caern. Early, hours early, but even so, he'd almost been late. As he'd driven toward the Presidio from his condo near Marine Park, the radio traffic reports had told of fog thickening between Fort Point and Fort Baker, wreathing the Golden Gate Bridge and slowing traffic to a crawl. Then, just as he'd cruised past the Palace of Fine Arts, the reports had changed: an accident had blocked northbound traffic, and the authorities were considering closing the bridge entirely until conditions cleared. Sadly — he hadn't realized, until that moment, how much he'd been looking forward to *feeling* the music that was the mathematics of the bridge as he drove across it — he'd turned around and taken an alternate route, over the Bay Bridge, around the bay, and south to Muir Woods from San Rafael. Traffic had been snarled along the whole route, and by the time he'd parked, hurried through the shifting paths of the bawn and jumped the boulder that was the "main gate" to the clearing, everyone else had been present and waiting for the moot to begin. It had been harder than usual to ignore the stares of the Furies as he'd hastily taken on the Crinos.

And, after all that, the old words hadn't touched him the way he'd hoped. Again, he sighed.

"Like it here, don't you?"

Jim turned, startled.

Here, in the altered perceptions of the Penumbra, it took him a moment to recognize the hulking figure next to him. A Crinos, an arm's-length taller than his human form, fur silvered by the fading moonlight. He felt a sudden, unreasoned impulse to back away, but stifled it as he saw the characteristic pattern of scar tissue on the figure's throat.

He smiled — a real smile, for the first time tonight. "Didn't see you at the moot, Fraser."

The Crinos returned his smile, dark lips drawing back from polished white fangs. "I was there," Fraser said lazily. "I kinda get the feeling you didn't see much tonight. Hmm?"

Jim didn't answer at once. Among the Bay Area Garou, Fraser Martinsen had a reputation for being able to sense another's feelings, sometimes even thoughts. It wasn't a Gift, not as such — just an awareness of subtle cues. *And, Jim couldn't help thinking, an understanding of himself, a very deep self-knowledge, that lets him understand others as intuitively as he does himself.* Martinsen was of the Children of Gaia, a tribe distrusted by the traditionalists among the Garou almost as much as Jim's own. Yet only the most extreme of the hardliners didn't consider Martinsen himself to be a confidant and friend. *Even me,* Jim reminded himself. *I'm closer to Fraser than I am to some of my fellow Glass Walkers.*

Before Jim could decide how best to respond, Fraser shifted to human form, the transition effortless here in the Penumbra. Laurence considered the man that stood by his side — a hand's breadth taller than Jim, and narrower across the hips and shoulders. Ageless, in a way; his unlined face could be that of a teenager, or someone almost as old as Jim himself. The battle scars that had been so obvious in Crinos form now resembled a port-wine birthmark extending from Fraser's Adam's apple to below his left ear. Fraser's green eyes flashed in the moonlight.

"Troubles?" he asked. His smile was still in place, but Jim could hear the concern in his voice.

Jim shrugged uncomfortably. "Changes, let's say."

"Hmm. Changes." Fraser turned away to watch the setting moon.

The silence stretched between them. Finally, Jim couldn't hold it inside any longer. "Twenty-seven years."

His quiet voice was harsh in his own ears, his mouth tight as though the words themselves were bitter on his tongue. "I've been there 27 years."

Fraser didn't speak immediately, didn't even turn to look at Jim. Most importantly, he didn't ask the older Garou to explain. *Almost as though he knew already*, Jim thought. *Knew from some other source, or sensed enough to guess.*

"You don't need the job," Fraser said at last.

Jim felt his lips twist in something that wasn't a smile. "Be happy with my pension, is that what you're saying?"

"No. You don't *need* the job. You don't *need* any job."

"Gaia will provide, you mean?"

"Won't she?"

"Yes," Jim admitted after a moment. "But—"

"But that's not what you're concerned about," Fraser finished for him.

Jim nodded. "I'm not talking survival. You're right, Gaia *will* provide. Food, shelter, but not. . ." He trailed off.

"Fulfillment?" the other suggested softly. "Self-actualization?"

"Sounds like psycho-babble," Jim snorted. Then he relented. "I suppose so."

"You've talked to the other Walkers?"

"I've tried," Jim corrected. "They don't understand, or they don't care — I don't know. They talk about mechanical engineering being a 'sunset' industry, populated by dinosaurs who aren't aware enough to realize they're already extinct. They tell me jobs like mine are gone, they're never coming back, and I've got to get off my ass and get into a 'sunrise' industry. Computers, or something like that."

He snorted again. "They read all the articles about 'structural unemployment', they hear the experts talking about it. They don't believe it, though. It's not a systemic problem, the way they see it. To them, 'structural unemployment' is just an excuse. It's dinosaurs like me trying to blame something outside ourselves for the fact we let ourselves get dead-ended. We didn't upgrade our skills, they say. We didn't see the writing on the goddamn wall, and we didn't react in time. Our willful blindness, our fault. My fault I didn't keep up to date."

Fraser nodded silently. Then, "Have you wondered," he suggested softly, "whether they might not be right?"

"Of *course* they're goddamned right," Jim snarled. Then he barked with bitter laughter. "Of course they're right," he repeated more quietly. "To some degree, at least. And I guess that's what galls me the most."

The younger Garou smiled and chuckled softly, a response that felt to Jim more comradely than a pat on the shoulder or a squeeze on the arm. Again, Fraser paused in thought as he watched the moon, now bisected by the dark horizon. "There are many things I don't understand about your tribe," he said at last.

"You and many others."

Fraser's smile broadened. "But the difference between me and them is that I *want* to understand." He took a moment to collect his thoughts. "I understand the Walkers' belief that the tools of the Wyrm can be used *against* the Wyrm" — he chuckled again — "the analogy of the double-edged sword moved out of the gladiatorial arena and into the arena of business, I suppose — and I applaud it. I also understand that to use tools like the machines of business, you've got to immerse yourself in them — become part of them. The willingness to do that — to enter the city and learn its paths and glens and dangers and opportunities. Well, that's enough to set you Walkers apart from the majority of our kind, and to taint you with the stench of *urrah* in the noses of many.

"Yet, you — you set yourself apart even from your fellow Walkers." What could have been an insult, even a challenge, if voiced by a Get of Fenris or a Black Fury, came as a mild statement of an interesting fact from the lips of the younger Garou. "You work, a full-time job. And not for a company that has any overwhelming importance in the fight against the Wyrm — not that I can see, at least.

"Why?"

"I don't have a good answer," Jim admitted. He rubbed the back of his neck, rolling his head in a vain attempt to loosen up tense muscles. "It's not like I haven't thought about it, either. I don't know how many times I've asked myself that same question, and I've *never* had a good answer. It's just what I am."

"A Garou?" Fraser asked quietly. "*That's* what you are."

"What I am is an engineer," Jim corrected with a mirthless smile. "That's what I was first — in my mind, at least, in my dreams as early as I can remember — before I was Garou."

"No." Again, the Child of Gaia's tone robbed the word of any insult. "You were Garou first; you were always Garou, you will always *be* Garou. First *and* last. The Firsting isn't a change; it's an awakening, a recognition of a fundamental reality."

"I've always tried to strike a balance," Jim said uncomfortably. "Balance is important. In everything."

"You've been walking a tightrope for. . . what, 60 years?"

"Sixty-two."

"It hasn't worked, has it?"

Jim looked away, over toward the stone hut that was the Penumbral image of the inn. In the growing "sundark" of Helios, the Weaver-patterns of technology flickered and shimmered like strands of spider web that had trapped a million fireflies. "No," he said at last. "It hasn't worked. I thought it had, but. . ." He shrugged again.

"Have you ever heard the human expression, 'What you are is what you do?'"

"Who hasn't?"

"I've been thinking about that," Fraser mused. "I think the humans remember only part of another expression, a more important one."

"Which is?"

"I think it's, '*If* what you are is what you do, when you don't you aren't'."

Jim had to smile, but sobered again immediately. "You say I'm confusing what I am with what I do?"

"Aren't you? You lost something you *do* — OK, granted, it's something that's important to you. But you still *are* what you always were — Garou. You have to get back in touch with that."

"That's what I was trying to do, tonight."

"Again, granted. But maybe you're looking for an answer in the wrong place."

"Where else would I look for it than among other Garou?" Jim asked with a frown.

"Well," Fraser replied quietly, "I might start right *here*." And he touched a slender forefinger to the center of Jim's chest.

• • •

Pamela Barnes hated to fly by public carriers.

No, she decided, "hated" was too insipid a word for the way she felt. Loathed with a detestation that drove her to the bitter, brittle edge of fury. It wasn't just the inconvenience, the hours wasted, when she had access to other means of travel — because of her position and her importance — that would get her to her destination in much less time. No, the worst part was being treated as just another one of the. . . the *herd* (she could think of no better word) of faceless, mindless travelers. As though she were *like* them; that was what was intolerable.

Well, at least the journey was almost over. They were still above the clouds, still on the periphery of the approach pattern and a good half-hour from touchdown. In her mind's eye, though, she could see the lights of San Francisco, the narrow ribbon of light that was the Golden Gate Bridge tracing the way to the sprawling sea of neon and sodium glare of the city. The plane surged momentarily as it struck turbulence.

Only idiots would travel this way, unless there was something valuable to gain from the process. The symbolism of the highly reputed "expediter" arriving from the East Coast, for example. She knew from experience how takeover negotiations always seemed to advance to a new level when the preliminary team of negotiators was replaced by a single "problem-solver" from "head office."

She smiled scornfully to herself. Such a simple ploy, but still so effective. She, and others like her, had used it more times than she cared to count over the last few years. Sometimes the mere arrival of an "expediter" like Pamela was enough to convince the directors of the target company to acquiesce. And if not, well, she and those like her knew what had to be done, and had no qualms doing it.

Which way will it go this time? she asked herself. This target was a private corporation, with most of the ownership and all the control concentrated in one man. Owner-managers were unpredictable. Sometimes they were smart, and went along with the inevitable. Other times they turned stubborn, requiring some of Pamela's more specialized talents to close the deal. Which way would this . . . what was his name? That's right — David Gibson. Which way would he react?

Stubborn, Pamela told herself silently. *Let him be stubborn. It's been too long.*

Barnes leaned back in her seat and closed her eyes.

Only to open them a moment later as she sensed a presence beside her. A flight attendant, she knew. She could smell the woman's tiredness after the long flight — and her nervousness. Slowly, Pamela turned toward the other woman — Marsha, her name-badge read.

Pamela knew what the flight attendant was seeing. A tall, slender woman in a severely tailored burgundy business suit. Black hair with two streaks of white — not gray, but pure white — at the temples. Green eyes in a fine-boned face, eyes that seemed to glint like glacier ice under an Arctic sun. She let her lips curve faintly in an expression that could almost be a smile, and relished the way Marsha's nervousness increased.

"Coffee?"

Pamela didn't respond at once, letting the silence stretch. Then she nodded curtly and touched the plastic coffee cup on her tray with a carmine nail. Hurriedly, the flight attendant leaned forward with the insulated pot and began to pour.

The plane surged again. Hot coffee splashed. Pamela hissed through her teeth.

"Oh my god, I'm *so* sorry." The flight attendant didn't know what to do — try to dry the spill with a paper napkin, or just turn and run. "I'm so sorry, can I. . . ?"

The woman's voice trailed off as Pamela looked up from the wet stain on her skirt. The scent of fear was strong in her nostrils. Again, she let the silence stretch, then smiled mildly. "Accidents happen, Marsha," she said quietly. "Accidents happen."

• • •

Christian pulled into a parking space marked "Visitors" and killed the engine. He glanced over at Jim with that innocent — irritating, sometimes — smile of his. "We're here."

Jim looked glumly at the younger Glass Walker. *If anybody saw us, they'd think we were father and son*, he thought dryly. Or maybe grandfather and grandson, the age difference was almost enough. And wasn't *that* a grotesque thought.

Christian took off his sunglasses — the small round lenses had holograms of eyes etched into them, that seemed to blink when the light struck at the right angle — and started to clean them on his T-shirt. "Well?" he asked lightly. "You going, or what?"

"I'm going." With a sigh, Jim opened the door and climbed out of the car. He made to shut the door behind him, but a thought struck him and he bent down to the open window.

"Don't worry," Christian said, anticipating his comment, "I'll still be here when you get out."

The Terra Nova Biometrics facility was a sprawling three-story building taking up almost half of one of the "industrial parks" that sprung up overnight out here in the valley, between Palo Alto and San Jose. Clinically clean, it looked — the kind of place Jim mentally equated with bean-counters and paper-pushers, not with engineers who did *real* work. With an effort, he pushed those negative judgments into the back of his mind. Terra Nova *did* real work, real engineering. Just a different *kind* of engineering — "bioengineering," they called it — and on a different scale from what Jim was used to. No bridge trusses, no high-load turbines, no dam penstocks here: Terra Nova's largest product was the size of a man's arm. But engineering was engineering, wasn't it? The base skills were the same.

He squared his shoulders and walked up the shallow steps to the front door. Reacting to his presence, the glass doors rolled silently back, and air-conditioned air — almost cold in contrast to the heat outside — washed over him. He could feel Christian's gaze on his back — reassuring, he thought, but also mildly amused — as he stepped inside.

The lobby was a fantasy of acrylics and brushed steel — striking to the eye, but cold and sterile. As he approached the curved reception desk, the receptionist looked up and flashed him a smile. "Welcome to Terra Nova." Her teeth were bright white in a tanned face, her blonde hair sculpted in an asymmetrical cut. Jim had the momentary impulse to reach out and touch that hair, to see if it felt as plastic, as artificial, as it looked.

"Jim Laurence," he said. "I have an appointment with Mr. Gibson."

• • •

David Gibson couldn't be more than a dozen years older than Christian, Jim thought as he sat in the president's office. Thirty-five, maybe 37 at the outside. The athletic, outdoorsy type — rangy, with the build of a swimmer or volleyball player. Chestnut hair, with sun-bleached highlights. Cornflower-blue eyes. He wore casual clothes, comfortable, but obviously expensive — no tie. (Come to think of it, Jim hadn't seen a single tie since he'd arrived. He fingered the collar of his suit jacket, a little self-conscious for the first time.) He radiated energy and enthusiasm, a healthy enjoyment of life.

Gibson sat across the acrylic-topped desk from him, reading from an open file folder — Jim's résumé, he assumed. Jim found his gaze drawn repeatedly to the knick-knacks on the credenza and dotting the shelves around the room. Some of them were typical "executive toys;" for example, a board set with a thousand sliding pins that conformed to the contours of anything pressed against it. But there were also some items that made Jim feel at home, the kinds of things he might display in his own office: framed black-and-white photographs of bridges, composed in such a way that their designs were rendered down to their mathematical underpinnings; manual drafting tools; even a large, 1960s-vintage log-log slide rule.

The president of Terra Nova glanced up, followed the direction of Jim's gaze and smiled. "The slide rule?" he asked, amused. His voice was quiet, but firm. "My father's." He chuckled quietly. "I assume you still have yours?"

Jim smiled. He felt comfortable with the man across the desk. They were separated by decades of age, and by a wide gulf of experience. Yet something told him they had some important things in common. "I'd frame it if I could figure out how."

Gibson's grin broadened. He tapped Jim's résumé with a broad forefinger. "An impressive background," he remarked. "Mainly civil and mechanical, but," he shrugged, "math's math, and engineering's engineering, I guess." He paused. "Mind if I ask how you found out about us, and about the fact we're looking for a machinist? The opening wasn't posted."

"From a friend."

"Who?"

"Christian Vederweld."

Gibson sat back in his chair and laughed out loud. "When you drop names, you drop big ones, don't you?"

"You know him, then?"

"Who doesn't?"

Jim filed that away for future reference. He'd known Christian had something of a reputation as a freelance system analyst in the Silicon Valley, but he hadn't known it was that good or widely known.

"He told you about the opening?" Gibson asked.

"He suggested I should apply." Jim had to stifle a smile. *Suggested* — Christian had damn near bullied him into calling Terra Nova and asking for an interview.

"Did he mention how he learned about us?"

"Not that I can remember," Jim admitted. "Why?"

"Doesn't really matter," Gibson said with a shrug. "Just curious. Did he tell you exactly what it is we do at Terra Nova?"

Jim shrugged. "He told me some things," he replied. "I know you're working on artificial limbs and prosthetics."

"The neural interfaces for prosthetics."

He accepted the correction with a nod. "But Christian told me you *are* producing complete prototypes, the whole limb, not just the neural interface. And that's why you need a precision machinist. Right?"

"I assume Mr. Vederweld told you what the job pays?" Jim nodded. "It's quite a step down from what you're used to."

Jim shrugged again with a smile, remembering the satisfaction of adjusting the manual controls on a precision lathe and watching the metal spooling off from the workpiece, so thin as to be almost transparent. "Maybe, but it's good, honest work."

"You can bet on that," Gibson confirmed, grinning broadly. "Just a couple more questions and I think we can settle things. What kind of equipment are you used to?"

"Cincinnati Milacron."

Gibson's eyebrow shot up. "Five-axis?" Jim nodded.

The younger man pursed his lips in a soundless whistle. "You're doing that name-dropping thing again." Jim shrugged. "Well," Gibson went on, "this ain't Rocky Flats, and we don't need *quite* that level of precision. What we've got isn't CM, but it's pretty good. I think you're going to enjoy it."

It took Jim a moment to realize just what the younger man had said. As the meaning struck him, Gibson was already standing and extending his hand across the clear-topped desk. "There's still some paper to be pushed, but as far as I'm concerned, things are settled. Welcome to Terra Nova, Mr. Laurence. I'm looking forward to working with you."

● ● ●

It was all happening so fast. Not that that was bad, of course — quite the opposite. It was just that the absolute best Jim had allowed himself to expect from the meeting was an invitation to come back for a second interview, and the most likely outcome a polite "thanks, but no thanks."

Gibson had been right about the paper-pushing. Jim had spent an hour filling in forms in the office of the Human Resources Manager, Frances Amaraglia. Finally, though, he was done. The officious woman — young; *everyone* seemed so young here — had finally given him a brusque smile, said, "See you next Monday," and that was it. Employee package clutched in his hand — contract, booklet explaining compensation and benefits, plus a slip of paper telling where and when to show up to be photographed for his security pass — Jim found himself out in the lobby again, walking out past the reception desk, dropping his laminated visitor pass into the small basket.

So fast. He felt numb, stunned — no, *disconnected*, that was the right term. So disconnected he couldn't even respond to the receptionist's cheery good-bye.

The glass front doors were ahead of him. He reached out for the nonexistent doorknob, remembering at the last moment that they operated on proximity sensors. With a barely audible *hiss*, the doors slid open before him, and he stepped out—

—only to step hurriedly aside — *flinch* aside, almost. A group of people — all dark, conservative suits and grim attitudes — were coming up the low steps; five of them: four men and a black-haired woman in the lead. For an instant, Jim's gaze met hers. Something seemed to twist in his chest — something inexplicable.

Then they were past him, through and into the lobby, the doors sliding shut behind him. There was tension in the woman's shoulders, he could see it — almost as though she wanted to turn back and look behind her, but wouldn't allow herself.

But then the feeling was gone. He felt his own tension — sick tension in his chest — fade away as though it had never been. *What the hell just happened?*

Nothing, he told himself firmly. *Nothing just happened. I was startled, and I overreacted.* That was the truth of it, of course. He glanced in through the glass doors again.

The receptionist with the asymmetric hair was ushering them through into the heart of the building. *Just businesspeople, that's all.*

He looked around. The car wasn't out front where Christian had parked it.

Damn it! Wouldn't that just be like Christian if the young Walker had taken it into his head to go for a drive or something, and forgotten about Jim? With a muffled curse, Jim strode out into the middle of the parking lot, fists planted on his hips. *Damn it!*

No, there was the car. Pulled round the corner, parked in the shade of the building. Through the windshield he could see Christian, kicked back in the seat, head hanging limply, mouth open. From this angle, even the holographic eyes etched into his sunglasses were closed.

Jim walked up and rapped sharply on the roof, chuckling as the younger Garou jolted awake.

Christian looked up at him sourly. "Why's it always in the middle of a good dream?" he grumbled.

A sudden thought struck Jim. "Did you see the business types going in the front door?"

"Suits, huh?" Christian shook his head. "Didn't see anything, had my mind on other things." He paused. "Why?"

Jim forced the last remnants of his reaction from his mind. "Nothing."

"So how'd it go?" the other Glass Walker asked as Jim climbed into the passenger seat.

"Say hello to the new precision machinist at Terra Nova Biometrics," he said.

• • •

Who was he?

Pamela Barnes felt her thin lips twist in a snarl. A Garou, that was clear, his smell — his *reek* — was still in her nostrils. But who?

And, more important, what in the name of the Abyss was he doing here? Coincidence? No, she couldn't accept that. Only weak-minded fools believed in coincidence. Coincidence was a working of the Wyld or the Weaver, always.

So he knew, why else would he be here? He knew *something*. But what? That she'd be here, today? No, that was too great a leap. If he *had* known, would he have been alone? No, he'd have brought with him more Wyld-dazzled fools like himself, and she'd have been in a fight for her life.

Should she have gone for his throat when she'd had the chance? Even now her tongue ached for the taste of his blood.

Again, no. Patience always came hard to her kind, but this was one of those times when patience was the only logical course. The Delirium, the Veil, would have made sure none of the monkeys accepted what it was they were actually seeing — one Garou throating another, in the heart of a Silicon Valley industrial park. But however they'd interpreted it, however they'd framed it so it fitted with their blinkered view of the universe, it still would have disrupted her mission here. Nobody talks business when a knife-wielding maniac, or maybe a cougar come down from the high country, has gone berserk in the parking lot.

A scout, then? An agent of a kind, sent to learn. . . what? What had he been here to learn, and had he learned it? She had to find out.

First, she had to find out who he was. Fortunately that was easy from this vantage point. She reached out and grabbed one of the many Net-spiders that scurried along the laser-burning datapaths that surrounded her. As the small spirit thrashed and flailed in her claws, she snarled her instructions to it, focusing the power of her will through the technofetish that had brought her to this place. Slowly, the spirit's struggles stilled, until it rested, placid, against the pads of her paw. Satisfied, she tossed the Net-spider back toward the datapath, watched as it grabbed onto the construct with tiny claws, and scurried off into the shimmering distance.

Terra Nova took its security seriously, she knew. Every guest had his or her image scanned via a video camera, and that image was stored in the security database along with every datum the company had on the visitor. These datafiles were locked and encrypted — tight enough security to keep out all but the best monkey hacker. To a Net-spider, though, the primitive security might as well not exist at all. Soon enough she'd know everything that Terra Nova knew about the strange Garou. And then she'd make her decision on how to proceed.

For the moment, though, she had other matters to deal with. In an instant, she shifted from Crinos to human. Again she focused her attention on her technofetish — represented here by a swirling, writhing web of Weaver-patterns — and brought her will to bear. The harsh, fractal imagery of the Computer Web faded around her.

Barnes slipped her pocket computer — the manifestation of the technofetish in the physical world — into her purse, and straightened her severely cut jacket. She pushed open the door and stepped out of the washroom into the hall.

The administration drone who'd been assigned to escort her looked relieved. "Are you okay, Ms. Barnes?"

"Airline food," Barnes said flatly. "Now take me to Gibson."

• • •

Arrogant, this monkey. Arrogant, and stubborn. With an effort, Barnes kept her face calm and expressionless. Her eyes were drawn, again and again, to his tanned throat framed by the open collar of his shirt. She imagined how that shirt would look stained by pulsing gouts of his blood.

"I'm sorry, Ms. Barnes," Gibson said, his tone of voice making it abundantly clear he wasn't sorry at all. "You've wasted your time coming out here. I told that to your colleagues, and I told that to you yesterday over the phone. I'm not interested in selling."

Barnes let her lips twist in a faint, knowing smile. "Every man has his price, Mr. Gibson. I came here for the opportunity to discuss yours, if you take my meaning."

She could smell his anger, and his effort to conceal it. "Every man probably *does* have his price," he said flatly, "me included. But that price varies depending on who's offering it. If *you* take *my* meaning."

"My principal has made a fair offer—"

He cut her off sharply. "*Which* principal, Ms. Barnes? See, I've done some digging. You claim you're working for Tsubai Technologies. But Tsubai's just a shell company, isn't it? Another outfit's pulling its strings, some multinational called Pentex.

"Like I said, I've done some digging," he went on, his tone almost conversational again, his anger suppressed. "Nobody much has heard of Pentex, but those who have heard of it would rather they hadn't. Shady business practices, direct manipulation of regulatory agencies, willful disregard of environmental regulation, dirty tricks against competitors — including the way the corporation bought out Tsubai itself, by the way — you name it. Even if I was looking for a buyer — which I'm not — you think I'd sell to Pentex? Not on your life."

Barnes was silent for a moment, regarding him with hidden amusement. *Stubborn*, she thought again. *Good*. "And that's your final decision?" she asked quietly.

"What do *you* think?"

She smiled. "I think things change." She rose smoothly and started for the door. "I'll be seeing you," she told him over her shoulder.

"I doubt it."

She felt her smile broaden. *I don't*.

• • •

The sheer brass of the woman.

David Gibson leaned back in his chair, rolling his head to release the tension in his neck and shoulders. He turned off his halogen desklamp, the only illumination in the room now the small spots that highlighted favorite items on his bookshelves. He sighed. Gibson normally did his best work at night, after the bustle of the day had died down — no interruptions, no phone calls, no visitors, no distractions.

Not tonight, though. He couldn't focus; his anger kept welling up, eliminating his capacity for clear thought.

Who the hell does she think she is? he asked himself. *And who does she think I am?* No subtlety at all in her approach, no acknowledgment of the fact that he might have more interest in Terra Nova's business than money. No recognition that he might care what happened to the neural interface technology he'd developed, and to what use it was eventually put. Had she thought he'd just sell, without doing any research into who was offering to buy? Or had she complacently expected that one layer of shell company would be enough to conceal her real allegiance? *Pentex.* Sell out to the multinational, and within a year the technology he'd envisioned as a way of helping the disabled and amputees would find its way into horrific new weapons, or worse.

He jumped at the sound from outside his office door — a sharp *clack*, as of something hard striking the composite-tile floor. Gibson shook his head, laughing silently at his own reaction. *Edgy, am I?* It was almost 10 in the evening, long after official business hours, but there were always people in the building. System designers and programmers working on flex-time, janitors. That was it, he decided: a cleaner had probably set down a bucket or something. That's what he'd heard.

The sound came again, closer this time, and again he jumped as though he'd been stung. No bucket, that. No, it was something else.

He tried to laugh again at his reaction — *foolishness* — but the tension in his throat and chest stifled the sound, turned it into a sick croaking. *Stupid to be afraid.*

But he *was* afraid.

Another sound, the soft brushing of. . . of *something* against the outside of his closed office door. Slowly, the doorknob began to turn.

Gibson pushed his chair back from his desk. *Nowhere to run.* The thought struck him like a physical impact, as something from outside him, the mental equivalent of a spoken taunt. The door began to swing open. All he could see beyond it was darkness.

Without taking his eyes from the door, he reached for the phone. Hit the speaker button, and the speed-dial key for building security.

No response. Silence, not even the internal PBX dial-tone. For an instant he wished he had a gun in his desk drawer, like corporate executives always seemed to have in bad TV movies.

The door was wide open now. The hallway beyond was pitch black — not the half-lighting that was on around the clock, not even the dim red emergency lights.

Movement! Something was moving beyond the door. Impossible to make out what it was, black on black, darkness in darkness, hints of a shape. His mind tried to make sense of it, failed.

With an effort, Gibson tore his gaze from the door, glanced at the window. His office was on the third floor above the parking lot. If he jumped, it would be a 30-foot fall onto concrete. Possibly fatal. He imagined the glass shattering as he hurled himself through the window, the night air whipping at his clothes and hair.

Another sound, and his gaze snapped back to the door. The darkness writhed.

Belatedly, he remembered his desklamp. Gibson flipped it on, grabbed the swiveling head, feeling the hot metal sear his flesh, and pivoted it toward the door.

He saw the shape, in the moment that it flung itself toward him. Twisted, impossibly large, reaching for his throat with claws like small daggers. It was too late to even scream.

• • •

Jim heard the news at breakfast. The radio newsfeed was playing softly in the background as he sat before the condo's picture window, gazing out over the bay toward Alcatraz and Angel Island. He wasn't really listening, but somehow the words still managed to penetrate. He jerked upright, slopping coffee onto the off-white leather of the chair.

He checked his watch. Just past eight; the local news should be on. Setting the mug down, he crossed to the TV and turned it on.

David Gibson, president of Terra Nova Biometrics, had committed suicide. That was the story. His body had been found less than an hour ago by Frances Amaraglia, Human Resources Manager, who'd gone to his office to discuss staffing requirements. She'd found him behind his desk, his cold hand still clutching the 9mm pistol he'd fired into his right temple. The police were reporting no signs of forced entry, no indications of a struggle or foul play — an open-and-shut case of suicide. A business analyst speculated that Gibson's company might be under financial pressure, and that a recent refusal by Tsubai Technologies to buy the troubled organization had driven him to despondency and suicide.

Jim turned off the TV and returned to his chair by the window. He picked up his coffee again and sipped at it thoughtfully. It all sounded logical enough, particularly in the Valley. Boom and bust was a common story, start-ups that took off like a rocket, only to drop faster than a rock years, months, or even weeks later. It was all so believable.

Yet Jim didn't believe it — *couldn't* believe it. Financial trouble? Possibly, even though he hadn't seen anything at the Terra Nova facility to make him think it was hurting in any way. But despondency and suicide? That just didn't fit with his memory of David Gibson, didn't fit at all. There was no way — no way at all — he could accept the fact that the man he'd met had, less than eight hours later, put a gun to his head and pulled the trigger.

Yet the police had found no evidence of foul play, so the new report had claimed. What had happened? *Could the failed buy-out have driven Gibson to take his own life?*

Suddenly, in his mind's eye he saw the group of businesspeople — "suits", Christian had called them; the four men and one woman — he'd passed outside the Terra Nova lobby. Were they the contingent from that company the news had mentioned — what was it, Tsubai Technologies? There was something about them. He'd felt real fear when he'd first seen them. No reason for it, and he'd had so much on his mind that he'd denied the feeling, suppressed it so fast that he'd hardly been aware of it. But, denied and suppressed or not, the feeling had been there.

Why? What was it about a group of "suits" that could frighten him on such a profound level? Was there some connection with Gibson's death?

His eyes still on the bay, Jim reached over and picked up his phone, dialed a number by feel. The ringing tone sounded a half-dozen times, a dozen. When he finally heard the *click* as the connection was made, he expected a voice mail system.

"Yeah, what?" The voice was thick, muzzy with sleep.

He smiled to himself. "Sun's up, Christian. You should be too."

"Sun's up only because it doesn't have a choice in the matter. What's happening?"

"What do you know about Tsubai Technologies?"

There was a pause at the other end of the line. When Christian spoke again, his voice was clearer. "Somebody tell you about Tsubai?"

It was Jim's turn to hesitate. There was something about the other Garou's voice that nagged at him. He set it aside for the moment. "Something on the news."

"Huh, well. Biotech company, originally out of Kyoto, but they've got subsidiaries in New York, Toronto and somewhere in Australia. Canberra, I think. Never heard of them until a year or two back, don't know where they're getting their funding. But funding they've got, that's for sure. They're picking out the best and the brightest biotech start-ups and buying them out. Senior management seems to know where it's going, and it's willing to spend the money to get there."

Jim shook his head. *I'm missing something here.* "You said they're buying start-ups," he repeated. "Like Terra Nova?"

Again there was a pause, silence except for the ghost-voices of other lines, other conversations. "What's given you such a hard-on about Tsubai?" Christian asked at last.

"Like Terra Nova?" Jim repeated.

Christian sighed. "Yeah," he admitted, "that's the buzz I hear. Now answer *my* question."

Curtly, Jim filled the younger Walker in on the news report. When he was done, Christian gave a low whistle. "Interesting. *Mucho* interesting. Old Money Bags is going to want to hear about this," he mused.

Jim raised his eyebrows at that. Roderick Harrington — "Money Bags" to the younger Garou — was the leader of the local Glass Walkers, known throughout the Valley for providing venture capital to innovative start-ups and buying out organizations that were financially shaky, but working in technological areas that intrigued him. "Why would Harrington be interested?" Jim asked.

Christian snorted, the verbal equivalent of a shrug. "Pretty damned obvious, isn't it?" he suggested. "With Gibson gone, Tsubai's going to move in. And Tsubai's going to be a lot more likely than Gibson was to let Money Bags take an equity position in the company."

"Wait." Things were suddenly more complicated than Jim could immediately deal with. "Harrington was interested in buying Terra Nova?"

"Not all of it," Christian corrected. "That's not his way unless the company's in real trouble. He's just into buying a percentage in companies developing technology he likes."

"He likes what Terra Nova's doing?"

"*Loves* it."

This didn't make any sense. "Does Tsubai like it too?"

"If they had any brains, they would," Christian answered flatly.

"And David Gibson was looking to sell to them?"

"No way. They were coming after *him*. I hear he shut them down hard, just like he shut Money Bags down." Christian hesitated. "Course, that could have been a bargaining ploy — you know, a move to jack the price up."

"But the new report implied he'd been *trying* to sell out to Tsubai," Jim reminded him, "and when they turned him down; he was supposed to kill himself."

"Yeah," Christian growled, "well, I think the press kinda got it ass-backward on this one — not an uncommon occurrence in this town. What makes more sense is that they made a bid, Gibson came back with a counter — way higher than they wanted to pay — and they walked away."

Jim shook his head again. "Then why would he kill himself?"

"Who knows? Why do monkeys do anything?"

"Not good enough." Jim frowned in thought. "What if Gibson *didn't* kill himself?"

"Why does it matter?"

"I *liked* him, that's why it matters. What if Gibson didn't kill himself?"

"You said he shot himself," Christian said patiently. "Gun in his hand, right? No signs of a struggle; would *you* let someone put a gun in your hand without fighting back?"

"It can be done."

"In the goddamn *movies*, maybe." Jim heard Christian take a calming breath. "Anyway," the younger Garou went on, "it's a secure building — alarms, electronic locks, security cameras, probably patrolling security guards. No signs of forced entry, not a peep from the security systems. Who could have done it?"

"*You* could," Jim said flatly. "Maybe even I could."

"Are you saying a *Garou* killed him? Come on."

"All I'm saying is there are possibilities — possibilities the monkeys aren't going to think of."

"You're reaching."

"Maybe. But I don't think so." Jim paused. "What if I'm right? Who stands to gain?"

"Tsubai, mainly," Christian answered slowly. "I don't know who inherits with Gibson gone, but they're much more likely to sell out to Tsubai at a reasonable price."

"That's what I thought." There was a strange tension in Jim's chest, like a fist squeezing his heart. Puzzled, he examined it mentally for a moment. Then he recognized it: *Anger.* "And from what you've said, that means *Harrington* also stands to gain."

There was a long silence. "I don't think you'd better be saying that in certain circles," Christian said finally, his voice quiet.

"You said it, not me," Jim corrected. "Not in so many words. But you did say Tsubai would be more willing to let Harrington aboard. Right?" The younger Walker's silence was answer enough. "Is there some kind of link between Harrington and Tsubai?"

"Link?" There was something new in Christian's voice, the first hint of uncertainty, as though he were considering something for the first time. "Not directly. I know he admires some of what they're doing; he considers them a lot more right-thinking than a lot of similar outfits. They're always digging up the best and the brightest." He snorted quietly. "You're not going to get much of a hearing from Harrington — or from anybody else, for that matter — if you're going to start bad-mouthing Tsubai."

"There's something wrong here." The words were out of Jim's mouth before he was even aware he was going to speak. But, once he'd said it, he knew — deep down *knew* — it was true. "There's something going on that we don't know about."

"It's called 'business,'" Christian shot back immediately, but the thoughtful tone was still in his voice.

"More than that." Jim paused. "I want to find out more about Tsubai. Can you help me?"

After a long pause, Christian answered, "I don't know."

"I think this is important." Jim was surprised by the intensity in his voice. "It's important, and I need your help. I can't do this by myself."

"You would be able to, if only you'd—"

Jim cut him off in mid-grumble. "I know. 'If only I'd stop being a technopeasant and open my eyes.' OK, I know I've been a technopeasant, but now I *want* to open my eyes, and I need you to help me do it."

Another pause followed — so long that Jim wondered if the connection had been broken. Finally, he heard Christian sigh in resignation. "I'll be round as soon as I can."

• • •

Jim opened the door at the first knock. Christian strode in, a notebook computer under his arm. He shot Jim a baleful look. "You sure you still want to do this?"

"I'm sure."

The younger Garou sighed. "I was afraid you'd say that." He set the computer down on the table and brushed the matte-black case with his fingertips. "If we're going to go, let's go."

Jim indicated the computer. "You need to plug that into the phone, or something?"

"Uh-uh. Cellular link." Briskly, he flipped open the clamshell cover and powered the compact unit on. "Have you done this before?"

"What exactly are we going to do?"

Christian chuckled. "I guess that answers my question." He typed a quick command into the computer, and nodded in satisfaction as the display on the screen changed. "We're visiting the Computer Web."

"The. . . ?"

"Part of the Umbra," Christian explained. "Some people call it the 'Virtual Umbra' or the 'TechnoUmbra'." He glanced wryly at Jim. "Are you *sure* you're a Glass Walker?"

Unbidden, memories of his conversation with Fraser Martinsen in the Umbrascape of Muir Beach filled his mind. *A good question: Am I sure I'm a Glass Walker?* "Just get on with it," he said gruffly.

Christian played another blindingly fast riff on the keyboard. Eyes fixed on the screen, he extended his left hand to Jim. "Take hold." Jim gripped the younger Garou's hand. "OK, here we go."

Jim felt the shift before he could see it: the momentary *discontinuity* — there was no better word — he associated with stepping sideways into the Umbra. There was a difference, though: the lack of control. He wasn't doing this himself; he was a passenger, drawn along by the power of Christian's Gift.

Now the visible changes began. The screen of the notebook computer started to glow, brighter and brighter, until it was physically painful to look at. Jim averted his eyes, but still he could *feel* the light, as though it were penetrating skin and flesh to fill his bones with a strange new energy. The view out the window faded away, as though a gray, diffusing fog had come up out of nowhere. In a matter of seconds, the bay, the island of Alcatraz, everything was gone. . .

. . . to be replaced, a moment later, by a shimmering light. It was amorphous, unfocused at first. But quickly it coalesced, forming a glowing spider web of luminescence. Its complexity drew Jim toward it. There was no order to it, no overall structure — not that he could see, at least. But somehow Jim could *feel* there was order — order he'd perceive if only he studied it long enough.

He felt a tap on the shoulder, turned quickly.

Christian was grinning at him. He held something in his hand: a glowing object about the size of a cigarette pack. It took Jim a moment to realize it was a manifestation of the notebook computer — *A technofetish*, he realized belatedly. He looked around him, noting with surprise that the walls of his condo were gone.

"Welcome to the Pattern Web," Christian said. His voice had a strange timbre to it, almost as though the sound had been phase-shifted. "Ready for step two?"

The next transition had begun even before Jim had nodded his agreement. The glowing network — the Pattern Web, Christian had called it — rushed toward him, or they toward it — he couldn't be sure, since there was no sensation of movement. It expanded in his vision, expanded exponentially, somehow warping itself around him as space itself — or whatever was its analog here — twisted in on itself. The net, the web, extended off to infinity in all directions. For an instant his mind spun, as though he stood, balancing precariously, on the edge of madness. But then he found an image that made sense to him.

Yes, he told himself, *that's it. I'm in the middle of a bush, and a thousand spiders have built their webs throughout the branches and twigs. It's near dawn, and there are droplets of dew on the strands of silk, except that the droplets burn like stars, and they move independently of each other.* It wasn't a perfect analogy, but at least it was *something* for his mind to cling to.

"The Computer Web," Christian said. The phase-shift effect was even more pronounced, making it difficult to understand his words. "This is the first step to *anywhere*, data-wise. Where do you want to go first?"

Jim hesitated, then, "Terra Nova," he said, his voice ringing strangely in his own ears. "Let's start there."

"You're the boss." Christian chuckled. "Here we go. Hang onto your brain."

With shocking suddenness, the Computer Web shifted around them, spinning into a new orientation as they hurtled forward.

• • •

Her view out into the "macro" level of the Computer Web was narrow and grainy, limited as it was by the "bandwidth" of the Net-spider Pamela Barnes was using as a "remote" for her senses. Still, it was more than good enough to see the two figures speeding through the network of datapaths. In her extended vision, one burned almost as brightly as the technofetish in his hand, glowing with the power of the Gift he used to convey them both. The other was dim, lit only by the faint "signature" that identified him as Garou. Her thin black lips drew back from yellowed fangs as she recognized the dim figure.

James Laurence. The Garou she'd seen at Terra Nova, the one she'd sent a Net-spider to investigate in Gibson's security computer system.

So she'd been right all along. It *hadn't* been paranoia. (*Paranoia.* She hissed wordlessly. Some of her colleagues in Pentex's Acquisitions Division had accused her of paranoia — never to her face, of course — in the past. By the blackness of the Abyss, what did *they* know?) She'd been right about that Wyld-blinded fool. He *knew.* He *had* to know — some of what was going on, at least. Otherwise, why would he be here? Smarter than most of his kind, he'd obviously sensed at least the basic shape of her activities, and of Pentex's plans.

Smarter than most, yet not smart enough. Otherwise, why would he be coming here with only one comrade, blundering into the ambush she'd laid in anticipation of his arrival? No, if he'd truly been smart, he would have brought a whole contingent of his fellows. *Unless.* . . Her red-rimmed eyes narrowed.

Unless this James Laurence judged that he and his colleague — and the fetish; don't forget the fetish! — were powerful enough to deal with any opposition on their own. She focused her will on the Net-spider remote, narrowing the range of her vision.

Neither Laurence or the other showed the signatures of great power. The nameless one was using a Gift the Garou called "Virtual Umbra," and that was the only power that was upon him at the moment. Laurence himself was exercising no Gift at all, as though he possessed no Gifts usable here in the Computer Web. (Either that, or as though he were conserving his strength for a coming fight —*No!* She shook her head, driving that thought from her mind.) No, the real unknown — the factor that could sway the balance one way or the other — was the technofetish, the bright-burning spiritual construct the nameless one clutched in his hand.

She nodded to himself, fingering the bone hilt of her baleklaive. The nameless one would be the first to die.

She laughed, the sound harsh and alien in her own ears, as she watched the two figures approaching the data junction — the "doorway" — that led to the Terra Nova computer system.

• • •

The shapes were on them — all over them — the instant they came through the doorway. The data junction, a shimmering, shifting dodecahedron, had responded to their approach with an almost-supersonic keening. At Christian's touch, it had warped, shifted — almost as though reality were turning itself inside-out — and engulfed them. For a moment Jim had been disoriented, finding himself inside a kind of low-resolution rendering of a computer room. And that's when the shapes had hit them.

Instinctively, Jim batted aside the small black form that hurtled at his face. In the instant of contact, he felt tiny claws tearing at the flesh of his hand, trying vainly for a grip. The wounds they left burned, like vinegar in a paper cut. Another shape flew at him from a new angle, but he managed to duck aside. As it sailed by, he got an impression of spider-like legs tipped with hooked black claws.

From the corner of his eye, he saw Christian beset by the spider-things. While only two of the creatures (*so far*) had gone for him, there were almost a dozen of them clawing at the younger Garou. With a silent curse, Jim stepped toward his friend, swinging a fist to knock away one of the attackers.

But before the blow could even land, Christian spoke a work in the Old Tongue, and the light from the technofetish in his right hand flared, multiplying a dozenfold. Throwing up a hand to shield his eyes, Jim reeled back. The air crackled with power around him, and thin, batlike shrieks tore at his ears.

The energy discharge was over in an instant. Jim forced his eyes open, blinking back tears. Through floating blue afterimages, he saw the scorched and smoking bodies of the spider-things twitching spasmodically on the floor.

Movement.

He spun in response to the flash of motion caught in his peripheral vision. A huge figure was lunging at him, a female Crinos with pure-white ears contrasting brilliantly against night-black pelt. Her eyes glowed with a faint green radiance, and the kris-bladed klaive in her hand glinted with the cold, unmistakable light of silver.

Jim felt his body instinctively shift into the Crinos, the transition effortless in the Umbra. Powerful muscles tensed to counter the black-pelted attacker's charge.

But at the last instant, the attacker danced aside. Her klaive flashed in a short, fast arc.

To plunge deep into Christian's gut. The younger Garou was still in the human — he hadn't shifted. His eyes were wide in alarm as he desperately worked the tiny keyboard of the technofetish. He doubled forward as the silver blade drove into his flesh, spittle and blood spraying from his lips with the force of his scream. The fetish fell from his hand, and the death-black Crinos kicked it aside. For a moment Christian remained on his feet, bent forward over the blade still buried in his belly, the strength of the attacker's arm supporting him. Then the Crinos withdrew the blade — Christian's moan of agony almost covering the wet, sucking sound — and the young Glass Walker crumpled to the floor.

The black-pelted Crinos turned to Jim, her lips drawing back from her fangs in a rictus that could almost be called a smile. "Your turn," she growled.

Rage twisted in Jim's chest — rage, and a terrible fear. A *Black Spiral Dancer.* "Why?" he gasped.

Slowly, the Dancer advanced on him, a supple wrist twisting the silver klaive in a serpentine, almost hypnotic pattern before his eyes, somehow echoing the spiral bone fetish she wore on a leather thong around her neck. He backed up a step, then another. "*Why?*" he asked again.

The Crinos laughed, the phase-shift effect making the sound even more horrible. "You thought to stop us, did you? Foolish, like all of your kind."

Another step back. Jim wanted to glance over a shoulder to see if there were any further threats behind him, but he couldn't tear his gaze away from the circling silver blade. Instinctively, he tried a step to the side, an attempt to get them circling. But the Dancer countered simply, by mirroring his step. The fear and rage churned within him. He felt the Fox stirring in the primitive shadows of his mind. *Flight rather than fight.* But where would he run to, here? "Stop what?" he asked. Then suddenly something clicked into place. "You were at Terra Nova, weren't you? Outside the lobby."

Her grin was answer enough.

In a cascade, unbidden, unrelated thoughts and facts came together, forming the rudiments of understanding. *Christian said Tsubai wanted to take over Terra Nova. Tsubai had the funding, but he didn't know where it came from. Funding from a larger corporation, a corporation associated with the Black Spiral Dancers.*

"You're of Tsubai," he gasped. "Tsubai is of Pentex, and Pentex is of the Wyrm."

The Dancer's eyes widened. "You *didn't* know?"

"I know now."

She laughed again, her momentary surprise gone. "For all the good it'll do you. You die here. We take Terra Nova. We let Roderick Harrington and his Glass Walkers take an equity position. We feed him prototypes, for him and his friends to use — *special* prototypes. And we feed the truth of the Wyrm right into the brains of the Garou."

Jim's skin felt cold. *Could it happen that way? Yes,* he realized, *all too easily.* Christian's reaction had shown that very clearly. Harrington wanted Terra Nova, and what it represented. Tsubai represented a way around Gibson's stubborn refusal to sell. And, because the corporation was giving Harrington and the other Walkers something they wanted, none of them wanted to look too closely at Tsubai.

Lost for an instant in his thoughts, he'd let the Dancer move too close. The klaive licked out like silver lightning toward his heart. At the last instant he flung himself back, swinging up a powerful forearm to deflect the blow. The Dancer twisted her wrist, and the keen edge sliced skin and muscle.

Jim howled with the agony of it. Frenzy boiled, and it took every iota of willpower in him to fight back the siren-song of the Fox. Through a red fog of pain, he saw that the Dancer hadn't withdrawn her knife-hand after the thrust. Wildly, he lashed out with his right paw, feeling his claws score the back of her hand. She hissed with her own pain, drawing back. He took a half-step toward her, but stopped as the klaive resumed its sinuous pattern.

The Dancer's smile became something terrible to see. "Good," she cooed. "Good. A worthy adversary. A true Garou. Not like *that*." Without looking, she gestured down with her free hand at Christian.

In reflex, Jim glanced down at the crumpled body of the young Walker. And in the instant his attention was diverted, the Dancer came for him again. He caught the flash of movement in his peripheral vision, and just managed to duck under the cut, hearing the silver blade whistle past a hair's-breadth from his skull. He lurched back out of range.

As the Dancer resumed her slow advance, he tried to split his attention between her movements and what he'd seen.

Christian wasn't dead, as he'd thought; sorely wounded, perhaps mortally, but still conscious for the moment. He'd seen the younger Garou dragging himself forward, agonizingly, along the cold, white floor of the data node, leaving a broad smear of blood behind him. Dragging himself, an inch at a time, toward the technofetish that the Dancer had kicked aside. He fought to keep his gaze fixed on the circling klaive. He took another step to his right, away from Christian. As she echoed the move, he started a weaving motion with his own clawed paws, an imitation of a karate *kata* he'd seen in a movie — *anything* to keep the attacker's attention on him, and away from Christian.

But somehow he must have given his thoughts away — a subliminal glance toward his fallen comrade, *something*. With a rush of sick horror, he saw the Dancer's eyes widen in surprise. She looked down at Christian, saw him reaching feebly toward the technofetish still a yard away from his shaking fingers. With a shriek of rage, she lashed out with a vicious kick, the claws on her feet laying the young Garou's throat open to the spine.

"*Noooo!*" The scream tore Jim's larynx, and he tasted his own blood, copper-bright. In that instant, he felt the Fox flee from his mind, the Berserk come down upon him.

In slow motion, it seemed — detached, almost as though he were an observer, not a participant — he felt himself launch forward, driven by the powerful muscles of his Crinos, claws ready to rend and tear.

The Dancer's reactions were almost as swift as his; she was moving before he'd traversed a fraction of the distance between them, dropping into a crouch. She had a fraction of a second to decide on her response.

In her eyes, he *saw* her make the decision, saw her make the wrong one. If she'd fallen back, she'd have avoided the violence of his initial charge, and would have been able to cut him to pieces at her leisure. But her own rage bloomed — he saw it, the green radiance in her eyes flaring — and overpowered her judgment. She held her ground, driving the klaive straight toward him.

He roared in transcendent agony as the tainted silver slid into his chest. But his claws were already sinking into her throat. Convulsively he dragged her body against his, driving the klaive even deeper, but trapping it between them so she couldn't withdraw it and use it again. The corruption of her breath washed over him. Her eyes widened again — in fear, now, not in rage. And then he could see nothing as he buried his face in her throat, jaws working, tearing. Blood gouted over him — hot, bitter blood. Her scream became something hideous, burbling.

And it was over. Jim flung the limp body from him. Through a narrowing red tunnel, he saw the massive form of the Crinos shift into the human as death took her: a coldly beautiful woman, blood matting her white-streaked black hair.

He heard a rushing sound around him, within him. *Surf; the surf of Muir Beach.*

The blood-red tunnel closed before him, became an endless sea of blackness. He fell headlong into it.

● ● ●

"We had the Wyrm's own time finding you, you know."

Night. The gibbous moon sailed among the clouds like a ghostly galleon. Jim Laurence sat on the sand of Muir Beach. The cold salt air intensified the dull ache in his chest. Absently, he slipped a hand inside his shirt, felt the soft weal of scar tissue. He looked up at Fraser Martinsen, standing over him. "Thanks," he said softly.

The Child of Gaia shrugged. "You fought well," he said after a moment. "You brought glory and honor upon yourself and your tribe. So say the elders." He hesitated, his lips twisting in a wry grin. "Given any more thought to what we talked about last time?"

Jim turned to look out along the moonlight reflecting off the waves. *Like a road of silver I could follow to. . . where?*

"We talked about balance," he said, without taking his eyes off the silver path. "Finding it, losing it. Do *any* of us have it?"

"That's an interesting question. And an important one. Do you have an answer?"

"When the Dancer attacked us," Jim went on as though he hadn't heard, "I took on the Crinos; instinct, no conscious thought involved. Christian kept the human, and he tried to use his fetish. Even when he was dying, he kept trying to use the fetish. I acted from instinct; I think he acted from conscious thought." He looked up at his friend. "Which one of us acted like a true Garou?"

"You survived," Fraser pointed out. His smile faded. "Which do *you* think?" he asked softly.

"Both. Neither. I don't know." Jim paused. "Thought, instinct; is it possible to strike the balance?"

"Another important question. Where are you going to look for the answer?"

Again Jim touched the wound in his chest. "Here." ///

Fang of the Wolf

by Owl Goingback

They were out there, somewhere, beyond the arena where dancers moved and swayed to the beat of a northern drum, out past the rows of teepees, tents, and RVs. They lurked in the shadows, unseen, undetected, but Sam Nakai knew they were there. He could smell them. The wind carried their scent, foul and loathsome. They were the servants of the Wyrm.

Sam felt old, very old, much older than a man of 55 should feel. He stood in the doorway of his RV and looked out across the pow-wow grounds, searching for a sign that the end was near. that the one who would take up the battle had finally arrived.

A member of the Wendigo tribe of the Garou, Sam had left the dense forests of Canada years ago. He traveled alone, an Anruth, the pack just a distant memory. In the past 10 years he had faced death more times than he could remember. His body told the story, each scar a different battle. The black patch that covered his sightless right eye was testimony that not all battles were easily won.

He wasn't sure why he had come to California, to this particular gathering. There was something in the wind, a premonition of things to come, that had drawn him to the Coyote Hills Regional Park, just across the bay from San Francisco. A tense stillness clutched the night, unnoticed to those whose ears were filled with the beating of the drum and the haunting voices of the singers. But Sam noticed the uneasy quiet. It was a warning that the evil one was near.

Sam let his gaze again roll across the pow-wow grounds. The spirits had promised he would find someone worthy of passing the sacred stone on to; a person who would protect it with their life from the evil that threatened to destroy it. So far, that someone had not shown up. But they would. Sam had faith in the spirits. In the meantime, he would continue to wait. . . and pray.

● ● ●

Heather Ocoee knew she was going to be sick. She staggered to the shoulder of the road and dropped to her knees. Her vision blurred, and she broke out in a cold sweat, but she didn't black out. Not this time. Instead, she gagged, throwing up what little food she had eaten.

What's wrong with me, God?"

She had been sick for weeks, barely able to keep anything down. Food, smells, even the sight of certain colors made her nauseous. The nurse at the orphanage said it was because her body was going through changes. But Heather had already had her first period and knew that the sickness and dizzy spells were more than just the onset of puberty. And she wasn't pregnant!

Even the feeling of her own clothing had become a source of irritation. She longed to tear off her jeans and shirt and run naked through the night.

Like in my dreams.

The dreams had started about the same time as the sickness. Strange, bizarre visions that tormented her sleep, leaving her soaked with sweat and physically drained the next morning. In her dreams, she ran naked across the moonlit desert, the caress of the chill wind cleansing her body, exciting her. There was a sense of freedom she had never known in real life, a feeling of longing that made her waking hours all the more unbearable.

Though she had lived there all her life, the orphanage with its dark corridors and grimy windows, became a prison to her. She felt like an animal in a cage. Finally, unable to stand it any longer, she crawled through a window on the second floor and shimmied down a gutter drainpipe to freedom. That was six weeks ago. Since then she had learned that life on the open road wasn't so hot either.

Death had come to California. Silent, carried on the wind from the nuclear weapons factories and testing grounds, it had swept across the land like a plague of hungry locusts, turning grass and flowers brown, and twisting trees into grotesque deformities. Gone were the animals that once called the countryside their home. Gone, too ,were most of the people, their houses left to crumble and rot like the bones of ancient dinosaurs. Deserted roads ran like scars through the barren hillsides, and rusting road signs told of towns that no longer existed.

The nausea finally passed leaving a dull ache in the pit of her stomach. Heather leaned back, brushed the hair out of her eyes, and took a deep breath. The breeze off the ocean carried the stench of pollution and toxic chemicals buried deep beneath the ground. She wrinkled her nose in disgust. And from somewhere in the darkness came the putrid odor of death and decay.

Probably an animal, Heather thought as she stood up and walked back to the center of the road. Ahead in the distance, less than a mile away, a circle of lights beckoned like an oasis in the night. She studied the lights, wondering what they were for. Perhaps it was a farmhouse, or a refugee settlement. She was tired and wanted to find a safe place to curl up for the night. With her luck, it would turn out to be another hazardous waste facility.

As Heather stood there, gazing at the lights, she heard something move behind her. She turned in time to see a dark shape dart across the road and disappear into the shadows on the other side. She only saw it for a second, long enough to send tremors of fear down her spine.

The thing looked like a man, but had arms that stretched all the way to the ground, and a head the size of a pumpkin. A pair of eyes flashed green in the moonlight as it crossed the road, bent over, running on all fours.

Heather's heart pumped wildly. In the middle of nowhere, on a dark night, was no place to bump into anything as scary as what she had just seen. With no desire to stick around for a second look, she turned and fled toward the oasis of lights. Behind her, a strange cry split the night. It was answered by a howl from off to her left.

Oh, God, another one. And Halloween isn't over until next weekend!

The road curved to the right. The lights drew nearer. She could see tents set up along the edge of light. A rhythmic beating, like the pounding of a giant heart, filled the air.

Her gaze focused on the lights. She didn't notice the road curve back to the left. Heather cried out as she slipped on the loose gravel at the road's edge, lost her footing, and fell. Sharp rocks bit into her knees and punctured the palms of both hands. She started to stand back up when something tackled her from behind.

The creature slammed her into the ground, rolled her over, and climbed on top of her chest. No longer just a shadowy shape, Heather could see it clearly now. And what she saw terrified her. A thin, muscular body of pallid, gray flesh supported a head that looked like an apple dried in the sun. The nose was barely visible amidst waves of wrinkled skin, but the eyes were large and dark, like those of a reptile. The mouth also looked reptilian. Wide and lipless, it was lined with a double row of serrated teeth. The breath of the creature made Heather gag, for it reeked of blood and decayed meat.

She struggled to get free. but the creature pinned her to the ground. Cold, clammy fingers clamped around Heather's neck, choked her, caused her vision to dim. She knew she was going to die, but was determined not to give up. She felt around on the ground beside her for something to defend herself with, but her trembling fingers found nothing: no stick, no rock — nothing she could use. In desperation, she scooped up a, handful of dirt and flung it into the eyes of the monster.

The creature hissed in anger, covered its eyes, and rolled off of her. Heather jumped up and ran, fleeing for her life. Sounds of pursuit came from behind her, but they were confused and wandered in different directions.

Her heart about to burst, Heather finally reached the circle of lights. She didn't slow down, but raced madly between tents and campsites, colliding with a man dressed in feathers: an Indian. Heather would have screamed, but all her constricted throat could manage was a faint hissing of air.

"Watch, it kid," the man growled. "Don't you know how to act at a pow-wow?"

Heather blinked and looked around. A pow-wow. That's what it was. She had read of such things, but thought all the Indians had died out long ago. She would be safe here. The creature that attacked her wouldn't dare come around so many people.

A feeling of weakness washed over her. Heather's legs quivered, and her bladder felt uncomfortably full. A smile touched her lips as she spotted a row of portalets. Things were already looking up. Maybe she could also find a shower and some food.

• • •

The song ended. The dancers returned to the wooden benches that circled the arena. Sam Nakai studied the dancers and felt a wave of disgust wash over him. He had no particular love for humans in general, but even less for the white race — especially those who dressed up in feathers and bells, and tried to pass themselves off as Native Americans. Only a handful of those who danced were real Indians. The rest were white impostors from the concrete jungle of the cities, their spirits corrupted by the Wyrm. And now they, too, were corrupting, attempting to defile and claim as their own the sacred ceremonies of the Indians.

Sam stepped back from the doorway and grabbed the coffeepot off the stove. He had just poured himself a cup, when he heard the cry of an owl. So distinct and so clear was the cry, and so noticeable above the singing, that it got his immediate attention.

It comes from the east, the direction of a new beginning.

Sam climbed down out of his RV. He stood for a moment, listening, almost afraid to breath. A few seconds later he heard the owl again. The cry came from a strand of trees where the tents were set up.

A feeling of great urgency came over him as he cut between the dealer's booths, the tables crowded with everything from imitation turquoise jewelry to sweet grass. He knew the chosen one was near, but did not feel that they were among those who danced in the sacred circle, or even among those who watched.

He, reached the campgrounds, carefully navigating the shadowy darkness between tents and teepees. He had just past a row of portalets. when the little voice inside his head told him to pay attention. Sam stopped and turned around, looking for what his spirit guide wanted him to see. Just then, the door on the very last portalet opened and someone stepped out. The chill that exploded along his spine told him he had found the one he was looking for. Sam's mouth dropped open in surprise. He never expected the chosen one to be a little girl.

This cannot be. She is too young!

She was about 12 years old, thin and muscular, with raven-black hair reaching to the center of her back. She wore a pair of torn blue jeans, a T-shirt, and sneakers, and carried a small backpack in her left hand. Sam was sure she was Native American, though her complexion was light enough to be of mixed blood. Her face, streaked with dirt, had the innocence of youth. But as she turned toward him, Sam saw something in her eyes that spoke of deep, dark secrets.

Sam sniffed the air and picked up a familiar scent. He smiled. The girl was a Garou, although it was doubtful if she was aware of it. She needed to go through the Rite of Passage, and survive, to become one of the pack.

Sam was elated to find that the chosen one was also a Garou. His happiness was short-lived, however, for just, then, an eerie cry split the night. There was no mistaking the howl. He had heard it too many times before. It was the hunting cry of a Black Spiral Dancer.

A deep growl formed in the back of his throat as he turned in the direction of the howl. The Black Spiral

Dancers were enemy to all Garou. Though they, too, took the form of the wolf, they had sold their souls to the Wyrm. Now, twisted demons of the night, they did the Wyrm's bidding as they hunted down and destroyed all those who fought to protect Gaia, the Sacred Mother.

A second howl came from somewhere off to the right, just beyond the campgrounds. Sam shuddered as he realized there were two Black Spiral Dancers — two servants of darkness. They must have felt the girl's spirit, which burned like a beacon in the night. There was no time to lose. Her life was in danger.

Sam stepped forward and grabbed the girl by the wrist. "If you want to live to see tomorrow, you must come with me — now!"

Heather resisted, pulled back. "Please," Sam said. "There is no time to explain. We must hurry."

Another howl echoed through the darkness, much closer than before. The girl's face paled, and she stopped struggling. She looked at Sam, looked into his eyes, and nodded.

As Sam and Heather raced toward his RV, a strong wind sprang up out of the west — from the direction where darkness lived — and tore across the campgrounds. The wind shrieked like an animal caught in a trap, as it blew down tents, toppled teepees, and sent campers scurrying for their lives. Trees swayed and branches snapped, filling the air with deadly projectiles.

Dancers and singers fled the arena as the wind tossed folding chairs and benches high into the air. There was a hollow booming as the drum was flipped on its edge and went rolling across the ground.

Everything was chaos as Sam led the girl between the rows of traders' booths. Display cases and folding tables were upended, their shiny trinkets spilled upon the ground. And canvas awnings flapped like giant birds' wings in the wind. They had to dodge and weave to keep from being trampled in the confusion as traders cursed and scrambled to save their handicrafts from blowing away.

They finally reached the RV. Sam pushed the girl in ahead of him, slammed the door, and locked it. The RV rocked and groaned from the wind, rattling cups and saucers in the tiny cabinets. Sam listened carefully, waiting to see if the RV was in danger of being torn apart. Satisfied that the structure was reasonably sound, he turned around to study the girl.

She stood facing him, her eyes narrowed in concentration, her mouth set. Sam smiled when he spotted the steak knife taken from his sink, clutched tightly in her right hand.

Ah, this little one is no helpless rabbit.

He had to convince her that he was on her side, and he had to do it quickly. They didn't have much time.

"Do not be afraid. I will not hurt you," he said. The girl moved sideways. Sam took a step to the left, keeping himself between her and the door. He tried a more direct approach.

"In your dreams you are running through the forest at night, with the wind in your hair, free, strong, and naked."

His words caught her off guard. He saw confusion in her eyes.

"And the smell of other people makes you want to puke," he added. Sam definitely had her attention now.

"Who are, you, and how do you know about my dreams?" she asked, her voice scratchy. He noticed three blue lines across her neck: bruises. Someone had choked her.

Sam showed his best smile. "I am a friend, someone you need very badly right now. My name is Sam Nakai. And you are?"

"Heather Ocoee," she said, slowly lowering the knife. "How do you know what I dream? Are you a mind reader?"

Sam shook his head. "No, but when I was your age I had similar dreams. And I, too, was sickened by the smell of those around me. We are different, you and I. Special. We are Garou. And like me, you, too, have been chosen by the spirits to be the guardian."

"Guardian?" she asked.

He reached beneath his shirt and pulled out a leather pouch that hung from his neck by a thong.

"Long, long, ago, back before the white man ever came to this country, there were only the Indians and the Garou — the people of the wolf. The land was green and lush back then, and there were many sacred places — places of power where those of medicine could connect with the great mystery.

"One such place was at the crest of the Cumberland Plateau, near Monterey, Tennessee. Here, the Sacred Mother had left a gift to her children: a large monument of stone, carved in the shape of a sitting wolf. Nee Yah Kah Tah Kee, as the sacred standing stone was called, towered over 30 feet tall and contained great magical powers. Warriors and medicine men came from across the land to meditate and learn from the wolf. But the white man, his mind already corrupted by the voice of the Wyrm, looked upon the monument with fear and hatred. He blew up the stone with dynamite and built his railroad upon the spot, destroying forever the medicine of the Great Wolf."

Sam opened the pouch and slipped a small gray stone into his palm. The rock was about four inches long, narrow, and jointed at one end, like an icicle. "This is all that remains of Nee Yah Kah Tah Kee. One tiny sliver, the Fang of the Wolf."

He closed his hand around the stone and whispered a short prayer. A tingling shot through his arm, and the rock began to pulsate like a tiny heart. As the Fang came to life, it gave off a shimmering blue glow. The glow leaked from between Sam's fingers and engulfed his hand.

"But even this tiny piece of stone has great powers," Sam said. "With it, one can heal the sick, see into the future, and open doors to other worlds. Such powers could be deadly in the hands of the wrong person. That is why the Fang is passed from one guardian to another. I have been the guardian for over 20 years, but my time has come to an end. It is time to pass on the Fang. You are the new guardian, Heather."

Sam held the stone out to her, but Heather shook her head, refused to take it. "Get somebody else," she said. "I don't want it."

"It is not my decision," Sam said. "The spirits have chosen you."

"Then tell them to choose another," she said.

"Even if they would, it is too late for that. The Wyrm knows that the choice has been made, and that you are the chosen one. His followers will hunt you down and kill you, even if you do not take the Fang. Only the power of the Fang can protect you."

Heather glanced toward the door. "These followers — what do they look like?"

"They are creatures of darkness and can take many shapes."

"Do they ever look like men, but deformed. . . like monsters?"

Sam nodded. "Sometimes. You have seen one?"

"I think so." Heather described the creature that attacked her. Sam explained that it had probably been a Banth — an evil spirit that could come into this world and take over the body of a person, deforming it, changing it into something less than human. Like the Black Spiral Dancers, the Banths were followers of the Wyrm.

"And even if I refuse to be the guardian, they will still come after me?" Heather asked.

Again, Sam nodded. "It makes no difference. You are the chosen one, therefore, you are a threat to the Wyrm."

"But I'm only a kid. How can I be a threat?"

"You are a child only on the outside. And once you pass the Rite of Passage you will—"

A howl sounded from just outside, interrupting him. "I can explain later," Sam said, "but we must leave here, now."

Heather looked at the door, back at Sam, and nodded.

Sam squeezed the Fang tighter. The blue glow increased in intensity. As it did, a rectangle of darkness appeared in front of the wall: a doorway, black as a void. Sam took Heather by the hand and started to lead her through the doorway, when all of the windows in the RV exploded inward with the force of a bomb going off.

Pieces of glass flew everywhere. Sam pulled Heather to his chest, shielding her from the deadly shards. Something struck the door a thunderous blow, causing it to buckle inward. Another blow tore it off its hinges.

The door hit Sam in the back and drove him into the wall. The blow stunned him, made the room spin sideways. He shook his head, fighting off unconsciousness. A howl sounded.

Sam's vision cleared. He turned and saw Heather lying in the middle of the floor. A thin trickle of blood ran from a cut on her forehead and down her face. She lay motionless, her eyes wide with terror. Towering over her, his back to Sam, was a Black Spiral Dancer.

The Dancer no longer rode the wind. He stood over Heather in his werewolf form, fangs bared, claws threatening. The sight of the Dancer brought on the Rage in Sam — brought on the change.

Sam's veins quivered like electric wires, and the bones in his back crackled and popped. He stood up and tore off his shirt. The muscles in his shoulders, chest, and arms thickened. Hair grew. His fingers became longer; claws sprouted from each tip.

Sam's face reshaped itself, grew longer. His nose became a snout and his teeth became fangs, deadly and sharp — the fangs of a predator. The transformation to werewolf was complete. Sam threw his head back and howled a war cry.

The Black Spiral Dancer spun around to meet the challenge. But before he could complete his turn, Sam tackled him.

The two slammed into the counter. Wood splintered, cabinet doors flew open, and dishes crashed to the floor. But neither one cared. Each fought with the fury of their Rage, the fury of hatred. Claws sliced the air like sickles as they severed flesh; fists, elbows, and knees struck bone.

Sam, already bleeding in a dozen places, attacked the Black Spiral Dancer with blow after blow. He didn't let up, never gave his opponent a chance to recover from the attack, robbed him of the opportunity to go on the offensive. The Dancer, knowing he was losing, tried to twist loose, but Sam held on. He sank his fangs deep into the Dancer's left shoulder and jerked his head to the right. Muscles ripped and tendons snapped like rubber bands. Blood flowed.

Pain exploded through Sam's side as the Dancer raked him with his claws. But Sam refused to let go. He bit down again, grabbed his enemy by the neck. The Dancer jerked his head back. . . and ripped his own throat out.

Sam let go. The Black Spiral Dancer rolled across the floor, grabbed the counter and tried to rise, only to fall again. Blood pumped from the wound, slowed, and finally stopped as the Dancer died.

And as the Black Spiral Dancer died, so, too, did the Rage of Sam Nakai. He allowed himself to slip back into human form, wiped his bloody hands off on his thighs, and turned around. Heather sat with her back against the wall, watching him, her face a mask of fear. At first, he thought that she was afraid of him. But then he heard sounds of movement in the doorway behind him.

As he turned. Sam realized the mistake he made by not remaining in Crinos form. The blow that struck him across the side of his head was solid, hard. His teeth rattled, and he felt a vertebrate pop in the back of his neck. Tiny, crimson droplets of blood spattered the wall.

The Banth stalked across the floor after him, the board gripped tightly in both hands. Behind him a second Black Spiral Dancer appeared in the doorway. Sam raised his hands to protect himself, willed himself to change, but the board descended again.

Ribs snapped like popsicle sticks and pain lanced through his side. He tried to howl, to scream his Rage, but couldn't catch his breath. Sam Nakai stumbled backward, tripped over the body of the dead Dancer, and fell. He watched through a red haze as the Banth raised the board for a killing blow. He also watched as Heather sprang to her feet, snatched the Fang off the floor, and fled through the shimmering doorway to another place. The Banth turned and raced after her, followed by the Black Spiral Dancer.

They're after the Fang. I can't let them catch her.

He had to stop them. He could not allow the Fang of Nee Yah Kah Tah Kee to fall into the clutches of the Wyrm.

Sam got slowly to his knees. Pain ripped through his side, making breathing difficult. He tasted blood.

I've got a couple of broken ribs, and maybe a punctured lung.

Blood continued to flow from the wound on his head. His scalp felt loose.

He got to his feet. The doorway started to dim and grow smaller. In a few more seconds, it would close completely.

Sam staggered forward and dove through the doorway. Dizziness overtook him as he spiraled downward, fell into the void between worlds, passed into another place and maybe another dimension. He never knew where he would end up when using the doorway. It was always the Fang's choice. There was a blur of green as he reached the other side: trees, grass. Then the blackness overtook him.

• • •

Heather hit the ground and rolled. She jumped up and tried to run, but her feet slipped on a carpet of loose leaves and she tumbled down a steep hillside. Over and over she rolled, her face and hands torn by briar bushes, the stars whirling overhead. She might have rolled forever, had not an oak tree blocked her path. Heather struck the tree hard, her forward momentum halted.

She lay on her back and breathed deeply, feeling each tiny cut come painfully alive. She couldn't move and could offer no resistance when the Black Spiral Dancer and the Banth caught up with her.

They flipped her over on her stomach and tied her hands behind her back. They also removed the Fang from the hip pocket of her blue jeans. The Banth then grabbed her by the hair and drug her back up the hill, where she was left to lie, face down, in the middle of a small clearing.

Heather was terrified, but she had to get a better look at her captors. Slowly, so as not to draw attention to herself, she raised her head and looked around. The Banth was the same misshapen creature that had attacked her in the Oklahoma countryside. Naked, he crouched in a position of obedience at the other's feet.

The Black Spiral Dancer had changed into human form, which Heather found more disturbing than that of a werewolf. The man was in his middle to late thirties, thin, muscular, and bald. He wore black leather pants and matching boots. His upper body was covered with tattoos, and his ears were adorned with several earrings. The light of madness shown in his eyes as he talked to himself and slashed at the air with the Fang. He turned suddenly and noticed Heather watching him.

"Pretty's awake, is she?" He dropped down on all fours and crawled to where she lay. "Awake, awake, awake. He held the Fang in front of her face. "Make it work."

Heather shook her head. "I can't. I don't know how."

The slap caught her by surprise. "Liar! Make it work, or I'll tear out your tongue and eat it." He laughed. "Don't know how? Well, no matter. The Wyrm will teach you. He'll teach you many things — many, many things. Just you wait and see."

He had just stood up when the wolf pounced from the darkness of the forest: a giant gray timberwolf, its fur matted with dry blood.

As the Black Spiral Dancer went down beneath the wolf, he changed into his werewolf form. The wolf also shapeshifted into a werewolf — the same one Heather had seen before. It was Sam.

Over and over they rolled, each trying to strike a killing blow to the vitals of the other. Fur flew, blood flowed, and the night was rent with the fury of their combat. The Banth joined the fight. He jumped on Sam's back, trying to pin his arms.

Heather knew Sam was injured and could not defeat two opponents at once. It was only a matter of time before they wore him down, overpowered him. She struggled against her bonds, desperately trying to free herself so she could help. But her efforts were futile. The cords were too strong, too tight.

Anger engulfed her: Rage. Like an all-consuming fire, it burned through her, turned her soul to ashes. She wanted to attack, to kill.

Something happened. There was a popping in her head and a blinding pain ripped through her. Another pop and the blood in her veins became lava. Still another, and her spine contorted, almost snapped. Heather screamed. She looked at her legs, saw them change.

Sam was right. I am different. I am special.

Heather took a deep breath. She welcomed the change, opened her mind and spirit to it. Strength and energy coursed through her. She flexed her muscles and the ropes that bound her snapped like rotted string. She threw back her head and howled. And then she attacked.

Heather hit the Banth low, and she hit him hard. The Banth tried to ward off the attack, but Heather was at his throat. Her fangs tore into the corded muscles of his neck, severed tissue and flesh, ripped through tendon and bone. Blood, black as Texas oil, squirted from the wound and soaked the fur around her muzzle. Heather tasted the blood, oily and repulsive.

Heather slashed upward. Her claws ripped through the Banth's stomach, spilling his intestines on the ground like a nest of wet snakes. He hissed in anger, sank to his knees, and died.

She turned away from the Banth, only to be attacked by the Black Spiral Dancer. The Dancer was bigger, stronger, and more experienced. Heather had never been in Crinos form before, wasn't sure how to move, and didn't know what her body was capable of. She was hard pressed to defend herself as the Dancer attacked.

Sam Nakai lay on the ground. Heather didn't know if he were alive or dead, and had no time to find out. The Dancer continued his assault. His claws left bloody furrows in her forearms. Heather knew she couldn't last much longer. Any second he would get past her defenses and sink his teeth into her neck. She needed a miracle to survive. . . and saw one lying on the ground in front of her.

The Fang of the Wolf lay only a few feet away, where it had fallen when Sam was attacked by the Black Spiral Dancer. Heather wasn't sure if the stone would work for her, or if she could figure out how to use it, but she had no choice but to try.

She pushed the Dancer away and lunged for the Fang. As her fingers closed around it, a blue flame shot from the stone, encased her hand, and raced up her arm. The Dancer grabbed her legs, dug claws into her flesh. Heather howled in pain, but did not let go of the stone.

She raised the Fang of the Wolf high above her head. The flame ignited into a blinding brilliance. The Black Spiral Dancer shielded his eyes, turned away. As he did, Heather drove the Fang's point deep into the back of his head.

There was a loud *bang*, like a clap of thunder, and the Black Spiral Dancer exploded into a million pieces.

And, as his smoking molecules splattered across the clearing, a giant black wolf appeared before Heather.

Nee Yah Kah Tah Kee gazed down upon her, questioning, demanding. He spoke to her in a language as ancient as the land, and filled her mind with the teachings of the old ones. Tears rolled down Heather's cheeks as she learned what it was to be Garou, to finally belong. The image of the Great Wolf only lasted for a minute, long enough for her to understand what it meant to be the chosen one. . . the guardian.

• • •

Sam Nakai had many serious wounds and would have died had it not been for the Fang's magical powers. As soon as she changed back into human form, Heather went to work on him, slowly rubbing the stone back and forth over the wounds. Instantly, the flow of blood stopped and the flesh began to knit back together. With a little rest, he would be completely healed — though he would have several new scars to add to his collection.

Heather breathed a sigh of relief when Sam finally regained consciousness and opened his eyes.

"I am not dead yet?" he asked.

Heather shook her head. "The Fang of the Wolf brought you back."

Sam eyed her suspiciously. "Who taught you how to use the Fang?"

"Nee Yah Kah Tah Kee taught me."

Sam was shocked. "You saw the Great Wolf?" He looked around, and the light of understanding came to his eyes.

"I thought I recognized this place," he said. "This is the crest of the Cumberland Plateau, the very spot where

Nee Yah Kah Tah Kee once stood. I didn't know where the doorway lead to — I never do — it is always the spirit's choice. They brought you here for a reason. To teach you. Now will you accept the guardianship?"

"I have already accepted," she smiled, "but there is a lot I need to learn — and I still have to go through the Rite of Passage."

Sam shook his head. "You have already gone through the Rite. I saw you change. You are one of us now. A Garou. From this moment on Heather Ocoee, the little girl. no longer exists. You are Wa Ya Ny Wa Ti, Medicine Wolf, the woman. ///

Hunter's Blues

by Scott Ciencin

They had to shout to make themselves heard over the sound of the chopper's blades and their own weapons fire. Larry and Joe didn't mind. Getting used to the noise had been no more difficult than acclimating themselves to the freezing cold temperatures and hostile living conditions in northern Alaska. Both men were used to making changes. In their business, they were constantly reminded of the old adage: adapt or perish. Younger, stronger, and faster competitors came out of the woodwork on a daily basis, yet Larry and Joe were survivors.

They were *professionals.*

"You remember Sienkevitch?" Larry asked as he switched to a scope rifle and took aim at a fleeing form below. "That asshole from Corpus Christi? Said he was the best hitter in the Lone Star state."

Joe nodded. "That one."

"Hang on," Larry said. It had taken him a little while to get used to the harness that allowed him to sit with his feet dangling out of the helicopter's passenger side. His first few shots this way had been misses, but he quickly got the hang of it. He was 6' 2", with blocky features and pockmarked skin. His black hair was slicked back and held in a ponytail. Joe teased him that he was trying to look like Stephen Segal. Larry didn't care. "Got me some easy money down here."

Below, the glaring white carpet of snow was not enough to hide the frantic movements of a light gray wolf and the animal's nightmare black companion. Larry squeezed the trigger and the head of the gray wolf exploded. The black wolf that had been running beside the fallen creature stopped suddenly and let out a howl that cut through the screaming winds and the monotonous sounds of the helicopter.

"What did you load that thing with?" Joe asked. He was a little shorter than his companion, with a shock of red hair, doughy features, and an honest-to-God dimple. His professional name was "The Choirboy." Larry was known as "The Pilot" for a job early in his career. Both men were in their mid-forties.

"I tried out some hollow points."

"Damn. Well, there's the last one. Big son of a bitch. He's all mine."

"Have at it, partner." Larry settled back in his harness and allowed Joe to get comfortable. Beneath them, the black wolf obligingly padded around the body of its dead companion in aimless circles. The chopper pilot held their position. "Anyway, like I was starting to say, this guy, Sienkevitch."

"Right. The asshole from Corpus Christi."

"He's like, what, 23 years old. Thinks he knows everything. Going on and on about how crisp and clean he makes his kills, how he gets to know them so well, even bought his last one a drink in some bar an hour before he ran him down on the street."

"Gotcha." Joe readied his automatic weapon. He wanted to wait until the black wolf looked up. Then he was going to turn the creature into pulp, just as they had the other seven members of the pack they had stalked this morning. Their agent, Old Lou the Repairman, said the boys needed to get away from it all. He suggested they take a *rest cure* somewhere, try to unwind. Their last couple of assignments had been performed with such enthusiasm that even Old Lou was taken aback. Larry and Joe said they were just doing their jobs. Old Lou changed his tune a little, said he respected that and wanted to reward them. So here they were in Alaska, doing for fun what they normally did for $100,000 a head:

Spilling blood.

"I told this snot he didn't have to be so anal. Most times, you got to take someone out; they pretty much help you do it. People are idiots."

"Got that right," Joe said, waiting patiently for the wolf to look up at him.

"I made a bet with this dick. I told him, I had this guy to get rid of the next day. Simple job, no big deal. Seven or eight sticks of dynamite rigged up to his ignition. Start her up, *bam*, it's all over folks, one less moron eating oxygen."

"Sure."

"I told him, this guy's car looks like it hasn't been washed for six months. A black car, foreign. Doesn't take care of it at all. I said, before I plant the stuff, I'm gonna hot wire the car, take it through a car wash, then put it back and see if this guy notices anything different."

"I love it."

"Well, our pal Sienkevitch, he says, of course the guy's going to notice. No one could be that dumb. So we go out there together. I show him the car. It looks almost gray, there's so much muck on it. We take it out, put it through a car wash, even get one of those lemon scent things to spray around inside. Sienkevitch is like, gimme a break. Even if the guy's so stupid he doesn't notice the way his car's all black and shining after this wash and wax, he's gonna smell the scent and know something's up. I tell him, he's got to have a little faith in human nature."

On the ground below, the wolf looked up. Its green eyes sparkled in the intense sunlight. Joe opened up on the wolf as it bolted. Impossibly, not one of his shots connected.

"Follow that piece of shit!" Joe commanded. The helicopter pilot was already tracking the wolf, giving the assassins a clear shot at all times. "Sorry. What happened? Who won the bet?"

"Let's just say, when our buddy Sienkevitch went to pay the rent that month, he was a little short."

"You sent that asshole packing."

"To the moon, Alice. To the moon."

Joe grinned. The black wolf was still in view. He went to single shots and started firing. This time he was certain he tagged the animal at least twice. The creature flinched, but didn't stop running.

"Better get him now," Larry said. "Son of a bitch is making for the woods."

"I see that." Joe fired until his clip was gone. He reached out and Larry handed him the rifle filled with hollow points. Joe grabbed it and kept shooting.

One of the shots connected. A geyser of blood blew out of the creature's side, but it kept running. Joe blinked, wondered if he was going snow blind, despite the special polarized lenses he wore. The wolf seemed to be growing, changing into something less like an animal, more like a man.

Crazy. Not only crazy, irrelevant. He had that thing's head in his sights. The chopper came to a dead stop as he squeezed the trigger and his shot went wild. The wolf bolted into a copse of trees and was gone.

"What the fuck you do that for?" Joe screamed to the pilot.

"Chill out," Larry said. "We can't go any farther. Look up!"

Joe saw that they were on the edge of a forest. If they tried to get any closer, the chopper would crash.

"Don't worry about it, partner. There's plenty more where that came from. Besides, the way your last shot ripped open that thing, it won't last long."

Joe was silent as the chopper pilot took them away. He kept staring at where the wolf had disappeared. An instant before the woods went out of view, he thought he saw movement, something stumbling their way. He couldn't tell if it was an animal or a man.

"Bothers me," Joe said. "I hate leaving a job half-finished."

"We're here to have fun," Larry said. "Relax!"

Joe nodded, but somehow he sensed that for the rest of their vacation, and for some time after that, the shape at the mouth of the woods was going to bring him nightmares.

• • •

One year later

Desmond Willits was surprised to see the large figure framed in the cold, white morning light filtering in from the open doorway. He wondered if *he* had been the fool who left the club's front door unlocked. "Sorry, man; the

Blue Note Cafe won't be open again until seven. You come back then, we'll serve you up something right, like some homemade jambalaya and a little music to soothe the soul."

The figure did not retreat. There was something familiar in his shape. Desmond studied the fall of his wild hair and the manner in which the intruder carried himself — shoulders pushed forward, head down a little, like a fighter about to take someone on. Desmond had been a fighter once, when he was younger. Now that he was in his seventies, the only thing he fought was his arthritis.

"It's me," the man in the doorway said.

Desmond Willits felt his entire body stiffen. He hadn't heard that raspy voice in 10 years. Desmond tried not to think about the past. Too much pain waited back there. When he was young, he had won several title bouts. Some men in fancy suits told him to take a fall during the fight that would have made him a champion. If he didn't, his wife Bobbi would find out what life was like when you didn't have any arms or legs. The money he earned allowed him to open the Blue Note, which had gone on to become the oldest blues cafe in San Francisco. Ten years ago, when he had last heard this man's voice, his Bobbi had just died. Too much pain.

The man stepped forward, into the light. He had blazing emerald eyes, swarthy skin, and proud, noble features. The man's chin and cheekbones were elegantly sculpted, his Cupid's lips vulnerable. Steel-tipped alligator boots glinted in the light, along with turquoise rings and bracelets. A flak vest revealed a host of tattoos along his solid biceps. Above his button-fly jeans a black fishnet T-shirt covered a washboard stomach and a male model's chest.

"It's me, Old Paw. Donovan McKinley."

Desmond tried his best to be nonchalant. "I got eyes. You think someday you'll tell me why you call me that?"

"Call you what?"

"Old Paw."

"Habit."

The old man shook his head. "Didn't think you were ever coming back."

"Me either. I need work, a place to stay."

"Come right to the point, don't ya?"

Donovan shrugged.

"Ever wonder which side you got to thank for that?" Desmond asked. "Indian or Irish?"

"Don't think about it much."

"No, I imagine you don't." Desmond looked over to the stage. A set of instruments lay around in their cases. "You want some work, you got to show me what you can do."

"Have you forgotten?"

"Time messes with everyone," Desmond said. "I got to know if you still have the old magic."

"Fair enough." Donovan leaped onto the stage with a single, effortless stride. He took an electric guitar from its case, turned on an amp, and plugged in. After checking to see that the instrument was tuned, Donovan loosed a heavy metal riff that would have made Eddie Van Halen duck and cover.

Desmond frowned. "What was that?"

The guitarist smiled. "You said times change. I wondered if maybe you had changed with them."

"You wondered wrong. Now gimme some sugar, baby."

Shaking his head, Donovan took a step back and allowed himself to feel the old rhythms. A moment later his fingers touched the frets and the sounds that came out were so mournful they reminded Desmond of a dead man weeping at midnight.

The old man closed his eyes and let the haunting sounds wash over him for several minutes before he allowed a smile to spider across his deep brown, wrinkled face. "That's nice, old son. Like a butterfly looking for its dead love."

Donovan finished the tune. "Do I have the job?"

With a half-laugh, Desmond said, "Not everyone can play the blues. You got to have hurt way down deep in your soul."

"So nothing's changed?" Donovan asked, only a little unsure of himself.

"I didn't say that. You're not bad. Not like you used to be, but not bad. I remember when you first came back from 'Nam. You played like that. But you got better."

"I'm overwhelmed."

"You want coddling, you go somewhere else. Always been the deal."

"I need work," Donovan said.

"You got that," the old man said. "It's the old magic you're lacking. Don't worry. Time wears on us all. You'll get it back."

"Thanks."

"Thing is, you couldn't have picked better time to come back. Guy I had playing with us disappeared last night. Asian kid, coaxed the notes out of that guitar like he was kissing his lover's neck. Cleaned out his room. Didn't leave a forwarding. Damn deadbeat. You want the gig?"

"I do."

"It's yours."

• • •

The images came in a jumble, a chaotic mix of darkness and light. One ripped from the other as if they were being reflected on the blade of an overworked scythe. He was in the wilderness, with the pack. They were on the hunt, playing, making love, singing and dancing in the moonlight.

A chainsaw cut to the next scene.

The sun baked him and explosions came from above. One by one the wolves fell. Strange thoughts started to wake in his animal skull. Horrid, unwanted thoughts.

Human thoughts.

A painful tearing and suddenly it was just a little later. He was running beside one that might have been his brother. A final crack of thunder came from above. A torrent of blood, brains, and fangs spilled upwards.

Assault rifles, helicopters, two-leggers, laughter, speech — all the myriad shades of damnation. He didn't want to change again and become a man. More than anything, he wanted to stay in the wild, needed to stop the process dead in its tracks, stay pure, regain what had been lost, but it was too late, his human brain was waking after its long slumber, and it was turning his heavenly dream of peace into a nightmare!

Torture! Intolerable!

A knock came at the door. Donovan vaulted awake, thankful that the nightmare was at an end. He raised his trembling, human hand before him, and saw that he was wrong. The nightmare of human existence was his again, and this time seemed neverending.

"Coming," he said as he hopped off the bed and slipped into a pair of blue jeans. The room Desmond had given him was small and poorly furnished, but it was all he needed. He went to the door and breathed in a familiar scent. Steeling himself, he opened the door.

A beautiful, dark-haired woman stood before him. She wore sunglasses, a white shirt, a black vest, and jeans ripped at the knees. Her lips were blood red. She pursed them indecisively and leaned against the door frame.

"Want me to come in?" she asked in a husky voice.

Donovan stood back and allowed Melinda to enter the small bedroom. The window was lacking a curtain. Crossing the room, she stood before the fiery light of the sun and stretched, raising her arms high over her head. The vest fell back, allowing the full, sensuous curves of her breasts to be revealed by the light.

Donovan was unashamed by the animal desire that rose within him. Melinda caught the way he looked at her and grinned. She would have been offended only if he was not aroused.

"Thank you for coming," Donovan said haltingly.

"Leitch called," Melinda said as she threw herself to the bed on her belly. Rising to her elbows, she looked up at him, certain to give him a perfect view of her ample cleavage. "I figured he was crazy. I didn't think you were ever coming back, not after what happened with Calle Ann and your son."

Donovan looked away.

"What is it?" she asked. "The *harano* get you?"

"The suffering of Gaia plagues us all."

"Come on," she said. "Don't give me the company line. You haven't been active in the cause for a long time. Besides, this is me you're talking to. You know what I am. I see past the shadows."

Donovan watched as Melinda rolled onto her back and looked at him upside down. She reminded him of a cat as she slowly and sensuously writhed.

"Long drive," she said. "Could use some rest. Want to lie with me?"

"Maybe later."

Melinda rested her open hand on her forehead. "This *is* serious."

"Yes."

She rose to a sitting position, slipping off her sunglasses and depositing them on the bed. "Did you take out Jimmy Wang, the guitarist? I hear he was a good kid. Hope you didn't hurt him. I mean, you used to be a healer, at least in the army. Hate to think you've gone the other way."

"Made some calls. Got him a better gig with a band in Seattle."

"That's my *Wakiza*. No innocent blood on your hands."

Donovan flinched. "Please. Don't call me that. Wakiza's dead. He died with my wife and child."

Melinda reached out and caught Donovan's hands. She was determined to remain quiet until his gaze met hers. The last time she had seen Donovan, he claimed that he was never coming back to the human world. Killian Cross was dead. Donovan had been cheated out of his revenge on the murderer of his wife and child by yet another Black Spiral Dancer, one that Cross had betrayed.

Finally, Donovan looked into Melinda's ruby eyes.

"What made you change your mind?" she asked. "Why are you here?"

A ragged breath escaped him. The first time he had seen Melinda's eyes, he worried that she was an Enticer, a human seductress who served the Wyrm, a fomora, the enemy.

The truth had been far stranger. Their friendship stranger still. He remembered what she told him when he confronted her about her origins: "You know what they say: I was Snow White, but I drifted."

Donovan shrugged. "I had what I needed: peace. That was taken away. I've come here to get it back."

"There's going to be blood, isn't there? With you, there always is."

The dark-haired man said nothing. He lowered his head and looked away. "You didn't bring my guitar: Blue Light."

"You're the only person I know who would give a name to a guitar."

"It meant a lot to me. That's why I entrusted it to you before I went into the wild."

"It's safe. I wasn't sure it was really you. I'll bring it next time."

Donovan nodded, his gaze averted.

Melinda released his hands. "What do you want me to do?"

In his low, raspy voice, Donovan told her. Waiting for her reply, he went to the window and stared out at San Francisco. It was the last Saturday before Halloween. A full moon was due. That was not his auspice. His was the Galliard, the gibbous moon. No matter, it would do.

"Will you?" he asked, breaking the silence.

"Gee, I don't know. I might be busy. AMC's running *The Princess Comes Across* tonight. Carole Lombard, Fred MacMurray. 1930s innocence. Hard to pass up. Though, I'll tell ya, I always thought that title sounded a little like a porn film, you know what I mean?"

Donovan was unmoved by her attempt to lighten the mood.

"What do you think?" Melinda said with a sigh. "You know me. I'll do anything for old times' sake."

"Yeah, I know you." He waited a few more seconds, then glanced back at her. The room was empty. He didn't even hear her leave. The brief flickering of a smile touched his face. He whispered, "You've gotten good since I left."

From somewhere below, in the main chamber of the club, he thought he heard a woman's appreciative laughter.

• • •

Donovan was lost to the music. The Saturday night crowd was always the best. He had forgotten how sweet the release had been when he had played the circuit, traveling from city to city, playing a live gig here, a studio set there. Always moving. Calle Ann had changed all that. She wanted a stable environment in which to raise their son. He gave her that.

It cost him everything.

"Man, you make that thing weep," one of the other musicians whispered to him as he continued to play. The band had accepted him without reservation. The evening was passing in a haze of soft, sensual music, pierced by the haunting wail of his anguished guitar.

The club was about three-quarters filled. Only a few tables were empty. Donovan waited patiently for his visitors to arrive. They would be cautious, on the lookout for any kind of trap. Only when they were assured that no danger waited inside the Blue Note Cafe would the pair of men enter the club and find the table that had been reserved for them.

Another hour passed, and finally they arrived. Donovan did not miss a note. He played two more blues standards and a scorching rendition of "Hellhound on My Trail" before he bothered to glance their way. His senses had not betrayed him. The two men seated at a table in the far corner were indeed the ones he had been hunting for close to a year.

The Choirboy and The Pilot.

The killers of his pack, the monsters who had shattered the sanctuary he had found, and all for a few hours of amusement. He had used all his talents, all his Gifts, to learn their names and how to contact them. Returning to the world of man had been jarring, but Donovan knew there was no other way.

His friend Leitch, a man with money and contacts, had made all the arrangements. The assassins didn't like the idea of meeting their "client" face to face. Leitch had insisted. If they wanted the job, which paid a million dollars, 10 times their usual fee, they would arrive on the Saturday before Halloween, at the Blue Note Cafe in San Francisco.

Despite their misgivings, the killers had made their appearance. A sizable wire transfer of funds from one of Leitch's dummy corporations had ensured their cooperation. Whoever said Glass Walkers were good for nothing had never met Archibald Leitch.

An odd sensation came over Donovan — a strange longing for the life he once led. After turning his back on his friends for 10 years, Donovan had worried that they would want nothing to do with him. Instead, they welcomed him back and agreed to help. Explanations were unnecessary and unwanted.

It was Calle Ann they all loved, he tried to tell himself. *They're doing it out of respect to her memory.*

The velvet notes he coaxed from his guitar told another story.

Donovan looked over to his guests, Joe Entwhistle and Larry Santos. The set ended and he put down his guitar, smiled perfunctorily as the crowd applauded, and stepped off the stage. On his way to the men's room he walked past them. Once inside, he reveled in the foul scents he had taken from each of the men. The redhead, The Choirboy, smelled like embalming fluid. The black-haired one, The Pilot, bore the odor of copper-tainted blood. He had them now. They could run to the ends of the earth and never escape him.

Soon, the hunt would begin.

He left the men's room, took a longer route around the men, and was pleased to see them fidgeting nervously. Their "client" had already shown, only they would never know that.

Donovan picked up a snippet of their conversation. The redhead was bothered by some people he had seen on the street. A few had a single red eye, always the left one. He had never seen anything like it. Bunny eyes, he called them. Weird.

"You ain't seen nothin' yet," Donovan whispered as he walked back to the stage.

Another hour passed. The assassins were getting ready to leave. Before they could rise from their table, Melinda appeared. She wore a sexy red dress that revealed her hourglass figure. Contacts covered her crimson eyes, making them look bluish black. It wasn't much effort for her to talk them both into a night of fun in her hotel room. They negotiated what they believed was a fair price, took one more look around for their absentee client, and left the club with Melinda.

Donovan's second set was almost finished. The last chord was played and he set down his instrument. There was no reason to hurry. He knew exactly where Melinda was taking them:

Straight into the jaws of hell.

• • •

Donovan stood outside the door. He had been worried that the floor would be teeming with people. Instead, it was deserted. Gaia was smiling on him tonight. He knew that even if a few humans stumbled by at an inopportune moment, the delirium would take care of them. Nevertheless, he wanted to be a nightmare solely reserved for the two men waiting in the room beyond this door.

He waited a few moments, choosing to give Melinda a little time with them. That way they would be all nice and comfortable. Completely relaxed. That was how the first of his pack had been when the assassins had blown his guts out. The wolf had looked down stupidly, unable to comprehend what had been done to him, why his steaming entrails had sprung out of his belly, when death overtook him and came charging after the other members of the pack. In the beginning, the killers had been on foot. If Donovan had remembered who he was, what he was, just a little sooner, he might have saved at least of few of his wolf-brothers. That had not been the case. It had not been until the hunters were airborne that his human mind had resurfaced, and by then it was too late.

Now all he had to look forward to was paying these bastards back for the blood and terror they had delivered onto their victims. He thought he would be looking forward to their screams, but all he wanted was to get this over with so that he could go back to the wild where he belonged. Perhaps he wouldn't chase them into the streets after all. It might be best to end it quick and clean. Not for their sakes, but for his own.

He had dressed himself in a long leather raincoat and his favorite boots. Nothing else. He kicked off the boots and set them beside the door. Shrugging off the raincoat, he folded it neatly and set it beside his footwear.

Closing his eyes, he willed the change to come over him. A fire raged through his soul, boiled his blood, and consumed his flesh. Hair sprouted on his skin in great gouts, and his bones quickly unfolded and grew into shapes no longer meant for human flesh. His skin bubbled and changed, crawling and expanding. Donovan's ears yanked back and drew long, while his jaws extended and filled with razor-sharp teeth. His forehead became hooded and his snout itched. He touched the doorknob and began to turn it. As they had agreed, Melinda had left it unlocked. In seconds his hands would become sharpened talons and the human part of him, which told him that doorknobs were meant to be turned, not ripped from the wood that housed them, would begin to retreat. He pulled his lips back and could not resist a snarl as he started to push the door open.

A bright light and a sound like the world's end came to him as the door exploded outward. Splinters and fiery shards of metal slammed into him, sending him back against the opposite wall. His mind scrambled to reach beyond the surge of agony that had torn through his chest.

A gunshot! Someone had opened up on him with a shotgun!

He didn't have to wait long to learn the identity of his assailant. What was left of the door swung inward and the Choirboy stood before him, gun leveled.

From deep in the room, he heard a cry that could only be Melinda. Stupid, he thought. Walked into it, just like my wolf brother. Stupid.

Shuddering, he tried to cover the gaping wound in his chest and willed the change to continue, but the convulsions ripping through him had other ideas.

• • •

Melinda felt the cold metal of the gun pressed against her skull. She had been shocked when her victims had so easily slipped out of her spell. Were they Fomori? Is that why her power hadn't worked against them? No, judging from the way the delirium was beginning to affect the redhead, the one who had shot Wakiza, that was not the case. A more simple explanation came to her: The killers had no souls, nothing for her to manipulate and tempt. She should have guessed that when she had looked into their flat, dead eyes.

Even more surprising had been Wakiza's dulled instincts. She was certain that he would have sensed the trap waiting for him on the other side of the door. He would have found another way in, some other means to take out this trash that had performed some deep and unforgivable hurt on him. Instead, he had acted like a human in wolf's clothing, forgetting his many Gifts. His sloppiness had damned them both.

Ahead, the red-haired assassin advanced on Donovan's shuddering form. The man's limited, human mind was shutting down at the sight of the werewolf in transformation. His partner, who could only see a vague, black shape, was far more in control of himself. Melinda saw that Donovan was still changing, but now the changes were coming very slowly. Given time, his wounds would heal. If the killers had their way, Donovan would be dead in a few seconds.

Not enough time.

"What is he?" the redhead asked.

"Who cares, just finish him off!" The black-haired murderer couldn't understand the reason for his partner's hesitation. He tightened his grip on Melinda and hissed in her ear. "Christ, what did you fuckers think you were dealing with here? Amateurs? This is the oldest goddamned lure on record."

Joe Entwhistle, The Choirboy, pointed his gun at the werewolf's head. A sudden calm descended on him. For a moment, he had seen the man on the floor as some kind of animal, a creature from a horror show when he was a kid. Fear like only his father could provoke — before he sliced off the old man's hands, feet, and dick, and left him chained to the sink to die screaming — had washed over him, engulfing him, drowning him. He felt a wet stain by his crotch and knew that he had peed himself. Christ, how embarrassing. Maybe the bitch had slipped something into their drinks.

Right now, he could see his victim for what he was: a mark, a bleeding, spasming human being who had come willingly to his own personal end of the world party.

"Yeah, pal, only its your world that's ending."

He had no idea that his will was so great, his denial so encompassing, that his mind had created this fantasy of a human being at his feet. When the dying man rose to his knees, Joe did not blow his head off, though his partner was hollering for him to do just that.

"What, he's naked, he got no weapons, what's he gonna do, swat me to death?" Joe asked, cutting a look back to the Pilot. He had phrased it this way because a second before he looked away from his victim, the man pulled his hand back, as if to swat an insect. The image had amused Joe.

He looked back, about to say, "Fuck it, let's do this asshole," when he saw a blur of motion and felt the shotgun drop from his arms. He looked down and saw that his hand was gone. Blood spurted from the ragged stump.

"Hey," Joe said, his voice high and strained, like that of a confused little boy.

Donovan roared like an engine out of hell's lowest pit as he sprang up and gutted the man with his other claw. Snarling, he yanked back his hand, unraveling the killer's insides. Joe Entwhistle, The Choirboy, dropped to the floor, jerked a few times, then died.

The werewolf entered the room, its fur matted with blood. Melinda stared at the creature, wondering if the crimson stain on its pure black pelt had come from his own wound or the flow of his victim. Not that it mattered. One look into the creature's glowing green eyes told her that it would be all right. Wakiza was going to make everything all right.

The Pilot quaked with fear as the werewolf came closer. "Stay back! I'll shoot the slut, I swear I'll do it!"

Melinda's fear returned. The way the assassin was shaking, he might discharge his weapon by accident as easily as by design. She had no idea what he was seeing. Wakiza was very strong, he could use his power to allow the killer to see him in his true form. One way or the other, the situation was again becoming untenable. If Donovan's rage outweighed his reason, he might ignore the gunman's threat and she could end up very dead.

There was only one thing for her to do. She was actually grateful that she had worn heels tonight, though they were uncomfortable as hell. She brought her foot up then jammed it down on the killer's instep. He hollered and fell back, squeezing the trigger. Melinda darted forward, certain that she would be out of his line of fire.

She was wrong.

As Wakiza moved forward, a black, inhuman blur advancing on his prey, the bullet cut through her neck, entering on the left side and exiting on the right. She felt as if she had been slapped, but there was no real pain. Only, she couldn't breathe. Shuddering, she grabbed her throat and dropped to her knees. She felt the ragged holes in her flesh and slumped back, quivering, gasping for a breath that would not come.

For Donovan, it all happened so quickly that he also believed Melinda to be out of danger. He reached out and tore The Pilot's head from his shoulders with one clean swipe of his claw. The severed head struck the ceiling, ricocheted off a lamp, and fell neatly onto a recliner, its jaws quivering as it tried to form a word. The werewolf looked at his dying victim in satisfaction, howling as life fled from the killer's eyes.

His satisfaction was short-lived. He looked down and saw Melinda's bloodied, twitching form. At first, he couldn't believe that she had been hit, then his old training, acquired over a two year stint in the army as a medic, kicked in. Picking her up, he was relieved to note that the wound had only grazed her arteries. She had to breathe. He saw a can of soda with a straw nearby. Somehow he summoned enough presence of mind to snatch the straw as he looked to the window and launched himself, with Melinda in tow, at the glass.

• • •

Donovan landed three stories below, the impact hurting his ankles, but not shattering them. The street before the hotel was filled with traffic. A car was stopped before him, waiting for a light to change. Donovan reached out, tore the passenger door from the vehicle, and stuck his head inside as he let out a terrible roar. The driver scrambled out of his seatbelt as Donovan slammed the gearshift into Park. The man was in tears as he fled the vehicle, almost running into an oncoming car. Donovan was beyond caring about anyone except Melinda. It was happening all over again. He had been careless and because of that, someone he cared about was dying.

Forcing himself to concentrate, he willed the change to reverse. As his body slowly lost some of its bestial aspects, Donovan gently set Melinda down on the car's backseat. People were watching, but he didn't care. The delirium would keep the Veil from being pierced. He tore a section of fabric from her dress and wound it around her neck, cutting off the flow of blood. Then he took one of his sharp nails and poked a hole in the hollow of her throat. The straw he had somehow managed to keep hold of was delicately inserted and he started to relax as he heard her breathing through the tube. He ran around to the driver's side, half-man, half-wolf, wholly unrecognizable, and shoved the gearshift into drive.

He drove through traffic like a madman, his inhuman senses allowing him an edge against the other drivers. He screamed and cursed in his guttural, indecipherable speech at the limits of the foreign import at his command.

In his mind, he cursed himself again and again. It had been such a simple set-up and he let it all get away from him, just like before. Melinda was dying, like Calle Ann, like his son, like the other members of his pack.

A bloody hand reached out from the backseat. Donovan was so startled that he nearly lost control of the car. He swerved into a lane of oncoming traffic then back again instants before he could be hit. Melinda was shuddering, spasming, trying to speak.

Lie still! he commanded in his Mindspeak. *You're not going to die! You're not!*

In the rearview mirror, he saw her blood-red eyes. She seemed desperate to tell him something. A message screamed out from her stare, but he refused to listen. He took a sharp turn and Melinda fell back. Cutting a glance over his shoulder, he saw the bloody straw on the seat beside her and heard her gasping for breath.

Ahead, the lights of a hospital winked into view.

Take the straw, he commanded in the confines of her thoughts. *Put it back in! Do it!*

He leaped the car across two lanes of oncoming traffic and kept advancing until the tires squealed to a stop a few feet before the hospital's emergency entrance. Donovan turned back, saw Melinda holding the straw to her throat, gasping for breath. Relief surged through him as he jumped out of the car, opened the back seat, and pulled her out.

The seat was soaked through with blood. The wound on the right side of her neck had torn wider, allowing a steady flow of blood to drip upon the seat. Was this what she had been trying to tell him?

He hauled her into his arms, and ran into the emergency room. The doctor on call shuddered as he saw Donovan's inhuman form.

Help her! he screamed in his Mindspeak.

No one moved near him. He considered changing back to human form, but there would be too many questions and his presence would be too great a distraction. The delirium was already striking the emergency room personnel. Setting Melinda down on a table, he turned and ran, praying that the effects of the delirium would fade once he was out of view.

An hour later, after he had stolen some human clothing, Donovan returned to the emergency room and asked about Melinda. The news made his heart slow and almost stop. She had died a few minutes after being admitted. The blood loss, the shock — it had all been too much for her.

The nurse asked if he was a relative, if he would be the one claiming the body.

"A distant relative," he said softly, tears welling up in his emerald eyes. He knew that by dawn there would *be* no body. Others of her kind would come and collect her. They always did. The Garou's was not the only Veil that must never be pierced.

On the way out, he heard an orderly and a nurse talking. They stood just outside the doors of the emergency room, staring up at the stars.

"Look at that," the nurse said. "I haven't seen a moon shine that bright in a long time."

"You know what my grandpa used to say about nights like this?" the orderly asked. "He said, 'The moon only shines this bright on nights when God pulls the wings off an angel and sends them home.' That's what he said."

Donovan shuddered and walked away.

• • •

The next morning, Donovan returned to the club. Desmond was waiting.

"The way you rabbited after your second set last night, I thought I'd seen the last of you." The old man looked into Donovan's face and frowned. "So what do you have to say for yourself?"

Donovan's lips trembled for a moment, then fell still. Instead, he walked up onto the stage, took out his guitar, plugged it into his amp, and powered up. His fingers stole over the frets as if they were desperate to recapture something that had been lost, an elusive, ethereal quality that might have been his again.

Peace.

He had found it in the arms of his wife, but she had been taken from him. He had found it in the chill of the wild, but that, too, had been taken from him. He had even glimpsed it in the wanton smile of an angel who had fallen, but not so far that she could not be picked up again and carried home.

For the first time in 10 years, the music poured entirely out of his soul. The music of sadness and mourning, the fragile moonlit concerto of hopelessness and despair that had become his world.

The old man settled into a chair and grinned. "You got it, man. Don't know how you did it, but you got it back."

Donovan ignored him. The notes came freely now and in them he could sense some vestige of the escape he sought. Perhaps when he found it, he could move on again.

For today, the music played on. ///

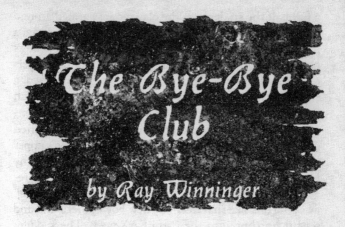

The Bye-Bye Club

by Ray Winninger

"Your mom is in the ground, isn't she?," whispered a thin boy with ash eyes. "And your papa's dead too!"

The new boy was too young or too unsophisticated to realize that ash-eye's own parents must be dead or missing. No one is admitted to the Child Services Northrock Facility for any other reason.

"Did they choke each other to death 'cause they couldn't stand your shitty reek?"

The new boy couldn't respond. He stared at ash-eye's face and nervously examined the boy's features, hoping they concealed a clue to the mystery that had tortured him all nine years of his life. As ash-eye turned to face him, the new boy instinctively locked his fingers around the plastic kaleidoscope resting on the desk in front of him. He was determined to protect the kaleidoscope. It was the only thing he had left.

"What's that?" Ash-eye grabbed for the kaleidoscope himself and raised his voice, obviously signaling for reinforcements. "You tryin' to hide that from *us*, you shitsmelling pussy? Maybe we oughta break you off!" On cue, a full half the students in the classroom swarmed around ash-eye and added their own voices to his taunts. One, a pasty boy in a GI Joe sweatshirt, grabbed the new boy's hand and began methodically prying each of his fingers off the kaleidoscope. When only two fingers remained, a sharp elbow to the stomach allowed ash-eye to snatch away the kaleidoscope and disappear into the crowd.

The instant his grip slipped away, the new boy started drooling and thrashing wildly. He grasped GI Joe's upper lip between his index finger and thumb and tugged the boy's sweaty face down toward the desktop. GI Joe reacted by bringing both hands up in an attempt to break away—a mistake that freed the new boy's other hand and sent it hurtling into the pasty boy's neck. The sudden, violent blow sent GI Joe gasping and startled the gang of tormentors. Ash-eye made his way to the corner of the classroom and steeled his fists. He recognized that he would face the enraged boy alone. No one else, save the incapacitated GI Joe, had invested reputation in the encounter.

As the students rushed back to their seats, an empty corridor opened between the new boy and ash-eye, allowing the new boy to charge with outstretched arms. As he approached, he spread his fingers and angled his thumbs, hoping to thrust them into his tormentor's eyes and gouge into the skull. Horrified by this savagery, ash-eye lifted his knee in a panic and drove it into the new boy's diaphragm, sending the berserker sprawling. In another beat, he pounced upon his floored prey, cocked back his fist, and grit his teeth. The new boy closed his eyes tight and brought both hands in front of his face.

Before ash-eye could strike, something yanked him to the floor. "GOD DAMN YOU! YOU LEAVE HIM ALONE RIGHT NOW OR I'LL TEAR THIS HAIR RIGHT OUT OF YOUR HEAD! Christ! I'm five minutes late and you're already causing problems!" Ash-eye let out a yelp and started mumbling. Another shout— "Now give me that thing and go see the administrator!"— was followed by the panicked squeak of sneakers and the sound of a small plastic object rebounding on the cold floor.

The new boy opened his eyes to the sight of a chubby woman on her hands and knees, retrieving the kaleidoscope. He supposed that she reminded him of his mother, though he hadn't been able to imagine anything about his mother for weeks. "Here you go, honey. Don't be afraid; I'll make sure those little bastards leave you alone. I'm Mrs. Tremond. I'm your teacher. If you have any problems, come see me." The new boy struggled to his feet, scooped the kaleidoscope from her hand and returned to his seat. Mrs. Tremond gave him what she hoped was a comforting pat on the top of his head and went to gather her papers.

The teacher's departure cued a whisper that filled the new boy's ears with a tickling wind. "Hey, Friend." The new boy recognized the lisp. It came from one of his tormentors, a gap-toothed boy in black overalls who was seated directly behind him. "Hey, I think I like you. Umm, we have this club here at Northrock. We call it the Bye-Bye Club. If you... if you wanted to join, I'm sure it would be okay."

The new boy turned and greeted the invitation with a vacant stare.

"Oh. Don't worry about that other stuff—we were just teasin' ya. I'm sure we'll get along from now on." Gap-tooth paused to read the new boy's expression, which hadn't changed much since the scuffle ended. "If you decide you want to join the club, we meet in the tool shed every fifth Wednesday after lights out. We're meeting tonight. Just sneak out through the fire door and head for the shed. You'll find us there. And don't worry about the door—the alarm doesn't work."

The new boy turned and pretended to focus his attention as Mrs. Tremond began the day's lesson. He still felt gap-tooth's breath on his neck.

"Um. One last thing." Gap-tooth waited for Mrs. Tremond to face the chalkboard before finishing his thought.

"My mom's dead too."

• • •

That evening, the new boy awoke to the sound of his bunkmate, rust-top, sliding down to the floor and opening a drawer. Feigning sleep, he watched through squinted eyes as rust-top pulled on a pair of trousers and slipped out into the corridor. It wasn't until the new boy noticed that rust top's exit failed to attract the attention of any other resident that he realized he was completely alone.

Then he remembered the tool shed and gap-tooth's invitation. He thought about his mom in the ground and his kaleidoscope and then slipped out of bed to find his trousers.

Ten minutes later, he was gliding through the darkness. As he neared the shed, he noticed that its door was slightly ajar. A red light emanated from within and stretched along the walkway leading back to the dormitory, cutting the courtyard in half. Something about the light sent strange signals to the new boy. It soothed him, though he couldn't understand why. It reminded him of that distant evening and the traffic light he noticed and his father missed.

As he approached the shed, he heard a low whisper that abruptly dissolved into total silence. Those inside were alerted to his presence. He should have been startled, but he wasn't.

"It's okay. It's the new kid," he heard gap-tooth whisper. "I told him to come." More whispers and a brief pause before the shed door finally creaked open.

Inside, the new boy saw his classmates seated in a semi-circle that faced the shadows blanketing the back of the shed. The red light came from a stained bare bulb that projected from a broken Mickey Mouse lamp. The glow it cast upon the faces of the assembled children lent them an unexpected familiarity. The new boy was certain that gap tooth was right—from now on, they'd all get along just fine.

As he entered the shed, the new boy sensed an unfamiliar presence. Disoriented, he looked around for a few moments before he noticed the two adults seated deep in the shadows. One was a fat, greasy man wearing a Marlboro hat and a dirty black t-shirt. The other was dark, lithe, and dressed in black leather. Something about the dark man fascinated the new boy. Perhaps it was the dull red glow that may have been another reflection of the Mickey Mouse lamp, but instead seemed to emanate from deep within the man's eyes.

The dark man was the first to speak. "And who are you?"

The new boy didn't answer.

"Well, little cobra, welcome to our club. Do you know who this man is?" The dark man looked at fat-and-greasy.

The new boy paused for as long as it was comfortable before nodding "no."

"I see. Do you dream of electricity?"

The new boy never remembered his dreams, but he knew the answer was "yes"—another nod, quicker this time.

The dark man smiled and a hint of recognition crossed his face and quickly submerged beneath his icy features. "I am your friend."

"Who is the other man?" The new boy surprised himself with the words, his first in a very long time.

"Let's ask one of your classmates. Chatterjack, tell little cobra about George."

Across the shed, ash-eye stood and stared at the new boy with contempt. "His name is George Feeney. People call him the Seaside Strangler. No one knows his real name but us." Ash-eye gave an abrupt nod to signal that he was finished and sat back down.

"Chatterjack, you're not finished." The dark man shot ash-eye a cold leer, spooking the boy and urging him to stand and continue.

"George likes to cut sluts. So far, he's killed twelve of them."

The dark man was obviously appeased. "Eleven actually, but very good, Chatterjack; I see you've read those books I left you the last time George and I were here." Ash-eye sat down with a wide grin poking out from under his deep brow. "You see, little cobra, George has a mission—he and many others like him, scattered all across the globe. George is part of a grand plan."

"What plan?" More words—the new boy was becoming intrigued.

"I'm afraid you wouldn't understand if I told you. But no need to worry; if you're like George, you'll figure it out for yourself one day."

Fat-and-greasy giggled out loud, pleased with the compliment.

"George was once one of you. He wasn't a member of this particular club—there are many such clubs scattered across the United States—but he was a club member.

Where was your club located, George? Kayenta, Arizona, wasn't it?"

Fat-and-greasy nodded vigorously and a stupid grin cut across his bloated face.

"Yes, Arizona. That's where George and I met. I remember that particular club *very* well."

"Who are you?" The new boy spoke for only the third time in almost two weeks.

"My kind are friend to George and friend to you all. George and his associates travel across the country visiting secret clubs like this one, always accompanied by a special friend like me. Tonight, George and I are here in Northrock. In five weeks, we will be in Tom's River, New Jersey and Paul Todd Earley will be here in our place."

"Who's Paul Todd Earley?," asked ash-eye, trying to take the dark man's eye off the new boy.

"You know him as the Red River Ripper, Chatterjack." Despite ash-eye's best efforts, the dark man's attention soon returned to the new boy. "So far, George and I have visited Pennsylvania, New Jersey, and Connecticut."

"And Delaware," added ash-eye. "The books say Delaware too."

"Yes, but I'm afraid the books are wrong. George had nothing to do with that woman in Delaware. Sometimes journalists get a bit carried away."

"How do you know where to go next?," asked a petite blond girl seated near the shed door.

"Again, I'm afraid you wouldn't understand if I told you."

Gradually, the new boy came to notice something. His classmates were completely silent and attentive, almost reverent. He could feel them clinging to the dark

man and his words, reaching out for attention, guidance…
something.

"There's something else you should know, little cobra. George and his associates are not the only men and women with a mission. You and the other members of this club have a mission as well. It is George's job to make people go away." The red light that inhabited the dark man's eyes grew so bright that the new boy was now sure it was not a reflection of the Mickey Mouse lamp. "It is your job to decide *who* goes away."

The new boy's classmates were obviously growing anxious. Each was coiling as if to spring upon some unseen prey.

"So," the dark man produced a thick Culver Country phone book from under his seat. "Who wants to choose?"

The moment the invitation was extended, the assembled children lashed out like sprinters starting a race. Each was trying to attract the dark man's attention by waving, grunting or shouting. Just before the noise level grew loud enough to attract the staff members stationed at the nearby dormitory, the dark man cut it off with a cold stare that quieted all the children save for the small blonde girl who spoke earlier.

"I don't want to use the book," she mumbled. "I want George to make Peter Pan go away."

A few of the other children giggled, but the dark man remained patient. "We needn't use the book, but I'm afraid George can't make Peter Pan go away, dear. Peter Pan is only a story."

The little girl hung her head and slumped to the back of the crowd. The new boy noticed a pair of tears start to slip down her face.

"I have an idea, my young friends. Since this is little cobra's first meeting, why don't we allow him to choose?"

The children obviously didn't like the idea, but they were afraid to question the dark man's wisdom. All eyes were drawn to the new kid. "So little cobra... who should go away?"

The new kid paused and stared into the Mickey Mouse lamp. He had questions. As long as he could remember, he had questions. But something in the dark man's eyes told him that answers were finally within his grasp. He realized the dark man was right. One day, he would figure it all out for himself. Like George. He sank into the dark man's shadow and reached out for the phone book.

At the last moment, the dark man snatched the book away and tilted his head upward, obviously deep in thought. When he finally looked down to face the children again, there was a hint of a smile on his lips. Something was wrong. The dark man's voice grew tentative, almost inquisitive. "I think your classmate is right, little cobra. Let's not use the book this time. Who should go bye-bye?"

Suddenly, the new kid felt like an outsider again. What did the dark man want from him? Why did he take away the book? More questions. Why no answers? He needed answers more than anything in the world. He struggled to remember a name, but the only name he knew was his father's, and his father was already gone. His eyes darted around the shed in a nervous panic, looking from child to child, silently asking for help. When he noticed ash-eye and the touch of amusement in the boy's expression, it came to him. He knew exactly one name.

Little cobra cleared his throat. "Um. Mrs. Tremond... she's our teacher." The blonde girl resumed her sobbing. The other children were quiet and interested, almost fascinated.

The dark man seemed to relax again. A broad smile cut across his face. "Mrs. Tremond it is," he said, shooting a glance toward George. "Our business is concluded then. Goodnight, children. You must return in exactly five weeks…" For a moment, his expression grew sour, "…and I'm sure I needn't remind you of what happens to boys and girls who talk to anyone about our club meetings."

The other children slowly filed out of the shed and started sneaking back down the path to the dormitory, but little cobra couldn't leave—not yet. There were still so many questions. The dark man gave George a nod of assurance, prompting the greasy whelp to make his own exit. On the way out, George grabbed the Mickey Mouse lamp.

Little cobra and the dark man sat alone in the shadows, staring at each other. Little cobra was afraid to speak. After a full fifteen minutes, little cobra finally mustered his courage. "What…"

The dark man cut him off in mid sentence. "No." A knowing smile took root in his dark lips. "One day, little one." The dark man gave little cobra a comforting pat on the head before standing and exiting the shed.

A moment later, little cobra came to his senses and followed. As he stepped out of the shed, he tried to catch a glimpse of the dark man walking off into the night, but there was no man in sight. He saw only what appeared to be a large black dog bounding across the courtyard toward the highway.

• • •

"I said give it to me right now, you cunt!" Little Cobra tore the seashell from the new kid's hand while ash-eye watched the hallway. Feeling his grip slip away, the new kid burst into tears and started flailing his limbs. A wild left fist caught Little Cobra in the lip, but served only to enrage him.

"Quick! Someone's coming!" Ash-eye heard the click of high heels against the polished floor of the corridor. At first, he presumed that Ms. Suarez, the boys' teacher, had finished her daily chat with the social worker a bit early, though it was actually the hefty, graying administrator who rounded the corner, heading toward the classroom.

Ash-eye leapt toward his seat, but Little Cobra was too interested in the beating he was dishing out to the new kid. He was still pounding his fists into the boy's chest when the administrator entered the room.

As she crossed the threshold, the administrator froze for an instant, then bolted for Little Cobra. "GET OFF OF HIM, YOU DEVIL!" She remained surprisingly strong for her age—one swipe of her long arm easily separated the two boys. She grabbed Little Cobra's shoulders and brought her face within inches of his eyes, as if she was trying to peer into his soul to uncover a clue explaining his behavior. "You'd think you of all people would have some sympathy for a new face. You've only been here a couple of months yourself." Little Cobra just stared back. Sensing she'd get few answers from the boy, she turned to face the new kid. "Now, what's this all about?"

"He... he... he stole my favorite shell."

The administrator rolled her eyes, grabbed Little Cobra's ear, and gave it a tug. "Did you take the shell?"

Grabbing the administrator's wrist to ease the pain, Little Cobra gently nodded his head "no."

"Empty your pockets!"

Little Cobra stood motionless, staring at her with clearly defiant eyes. Already tired of the whole incident, the administrator reached into the boy's hip pocket herself and tugged outward, spilling the pocket's contents on the ground. Maintaining her grip on the pocket, she stooped to pick up three items: the seashell, a plastic kaleidoscope, and a curious flat stone emblazoned with an unsettling painted rune in the form of a tight black spiral. Something about the stone sent a chill down her back. When she first touched it, its purpose and nature seemed to lie on the fringe of her conscience, just out of reach. Then, an instant later, the feeling was gone. "Where did you get this thing?," she asked, rolling the stone through her fingers.

"A friend gave it to me."

Once she decided she couldn't unravel the mystery of the stone, she placed it and the kaleidoscope back in Little Cobra's pocket and held the seashell in front of his face.

"Didn't steal it, eh? What do you have to say for yourself?"

Little Cobra stood quiet and defiant.

"Nothing at all?"

Unexpectedly, the boy's defiant expression melted away, replaced by an unsettling grin. "Nothing to say, ma'am, but may I ask a question?"

The administrator felt a sudden chill and took an unconscious step backward. "You may."

Little Cobra's grin melted away. "What's your name?"

Wolf Trap

by Richard Lee Byers

The fence was wrought iron, 16 feet high, and topped with sharp-edged arrowheads: a heavy-duty perimeter defense for a hospital. But I'd climbed tougher barriers, and didn't need to shift out of human form. As I swung myself over, the full moon, my birth moon, came out from behind the clouds. A thrill sang down my nerves.

I did my best to quash the feeling. That sort of exhilaration's nice (in a mindless kind of way), but I didn't want to bounce around like a puppy while I was trying to sneak into an enemy installation. I adjusted my ski mask and slunk on, creeping from one patch of cover to the next.

The well-tended grounds were extensive. It was a while before I caught a glimpse of the hospital itself, and that first look surprised me. My client had mentioned that there'd been some kind of insane asylum here since the mid-19th century, but I hadn't expected to find the original building still standing. The sprawling, three-story structure was as ugly as its surroundings were pleasant. The brick walls were grimy, the few small windows, barred.

The place reminded me of every nasty thing I'd ever read about Victorian England, of Bedlam, Newgate Prison, and the workhouse. It seemed out of place on the outskirts of contemporary San Francisco.

Still, aesthetics aside, I was glad it was old. Old buildings are usually easier to crack than new ones.

I looked about, didn't see anyone, and eased around the structure until I spotted a side door. As I'd expected, I needed my picks. The lock was a good one; it put up a fight, and despite decades of practice, the gloves still made my fingers a bit clumsier than they would have been otherwise. I'd nearly made up my mind to peel them off when the latch finally clicked open.

I cracked the door open and peeked inside. Beyond the door was a deserted hallway. It wasn't too dark to see down, but it was gloomy; most of the ceiling fixtures were switched off. The air smelled of disinfectant. Somewhere, a sound whispered, too faint to identify.

I headed down the passage. Doors with little windows lined both walls. On the other side were small, cell-like bedrooms, all vacant. Evidently, the hospital wasn't overcrowded.

I turned a corner, kept moving toward the noise. Eventually, it resolved into Jimmy Stewart's stammer. Brighter light shone ahead.

Skulking on, I discovered that the hall ended in a sort of lobby adjacent to the main entrance. Other passages ran off it, a staircase led upward, and one corner was glassed in; the nurses' station, by the looks of it. Inside, two guys in white coats sat watching a colorized movie on a portable TV. Apparently, they didn't have any work to do (one of the perks of the graveyard shift).

There was something odd about the scene, and after a second, I realized what it was. The lobby was too bare — just tables and chairs; no decorations, even though it was Halloween night; no projects that the patients had made in art therapy, or whatever on display; no ping-pong or pool table. Come to think of it, I hadn't noticed a baseball diamond or basketball court outside, either.

But hell, what did I care? I hadn't come to critique the facility — just to bust somebody out. And to do that, I needed to get to one of the other corridors and continue my search.

So I just walked out into the open. With luck, the attendants wouldn't look away from the TV. And if they did, well, that was why I'd brought the mask and my Beretta.

The men didn't turn. I chose another hall at random and discovered that its bedroom doors had name cards mounted on them. Bingo.

I found Jennifer Ryan's room halfway down the corridor. She was locked in, but this one only took a second to pick. I eased the door open, then stiffened in surprise.

The teenage girl was in four-point restraints. Leather cuffs bound her wrists and ankles to the bed. An IV ran into one pale, skinny arm. Someone had shaved her head, the better, I assumed, to attach the wires that ran to some sort of monitor. A visor, linked by a cable to the same console, covered her eyes and ears and hooked metal prongs into her nostrils. Dressed in a pungent, urine-stained hospital gown, her coltish body twitched and writhed. Somehow, I didn't think it was going to be a problem to convince her to leave with me.

Intent on pulling the hardware off her, I moved toward the bed. The soft scuff of a footfall sounded behind me. When I whirled, there was a figure silhouetted in the doorway. I lunged, but I was already out of time. The stubby, black gun in its hands made a funny whir. For an instant, my face and chest burned, then I couldn't feel anything. My knees buckled, and the room got even darker. As I passed out, I marveled at just how quickly and completely the job had gone south. And to think that when I'd heard about it, I'd figured it was going to be a cakewalk.

• • •

I supposed that Nikos Ripthroat and I were a study in contrasts. He was slim, handsome, his skin so smooth and his bones so fine that his face just missed effeminacy. He was elegant with his sculpted hair and pearl-gray Armani suit. I was hulking, shaggy, and, I knew, somehow uncouth despite a decent suit of my own and a stylish black leather trenchcoat. Plus, he was in a wheelchair and I was on my feet.

"Erik Mikkelsen." He said my name as if he were tasting it, not sure he liked the flavor. Maybe he thought it discreditable that I no longer used my bombastic Get of Fenris handle. "They tell me you don't like to shake hands."

I fought the urge to shove my fists deeper into my pockets. The urge won. "I'd just as soon you didn't sniff my ass, either."

Nikos flushed. "They also told me you were insolent."

"I'm guessing you didn't fly me 3,000 miles to talk about my quirks. Why don't you tell me what you do want."

He grimaced. "All right. Please, sit down." I dropped into the armchair in front of his huge teak desk. "You understand this has to be kept completely confidential."

"Uh huh."

"All right, then." Nikos paused, hitched the wheelchair around as if looking away from me would help him get started. Or maybe he was just checking out the view.

It was worth it. His office took up most of the top floor of a skyscraper in the financial district, and the walls on two sides were made of glass. Behind him I could see the Transamerica Pyramid, the Oakland Bridge, freighters and sailboats traversing the sun-dappled waters of the Bay.

"Sixteen years ago" Nikos explained, "I had a human secretary named Peggy Travis. She worked here, in the legitimate part of the operation. She was a wonderful girl, full of joy and fire, and we fell in love, or at least I loved her — enough to want to marry her. But while I was still trying to find away to tell her what kind of being I really am, she ended the affair and quit her job. To this day, I don't know why."

I figured I did. She'd caught a whiff of the beast inside him. It was the way ape-werewolf romances usually ended, or so I'd been told. There was no way I'd know firsthand; my sex life was limited to hookers and one-night stands.

"Anyway," Nikos continued, "I kept tabs on her to make sure she didn't run out of money before she found another position — that, in general, she was going to be all right. I knew when she married her high-school sweetheart, a boy named Scott Ryan, three months after she left me, and when she gave birth to a daughter named Jennifer, four months after that."

"Yours, unless she cheated on you," I said, showing off my arithmetic. "I assume that after that, you kept an eye on the kid."

He hesitated. Nikos reached the part of the story he was ashamed of. "At first. If she was only Kinfolk, I meant to leave her alone to live a normal human life. But if she was Garou, she'd need my help."

"Unfortunately, it hurt me to think about her, because I still loved her mother; loved her, too, in a way, even though I'd never met her. I had plenty of other matters to distract me. Jennifer turned 11, 12, 13, without showing any sign of the Change. The upshot of it all was that, gradually, I just stopped checking on her."

"Until recently, I gather. When you found out things were different."

"Yes. She'd started having nightmares and temper tantrums, fighting, destroying things, and running away. The usual picture. Naturally, Peggy and Scott thought she was having some sort of breakdown and dragged her to a shrink. The shrink recommended Jennifer be hospitalized, and when her first placement couldn't handle her, she was transferred to what I'm told is a state-of-the-art experimental program for explosive teens."

Nikos paused, rubbed his forehead, and continued. "I want you to break her out, so I can guide her through the Change before she really does lose her mind."

"One question," I said. "You're a pack leader. You have plenty of flunkies you could send. Why do you need me?"

Nikos scowled. "Because of this." He rapped the arm of the wheelchair. "A Bane got me. The wound's slowly healing, but until it does—"

"You'll worry," I said, suddenly comprehending, "that one of your underlings will try to grab your throne. You Shadow Lords are notorious for that kind of crap." Actually, as far as I was concerned, most Garou were too locked into the senseless, endless struggle for dominance, but Nikos' tribe was a particularly egregious example.

Nikos nodded. "I don't know who I can trust. And if a rival got his hands on Jennifer, he could use her against me. So, will you help me? I'll pay you $20,000 and make a place for you in the pack."

I'm sure I gaped at him, stupidly, in fact. It was the first time in a long while that I'd found myself so completely at a loss for words.

"I guarantee you'll be welcome," Nikos continued. "Everyone's heard about the victories you've won—"

"I fought for money," I said, more harshly than I'd intended. "Not for your precious Gaia, and certainly not to impress anyone. You can give my 'place' to the next ronin who wanders through here."

Nikos frowned. "Are you sure?" he asked. Modern as he looked in his high-tech, corporate surroundings, complete with the computer and conference phone on his desk and the big-screen video system in the corner, he was really an old-fashioned Garou at heart. He couldn't fathom why any werewolf would opt out of the hidebound system of tribe, sept, and pack if given a halfway reasonable alternative. No doubt he'd been certain the invitation would clinch the deal.

"Yeah," I said. "Hard to believe, isn't it? I mean, you make the Shadows sound like such a true-blue, fun-loving bunch of folks."

"All right," he said. "Then will you do the job for just the cash?"

"Sure," I said. "Why not?"

Ah, why not, indeed?

• • •

I dreamed I was lying in the bottom of a pitching rowboat with a fat fly buzzing around my head. Gradually, I realized the cold, hard surface beneath me wasn't moving. I was just dizzy and sick to my stomach. And the buzz became a droning baritone voice.

I cracked my eyes open and found that my vision was blurry. But I could see that I was sprawled naked on the linoleum in the middle of the lobby. A crowd of people surrounded me, many wearing blue coveralls and a number pointing guns at me — not tranq guns like the one that had knocked me out, but killing weapons, all loaded with silver bullets, I suspected. The voice belonged to a pudgy, pink-faced guy with a wispy, ginger mustache. He was holding one end of a three-foot rod. The other was attached to the steel collar encircling Jennifer's neck. The visor was gone and she was standing unassisted, but it was obvious from her slack jaw and glassy blue eyes that she was still only semiconscious.

"Look at him," the pudgy man said, "and you'll see that he's only flesh and blood. Nothing to be afraid of, just an odd kind of animal driven by instinct. That's why we caught him so easily. Despite the tricks he can do, he's no match for a rational human being."

"What's the deal with his hands?" an Asian woman asked.

"Ordinarily, a Garou mates with a human or a wolf. Sex between two werewolves is as unnatural as incest between a human brother and sister. The offspring of such a union is called a metis, or mule. They're always born deformed and are regarded as freaks even by their own race of monsters." He sounded as if he relished the thought of my childhood loneliness and humiliation.

"Actually," I said, "the other Garou always told me I had an endearing pixie-like quality. And everyone adored my blueberry muffins."

When I spoke, some of my captors jerked in surprise. The pudgy guy said, "I thought it was about time you were waking up. Who are you and what's your interest in this girl? Answer, or we'll hurt you."

"My name's Rolf Hendricks," I said. "Jennifer's my daughter, though she doesn't know it. I came to get her out of here and help her through the Change." A good merc always protects the client, though at moments when my own head is on the block, it's hard to feel enthusiastic about it. "Now, who are you and what were you doing to her?"

The pudgy man sneered. "Why should I tell you?"

Because it will give you a chance to gloat and strut, I thought. He seemed like the type. I just needed to provide an excuse. "Well, it sounded like you want to teach your buddies about the Garou. If we chat for awhile, maybe I'll display the inadequacies of my dimwitted animal brain." More to the point, from my perspective, if I stalled for time, maybe I could shake off the effects of the tranq before he and the goon squad started hurting me.

The pudgy man chuckled. "All right, when you put it like that, why not? It's not as if you'll get a chance to repeat what you hear, and it might be educational for the students to observe your reaction." He glanced around at his audience. "He could fly into one of the werewolves' legendary psychotic rages, so stay ready to shoot. My name is Howard Cooper. I'm a psychiatrist, a neurophysiologist, and a Project Head for the Aesop Research Company."

"A division of Pentex," I said. No wonder he knew all about the Garou. The tribes didn't have a deadlier enemy than the Wyrm-controlled megacorporation. I was in about as deep as I could get.

Cooper frowned. He didn't like it that I knew that much about his organization. "Well, yes. Recently ARC acquired this facility and informed the psychiatric community that we were converting it into a residential treatment program for troubled adolescents. Since our goal was research, we'd be offering our services free of charge. Naturally, we were inundated with referrals. After that, it was just a matter of using genetic testing to identify the children we actually wanted to work on—"

"Mislaid Garou-to-be," I said.

"Precisely." He stood up straighter, preening. "Needed to test a hypothesis of mine — namely, that the right combination of aversive conditioning and chemotherapy can make it impossible for a young werewolf to complete the Change."

I blinked and squinted. My eyes still refused to focus. "So what? The majority of lost cubs never achieve their potential anyway. And most kids aren't forgotten. Their Garou parents take them in hand as soon as they start showing signs of their heritage. So what do you hope to accomplish?"

The pudgy guy smirked. "As I expected, you lack the abstract reasoning ability to grasp the implications. Once I invent the treatment, I can refine it into a form we can administer to the entire population. The drugs will go into the food supply. The hypnotic stimuli will air subliminally on television. Every Garou child growing up in a human community will be affected. And since there aren't many being raised by wolf packs anymore, in just a few years the supply of new werewolves will dry up without your people ever even knowing why."

The gunmen tensed just in case I did go into a frenzy. "They would have loved you at Auschwitz," I said mildly. "But it'll never work." I wished I were certain of that.

"Oh no, I assure you, it will. I'm on the brink. Too bad you won't be around to see it."

"Why not? I figured there was an IV and a tin blindfold in my future."

"Sorry. You've already accessed your powers. The treatment was never intended to work on someone like you. But we do have a use for you."

"What a relief," I said. "I'd hate to think I couldn't pull my weight."

"I wear a lot of hats at Pentex," Cooper said. "One of my responsibilities is training First Team operatives.

Garou killers. They reside here, providing security, until they're ready to go into the field. You're about to become the object of a training exercise."

"Let me guess," I said. "Slow me down with dope, turn me loose, and let the posse hunt me down. Only, what if I refuse to play?"

"Then we'll regretfully blow you apart where you lie."

"In that case, I'll play."

He grinned. "I thought you might." He gestured, and the ring of people surrounding me opened, clearing a path to the door. "We'll give you a head start. By the way, the fence is now electrified."

"Well, gosh," I said, rising. "If there's no way out, I'll just have to kill every one of you monkeys, won't I?" Unfortunately, at that point my legs went rubbery and I staggered, making my threat less intimidating than it might otherwise have been. A couple people laughed. Trying to look undaunted, I ambled to the exit.

Once outside, I started running, putting distance between me and the enemy. I wracked my brains for a plan. Hell, I ought to be able to think my way out of this, no sweat. After all, I'd been a real Einstein so far.

For instance, I could have found out who owned the hospital *before* coming out here, could have retreated when I sensed there was something strange about the setup, or at least proceeded more cautiously, maybe avoided tripping the alarm or whatever it was I'd done to give away my presence.

But no, I'd waltzed blindly up the gallows steps and stuck my head in the noose — proof positive that a Goof of Fenris could take himself out of the tribe, but that there was no way to take the infamous tribal recklessness out of the Goof.

I did my best to stop kicking myself. It couldn't help me now. Instead I'd better decide what form to take. Either of the four-legged forms, Cujo or Rin Tin Tin, would have advantages. With sharper senses, I'd have a better chance of detecting enemies before they saw me, while being built low to the ground would help me hide.

But as Cooper had pointed out, I'm a freak. No matter what shape I shift to, my oversized Larry Talbot hands stay the same regardless of form. They don't shed their talons and fur when I turn human, and they don't shrink into paws when I go lupine. That makes the four-legged forms clumsy, and I didn't think I could afford clumsy.

Be Larry Talbot, then: the wolfman, the powerhouse. Except that that would make me 10 feet tall and very easy to spot. Okay, then be the troglodyte, Alley Oop. At least I'd be a little stronger. I crouched behind a purple-flowered glorybush and willed myself to transform.

When I did, I got another nasty surprise. I'd hoped Oop's high-performance metabolism would burn off the lingering effects of the drug. It didn't. Apparently the stuff was Wyrm-tainted.

Well, no use worrying about it. It wasn't as if I had much of a chance in any case. It occurred to me that if there was a tall tree growing near the fence, I could climb it and jump over the barrier without getting fried. I dashed to the edge of the property.

No dice. There'd been big trees here once, but somebody had cut them down. Somehow, I wasn't surprised.

Behind me, I heard doors opening, the hunters spreading out into the night. Afraid of being pinned against the fence, I ran back toward the hospital, hunkered down behind a fragrant eucalyptus, and strained to come up with another idea.

After a minute, I got one. I could at least screw up the enemy's night vision. Concentrating, I tried to activate one of my Gifts.

It was hard. The tranq didn't just throw off my balance and coordination; it made me feel drunk, undercut my ability to focus my will. Finally, just when I was about to give up and move on, I felt the power kick in, like a key turning inside my head.

Through the darkness sounded a quick succession of *pops*, like a bunch of inflated paper bags being swatted all at once. Small fires burst into existence in bushes and trees. Unfortunately, with only green growth to consume, most would gutter out quickly, but I hoped that at least a few would burn for a while.

Startled hunters cried out. Grinning, I slunk on, shoes swished through grass.

I lunged behind an oak, flattened myself against the rough bark. The footsteps continued toward me. One man murmured and another replied. It was hard to believe they didn't hear my heart pounding.

Obviously they didn't, because they walked right past me; two of them, with assault rifles, Kevlar jackets, and helmets equipped with modular nightvision goggles and radios. I eased out of my hiding place to attack them from behind.

I clawed the first one's carotid arteries. Blood spurted, suffusing the air with its copper scent, and he dropped. As I pivoted, the other guy, a burly Chicano with two tattooed tears, did the same, bringing his weapon to bear. Feeling horribly slow and clumsy, I barely managed to slap the rifle out of line, then punched him in the jaw. His neck snapped and he fell, too.

For the first time, I thought I might have an outside chance of surviving. Now that I'd taken down the gunmen, I could seize a weapon for myself. Not only would it narrow the long odds against me, but I could use it to blast open the gate in the fence.

I wrenched the Chicano's rifle out of his deathgrip. With its box magazine and folding steel butt, it looked a lot like an AKMS with some extra bells and whistles; probably the latest design from one of Pentex's munitions companies. Wishing that the one of the helmet and jacket sets would fit Oop's beetle-browed, anthropoid body, I crept back toward the edge of the grounds.

I knelt behind a bush, held my breath until four goons went by, moved on, swinging left to avoid the halo of light cast by one of my fires. I sensed motion at my back.

I pivoted. Nothing there. I did my best to blink the haze out of my eyes and still couldn't see anything.

Maybe my nerves were playing tricks on me. After all, I wasn't even sure I'd heard anything. I just had a feeling. Backing up, I took a last look around, then turned and stalked on.

For four paces, it was all right. Then the hairs on the back of my neck stood on end. I spun around.

For a second, I still didn't see him. Then he was right in front of me, a piece of the night molded into human form. A more prosaic description: he was a guy in black pajamas, hood, gloves, and shoes, wearing black pigment on his upraised samurai sword.

Damn my cloudy vision! Still, it was all right. I'd spotted him in time, and now he was going to wish he'd brought a gun instead of relying on this ninja crap. I pulled my rifle's trigger. Nothing happened. Maybe the gun was Wyrm-tainted, too. At any rate, it was gimmicked somehow so a Garou couldn't fire it — one more way this game was rigged against me.

For one precious instant, I froze in shock. By the time I recovered, the sword was whizzing at my head. Frantically I jerked up the gun to block. The blade swooped around my guard and slashed my shoulder. The ninja whirled past me.

No pain yet. Ordinarily, that would come in a moment, but I invoked another Gift and shut it out. At the same time, I wheeled to keep the swordsman in front of me.

He lunged, cutting, feinting, bellowing kais. He was a better swordsman than I was, or might have been even if I hadn't had the tranq slowing me down. Over the next few seconds, my superior strength and reach barely sufficed to hold him off. Meanwhile, blood streamed down my arm; the gash wasn't closing. Evidently, the blade was silver-coated.

Finally I got lucky. Swinging with all my might, I managed to bash the sword out of his grip. Spinning end over end, it vanished into the shadows. I rushed in, trying to brain him, but he sidestepped and tripped me. By the time I scrambled to my feet, he had a dagger in each hand.

I suspected he was as proficient with those as he was with a sword. Still, he'd have to get in close to score with them, and that might give me the chance I needed.

I dropped the rifle, brandished my hands in a your-knives-against-my-claws gesture, then swayed, trying to make it appear that my wound was draining what was left of my strength. Since it wasn't that far from the truth, I figured I'd look reasonably convincing.

He pounced at me. I jabbed my talons at his face, a feeble thrust, and he brushed the attack aside with his forearm.

I guessed Cooper hadn't taught the class about the Gift that lets certain Garou drop an opponent with the slightest touch. Or maybe Sho Kosugi here had been absent that day. At any rate, his feet flew out from under him. I threw myself on top of him, ripped through cloth, flesh, and cracking ribs to shred his heart and lungs.

Afterwards, I needed to lie still, gasping in chestsful of air. But I could already hear running footsteps pounding toward me. The ninja's shouts and the clangor of sword and rifle had drawn the other hunters.

My shoulder throbbed. My gaze fell on the useless gun, and a black, despairing rage welled up inside me. Suddenly, I didn't care about eking out another few fearful, painful minutes of life. I wanted to turn and charge my tormentors, kill and kill until they brought me down. My spine and limbs lengthened. My teeth grew points and my jaws began to stretch into a muzzle.

Shuddering, I clamped down on my fury. I refused to go berserk, not when it would mean losing, not with so much at stake. After several moments, my head cleared, and the shift to wolfman form reversed itself. Clutching my wound, hoping I wasn't leaving a trail of blood, I jumped up and ran.

A gun barked. I threw myself flat, then realized that the bullet hadn't come anywhere near me. Someone had fired at a shadow, or maybe at one of his fellow goons. For the time being, I was in the clear.

Which meant it was time to hatch Plan C. Much to my surprise, I finally did dredge up one last idea. It was a long shot; it meant trying something I hadn't done in years, and hadn't been good at even when in practice, but it also looked to be the only shot left.

Unfortunately, I couldn't take it out here in the dark. I got up and headed for the hospital.

After a minute, the black pile of the building loomed out of the night. I crept toward the door I'd entered through before. Guns banged and chattered. Bullets split the air around my head.

I sprinted, zigzagging, certain every instant that the next shot would take me out. But the gunmen kept missing. Chalk it up to the dark, and the fact that the clowns were still trainees.

Knowing the door had relocked itself when it closed, I hurled my weight against it. It crashed inward and I fell on top of the wreckage, jarring a burst of pain through my injured shoulder. I scrambled up and ran on.

I was afraid the lobby would be full of hunters, but it wasn't. The only people there were the two attendants I'd first seen, still manning the nurses' station. Since I didn't want them telling my pursuers which way I'd gone, I charged the enclosure.

One guy frantically locked the door, so I leaped at a window instead. As the glass exploded, I noticed the other man had a red left eye. I wondered fleetingly what that was all about, but by the time I touched down, I'd forgotten about it. I had more pressing things to think about.

I tore red eye's face off, then pivoted to kill his partner. No need. A flying shard of glass had opened his throat for me. I smashed a console that looked like it monitored an alarm system, then grabbed a piece of window, Then, I dashed up two flights of stairs, around a corner, and stopped, panting, under a light.

Below me, radios crackled and voices called back and forth. Knowing I'd reentered the hospital, the hunters would seal and sweep it. I was treed.

So I'd better get to work, I thought.

I held the shard up, tilted it to reflect the maximum amount of light, stared into the sheen, tried to push fear, anger, and pain aside so I could slip into the proper meditative frame of mind.

I felt the power stir inside me, but nothing tangible happened. Ordinarily, that wouldn't have been any reason to panic. On my best day, I'd never done this trick in less than 15 minutes. But now I didn't have 15 minutes to spare.

I concentrated harder. Drops of blood plopped from my elbow onto the linoleum. Footsteps clumped from the first floor to the second.

I kept straining, heard the hunters ascend again, and felt the world shift.

The ceiling fixtures went dark and turned to spider webs, deepening the gloom. Now, the only light was a sourceless gray phosphorescence. The linoleum changed into wood, while the antiseptic tang in the air gave way to a faint stink of excrement and rot.

I laughed. I'd done it, stepped sideways into the spirit world. The enemy couldn't get at me anymore.

Or so I thought. Then two riflemen stalked around the corner.

One Garou can lead a band of comrades through the Gauntlet. Though it was supposed to be impossible, somehow I'd drawn my pursuers after me. Which meant my last ploy had crapped out, and I guessed I was going to die. Still laughing, I charged the riflemen as they drew beads on me. I saw that I wouldn't close with them in time.

But before they could shoot, a ring of giggling shadows materialized around them, clutched at them with gray translucent fingers. The humans squawked, punched, and thrashed, but feebly, as if the phantoms, touch had sucked away their strength. In seconds the shadows disarmed them, then hustled each into a different cell.

I dropped into a fighting stance, but the spooks didn't attack me. After a few seconds, shrieks and gunfire began echoing through the building.

It sounded as if the hunters suddenly had bigger problems than bagging me. Emboldened, I sneaked toward the stairs to check out the situation.

Down the hall, another band of wraiths was stomping a fallen goon. On the second floor, they were wrapping the hunters in straitjackets. A few yards away, cell doors swung open by themselves. Startled gunmen pivoted toward them, then found themselves unable to look away. Sobbing and shuddering, resisting with all their might, they shuffled through. The doors slammed behind them.

Meanwhile, still unmolested, I tried to figure out what was going on.

Nikos said the hospital had been an asylum since the 1800s. Maybe it had been a snake pit, and the old-time inmates who'd suffered here were getting their revenge. Not that the shadows were their souls, trapped in this place for generations (or at least I hoped not). But Umbral sites remember their histories, and sometimes create emanations to reenact them. Or to settle somebody's old score.

Evidently, my step sideways had somehow enabled the spooks to pull my enemies into their reach. Not that I was complaining, but I wondered why they weren't messing with me as well. Maybe it was because I wasn't human and had never held anyone prisoner here. Unlike the Pentex guys, I didn't have much in common with the people the inmates once hated.

So I guessed I was home free. Then someone yelled, "Hendricks!" It took me a second to remember that that was the alias I'd given, but I didn't have any trouble recognizing the voice, — now shrill with fear — of Howard Cooper. Perhaps, hoping to witness the kill, he'd been following some of the goons around, and so had been yanked into the Umbra along with them.

"Come out!" the scientist shouted. "I've still got the girl! Tell him!"

A shaky female voice cried, "Yes! I'm here, too!"

At last I understood why Cooper had taken Jennifer out of her cell: to use her as a hostage, just in case, against all probability, I somehow managed to turn the tables on him and his men. He was either remarkably farsighted or astonishingly gutless. "Where?" I called.

"In the lobby!" she replied.

"Don't be afraid," I said. "I'm coming down to help you."

They were standing by the front door. Cooper had a snub-nosed .38 revolver pressed to Jennifer's temple. He had choked up on the rod-leash to hold her in front of him human-shield fashion. Maybe that was why none of the shadows had taken him out.

The girl's eyes widened when she saw me.

"I thought you'd be interested in learning about another difference between us inferior Garou and you godlike humans," I said, advancing. "We can open the way into a place called the Umbra—"

"I know where we are!" Cooper yapped. "Stay back!"

"Or else what?" I kept walking forward. "If you understand what I did, then you know you need me to take you back to the physical world."

"It doesn't matter. I'll shoot her anyway!"

"All right," I growled, "I guess you win." Then I charged.

Cooper shoved the hostage at me. I tumbled her out of the way. The revolver pointed at my chest. I dove, trying to get under the shot. The gun banged once as I plowed into him, taking him down with a flying tackle.

As soon I got my claws in him, it was over, but I'd grown to hate him so much that I felt an urge to keep mangling his corpse.

Instead, I got up and turned to Jennifer. She was cowering with her back against the wall — scared, but not terrified, which made sense when I thought about it. On one hand, I was a naked, blood-spattered ogre who'd just torn a guy into cold cuts, but on the other, my victim was the doc who'd been torturing her. To some extent, it ought to balance out.

Hoping it would reassure her, I shifted back to human form. Jennifer gasped and recoiled, but once the change was done, her trembling abated. "I'm a friend," I said. "Really. I came to take you out of here."

"But you," she swallowed, "you didn't stop when he said he'd shoot me."

"Yeah, well, even doped up like I am, I'm pretty fast. Cooper couldn't count on having enough time to kill you and turn the gun on me. I hoped he'd realize that and be more interested in protecting his ass than carrying out his threat."

"I admit it was a gamble, but what was the alternative? I could have stood a safe distance away from him and tried to shift us all back across the Gauntlet, but since Cooper wasn't a Garou, ordinarily it wouldn't even work. Then again, I got the two of you here, so who knows? Say it worked. Next thing, he shoots me and locks you back in the brainwashing gizmo. I couldn't see much percentage in that."

Jennifer's lips quirked into a fleeting smile. "Easy for you to say. I'd still have been alive. Maybe the next rescuer would have gotten me out."

"Maybe," I said, "but there was another side to it, too. Cooper claimed he could destroy my people, who are your people, too, even if you don't know it yet. That made killing him more important than saving your life or mine. I couldn't even risk simply marooning him here because his organization has agents who could cross over and bring him out. Can you understand that?"

"Kind of," she said. "Could you be a little more vague?"

I grinned. "I still have work to do. I'll explain things as we go. That is, if you feel up to helping me."

"You mean, help you free the other kids?" I nodded. "Sure," she said.

The mop-up took some time, but it was easy. Despite the fact that my companion had yet to come into her powers, I had no trouble carrying her back to mundane reality. Maybe the shadows helped me, I don't know. Afterwards, I killed the noncombatant Pentex staffer I found hiding in the building. Jennifer bandaged my shoulder. Together we found clothing. Then we trashed Cooper's files, drugs, and equipment.

Finally, we walked mumbling, stumbling teenagers around until they came to, then parked them in the lobby. Some couldn't stop crying; others wouldn't speak; many flinched at any noise or sudden movement. Though they weren't emaciated, their demeanor reminded me of photos I'd seen of death-camp survivors.

"You wimps make me sick!" I bellowed in my best drill-sergeant snarl. The teenagers jumped. "Don't you know why Cooper picked you to hurt? Because you're special! You have magic powers and a heroic destiny. Fate has chosen you to defend the world. So act like it, damn it! Stop sniveling. Stand up straight, and don't huddle together."

It worked to a degree. I jolted some of them out of their funk. A chunky black girl said, "What are you talking about? What's going to happen to us?"

And I realized it was a good question.

I didn't doubt that Nikos's pack would take them in. Like most troops, Nikos's pack was almost certainly eager for new blood. In fact, a mass recruitment might shore up the crippled leader's shaky position considerably. The problem was what would happen after that.

Garou aren't known for coddling their young. Certainly, the grim, cold Shadow Lords didn't. The kids would face a grueling series of tests, and for all I knew, they weren't up to it. There was no way to guess how much damage Cooper's experiment had done.

It was a disgusting thought, but I was afraid they were going to need a friend.

"Soon," I said, "you can go home if you want to. But first you have to spend some time with a secret society of people like yourselves. They'll teach you how to harness your hidden talents. It's what you need, and they're a good group — so good that I'm joining them myself. It's part of my reward for shutting this dungeon down."

Which only goes to show that there's more than one kind of wolf trap, and it's hard for any one Garou to dodge them all. ///

Predator and Prey

by David Chart

Kaoru ran through the woods, his paws whispering over the litter coating the forest floor, barely disturbing the leaves. It was dark, but the moon was near full, and its light through trees was more than enough for Kaoru to see by: his surroundings were almost as clear as most would find them during the day. He dodged the trees and leapt to and from boulders, leaving as little trail as possible, but knowing it was hopeless. The quaking earth earlier in the night had lost him too much time, and the Hunter would catch him before he could reach any caern. The clean smell of the forest assured him of no nasty surprises, but there was also no sign of anything he could use.

Despite the still air, the wind raised his fur on his left, and he bore round to the right, away from the Hunter. His nose caught the scent of water, of clean water, and he turned toward it. Perhaps this would work, he thought. Soon, his ears could make out the sound of the stream flowing over rocks and gurgling in the little pools and eddies that they formed, and his heart fell a bit. Sure enough, the surface of the water was turbulent, and no image was reflected back at him. A scent he knew all to well came to him on the wind, and he knew he had no time for reflection. Turning upstream, Kaoru hoped there would be a pool, or something, farther up. The scent got stronger, and another noise grew louder as he ran. His paws were wet and cold, but he still ran in the stream, hiding his scent as far as possible. The noise sounded like a waterfall, and Kaoru offered a quick prayer to Phoebe hoping it would turn out to be something else. His prayer wasn't answered. Kaoru ran between two boulders and found himself in a dead end, standing in a pool of churning water into which a powerful stream of water fell constantly from above. He turned, brought to bay, and faced the Hunter.

The Hunter rode through the gap, mounted on a white horse and wearing a neat suit. In one hand, it carried a cattle-prod. Its face looked human and bland, expressing no emotion of triumph or fear, and the horse's hooves didn't disturb the water. Kaoru snarled and backed up, trying to keep out of range. The Hunter rode forward, reaching out with the prod, and touched the Garou as he felt the waterfall beat on his tail. In an instant, all the fight went out of him, and the Hunter disappeared into the Umbra.

Defeated, Kaoru made his way out of the pool and back into the forest, shaking himself dry and sniffing the air for the scent of prey. He was hungry, and the period of grace was the best time to hunt. A rabbit fell easily to him, although he lamented the absence of a pack, which meant that the deer he could smell so temptingly were beyond his capacity. As the moon sank and the sky brightened in the east, he searched for a secure place in which to rest, somewhere where he could sleep without the risk of the apes disturbing him. Not that that was likely anyway — their scent was faint on the air here, despite his closeness to a scab, so they couldn't come there often. He found a spot between a boulder and a bush that would provide some cover, and that didn't smell of recent occupation, and he fitted himself into the gap, laying his head on his forepaws. He slowed, deepened his breathing, and let himself pass into a trance.

Kaoru let an image form in his mind, the odor of a grassy plain, the smell of the dust and the grasses, the taste of the traces of pollen in his mouth, the grass lying still in the dead air. As the image came clear, he imagined the wind rising, blowing the grasses, ruffling his fur, raising the pollen to scent much more strongly in his nostrils. Then Oigimi was there, within the image.

The wind-blown blossom,
Whirling before the tempest,
Never sets its seed.

"I know, but what can I do? The Hunters always pursue me, and if I just let them catch me they are sure to draw other things that will damage my body as well as my mind."

A stream ever runs,
But a fish in the current
Is killed on the rocks.

"The running probably does harm me, I know, but what can I do? I tried fighting, and there is nothing to fight. They just touch me and vanish. I think I released spirits that will destroy me."

The deer hears the wolf.
If fear of death prevents flight,
Its death is assured.

"Yes, you're right. I shouldn't be defeatist. But what else can I do? I have tried fighting, I have tried running; neither is a solution. I know just letting them take me will not be a solution. I don't see that there is any way out."

The wolf stalks the deer.
If the panther stalks the wolf
The deer will be safe.

"That's all very well, but I don't have any panther to stalk my Hunters. Anyway, I'm the wolf: stop calling me a deer!"

The wolf is hunter,
The deer is prey: you are prey,
How then are you wolf?

"Oigimi, don't say that! I am a wolf, but even a wolf must flee from some things, especially such dangerous spirits as I have released."

As the wind must blow,
The wolf hunts: if you are wolf
You are predator.

"OK, so I should be the hunter, not the hunted. I know that! But how can I hunt the spirits? They have no scent; they leave no trail. I could never find them."

How to hunt shadows
That leave no trace of passage?
They follow the wolf.

"So I should try to fool the Hunter so that I can trap it when it tries to trap me? I don't know: the spirits seem to have many more senses than I do. I'd have to hide, and I think they'd trap me."

The hard-hunted fox
Leads his pursuer to the cave
Of the mountain lion.

"Aahhh. . ." Kaoru paused, considering this possibility. "So maybe I could lead the spirits somewhere where another power would destroy them? I think that could work. I hope it does. I don't think a mountain lion would be sufficient, though."

The cherry blossom
Forms a white cloud on the tree.
It does not float off.

"Yes, Oigimi, I know it was only a metaphor. I was teasing. Still, it is a real problem. After all, they seem to be quite powerful spirits, and I don't think the Wyld Hunter would disappear if I led it into a city. The Web Hunter survives the wilderness well enough. Hmmm. I wonder if the defenders of a caern would be strong enough? And will they find anything to fight?"

Your shadow is long:
Others may stand on its head,
Where you may not come.

"I suppose so, if they really are as exclusively after me as it seems. Maybe they won't even be a threat to anyone else, but I don't really think I dare hope for that. Still, if there is something to fight, I think caern defenders would be able to deal with it. After all, if they were that powerful, I don't think I'd still be around."

The cubs are carried
Unharmed in the lion's mouth.
Are her jaws, then, safe?

"OK, it's risky. But it's sort of your idea in the first place, and I don't really see any alternative. Do you?"

The raging torrent
Is not swum for pleasure's sake,
But must be in need.

"Then I'll try that with the next Hunter. I hope that it's the Wyld — I don't want to have to lead a Wyrm creature to a caern."

The torrent still floods,
Whether you face it alone,
Or carry your child.

"True enough. Anyway, I'd better use my respite to get some sleep. Will you watch me?"

While the cricket sleeps,
And the fox seeks his burrow,
The moon ever shines.

"Thank you." Kaoru let the image slip away from him, and the smells of the forest replaced those of the open plain as he came out of the trance. Settling down, he felt a wind on his flanks — a light wind that didn't ruffle the leaves of the bush in the slightest — and he relaxed into sleep.

The sun sank on the next night and the moon, just a sliver short of full, rose to cast its light over the land. Kaoru crept carefully from his hiding place and howled at the moon, acknowledging the rage at the ruin of Gaia that flowed into him as he gazed upon Phoebe's image. He padded down to a small stream, enjoying the smell of the wood as the day creatures went to their rest and the night creatures stirred from their burrows, and drank from the clear water. Then he went, boldly and without stealth, to the top of a boulder, whence he could see the forest around him. He heard and smelled the small animals scattering from his path, but they were safe, for the moment. There was something to be done first.

Kaoru gazed westward as the sun sank, watching the last glow fade from the sky with less apprehension than he had felt since his Rite of Passage. As the darkness became complete, a hideous howl echoed through his soul: a howl that spoke of pain and torment and the desire to bring both of those things to others for the joy of bringing suffering. It was the Wyrm Hunter, then. Kaoru flung his head back and howled in defiance, as he had never done before. The response was almost a screech, and he realized that the thing had learned his location from the howl.

Kaoru sprang down from the rock and began running, dodging among the trees as he ran for the stream. If the Hunter had learned something from his howl, then they plainly weren't as omniscient as he had imagined. If they had to seek information, then they could be fooled, and if they could be fooled, the trap might yet close about them.

That night was a furious chase as Kaoru employed all his skill and cunning in leaving as little trail as possible. He could hear the Hunter behind him, closer than he had bargained for, and he changed his course to head for the nearest caern. The Sept of the Western Eye guarded this area, he knew, and their caern was in the Muir Woods, which meant he had to head for the coast. As the sun rose, he had almost reached the scab. The rising sun brought a despairing cry from the Hunter, so close behind him, yet so far now, as it was forced to cease its pursuit. Kaoru moved to a small rise so that he could see the scab. Even from this distance the foul smell prickled in his nostrils, and the scent of the apes was heavy on the air and plants around him. This was their territory, theirs and the Wyrm's, and he did not want to pass through it during their time, even if it would buy him time over the Hunter.

No, he decided, it was time to hunt and rest. A couple of small birds formed an adequate, if unsatisfying, meal, but the only stream he could find was laced with the foul taste of the Wyrm, and he drank sparingly, grimacing as the water burned his mouth. He slunk deep into what cover was available as he sought a resting place for the day. It wouldn't do to have the apes find him while he slept.

In a safe place, well hidden by thick bushes and some convenient poison ivy, he let himself slip into a trance. This time the image was of mountains, the smell of bare rock and snow, and the cold as a bitter wind whipped up around him. Oigimi was there.

The river flows on,
Seeking union with the sea.
Why has the boat stopped?

"I can't go through the city during the day, Oigimi. It's too risky — the apes would see me and probably try to capture me. I don't know if I could control the Rage at this time of the moon, and I don't think slaughtering apes while the Wyrm Hunter is after me is a good idea."

The wind blows too hard,
And snow dances in the air.
Wolf leaves not his den.

"It's not an excuse. I think it would be too dangerous at the moment. I'm sure I can keep ahead of the Hunter long enough to reach the caern, especially if I use the apes' bridge across the bay."

A hovering hawk.
The wise mouse seeks cover now:
Too late when it dives.

"Look, Oigimi, I need sleep as well. I'm not a spirit — I can't keep going forever. Watch me while I rest."

The sage's wisdom,
Spoken soft in golden words,
Is lost in the gale.

And then Oigimi was gone from his trance, and the wind on the mountainside was still. Kaoru brought himself out to sniff at his surroundings, knowing Oigimi would be there. Indeed, he felt the light caress of the ethereal wind as he scented the air, finding only distant traces of the apes, and settled himself for sleep.

The day passed quietly again, and Kaoru rose as the sun set, sniffing the fresh, early evening air, almost entirely cleansed of the stench of the apes by a light shower. He made his way carefully out of his hiding place and worked his way through the undergrowth until he could see the full moon rising over the hills. He could feel the boiling instincts within him, and he growled quietly in acknowledgment, reluctant to give the Hunter any more than he already had. For all his confident words to Oigimi last night, he was not at all sure that he could get to the caern before the Hunter caught up with him. Quickly, he returned to the stream and drank, forcing himself to ignore the rank taste. It wasn't enough to actually hurt him, and he would likely need all his energy for the coming night. Then, as the last glow of the sun disappeared, Kaoru heard the call behind him, splitting the air and fouling the very taste of it with its sound as the Hunter took up the chase once again.

Running, Kaoru soon found himself approaching the scab. The smell of the apes, the stench of their oils and gasolines, assaulted his nose. Then he was among the streets, the harshness of the surface scraping his paws, the odor of corruption so strong on the air that he could almost taste it. Apes milled about him in strange costumes, mostly the young, he saw, the nearly innocent, dressed as leeches, witches, and shamans from the past — even as Garou. Kaoru suppressed the growl that rose in his throat, as it would not do to frighten them, and perhaps this night was the best he could have chosen for crossing the scab. With so much strangeness on the streets, his extra, small strangeness would surely go unnoticed.

He could sense the Hunter close on his tail, and so he couldn't afford the time to be slow. Running, his ears were assaulted by the harsh cries of cars, adding burned rubber to the assault on his nose as the car screeched to a stop bare feet away from him. His eyes were assaulted by the flashing of multicolored lights at the joining of two roads, and his mouth offended by the taste of gasoline fumes that hung on the air. His sense was confused by roads that ignored the lay of the land, traveling straight up and down hills at gradients that surely even the apes could see were ridiculous.

Kaoru tried to close his senses to everything except his goal and the Hunter behind him as he wove his way deeper into the scab, where the mountains of the Weaver towered on either side of him, cutting off the sky and the smell of the free wind, while between them huddled the corruption of the Wyrm. Smells of decay and hopelessness crept out of the dark openings, much as did the occasional ape, an animal clad in rags and unwashed, stinking not of his natural smell, but of some foully tainted perversion of it. Kaoru crossed more streets, almost stumbling on the foul slime underfoot, choking on the rot of food and flesh, the fumes of exhausts, and the litter that blew up in his face, heading always for the tang of salt on the air that told him he was nearing the bay.

And then he was there. In front of him, instead of the bridge, a wall of mist rose. Kaoru could smell aggression, fear, anger — all suppressed and boiling inside from the apes all around him — as they shouted at each other. Red and blue lights flashed from atop one of the cars, distracting Kaoru as he searched for a way through the press. Kaoru shied away from the near contact, retreating to the shadows from instinct until he found that the shadows were fouler than the light. A nervous growl rolled in his throat as the milling apes came too close, looked too curiously, nervousness and the beginnings of fear over-laying their normal, acrid scent. Another scent pierced through it; a scent fouler by far: the scent of pure corruption. Kaoru could hear that the Hunter was not far behind him.

Kaoru burst from the shadows, leaping onto cars, the slick metal burning his paws and the engine fumes making him gag. Apes scattered around him, the scent of fear strong now, sharp cracks from ahead and a brief, stabbing pain in his side as a horrible wailing assaulted his ears from in front as the awful cries of the Hunter assaulted him from behind. Then the mist was in front of him.

And around him. Kaoru ran through the blank silence, smelling nothing but water. Even the bridge under his paws seemed barely there, as if he was running in a void. The mist was unchanged around him, constant in scent, taste, sound, and sight. There was neither sound nor scent of the Hunter behind him, nor ahead. Kaoru ran on.

Beyond the mist, another chaos of apes awaited him, their cars polluting the air as they growled in an impatience that matched their owners' and gave off scents as frustrated as any produced by the apes present. Another red light almost blinded Kaoru, and he leapt through the crush again, scattering cries of fear and the scent of urine, rushing for the rising streets to take him out of the scab and into the wilderness, landing in a puddle that wasn't water, that wasn't natural, that seemed to cling to his fur as he ran on, away from the apes and into the shadows.

The fake stone of the ground burned and scraped the pads of his feet. The scream of cars assaulted his ears, the smells of urine, of vomit, of fouler things yet, things unnatural and Wyrm-tainted, assaulted him from the darkness of the alleys down which he ran for his life, for his sanity, seeking the calm of the wilderness, seeking to outdistance the Hunter who was once again on his tail, slightly further back, but still close enough to smell, a miasma on the air. As Kaoru ran, the buildings shrank around him, spilling a cleaner darkness onto the street, a smell of the wild, a hint of Gaia, even here in the scab. But still the apes were all around him, scattering from his flight, fear and aggression rising in the air all around him, almost hidden at times beneath stronger, unnatural scents that tried to drown out nature, to suppress the being of the apes as the false stone sought to suppress Gaia, cutting Kaoru off from her touch as he ran ever onwards, with the Hunter gaining, howling in a voice meant for him alone.

But now he was back in the wilderness, with Gaia under his feet and Phoebe riding in the sky above him. The scent of the plants around him, while tainted by the effluvia of the scab, was natural and good. He felt the pain dissipate from his feet as they brushed over leaf litter, and the sounds of the apes faded behind him. The Hunter's presence did not, but now Kaoru was on his own ground, close to the caern, and he felt a rush of confidence. He would be able to make it to the caern before he was caught, so maybe he wouldn't be caught at all.

Panting, Kaoru could taste the wholesome flavor of a place still in touch with Gaia, a place protected by the Garou and their Kinfolk. As he sprang lightly from rock to fallen tree, then to a patch of stony ground, he felt a pang of regret that he was leading a Wyrm creature into this place. He just hoped that the Garou would defend against it as eagerly as against any other. Kaoru's ears and nose told him that small creatures were scattering from his path, which was only right, only the proper respect.

The woods got thicker, the paths more tangled and more defined. This was obviously part of the defense of the caern. Kaoru was glad to see it despite the fact that the thicker undergrowth limited to his path to the obvious ones. He didn't really want the Hunter to lose him now, anyway. The creature's grinding steps, miasmic stench, and piercing moan were audible close behind him. Close enough, he hoped, for the guardians of the caern to notice, as he realized the paths formed a maze, and that he wouldn't be able to find the caern on his own.

Kaoru heard a step ahead of him and turned the corner to see a Garou in ape form standing across the path, dressed in some sort of uniform. Kaoru sprang hard, leaping straight over the Garou's head, and continued down the path, glancing back to see what happened. The Garou stood facing the Hunter, a creature out of nightmare, a rotting horse with the head of a crocodile, with two extra limbs sprouting from its shoulders — limbs that ended in enormous blades, dripping ichor. Then, impossibly, the Garou turned away, turned toward Kaoru and called out a challenge. Kaoru howled his despair as the Hunter ran straight through the Garou without even slowing and continued the chase.

Desperate now to lead the creature away from the caern, Kaoru ran through the paths, seeking the exit. This task proved much easier than finding the way in, and soon he was running through the normal woods again, painfully aware that the Hunter was just behind him and nearly close enough to strike.

Then it did strike. One of the blades passed through Kaoru's body, and he felt the chill of corruption as it struck and vanished, taking with it the aura of rightness that had hung over the woods. Phoebe was only a light in the sky and all sense of the presence of Gaia had gone, leaving trees standing alone, small animals fleeing in terror from predators that sought only to kill, the manic laughter of unthinking streams, the cry of lost flowers as they were trampled underfoot, the gloating malignancy of fungi growing on the trees, a place with sharp stones underfoot to cut his feet, drive him out. Kaoru fled, seeking a safe place to hide.

Beneath a full, evergreen shrub in a garden on the edge of the scab, Kaoru found his resting place. The apes might find him, but he was more afraid of the Garou. What would they think of his flight from what had been a perfectly reasonable challenge? And what about the fact that the sentry had been unable to see the Hunter? It was too much for Kaoru to deal with alone, and he composed himself to sink into a trance. He pictured an endless sea, stretching from horizon to horizon, its surface perfectly smooth. The wind picked up across the sea, raising ripples, then waves, and finally foaming caps to the waves. Oigimi was there.

"He didn't even see it," Kaoru said.

While the new moon rides
The sky seems dark and hopeless.
It will wax again.

"Yes, I know. Now of all times, I need to think. I need to do something. I don't know that there is a lot left."

Harried by cold winds
The wolf flees to the lion,
Who cannot fight air.

"Obviously. But since I am on my own, what is there left to try, or was this fetish purely and simply a trap? And if so, why was put in my Rite of Passage?"

Girls gathering plums
May leave a few on the branch
Every autumn.

"Yes, they do. But I would have thought this would have been rather obvious. Anyway, I don't want to think about that, since it means I can't do anything. If we assume there is something I can do, what could it be?"

I search for ripe plums,
But find only empty trees,
Laden with dead leaves.

"Oh well. I suppose you can't think of everything. I wonder where the Hunters come from? Maybe I could stop them at the source. . ." Kaoru paused, turning the idea over in his mind. "The source need not be another Hunter, I suppose, and that might be something I could affect." He paused again. "But if that's all I can think of, I might as well be as empty of ideas as the tree, since I don't know where they come from, and can't find out."

The wolf leaves his den
When he goes to hunt the deer.
Can it not be found?

"Hmm, maybe. I could try tracking the Hunters back, couldn't I? But that would mean heading towards them, and going back into the Umbra. I don't want to get caught in the Umbra again."

A flood wrecks the bridge.
Despite their fear the people
Must build another.

"Yes, yes. I suppose you're right. And I can't be much of a Theurge if I won't go into the Umbra, anyway. OK." Mentally, Kaoru drew his breath in, trying to bolster his courage. "I need to find a pool, then go into the Umbra when the Hunt starts tomorrow. So I can't wait here." Kaoru slipped out of the trance and reluctantly stood up from his hiding place, sniffing cautiously to make sure that there were no apes around. When he was sure the coast was clear, he stealthily made his way out and headed back into the wilderness.

The wilderness was still not as welcoming as it had been, and the daylight made Kaoru more nervous. There were a lot of apes about; he could smell them on the air, and he occasionally even caught sight of them. This made him even more nervous, especially since they were likely to be near any appropriate pools. He moved through the woods, searching for streams and following them back into the hills. Most yielded nothing, and the day was dragging on. Kaoru was tired, and he still hadn't found a pool. As Kaoru followed another stream, he caught the scent of apes in the water. A little later, he could hear them calling to each other and splashing in the water. His ears pricked up, listening to the sound of the splashing. There was no question. It was a pool.

Eager now, his tiredness forgotten, Kaoru followed the stream, keeping to the undergrowth so that he wouldn't be spotted, then slipped around so he could see the pool from above without being seen. Looking down, he could see that it was near perfect. The pool was fed from underground, and the surface looked as though it would naturally be still, although at the moment the four apes who were swimming there were churning the surface into a mess of ripples and scattered reflections. Kaoru looked around, checking that he would be hidden where he was, and settled down to wait for the evening.

Kaoru fell asleep and was woken by a powerful gale. When he opened his eyes, the bushes were unmoving, but the apes were dressing beside the pool, preparing to leave. The water was smoothing out, gradually becoming as still as Kaoru had hoped. He glanced to the west, and was relieved to see that the sun was still entirely above the horizon. There was still time. Kaoru found he was almost impatient to begin, now that he had another plan. Wryly, he thought back to a similar impatience a day or so earlier and hoped the results would not be similar.

Finally the apes left, making so much noise that he could hear them long after they were out of sight. Kaoru walked down to the water's edge and looked into the pool, careful not to disturb the surface. The wolf looking back at him was a solid black, well formed, with a proud bearing, shining eyes, and a full and healthy coat. Kaoru concentrated on the reflection and willed himself through the Gauntlet.

The world shimmered, but changed little. The forest was still around him, now even more peaceful, and the redwood trees still stretched for the sky, more vibrant and alive here than in the material world. Kaoru ran to the top of the nearest hill, looking west as the sun sank. As it disappeared, he scanned the whole of his view, ears pricked, nostrils quivering, trying to pick up something, anything.

It was a scent — a strange scent that changed even as Kaoru smelled it — that came to him. It was followed a moment later by the cry of the Wyld Hunter. This time, Kaoru didn't answer, but simply turned toward the source of the sound and the scent, and began running, chasing toward the source of the smell. Around him, a small breeze blew up, keeping other scents away. Then Oigimi spoke to him.

The running black wolf,
In chasing his rightful prey,
Grows in his spirit.

Kaoru yipped his thanks for the encouragement, and kept running, intent on tracking the scent to its source. Another howl — this time of triumph — came from ahead of him. Kaoru shook his head, puzzled. Why should it be triumphant? The Hunter hadn't caught him yet. Or maybe he was playing into its hands? Around him, the Umbrascape shimmered, as if catching on his thought, and changed.

The cleaner, more definite smell of the Umbra faded, to be replaced by the odors of a normal forest. Kaoru's paws disturbed the leaf litter with the sounds of the material world. The forest around him was of the wrong type for the area he had been in. Sniffing the air, Kaoru stopped running. He had lost the scent of the Hunter. He padded forward, ears pricked and alert, listening for the slightest sound of attack. There was nothing. Kaoru sniffed again. The smell of trees and leaf litter was heavy on the air, with the soft edge of blossoms and a hint of running water. But there was no scent of any animal other than Kaoru himself, and certainly none of the Hunter.

Familiar woods
In unfamiliar times
Threaten and confuse.

Kaoru started. "Oigimi? I'm still in the Umbra, then. What happened? Is the Hunter still around?"

No sound of pursuit:
The deep forest unawares,
Swallows the lone wolf.

Kaoru moved through the trees, sniffing at the boles and searching for any hint of another animal. There were no traces, no scents, no tracks. "I suppose this must be some sort of Realm," he said. "I wonder why I came here? And can I get out?"

The moon shines on high
And is captured in the pool
To brighten the depths.

Kaoru nodded and started following the scent of water. Soon, his ears picked up the sounds of a quiet stream flowing gently over a sandy bed. He reached it and turned upstream, looking for a pool. Phoebe was kind: the source turned out to be a small pool of calm water contained between several rocks. Kaoru climbed up onto the rocks and looked into the pool. His reflection stared back at him, and as he concentrated, he felt no shift around him, none of the characteristic feel of passing into the Umbra. "That doesn't work." He stood on the rock and sniffed the air again. There was still no sign of the Hunter. "And I don't think I'm being hunted any more. I wish I knew what was going on."

There was a sound of splashing from downstream. Kaoru swung around toward it, confused as the scent of another wolf suddenly reached his nostrils. It was a small wolf, a male with a good scent, — the scent of a wolf still in touch with Gaia — and it looked at him calmly. Kaoru wished he could return the calm gaze, but instead, he backed off nervously, a growl rumbling in his throat. The other wolf could clearly smell his unease and was slightly amused by it.

"Come now, Kaoru. That's no way to greet your teacher." Kaoru stopped backing off and sniffed the wolf's scent again. It was familiar, although it seemed younger, more vital than he remembered. The wolf looked familiar as well.

"Zeno?" The other wolf stepped out of the stream and shook its paws dry.

"Of course." Kaoru jumped down from the rock and rolled submissively in front of his teacher. Zeno merely sat back on his haunches and waited, silently, for Kaoru to pay attention. He quickly settled down, lying with his eyes fixed on the older Theurge.

"So, Kaoru, what have you learned?" The younger Garou thought carefully before answering.

"That I am a predator, not prey, that as long as I flee before a threat, I cannot truly be myself." He stopped, abruptly, and Zeno cocked his head to one side.

"Yes?"

"Was this all a test, then? Part of my Rite of Passage?" It was closer to a puppy whine than Kaoru would have wished, but he felt badly used.

"Your Rite of Passage finished long ago. What else did you learn?" Kaoru forced himself to think only about what he could gain from his experiences.

"I don't understand, teacher. What else was there to learn?"

"There is always more to learn, pup." Zeno said, and he sprang into the air, vanishing as he passed over Kaoru's head, fading from the world. Kaoru sniffed the air. The scent was gone completely. Kaoru stood and padded over to where Zeno had been sitting, but there was no trace of scent even there. He sat back.

"Oigimi?"

The sage speaks wisdom
And the students assembled
Hear the wind crying.

"No, I don't understand either. It must have all been a test, or a lesson. And I failed." Kaoru lapsed into a dejected silence.

Fair wind on the sea:
The wise fisherman stays home
With his leaking boat.

"Recognizing my ignorance is all very well, but I need to know at least what I'm supposed to do now." A new scent came to him on the air, the scent of a single rabbit. He looked around and saw the creature come out of the undergrowth to drink from the stream.

Predator and prey.
Can there be any question,
About the right path?

Kaoru bared his teeth. "I suppose not." He sprang forward, and the rabbit bounded into cover, fleeing. Kaoru sped after the rabbit, following the scent, trying to run the rabbit down. ////

Lone Werewolf

by Lois Tilton

The full moon was hidden by an unnaturally dense fog that obscured even the peak of Mount Tamilpais and lay thickly over the Coastal Highway as it climbed up from the bay. A dark, uncanny silence brooded among the ancient coastal redwoods.

Suddenly, it was shattered by the black coup on the highway, a low-slung, predatory shape with an opaque, tinted windshield (theoretically illegal in the state of California) and ghostly fog lamps that stabbed through the murk and spawned distorted shadows among the giant trees.

At the edge of the road, a startled yearling doe looked up at the sound, and the headlights caught her eyes, held them like a binding spell while the car swerved deliberately into her.

There was a sickening, dull *crack* of impact, and the deer flew into the air, landing brokenly off the road while the car spun, tires whirling in the gravel on the shoulder, and skidded to a halt straddling the center line.

Unblinking, yellow lupine eyes watched from the shadowy concealment of the huge trees as a moment later, the driver's-side window slid down, revealing a man wearing a high-necked black cape. The wolf's fur rose along his back in instinctive reaction when he saw the exposed fangs, but the scent was only human and alcohol — not the rank Wyrm-stench of a Cadaver, the ancient enemy. And the wolf understood: fangs and cloak were only a costume, meant to celebrate the travesty of the Samhain-feast, the night when spirits walked unbound. The drunken reckless driver had doubtless been to a Halloween party masquerading as a vampire.

Then the window slid back up, the car's engine coughed and roared to life and it sped away with a squeal and reek of smoking rubber. When it was gone, the watching wolf crept slowly on his belly toward the broken deer. His hackles were still raised, his ears lowered flat in suspicion. He mistrusted this fog, mistrusted it as much as the callous drivers who raced up and down the highway heedless of the risk to innocent animal life.

But there had been nothing obviously supernatural about the car and driver, and the deer's eyes were already filming in death, her blood ceasing to flow onto the pavement. The hot scent of it made the wolf shiver in delight and forget his misgivings. Whining, he licked it from a slender, shattered leg. This was meat. It was fresh; it was good. The wolf's massive jaws closed around the deer's lifeless neck, and he started to drag the carcass into the concealment of the forest.

In this form, he was a good-sized, young wolf with dull, gray fur, well muscled around the neck and shoulders. But the doe was heavy, and he was handicapped by a twisted left, rear foot that made him stagger frequently under the weight of the carcass. He paused, and in an instant a transformation occurred: his mass increased, his limbs lengthened and bulked out with muscle, his jaws became huge, capable of gripping the dead doe by the shoulders and lifting her half-off the ground.

Shapechanging had always come easily to him; he had been born Garou. But no matter how he tried to change, no matter what form he took, it was always the same: his left foot was never anything but misshapen, deformed. His curse was an essential part of him, the visible sign of his shameful birth. He was metis; his long-dead parents had broken the law of their kind: Garou must not mate with Garou.

On account of his limp, some of the younger human members of his tribe had cruelly named him Chester. He had no other name.

In his interactions with human society, he called himself Chet; in wolf-language he was Twisted Leg.

Despite the powerful near-wolf form, it still took the greater part of an hour before he had carried the carcass to his destination, dragging it the last few hundred yards up a broken rock face of a remote ravine in Mount Tamilpais State Park. Here, in a cleft in the rock, was where Moonlight had chosen to make her den, miles from the safety of the caern's protection, despite the misgivings of the other Garou who warded this bawn. But none of them could dictate to Moonlight. She walked her own path, alone.

Not with me, least of all, Chet thought sorrowfully, dropping his burden to resume his lupine shape. He knew she would never accept his presence near her cubs in any other form.

Now he yipped to announce his approach to the den. The entrance was hidden by a spell of concealment, and a stone at the entrance held a guardian spirit to ward off danger. Chet, being what he was, knew he could have passed by it unharmed, but not without inciting Moonlight's Rage.

She appeared at the narrow entrance, a magnificent silvery gray wolf with dark-tipped fur and teats swollen with milk. Her teeth were bared. "You. Twisted Leg. What are you doing here?"

Chet lowered head and tail in a submissive posture. "I brought food. For the young."

She approached the dead doe, sniffed it suspiciously. Her upper lip curled in a snarl of contempt. "Roadkill!"

He didn't deny it. How could he? "Fresh-killed. Deer meat. Accept it, please, for the sake of your cubs, Walks-in-Moonlight-Ranking-Far-Above-Me."

His use of the honorific mollified her slightly. Without a word of thanks, she seized the carcass in her own jaws and dragged it with difficulty through the narrow rock-cleft into the den where her pups were waiting. Daring, uninvited, Chet followed at a distance.

For the sake of the cubs: it was the first law of the wolf-pack, that the welfare and safety of the cubs must come before everything. It was the pack's duty to provide, to bring meat for the mother and young. It didn't matter to Chet that Moonlight wasn't part of his pack, or even his tribe. He had no pack. The others had never wanted him. He had no obvious gifts, talents. And he was Ragabash, born under the Dark Moon. His kind were loners; everyone knew that. Then there was always his leg. Not Chester. We don't want him with us. He can't keep up!

But he had seen Moonlight with the pups swelling her belly, had watched her lying on her side with them suckling at her teats, and his wolf-instincts had overwhelmed him. She was Alpha Female, she was Mother. It was her own choice to be alone, but he would have let her rip open his own belly to feed her young.

Ignoring him, accepting the meat without a word, as no more than her due, she dragged the carcass to the back of the den where the cubs tumbled and played. Chet could see that they were almost ready to be weaned. Even now, as their mother tore open the doe's belly, the scent of blood brought them to gather around it, lapping at the spilled blood, pulling at the entrails, jostling for the dominant position with small growls and bared milk-teeth.

Efficiently, Moonlight tore off chunks of flesh and bolted them down. Later, she would regurgitate the half-digested meat for the pups. Watching, Chet allowed himself for one instant to cherish the hopeless illusion that she was his mate, that the cubs were his own.

But that was the human in him, wanting what could never be. Chet, cursed by his illicit birth, could never have young of his own. It was as much as he ever could have hoped that Moonlight would allow him here, this close to her cubs, almost as if he were a part of her pack.

Not that she would ever admit to such a thing — not Moonlight — Pure Breed as she was from the proudest tribe of their kind.

Now, before she could turn on him and order him away, he backed out of the den, into the rose-gray dawn of a new day. The unnatural fog was lifting. There would be no easy excuse if he were late to work this morning.

• • •

The Sept of the Western Eye had its territory in Marin County, not the metropolis across the Golden Gate. But although the city had its resident Garou, these were not considered quite reliable by the sept leaders, not in important matters. One of these matters was the welfare of the wolf pack at the San Francisco Zoological Gardens, and they had for a long time considered the prudence of having their members on the staff there to guard the animals from harm or interference.

The need for such a policy had became obvious last year, too late, after the zoo's entire pack of 12 animals, including pups, had been abducted. Someone had entered their enclosure during the night and fed them meat dosed with tranquilizers. Scraps of the meat had been found on the grounds, but no trace of the missing animals, or any sign of the agents who had perpetrated the deed. Among the Garou there was no doubt that the act had been aimed at them — most likely perpetrated by unknown agents of the Wyrm — but with no evidence, no trail, there was nothing any of them could do but mourn the missing and take steps to ensure it could never happen again.

This was how Chet had found himself applying for a job on the zoo's maintenance staff. He had no other job, nothing else to do of any importance — this was generally agreed. It meant a lot of changes for him, driving into the city, dealing with more humans than he had ever seen in one place. But he'd discovered that he actually liked the zoo, the animals, and sometimes he even thought he might want to become a keeper, maybe. Of course, they wanted you to have college for that, and all Chet had was a GED. Still, he'd heard there were always classes you could take at City College.

Chet hadn't mentioned these ideas to anyone in the tribe; he figured they'd probably just laugh at him: Chester, going to college — yeah, right.

But that was before he'd seen Moonlight.

The zoo had obtained replacements for the missing wolves: six animals from Canada. It had been only a couple of days after their arrival, when the new wolves were still working out the social dynamics of their pack and the keepers were watching them with a certain level of anxiousness. Chet had been on the nightshift then.

He was emptying the waste receptacles when he first saw her: a silver ghost-wolf shimmering in the full moonlight. At first he'd thought for an instant that this was a spirit-vision, and he stopped still with a dry throat and a faltering heart, like a man turned to stone by the forbidden sight of a goddess. Then he realized what she was in fact: Silver, Silver Fang.

She was standing motionless, watching the wolves in their pen. They were clearly aware of her presence, but more interested at the moment in their new surroundings and companions, sniffing the scent-marks left by the others.

Sensing Chet's stare, she turned her head and looked through him, as if he didn't deserve to be recognized. Chet had never felt so totally unworthy, so painfully aware of his visible deformity, the stigma of his birth. As he well knew, it was custom for a stranger to announce her arrival in the territory of another tribe, but he could have torn out his own heart before he could have confronted her.

Moonlight did, in fact, present herself to the sept authorities in due course, meeting briefly with Able Heart, Warder of the Caern, who readily accepted her presence. But Able Heart was lupus, and she met him in lupine form, the only form she would willingly take. Chet, as a metis, might as well have been an untouchable.

But from the beginning, Moonlight kept herself apart from the rest of the Western Eye Garou. She had her own agenda. Two of the new Canadian wolves were her Kinfolk; generations of her tribe had interbred with wolves of this lineage.

Chet got used to seeing her at the zoo: always at night, silver ghost-wolf, prowling the perimeters of the wolf enclosure after the gates had closed, when only the maintenance staff and security was left. The human guards never seemed to see her, never seemed to notice on the nights when she led the pack in howling at the moon. Chet didn't dare transform and howl along with the rest when she was there, although it made his throat hurt, keeping silent.

When Moonlight went into heat, Chet couldn't stand it; he ran away to the woods and raced through the trees, howling his anguish and frustration aloud to the indifferent moon.

By the time he came back to San Francisco and talked his supervisor out of firing him, Moonlight had gone to ground in the ravine on Mount Tamilpais, preparing her den for the birth of her pups. In heat, in his absence, she'd mated with the alpha male of her kin-pack, her purpose all along in coming here.

But the pack at the zoo was not her pack. She was Garou, after all, not wolf. And she was alone. Chet was lupine enough to accept the situation without jealousy. Instead of illicit, forbidden lust, he was now driven by the pack-instinct to protect and provide for the pups in her belly. Slowly, submissively, he approached her, bearing offerings. Disdainfully at first, she accepted them — even, now that the cubs were growing and constantly hungry, even if they were roadkill.

• • •

Now, leaving Moonlight in her den with the fresh-killed doe to feed her cubs, Chet drove his cranky old Ford Pinto to work in San Francisco. He was on the day shift at the zoo these days, reassigned after his recent unauthorized absence. Traffic this morning was normal, which meant that even at 6 AM it was stop-and-go crossing the Golden Gate Bridge. But the weather-and-traffic guy on the radio kept talking about last night's "killer fog."

Chet scowled. Unlike the weatherman, he had reason to believe that last night's fog was of supernatural origin, and no good thing. Not that he had any particular powers or skills along those lines, but he knew that March Lion had led the elders of the Uktena in some kind of ritual last night to try to avert trouble.

Now, as he approached the gates of the zoo, he began to wonder if the rite had failed. A police car blocked the entrance to the zoo, and Chet was stopped briefly before being waved through. By now the sense of wrongness was making the hairs rise on the back of his neck. Instead of checking in for his shift, he made his way directly to the wolf enclosure, but he paused at the sight of a group of police and zoo security clustered around the area.

Before he could decide what to do, one of them called out sharply, "Hey, you! Hold it!"

Fortunately, another one of the security men was Carlos Ravenswood, a Garou from his tribe with a more responsible position at the zoo, and so Chet was saved from a prolonged interrogation.

"What are you doing over here?" Carlos asked shortly, scowling, visibly irritated at having to deal with this new complication in the middle of the investigation.

Even under the best of circumstances, Chet had never been extremely articulate. He stammered, "I was just coming to work. I saw — what happened? Did they. . . again?"

"Yeah, they did it again!" Carlos snarled, holding in his Rage only with obvious difficulty. "They're gone! All of them! The whole pack!"

"Do they know yet? Back. . . at home?"

"I phoned it in." Carlos looked back, distracted by one of his superiors calling to him impatiently. "Look, I don't have time for this, all right, Chester? Just. . . go home, or go back to work — something, OK? There's nothing you can do here."

But Chet was thinking of Moonlight. The abducted wolves were her kin. She'd be bound to avenge them. It was a sacred duty, especially among her tribe. And she was alone, without a pack. She needed him, Chet thought vaguely, as he went back to his car and headed north again, back to Mount Tamilpais. He could help her — somehow. There had to be something he could do.

By this time the news media had picked up the story. The radio was reporting it: All six wolves in the pack at the San Francisco Zoological Gardens were discovered missing this morning, in an incident that authorities say may be a repeat of last year's wolfnapping. . . .

Annoyed, Chet switched the radio off again. Did Moonlight even know what had happened? Had anyone told her yet? In his hurry to be with her, in his rage, Chet swore helplessly, caught in rush-hour traffic. He wanted to break free, to floor the accelerator and roar at 200 miles an hour past the lines of other cars — and heaven help the traffic cop who tried to pull him over. But he retained just enough hold on his reason to recognize that his clattering, third-hand Pinto was barely capable of breaking the speed limit.

At the edge of the park boundary, almost a mile from the place he had found the dead deer last night, he turned off the highway onto an access road, took it as far as possible into the trees, then got out of the car and transformed to the faster wolf form. Now, more then ever in his life, he cursed the deformity that held his pace to a limp. No wonder everyone thought he was useless, if he couldn't run any faster than this!

Less than a mile from Moonlight's den, he paused, warned by instinct before he even heard the sound of an engine blasting through the trees where no machines should be — and it was coming from the direction of the den! The noise grew rapidly closer, and now he could smell the burning hydrocarbons, the foul scent of petroleum exhaust. Then it came into view: a four-wheel-drive Jeep Wrangler, with two men inside.

Wrong! Wrong! screamed along Chet's nerves, and his reaction was reflexive, instantaneous. His body expanded, rose up on its hind legs, claws extended to monstrous size, fangs bared, and eyes glowing with the balefire of raw unfettered rage: Crinos, the werewolf in its purest manifestation.

At the sight of him rising up suddenly in their path, the Jeep swerved. With a roar, Chet sprang, directly onto the hood, a powerful, clawed fist punching through the windshield. Glass shattered. The Jeep skidded and slid into the trees as the driver fought for control, and Chet's claws raked flesh; he scented his enemy's spilled blood.

The second man was fumbling frantically for some kind of weapon in the back. Chet lunged for him, but before he could strike. The Jeep slid into the trunk of a redwood. Chet's hold was jarred loose. He was slammed violently against the tree, his bad leg pinned momentarily against it. Stunned by the impact, he was too slow to react as the driver gunned the accelerator. Wheels spun, caught hold, and the Jeep roared away, out of reach in a matter of seconds.

Groggy, in pain, Chet pulled himself to his feet. His leg was bleeding, fur and skin scraped away the length of his thigh, but the bone wasn't broken. He was werewolf; he would heal, especially in his present, horrifying form.

Suddenly he remembered Moonlight, back at her den. What had they done to her? And the cubs?

Limping badly, fighting the pain in his leg, Chet stumbled and crawled up the trail to the den, praying with all his strength that he would find her there, un-harmed. But his anxiety increased as he saw that the tire tracks led directly to the den, as if the men had known what they would find there. But what had they been looking for? Wolf or werewolf? Who were these men? Who — or what? And what cause did they serve?

As he came to the den, Chet could now see that the guardian stone at the entrance to the den had been dislodged, tossed aside. There was a blood-scent in the air. Chet's belly clenched with dread. Calling out to Moonlight, he pushed his way through the den entrance.

Moonlight lay on her side in a dark pool of gore, but she was alive, and in Crinos form — fangs bared in defiance, eyes glowing with balefire. Chet had never seen her in werewolf form before, but he knew her instantly, just as she could recognize him.

"The cubs!" she hissed through fangs clenched in agony, but Chet couldn't tear his eyes away from her wound. It was in her belly, and the way it was bleeding, it could only be caused by one thing: silver, deadly silver.

"You're hurt! You need help," he protested, but she struck him away with a snarl.

"The cubs! They took. . . my cubs. Find them! Bring them. . . back!"

"But. . . how?"

Her eyes met his, held them. "You saw the ones who took them. You know them. You can follow."

And when he protested again that he couldn't leave her in this condition, she raised herself up painfully on one arm. "Never mind me! I will heal! But find. . . the cubs! Go!"

"Yes," Chet stammered finally, and backed out of the den, reluctant to leave her like this. But she had asked him — asked him to find her cubs and bring them back to her. Just as if she was his pack leader. She was Alpha. How could he refuse?

His leg had stopped bleeding by that time, but he was still limping badly and he knew the leg must be bruised down to the bone. Running was impossible, but with every second the cubs' abductors were getting further and further away!

By the time Chet had followed the tire tracks as far as the road, only his Rage was keeping him going. But — where? Which way had they gone? They were probably miles away by now. How could he ever find them?

Despair clawed at him. Chet was nothing among his tribe; he was no one, with no powers, gifts, talents — only a few skills necessary for existence. Or so he had always believed, and so his experience had always proved. Up to now. But he was Garou, and born under the Dark Moon. Its gifts had lain within him, unclaimed, all his life. Now, with Rage and need seething through his veins, and the blood of his enemy still staining his claws, he remembered Moonlight's words, and what had been dormant awoke: some newborn sense inside him was drawing him, like a lodestone, in the direction of his enemy, his prey. *You know them. You can follow. North, up the coastal highway, away from the city.*

He brought his claws to his face, recalling the scent of blood as he raked the driver's flesh. That blood would continue to draw him, wherever it was, however far it went. Time and distance would be no obstacles to him.

His own body, however, was another matter. Even with his wound healing, he was still crippled. And his car was still a mile up the road.

His car. Chet groaned. The rusting Pinto, all he could afford, barely capable of reaching 60 miles an hour. And, he was afraid, almost out of gas.

He limped to it, cursing every wasted minute, resumed his human appearance and dropped exhausted into the driver's seat. Accelerated healing wasn't possible in this form, but it was the only way he could drive.

North. The prey-sense was still with him, a constant urging toward the scent of his enemy's blood, toward Moonlight's stolen cubs. He had to find them. He didn't deserve to exist if he failed.

The cubs. Chet wanted to howl, thinking of them: the five cubs with their soft puppy fur, their milk-teeth, the mock ferocity that would soon grow into the real thing — if he could save them. He had seen them with their eyes closed, suckling, had seen them take their first steps, had watched them tear at the meat he brought to the den. He loved them as he would have loved cubs or children of his own. Because they were Moonlight's — yes, that was part of it. His feelings for Moonlight were so confused. He wasn't sure if she were Alpha female to him, pack leader, or something else.

He knew he'd be better off not thinking about the possibilities of something else. But thinking about her reminded him how she was hurt. Worried, he stopped briefly for gas and made a call to the number at the park ranger station. A machine answered. Chet cursed, gave his message, got back into the car. He drove, following the sense of his prey, trusting in it because it was the only link he had.

By now he was into the wine country, unfamiliar territory. Though his prey sense never flagged, it could only tell him the direction his enemies had gone, not which roads they'd taken. Chet ended up backtracking up and down unmarked roads, stopping frequently to pause and check his sense of direction, sometimes not even sure if he could tell north from south any more. This new gift wasn't quite as simple to work with as he might have thought.

Finally, though, something changed. At first, Chet couldn't quite tell what was happening, what was different. Then he realized: his quarry had stopped moving, was gone to ground. From then on, the sense grew steadily stronger until the closeness of his prey was making his hackles bristle. Rage, smoldering all through the long chase, burst back into flame.

It was centered now on a nondescript, gray building about three miles outside a town named Claypool. Conspicuously nondescript, unmarked, almost windowless, there was nothing to indicate what it might have been — machine shop, warehouse — except for the high chainlink fence and locked gate surrounding the structure and parking lot. But the fence was the kind with the angled barbed wire at the top, and electrified. There was something hidden inside there — something they didn't want anyone to see.

Chet crouched in wolf form behind some overgrown shrubs at the side of the property. Sunset was fading now; it was almost dark.

The place seemed almost deserted. Four cars in the parking lot — one of them the Jeep Wrangler he'd followed all the way up from Mount Tamilpais, the windshield still shattered. It had to mean the cubs were in there. It had to.

But were they all right? What were they doing to them in that place?

And what was he going to do about it?

The Rage inside him, of course, wanted to assume his most horrifying shape, to tear down the fence with his bare hands, to rip the door off its hinges and rush inside to spill the blood of his enemies. But there were the cubs to consider. Saving them had to come first, even over the demands of blood vengeance.

Chet was slowly coming to think that he'd made a bad mistake in coming so far by himself. Of course, he was only doing what Moonlight had told him to, but now he was over a hundred miles away from any allies. What if he was killed? Who else knew where the cubs had been taken? Who else could save them if he failed?

Who else but an idiot would have driven off the way he did, not telling anyone else where he was going?

Full of shame, he drove back to the town and stopped at the first public phone to call the ranger station again. This time, someone answered: "Chester? Is that you? Where on Gaia's Green Earth are you?"

Chet briefly gave the details of his chase, explained where he was, what kind of situation he was facing.

"We'll be there as soon as we can. Just wait there. Don't do anything."

Don't do anything. Just wait. Right.

Back in wolf form, Chet resumed his watch, beneath the vigilant full moon. With his auspice, he had an ambiguous relationship with the moon; he never felt he could quite trust its effects on him, urging him now to wild and reckless acts.

To make the waiting bearable, he recalled what he knew about his enemies, making sure he hadn't omitted some vital information. The one whose blood he had spilled was human, no doubt at all of that, and free of the taint of the Wyrm. But they knew what they had been hunting. They had found Moonlight's den, despite the guardian spells. And their weapons were silver — silver bullets in at least one gun. Reason enough to be prudent; reason enough to wait.

The night was quiet — too quiet. What was going on inside there?

Suddenly, Chet tensed and went motionless. The door was opening! They were coming out! Three of them. The blood-sense screamed at him: this is the one, this is the enemy, your prey!

It was the man who'd been driving the Jeep Wrangler back on Mount Tamilpais, his wounds bandaged now, his walk unsteady as he crossed the parking lot. The other one with him, helping him — Chet wasn't sure if he recognized him. They got into the Jeep, the second man behind the wheel this time. The third one, a woman wearing a khaki coverall, went toward the gate.

As the engine started up, Chet frantically tried to decide: what now? On the phone, they'd told him to wait, not to do anything by himself. But what about the cubs? Were they still in the Jeep? And what about weapons? Should he try to stop them or let them go?

The woman unlocked the gate, the Jeep drove through, down the driveway toward the road. On his belly, Chet crept closer. The brush here concealed him from sight, a good spot for an ambush. This time he was going to do it right.

The wolf waited from the cover, the werewolf sprang. The transformation was instantaneous. This time, he went directly for the driver, ripping away the canvas roof already slashed from his previous attack. There was a scream, but it came from the wounded man in the passenger seat, seeing the blood spraying from the driver's torn-out throat.

The interior of the Jeep reeked with blood and terror. The wounded man's eyes were wide, staring helplessly up at the monster looming over him. Chet's hackles bristled, his fangs were bared: this is the one, his prey-sense was screaming — Kill him! Kill him now!

Chet grabbed his shoulders, pulled him closer, and the man whimpered as claws dug into his flesh and he felt the werewolf's hot breath on his face.

"Where are they? The cubs?"

The man's throat worked, trying to form coherent speech. It was terror in his eyes, but not Delirium. This human knew what he was seeing. He understood.

"In. . . lab," he gasped finally.

Lab. Dread images flashed through Chet's mind at the word: scalpels, hypodermics, cages — vivisection. He shook his captive. "That building — back there?" Crinos form made speech difficult, but the man understood. He nodded.

Chet snarled, "If you hurt them —"

"No! I swear it, we just brought them in!" The man sobbed, closed his eyes. "Don't kill me!"

Chet hesitated at the question raised. What was he going to do with his captive? And — he glanced down on the ground where he had thrown the driver's body — what would he do with the remains?

One thing was clear, at least: he couldn't let the Jeep stay here in the driveway, in full view of the road. He lifted the corpse and dragged it into the car to stuff it into the back. The sight of the gun there arrested him for an instant, while Rage howled: they shot Moonlight with this!

Fiercely, he crammed the body in behind the back seat, then changed to near-man shape so he could fit behind the wheel of the Jeep. About a half-mile from the lab he pulled off the road again, cut the engine, and turned to his prisoner, who flinched away from him. The man's bandages were soaked with fresh blood.

"Tell me," Chet demanded. "Who are you? What do you want with the cubs?"

"DNA," he whispered weakly.

Chet growled deep in his throat as he recognized the name. Then he glanced back at the gun half-hidden beneath the driver's body. The gun loaded with silver bullets. Not to mention what other weapons there might be in the DNA lab.

The genetic research corporation knew what kind of beings they were dealing with — and meant to know more, by any possible means. They were not to be underestimated, not by fools breaking down their door and rushing in alone, armed only with fangs and claws and Rage. Oh, but the thought of Moonlight's cubs in their hands, what they might be doing to them, even now. . . .

Again, Chet seized his captive, shook him, not sparing his claws. "Why the cubs? Why did you take them?"

"Testing. . . recessive genes. . . ." The man gasped in pain as Chet's claws tightened. "Just blood tests! They're not hurt! Don't—"

Chet bore down for an instant more, then released his victim. "How many of you are still in that lab?"

"Three. Just three. Technicians. That's all."

"Weapons?" Chet looked meaningfully into the back of the Jeep. "Like that?"

The man shook his head desperately. "No. No security. This is just a temporary lab. For testing the wolves. To see which ones have the recessive gene—"

Chet growled menacingly. "If you're lying. . ."

"I swear!"

From the darkness, a low voice said, "I think that's all the information we'll need."

Chet spun around. Gathered around the jeep stood a group of fearsome creatures, the warriors of the sept: Able Heart, Rowantree, the giant Silent Fist — all in Crinos form, ready to do battle. Chet could see that some of them were armed.

Able Heart put a huge clawed hand on his shoulder. "Good job of tracking."

The unaccustomed praise left Chet unable to reply. But no one seemed to expect him to.

Able Heart had turned to the others, was issuing orders for the assault on the lab. The mood was grim. DNA was a longstanding enemy, a dangerous adversary. Chet half-expected to be left out of the battle, ordered to stay behind, but Able Heart came to him at last. "You come in second. On my right." And handing him a gun, "Just in case."

Chet nodded wordlessly.

The werewolves deployed around the building, and at the signal, attacked, leaping the fence with superhuman strength, tearing the metal links apart. Glass smashed, doors were blown open as a half-dozen fearsome, howling, raging beasts assaulted the DNA lab.

There was no resistance. It was as Chet's prisoner had said: there was no security, only a few panic-stricken technicians who either tried to flee or crawled gibbering under the tables to try to escape what their terrified minds would not allow them to face openly.

And there were cages — cages holding wolves. Not only Moonlight's cubs, all five of them together in a single pen, but six other, adult animals — the wolves stolen that morning from the San Francisco Zoological Gardens.

While some of the Garou worked quickly to quiet the animals and stop their howling in case the authorities were alerted, Chet broke open the lock to the cubs' cage and lifted them out, taking all five in his arms, stroking and sniffing them to make sure they were unharmed.

After a moment, Able Heart came up, crouched down beside him. "I have bad news."

Chet's heart went cold with dread as the sept Warder went on, "Walks-in-Moonlight is dead. When your message was received, we went to her den, but it was too late. She was gut-shot. The bullets were silver. It was too much for her to heal."

Moonlight. Dead.

Chet's howl of bereavement rose from the bottom of his heart to fill the shattered lab. First Able Heart, then, one by one, the other Garou joined in the dirge until the building seemed to vibrate with the discordant tones.

Finally, Able Heart again put his hand on Chet's shoulder, and the howl subsided. "She was noble, and she walked her own path. But this isn't the time or the place to honor her.

"Come. Bring your cubs. They're safe. We can take them home now. ///

Shards

by Phil Brucato

"We've got to talk." Gerald's words had an ominous chill. Sara glanced up at him as they walked, and his eyes were as cold and distant as the San Francisco mist. *Here it comes*, she thought. She'd seen it coming, but felt no better for the knowledge. Tanglewood had meant what he had said. The loremaster's rites were more powerful than she would have guessed.

Gerald quietly refused to meet her gaze, but looked off into the fog. The cool sheen on his face reflected the orange glow of streetlights. finally, he spoke. "I think that it may. . . we might. . . maybe we shouldn't see each other like this any more."

A blow prepared for hurts just the same. Sara swallowed, and for a long time she said nothing, feeling the chilly, damp sand beneath her feet. They walked in silence for a time before she answered. "Just like that?" The words grated in her throat like glass. Gerald nodded. He had no answer. Sara hadn't expected him to. "Well, this certainly comes out of nowhere," she said, but she was lying. She had an idea of exactly where it had come from.

• • •

"Stand by the fire," Tanglewood had said. The loremaster's eyes reflected dancing flames as the bonfire bled its warmth into the August night. Sara padded carefully through the rock-studded clearing and took up a place by the fire, feeling the gaze of the pack upon her.

"You disappoint me," said Tanglewood. His voice was heavy with sadness and anger. "You are Garou, but you are not pack to us. You dwell in your own life and wall out those who are your family. You shirk responsibility and set yourself apart, and yet you still have no wholeness, no sense of Gaia in your heart. The wolf and the woman are not one within you. Your soul is selfish and alone."

"That's not true!" Sara shot back. "And it's not fair! I'm new to all this! I'm just trying to get my bearings! This stuff takes time—"

"You have had time," Tanglewood thundered, "and you have wasted it. You see our tribe as some great new game, but you do not aspire what you must become! You are separate now, as you were two years ago, still woman and wolf, and not a whole Garou!"

"But—"

"We try to help you," he continued, "and you do not care. Your old life is still too important to you, and you cling to it like a child! Until you let it go, we can waste no more time with you." Sara shivered, and she crossed her arms against the hostile glare of her tribe. "If you wish to stand alone," said Tanglewood, "You shall."

• • •

Tanglewood's words rang hollow in her mind. Primal Rage stirred in her gut, black, frightening, all too familiar. Gerald, oblivious, walked beside her, searching the night mist for answers. "So, how long have you been thinking about this?" she asked.

"A few weeks."

"How long?"

"Over a month," he admitted. Sara glanced up sharply. The Rite had been three weeks earlier. "Any particular reason?" she demanded.

He shook his head. "A lot of reasons. I can't put them all into words."

"How about trying?" She looked at her feet, sticky with sand, as they walked. Doubt, fear, anger swirled up the back of her throat like bile. She bit her lip, feeding Rage with her own blood.

"I haven't felt too good about us lately," he admitted. "It's a lot of little things. Look," he said, stopping, "we're pretty young, okay? " This was true; Sara was just shy of 18, Gerald a little older. "Things never last at this age. I'm thinking about college after all, and I don't want to go to Berkeley. I just wanna go somewhere else."

"And leave me here."

"You never needed me to take care of you or anything," he said. Was there an accusation in his voice? "You'll find someone else."

"And so will you." She started walking again. She felt scabs pulled off deep inside, and the cuts were still raw underneath. The blood from her lip tasted good. "Bastard," she muttered. Gerald didn't answer, and they both walked in silence for a while. "Well," she demanded at length, "don't you have anything else to say?"

He shook his head and extended his hand, but she refused to take it. "Sara," he implored, "don't be this way."

"What way?" Her tone was bitter. "I saw it coming, you know. I did. I just want a reason. I want an explanation. After almost two years, I think I deserve one. Why are you doing this?" The question was a plea for some normal, rational, human reason beyond Tanglewood's curses. She said it knowing that Gerald had no answer, but wanting one all the same.

• • •

She met him soon after the First Change, when her life was in fragments. The taste of bad wine had been strong in her mouth that night, and her eyes were swollen from crying. Gerald had touched her shoulder and asked if she were all right. Sara had always been a bad liar, but she had refined it to an artform since that night.

He'd been a sweet guy, then, not quite 18 and a bit awkward, too polite for his own good. It was always easy to keep her temper around him, and he accepted everything she told him with quiet deference. Sara had built a house of deceit to shield him from her new life, and had kept him as a barrier against the wolf. Gerald was soft, in a good way, a comfortable anchor, and she felt freer with him than she did with the pack. These walks on the beach became a ritual, a cleansing of her spirit. He had stood at the gateway to her humanity, the woman that the wolf could not command.

Now his voice was cold as the ocean and his eyes were hard as glass.

• • •

He stopped and turned away, looking out into the endless dark. Waves rumbled and hissed just out of sight, scattering the sands. "I'm not sure where we're going,

Sara." he said after awhile. "We've been together for a long time, but I don't see where we're going."

"That's a lot of crap." Her tone was quiet and sharp. She restrained a sudden urge to shove him down into the sand and scream out the fury just beneath her words. Deep inside, below her human mask, Sara felt another, darker urge to hurt. Something inside her twisted and uncoiled. "Don't give me that shit, Gerald," she snarled. "I know you too well. Be straight with me, dammit! Is there someone else, or are you just bored?"

The words stung him. "Fuck you!" he snapped. "This isn't easy for me, dammit!"

"It's a real treat for me!" she shot back.

"Listen to me!" he shouted. Their eyes locked. "You're asking for something I don't have." he said. "There is nobody else, Sara, no. I just. . . feelings don't always make sense. We can't. . . I have to go. I'm sorry."

You will be, said the wolf.

• • •

Sara had blinked back tears that night. The campfire stung her eyes, and she could not meet Tanglewood's gaze. Beside her, Bessa, in natural lupine form, snarled at the loremaster. Tanglewood glared in return as Bessa trotted up to her friend and brushed against Sara's legs, interposing herself in between the human cub and the angry loremaster. "Don't defend your charge, Bessa," Tanglewood growled. "She stands between two roads and will not choose. Until she does, she is of no use to us or to herself."

They performed the Outcast Rite and sent her away.

• • •

The wolf inside her reared its head. Sara felt its heat behind her eyes and fought to drive it down again. Gerald took her silence for speechlessness and reached for her. "Don't!" she snapped, and he flinched. Around him, the mist seemed to brighten. Sara's vision sharpened, and her heart jumped. The taste of Change, like a mouthful of summer grass, rose unbidden in her mouth. *Not now!* A voice inside her screamed. A sudden strong gust blew in from the sea, biting through her damp jeans and leather jacket, raising goosebumps on her bare skin. She shivered, but the chill went deeper, far deeper, than a cold misty breeze. She snarled. Gerald met her gaze, and she pinned him in place without raising a hand.

• • •

She had wandered the park for hours after the rite, daring some mugger to hassle her. None had. When she reached home, her Rage had built to a fever pitch, barely clenched by sheer will, and she paced the hardwood floor, muttering to herself until the dam broke inside and she hurled the first thing that came to hand — an incense burner shaped like a Chinese Foo Dog — and hurled it hard against the mirror. The bitter smash sent her into a frenzy of destruction, ripping furniture, trashing knick-knacks, baying in rabid fury.

The wolf had her in its jaws. Its Rage had shredded her apartment.

When her fury was spent, she sagged to the floor, weeping as she reverted to her human shape. Her clothes hung in tatters, and the mirrored glass bit into her knees. Blood welled up with the tears. She cried until she couldn't breathe, then reached for the phone.

When he came, he asked no questions. He only held her until she finished shaking, then helped her clean up the mess, his brown eyes clouded with concern.

• • •

"Sara?" Gerald's eyes were wide, his voice uncertain. The wolf in her wanted to rip those eyes from his head. It would be so easy, here, alone, to share her pain with him in ways he'd never forget. Words, torrents of fire, bloodlust, and worse boiled just out of reach. "Go home, Gerald," she said suddenly, breaking eye contact and turning away.

Was he to blame? Would things have ended this way if not for Tanglewood's rite? Did things run deeper than the rite, down below the surface of things they never talked about? Sara had built a wall of lies, to her pack, her lover, her self. What lies had Gerald built? He knew so little about her, really. How little did she know in return? She hurt too badly, now, to think about it. Better to puzzle through this later, when the wounds weren't raw.

"Hey, wait," Gerald called as Sara walked away. "We can talk about this!" Now he was beside her, reaching for her arm. She pulled away. "There's nothing to talk about," she replied. "You've said enough. Just go."

"I'm sorry."

"So am I, Gerald. Leave me alone. For your own good." Hurt lodged in her heart like a sliver of glass. Rage buzzed just beneath the surface. She had to get away.

"Is this it?"

"That was your decision." The wolf gnawed at her self-control; pain and loneliness, Rage, confusion and sadness washed through her like cold waves. Had she loved him, ever? Did she now? "Please just go." Too many questions, too many doubts.

• • •

Sara had sensed the difference in Gerald after that, the half-hidden glances when he thought she wasn't looking. No questions, ever. He hadn't thought to ask her what was wrong, not that she could've told him. He simply withdrew, like the pack, but without anger or recrimination. Less than three weeks after that night, Tanglewood's rite was complete. Or was it? Was this the loremaster's doing, or Gerald's, or her own?

• • •

"I'll take you home." He reached for her again.

"Go!" The word was a lash, and there was blood behind it. She dropped her human mask, and Gerald cowered, finally seeing the wolf in her eyes. Change bristled just beneath her skin. *Let me have him!* cried the wolf, and Sara stepped forward. Her prey stumbled backwards, sprawling in the sand. The fear in his eyes dimmed as she blocked the light, throwing her shadow across the sand. She could smell his sudden fear above the salty air. Her fingers curled into hooks, claws inching to extend from beneath the nails. Her teeth ached, sharpening into fangs. Only slivers of humanity kept her claws from his throat. Only shards of will kept the wolf inside.

"*Get out of here,*" she rasped. Gerald scrambled to his feet, eyes rabbit-wide. Sara trembled, wanting to hug him, wanting to kill him, and turned away instead, striding ankle-deep into the freezing surf. She waited there, hugging her sides, until the Rage subsided. When she turned around, he was gone.

She howled until her throat was raw. The sound was lost in the roaring surf.

• • •

Hours later, Sara stood alone on the beach, awash with memories and cleansed by the Pacific wind. Her eyes stung, but she refused herself the luxury of crying. The sliver moon was hidden, wrapped in shimmering mist that enveloped her like a mother's womb. This womb, though, was damp and cold, like the icy part inside of her. Sara's breath was mist before her face, and waves washed her bare feet. There was a chill, pristine beauty in the night, and both wolf and woman welcomed it together. The cool wind soothed Sara. Her sadness lingered, but the bitterness had faded. It was about time, she thought, to be reborn.

"The wolf and the woman are not one within you," Tanglewood had said. After the last few hours, though, Sara felt that they had come to some sort of understanding. With no one else to run interference, neither had a choice.

In the distance along the beach, the flicker of beach bonfires warmed the dancing mist. From one came the sound of drums, laughter, and off-key singing, all mingling with the roar of endless waves. Sara paused, recalling similar nights with Gerald, with Rick and Ray, Shelly and the mousy blonde with a name no one could pronounce. Cool wet nights in the fog with a fire and a beer and a pack of old friends. Gone now, only memories. It was a good night for sorrow, but sorrow was a waste of time. Her life was smashed to splinters, now. Better to bury the pieces and move on.

Down the beach a ways, firelight glittered on a rash of broken glass, bottles jutting from a blackened mound of sand. Sara swore as she approached the mess. The campfire embers guttered, smoke rose into fog, and the tracks of the bastards who'd left this disaster led up to the pavement and away. By the look of the fire, they were long gone. Pity.

She knelt beside the fire and carefully scooped up the largest pieces, tossing them into a paper bag. As she worked, Sara remembered Gerald, cleaning up bits of broken mirror. Maybe I'm not the only one, she thought, who got stuck cleaning up someone else's mess. The larger pieces were easy to find, Sara thought. The hard part was finding the splinters, the stubborn shards of glass half-hidden in the sand. No matter how carefully you picked them away, she reflected, some always waited below the surface, any one of them large enough to draw blood or to lodge painfully in bare skin. You could sift the sand all night and never catch all the shards.

But a few tiny shards in the sand evaded her grasp, leaving large, sharp fragments laying around. Given time, the sea would wear away the splinters until the shards and sand were one. Until then, she guessed, you just took your chances and hoped that you never stepped on the broken glass.

Her legs were cramped by the time she finished. She stretched and grunted, then carefully took the bag. The glass inside rustled thinly as she searched the sand a final time. You can never get them all, she thought. Sara brushed damp hair from her eyes with a sandy hand. It would have to do. She dumped the bag of shards in a nearby trashcan and headed back across the sand to the ocean's edge.

One less bag of glass. A few less shards to litter the beach. Not a clean sweep, but it would have to do. ///

A Day Off

by Thomas Kane

Clifford Rafferty processed one shipment form after another, no longer comprehending a thing. His mind hung in a dull limbo of fatigue. The terminal beeped; E-Mail from Rio appeared blinking on the screen, and Rafferty sent back a message to reassure the impatient Amazon Security Manager without even knowing what he had said. A phone jingled in an adjacent cubical. Dot-matrix printers buzzed like flies. Rafferty's hands moved mechanically, his eyes swept over text, his cursor roamed the screen, perspiration moistened his collar, his tie seemed to close around his throat, and still work built up.

For an instant, Rafferty glimpsed his reflection against the Rolodex. The rounded plastic case distorted his image into the vision of a madman with a bulbous head perched atop a tiny white collar and tie. Rafferty's jaw was firm. His skin appeared slightly weathered, and although the tracks of a comb furrowed his dark hair, a few strands shot up at rebellious angles. His gray eyes seemed permanently narrowed with buried rage. The frustration, the grinding tedium, the shame of leading a meaningless life had begun in grade school for Rafferty and never stopped.

At 8:30, Rafferty knew he had to leave. He had a two-hour commute across the Bay ahead of him. He thought of his wife Margaret and knew that if she was finished at work, she would already wonder why he was late. Rafferty gathered up the work he was taking home, organizing it in his security briefcase. He forced his jacket over his broad shoulders and numbly worked his way past the gray office dividers to the elevator. Orange streamers hung from Ms. Hubble's door; it was Sunday and it was Halloween. As Rafferty emerged from the glass doors of the Trans-Con Incorporated complex, a chilly mist assaulted him, penetrating every fiber of his suit. His car alarm keened a warning at him as he fumbled for his keys.

As Rafferty started the ignition, the radio hissed on. A strain of bad rock music let Rafferty know that he had lost his usual channel. As his hand rose wearily to the dial, the disk jockey's voice intruded on his consciousness. "More baaaaaad news for all you folks in commuterland."

At that, Rafferty's muscles went rigid.

"Traffic remains completely stopped on the Golden Gate Bridge due to heavy fog," the announcer drawled in his jocular, patronizing tones. "Weather Service sees no end in sight, possibly 'til morning."

There it was. Rafferty knew it would be most of the night before he made it to the Oakland Bridge and home. He would have perhaps an hour to sleep before heading back to work. He heard his own pulse pounding. All the frustration of the day built up inside him. He threw back his head for a madman's howl, but managed to contain it, and merely stared at the fuzzy car ceiling, releasing a prolonged sigh of helpless fury.

Minutes passed. Then knuckles rapped the window of the Mercedes. Rafferty heard a woman's voice through the glass. "Hey, are you OK?"

Rafferty shut his eyes, as tired and angry as before, and now embarrassed as well. His lips curled back with a snarl. "No!" Only after Rafferty shouted did he see the person he was speaking to. She was a woman in a denim jacket, her shadowy hair loose around her shoulders and beaded with droplets of fog. Rafferty stammered for a moment, regretting having snapped at her. He pressed a button, causing the window to roll down. "I'm sorry. Traffic's tied up on the bridge and I guess. . . you know, stress."

"Sure." The woman's voice had a lilt of sympathy.

Rafferty looked up at the woman. He felt comfortable with her young, slightly craggy face, and she maintained an easy eye contact as he regarded her. Rafferty blinked. "Have. . . Have we met?"

"I know who you are." The woman shrugged. "And you can call me Yolanda."

"Yolanda. . ." Rafferty wrinkled his brow at the woman's answer. Questions popped into his mind, but he did not get a chance to ask them.

"If you can't make it home this evening, I've got a spare couch you can borrow. My apartment is about a mile from here."

Rafferty swallowed once at that proposal. However, he considered his circumstances and realized just how convenient a nearby place to sleep would be. "I. . . I'll just take you up on that."

Yolanda's teeth flashed in a smile. She whisked around the car to the passengers' side. Rafferty flicked a switch, the door unlocked with a mechanical *click*, and Yolanda climbed in. "Straight four blocks, then turn left at Alpha-Beta." Rafferty returned her smile. His eye fell upon the telephone beside his seat, and the idea occurred to him that he should warn Margaret that he wouldn't make it home. However, no matter how innocent the situation with Yolanda happened to be, he could not imagine telephoning his wife at that moment without unbelievable awkwardness. Therefore, he said nothing, but drove on into the night.

Rafferty followed Yolanda's directions, steering into a neighborhood where he had never been before. Strains of music echoed into the mists. Rafferty glanced to his left and saw the raucous white lights of Club Calypso flashing against black, gleaming glass. Then his eyes strayed to Yolanda. Her eyes were shut, and although she looked still, Rafferty sensed an almost imperceptible movement of her head, nodding in time with the song.

Suddenly, Rafferty felt a burst of impulsiveness such as he had not had the opportunity to indulge for years. He cut his eyes across to Yolanda. "Want to dance?" She responded with a smile of real pleasure. And so Rafferty braked and dropped out of the traffic-stream. Rafferty knew he had work that needed to be done, and that he needed sleep before the next day, and he no longer cared.

At that moment, the car phone rang. Its muted, tiresome jingle filled the car. For an instant, Rafferty stared at the insistent machine, transfixed. Then Yolanda moved. With one fluid motion, she snatched the receiver and popped out the batteries, deftly disemboweling the instrument. Suddenly, Rafferty laughed with glee, Yolanda laughed too, and they both sat in the car chuckling in unison. Then they strolled into the Club toward the pulsing music.

• • •

Rafferty's gold, digital watch read 4:00 AM as he and his companion groped their way into Yolanda's darkened apartment. Yolanda flipped on a lamp, and Rafferty immediately dropped himself onto the cushions of her couch without waiting for further invitation. His muscles felt loose and completely exhausted. He stared for a moment at the picture on the wall, a painting of wolf with golden eyes, on the prowl in a forest of birch. Yolanda pulled up a wooden chair and sat beside him. For a moment, the two of them sat still.

Yolanda placed her warm hand on Rafferty's arm. "Cliff. . . I want to know how you feel about something."

After the evening, Rafferty scarcely felt the twinge of apprehension. He responded with an arched eyebrow and a happy sigh.

"Trans-Con Incorporated. Or, shall I say, Developer Forestry Group. How do you feel about working for them?"

"Oh." Rafferty shrugged, fighting off a tiny twinge of disappointment at the turn in the conversation. "I hate it."

"Do you mean that?" Yolanda's parted lips revealed a thin line of teeth in what did not appear to be a smile of any sort.

"Yeah." Rafferty himself felt surprised by the ferocity in his growl. "OK, I know, I'm lucky to have the job. A lot of people got the boot after we merged with DFG. But right now, I don't even want to think about it. It all seems so. . . fake."

"It's more than just fake." Yolanda's voice lowered to a canine growl. "It's *wrong*."

Rafferty gritted his teeth. He nodded. "That's it. I'm in on some projects that I'm not too proud of." He shook his head fiercely. "But what can you do? Day after day goes on, and what're you going to do?"

"I'll tell you." Yolanda's fingers closed on Rafferty's arm, as strong as steel bands. "Do you know why I spoke to you, Cliff? I spoke to you because you looked *angry*. I don't mean 'ticked off' or 'stressed out;' I mean genuinely furious, in a way that most humans have forgotten how to feel. And now you're going to have to make a decision. Are you angry enough to *do something?*"

Cliff scarcely realized what he was doing as he nodded his agreement.

"Then answer some questions." Yolanda's dark eyes had a feral gleam in the light of her little lamp. "Let us say that some friends and I are enemies of the Developer Forestry Group — very bad enemies, in fact. And we have just heard news which we find very disturbing. We know that Developer Forestry is purchasing weapons from the US Army. They want to use them in South America, against our brothers and sisters there. But we need more information. I want you to tell me the details."

Cliff convulsed. "That's sensitive stuff."

Yolanda did not say a word. Even her expression barely changed. But the reproaching crinkle around her eyes seemed to ask: Are you serious or aren't you? And Cliff felt an overpowering rush of shame.

Cliff let out his breath, forcing himself to relax slightly. "OK, sure, I'll help you. You're right. Developer Forestry Group wants to acquire specialty munitions for its subsidiaries in the Amazon basin. They're looking for dime/nickel howitzer rounds loaded with the VX binary nerve agent and I think aerosol vectored silver nitrate. Nobody understands what the silver is for, but VX, well, it's lethal—"

"I understand what the silver is for," Yolanda's teeth gnashed. "And you know when they're making the shipment."

"I do. That's my job." For a moment, Cliff found himself unable to meet Yolanda's eyes. He found emotions rising into his consciousness which had never troubled him before. He realized what it truly meant to go to work every day and manage the shipment of nerve gas. He felt the true meaning of shame, guilt, and sin.

However, under Yolanda's gaze, Clifford could only go on. "Department of Defense stores the shells at Pueblo Army Depot in Colorado. We're transporting them along the Southern Pacific Railroad to Military Ocean Terminal at Concord, just north of San Francisco. That's where the DoD releases them to one of our freighters for the trip to Brazil. Our rail permits expire midnight November 1st, so everyone at the office is busting a gut to make the shipment by tonight."

Then Cliff closed his fist, pulling free from Yolanda's hand as he turned his whole body to face her. "Listen — you're planning to stop the shipment, aren't you." He drew a breath through bared teeth. "Well, count me in."

Yolanda returned Cliff's gaze, her eyes calm, her features showing neither approval nor displeasure. "Why?"

"You need me." Cliff spluttered for a moment. "I have a security clearance. With a few phone calls, I can track that train's schedule, minute by minute."

Yolanda shrugged and smiled sweetly. "That really won't be necessary."

"OK." Cliff took a deep breath. "You should take me — to protect yourselves. I mean, what if someone grabs me between now and then and asks me questions about you."

Yolanda only shook her head with a faint sigh. "If we can't trust you, there's certainly no place for you on the raid."

"Yeah." Cliff screwed his eyes shut. "OK, OK. Take me because I *want to go*. It's something I have to do. I've done. . . terrible things. I owe it to. . . the earth."

"You owe it to the earth." Yolanda spoke in a deep, rich whisper. "Now that, Cliff, is a reason I can accept."

Cliff balled his fists. "Thank you!"

"You're welcome." Yolanda's voice suddenly became so matter-of-fact as to sound almost flippant. "Can you do anything useful?"

"I'm in shape. I was in ROTC for a few years. And — oh — I can shoot. I used to hunt when I lived back east." Cliff shrugged modestly. "Three bucks, three years, nine points on the last one."

"You won't just be missing a day of work, you know." Yolanda kept her soft gaze on him for several long moments. "We play this game for keeps. And even if you survive tomorrow, there will be people who are determined to punish you for what you did."

Cliff gulped, but nodded.

"Then if my pack agrees, you shall come. There are not so many of us left that we can turn down help from a brave man." Yolanda squeezed Cliff's shoulder. "Call in sick to your office. Then go to sleep. You'll need sleep." Then Yolanda plunked the cool batteries to Cliff's cellular phone into the palm of his hand. Cliff lifted himself from the couch for the trip back to his car and the phone. Adrenaline pumped feverishly in his veins as he recorded his message on the Trans-Con answering service, and at that moment, he could not imagine falling asleep. However, moments after he settled into the couch again, he lost all track of reality.

Many hours later, Cliff opened his eyes for a moment. He found himself on Yolanda's couch, still dressed in his suit, his tie askew across his chest. From the gentle light suffusing the room, Cliff guessed that it was mid-day.

Margaret still would not know where he was, and must be frantic. On any other Monday morning, he would have been at work for hours. However, he felt buried alive in the cushions. Sleep gripped his body, leaving him utterly unable to move.

Then Cliff sensed other presences. His eyes roved the room until they glimpsed movement. A dark form slunk in on four legs, slipping between the beanbag chair and the television table, its tail whisking the air behind it. Another such creature followed, then another. They resembled gigantic dogs, their gray coats thick and lustrous, their eyes glittering in the half-light. Cliff recognized them as wolves. He could not even twitch as the three wolves circled around his couch.

One wolf stepped from the shadows, approaching his couch. Its fur was nearly white, and it laid back its ears in an expression of hostility. Its black lips curled back to reveal rows of teeth. Then the wolf growled, and the tones of its canine groan clearly radiated the words, "I don't trust him." For the first time, Cliff felt electric fear, but he had no more will to move than before.

Then another wolf whined. This one had fur the precise color of Yolanda's hair. The Yolanda-wolf had a soothing tone to her voice, as if to reassure both Cliff and the large, pale beast before him. Then the suspicious wolf advanced step by soft step to the edge of the couch. It began sniffing Cliff's body. One by one, the other two wolves approached to do the same. He could feel their warm breath as they silently worked their way from one end of him to the other.

Finally, the Yolanda-wolf pressed her cool, damp nose against his cheek. Cliff sighed at this sensation, then, without warning, fell asleep to dream of wolves upon the snow.

Yolanda was in Cliff's dream, appearing as a wolf. He ran with her across the mountain trails, the horizon all ice-glazed peaks. Smudges of black stone marked the snow. "I am Garou," Yolanda keened to him. "I am both woman and a wolf, and I am the defender of Mother Gaia." Then it seemed to Cliff that they were back a thousand years of time, and as they ran, Cliff saw the years go by through the eyes of the Garou, the felling of woods and the raising of cities, the glory of human beings — but also their corruption.

Just as legends said, Cliff learned, silver was the bane of Garou. A silver bullet would pierce their mystic defenses, bringing death. The silver nitrate in the nerve gas would create a lethal mixture capable of exterminating them *en masse*. At last Clifford understood the purpose of Developmental Forestry Group's munitions order.

Then the great white he-wolf which had growled at Cliff appeared before them. Cliff pointed to the wolf and asked Yolanda the question that suddenly seemed more important than anything else in the world: if the two of them were lovers. Yolanda replied with a smile, a lovely enigmatic smile. "Garou do not mate with Garou. We couple only with humans or wolves, or else our bloodline dies out forever."

Suddenly bold, Cliff stepped toward Yolanda with his arms out, and she met him, in human form once more, and nude. Their lips touched. Cliff felt Yolanda's hand moving deliciously up his spine.

Then Cliff's eyes opened. Yolanda's apartment was dark again. A single yellow light burned in the room. Yolanda really was leaning over him, massaging his back, but her smile was more playful than romantic, and she was fully dressed, in black jeans and a desert-camouflage tunic with a bandolier of rifle clips slung across one shoulder. "It is time."

Cliff stretched and yawned beneath Yolanda's hand. He let her rub his back a moment more, then sat upright.

Cliff and Yolanda exchanged glances. Then Yolanda inclined her head toward the table. There lay a .50 caliber sniper rifle of German make, its dull, black casing giving it the look of some laser weapon in the bright-eyed, harmless world of a science-fiction movie. The broad infrared scope with its wires and external battery pack only added to the gun's futuristic appearance. Cliff walked to the rifle, hefted it, checked the bolt, and removed the clip to examine it. The working parts seemed clean and well oiled. "Let's go."

Yolanda led Cliff down her narrow staircase to the chilly air of the street outside. A battered Volkswagen van stood there, painted blue, with smears of white paint covering dents and rusty scars. Cliff boosted himself into the back, cradling the rifle. Yolanda followed him.

Then Yolanda gestured toward the van's driver. "Odin." Odin carried no weapons and wore tiny, round spectacles, but had the build of a linebacker. A white beard cascaded over his chest, and his olive jacket bore the screaming eagle patch of the 101st Airborne division. Cliff immediately guessed that he was the white wolf of the past day. The moment the van doors shut, the van's engine roared to life.

The next hours passed like another dream. The passengers sprawled on the metal floor of the van, among cartridge boxes and smelly olive-drab sleeping bags. Yolanda handed Cliff his cellular phone, and, without much ado, he dialed the Routing Office of Southern Pacific, gave an identification code, and asked for a schedule on DoD Hazardous Ordinance Shipment #450-HE/CW (High Explosive, Chemical Warfare). He repeated the railway timetable aloud, as Yolanda examined a series of maps, whispering to Odin. Then Odin nodded his head and steered toward the freeway. Nothing more needed to be said.

Cliff felt in the grip of fey excitement. He did not ever recall feeling so thrilled, or so terrified at the same time. He felt an unbearable urge to run, to fire off the rifle, or at least to break the tension by talking. However, Yolanda, who was short enough to stretch out in the van, cradled her head in her arms and went promptly to sleep. Somehow, Cliff felt that he must not speak to the white-bearded driver, whose brooding form loomed over the front of the van. Therefore, Cliff watched the amber lights of Oakland spread out behind the van until he felt hypnotized by them.

The van left the freeway an hour later and bumped on and on over mountain roads. Finally, it spun off the highway. The driver turned his head and bared sharp yellow teeth. "This is it." Yolanda rose from sleep instantly and released the baling wire which held the back doors shut. Cliff saw the black embankment of the railway running parallel to the road. The ground was rough with ridges and little gullies. Cliff remembered the mountain landscape of his dream, but these hills were dark, and clouds covered the stars.

"We time our charge to detonate under the cars, not the locomotive." Odin's growling voice made Cliff shudder. "Ten kilos of Semtex should brew them up even if they're armored. And remember what that train is carrying. Keep your distance and stay upwind of the blast — always. If you are touched by the smoke of the explosion, you will die; Garou or human, you will die."

"Human." Odin fixed Cliff with his blue eyes. "Cover us from that knoll. Watch for intruders from any direction."

Cliff scrambled up the gravel of the slope to obey. He crouched among the dry bushes, kneeling in a firing position, looking through his rifle-sight toward the railroad tracks and over the steep embankment on the other side of the ridge. Then Cliff flicked on the infrared scope. He used it to watch the hot, ruddy smears of the werewolves working around the track.

Odin lodged a package between the iron rails, cold and black in the thermographic scope. He spooled a pair of wires from the package, spliced them to a tiny device, and clamped the device over one of the rails. After fussing over it for a moment, he motioned, and the Garou retreated backward over a ridge, hundreds of yards from the railroad. At that point, Cliff licked a finger and tested the breeze. Both he and the Garou were indeed safely upwind.

Before Cliff even felt settled in his sniper position, he heard the rumble of an oncoming train.

The locomotive lumbered into view from behind a stony outcrop. Only three cars trailed behind it. In front, however, a squat little object scooted along the tracks, racing a hundred yards ahead of the ponderous train. It was a gray box on wheels, perhaps five feet high, with no features except an arm that suspended a platform of cylindrical paraphernalia above the track ahead of it. As the little device approached Odin's bomb, it screeched to a halt. Then whistles blew, and the larger train halted as well.

For a moment, all was silent. The train stood motionless against the black mountains. It was merely a silhouette looming in the darkness. The little car remained motionless as well. Moments passed. A pair of men in fatigues emerged from the first car of the train and advanced toward the site where the little car stood. Both men had rifles slung over their shoulders and carried square toolboxes. They crouched over the track as they went.

Then Cliff heard the long, feral howl of wolves.

With that sound in his blood, Cliff trained his rifle on the men who examined the tracks, fixing the crosshairs over their exposed infrared forms. He fired two shots. A man fell with each of report.

Cliff raised his head to see two lupine forms dashing toward the halted train. They ran a dozen yards apart, with Odin taking the lead. Odin was on all fours, his white fur flashing in the night. Yolanda ran on two legs, her body like that of a human, but her face distended like that of a wolf.

Automatic fire rattled from the train. Cliff turned his scope to glimpse a fraction of a warm, human form leaning from around the cool steel door of the freight car. The figure crouched low, directing the barrel of a weapon which seemed mounted on a tripod. Cliff fired once. However, the cacophony of the machine gun continued. A passing round tore through the brush with a rip before digging into the ground. Cliff pressed himself against the dirt as the burst of fire passed overhead. For the first time in his life, Cliff heard the whistle of bullets aimed at him.

The spent round gleamed dully from the ground where it had struck. It was a huge, ugly lump of brass ringed with metal of a different color: silver. Cliff's dreams had taught him enough about Garou to remember that silver was the metal that killed them.

Cliff lifted his head an inch from the dirt, squinting through the brush. The Garou had scattered. Yolanda lay prone, crawling forward through a brush-infested gully, occasionally raising her rifle to fire a shot. Odin's white form flashed across open ground, now far ahead of the others, dashing for the train.

The gun swiveled toward Odin. However, at that moment, Yolanda rose half-upright, firing from the ditch. The machine gun played back and forth for an instant. In that time, Odin leapt through the air in a broad graceful arc, landing in safety behind a jagged stone. Yolanda fired another shot before dropping to earth again. Cliff fired too, twice, aiming for the exposed crescent of the gunner's body, but his shots did not tell.

The machine gun opened fire with an extravagant burst. Second after second passed, and still the weapon clattered in the night. The gunner narrowed his sweep, playing across the gully. Cliff glimpsed Yolanda caught in the rain of bullets, huddled against the ground for protection. She jerked as projectiles punctured her flesh. Cliff glanced through the infrared scope to get a final, clear view of her and saw warm blood, pink in the infrared scope, welling up onto the cooler lavender hues of her clothing. Yolanda made no sound.

Yolanda lay still, her skull split open and her body pierced with silver bullets. Just like that, she was gone. There was no goodbye.

Cliff howled as he had heard the wolves howl and emptied his clip, firing more ineffective shots at the train. The machine gun swiveled toward him again, its barrel glowing pink in the sniperscope. It occurred to Cliff that he could stand up and follow Yolanda, but instead he huddled on the ground, scrambling for the slightest rise in the earth to hide behind, his belly and face scraping over the rough stones. At last, he rolled on his side and fumbled to snap a fresh clip into his weapon.

Meanwhile, Odin bounded to the tracks. He rose to his hindquarters and howled again as his forelegs ballooned into human shape. Snatching up the bomb, he ran for the train, weaving as he crouched forward like a hairy quarterback heading for the goal. But the machine gun turned to him again, and he was now exposed on the sandy railway embankment.

As Cliff rose to face the scene, he felt only a grim sense of calm. Time had seemed to slow down with Yolanda's death. As he watched Odin dash for the open door of the freight car, it occurred to him that unless the walls of the car were actually armored, a rifle bullet had every chance of punching right through them. Therefore, he sighted his gun again, aiming not for the visible portion of the gunner, but for the rest of the man's torso, hidden behind the steel. Cliff squeezed the trigger three times, firing three shots in a tight pattern. He heard the scream of bullets striking metal. Then the machine gun's warm, pink barrel drooped. The gun fell silent.

Odin leaped over the fallen machine gun, clutching the package to his chest. He scurried out of Cliff's sight into the freight car.

Seconds later, a white glare of unbelievable intensity lit up the infrared scope. Cliff moaned as the brightness seared his eyeball. The booming crash of a large explosion and a chatter of smaller ones echoed through the hills. Cliff's right eye stung and watered as he winked it shut. That eye saw only an angry patch of red, which did not fade even when he winked the eyelid shut. Through his left eye, Cliff glimpsed flames billowing from torn steel behind the toppled locomotive.

Then the cool breeze reminded Cliff of Odin's command and the train's deadly cargo. "If you are touched by the smoke, you will die; Garou or human, you will die." Odin had been at the center of the blast. Cliff realized that he was the last of the three. And if the wind changed, he would die as well.

Cliff considered the possibility of suicide, of joining Odin and Yolanda in death. However, the thump of his own heart beating reminded him that he had no desire to die. Therefore, he struggled through the brush with his limited vision, running away — upwind — from the ruins of the train.

The van still waited at the bend in the road. It seemed to be the logical means of escape. Cliff seated himself on the torn vinyl of the drivers' seat and groped around the compartment for keys. He found them in the ignition, turned them, and lurched out onto the mountain road. He drove back to the city slowly, his eyes watering profusely as his vision returned.

By dawn, Cliff reached his Oakland home. The moon hung low in the west, still nearly full, but ghostly faint against the blue sky. Yellow sun shone on the neatly clipped emerald grass of his lawn. Margaret's Saab stood on the perfect blacktop of the driveway. He drove past his driveway and glanced in the rearview mirror at his ruined suit and the shreds of a tie around his neck.

It occurred to Cliff that, in two hours, it would be time for work, and that nobody yet knew what he had seen or done. If he washed and changed and abandoned the van somewhere, he could go to the office as usual. He still had a mortgage to pay and a loan due on his car. However, in a few minutes, he would have to see Margaret again, and right then, he had no idea what he was going to tell her. And even if he tried to pretend things were normal, it could only be days, or at most weeks, before his life changed again forever. Sooner or later, either the Garou, or the police, or the corporate investigators would identify him, and then he would hear a knock on his door from one side . . . or the other. ////

Little Flea

by Scott Urban

This is going to be the lamest weekend in the history of the world, thought Justin Crandle as he walked back from the camp bath-house. *Any time you have to walk a quarter mile just to go to the bathroom, or take a decent shower, you know you need to run screaming back to the city.*

Not for the first time that Saturday morning, he sighed heavily. Sweeping damp locks of sandy-colored hair back from his forehead, he looked up at the spreading limbs of massive redwoods that formed arches 150 feet above him.

OK, OK, so I'm impressed, Justin thought, rehearsing the speech he planned to give his father. *I realize these trees were ancient even before white settlers came and ran the native Indians out of the neighborhood. I even think you ought to work to protect them. But now that we've gotten 'back to nature,' can't we please get 'back to indoor plumbing?'*

"I want you to see what I'm working to preserve," Nathan Crandle had explained to his wife and son two days ago when he announced this impromptu expedition.

"It's true that California is facing some tough economic times. But I can't believe that allowing the Developer Forestry Group limited cutting rights in Muir Woods is the answer. There *may be* hundreds of baby boomers who want redwood homes, but, dammit, I've worked *too hard* to see this land protected to let some asinine loggers come in and destroy this beauty." Justin had rolled his eyes to Kate, his mother, pleading to be left home, but it hadn't done any good. There was no way his parents were going to leave a fourteen year old home alone on a Halloween weekend.

And it wouldn't be so bad, mused Justin, *if I weren't going to miss the coolest party of the year.*

Thad Deacon, one of his few high-school friends, had invited him to a Halloween bash that Sunday night. Thad's parties were legendary. Everyone was coming in costume. A thrash band made up of high schoolers was going to be playing live. There was sure to be beer and maybe some hash floating around. And the babes!

God, *I can't believe I'm going to miss all those chicks in skimpy outfits,* he thought, biting his lower lip in frustration.

And here he was, stuck in Muir Woods. His father, a state senator, was making notes to help him defend Mount Tamilpais State Park from some corporation that wanted limited logging privileges. Both his parents were trying to rekindle the spark in an increasingly stagnant relationship. The three of them, with 19-foot camping trailer in tow, had arrived last night, just in time to feel the landscape rock under their feet from a moderately strong earthquake. The tremor had brought some heavy branches crashing down around their campsite, but no real harm had been done. Nathan had been on the cellular phone half the night, checking back with aides in Sacramento on damages.

Justin began to round the bend that would put him in sight of the trailer. *How am I going to kill the day?* he wondered. *I'm gonna kick myself for forgetting to bring my Walkman. Good thing I brought along some comics.* If his parents wanted to go for a hike, he hoped they would count him out.

Justin knew something was wrong when he brought his head up and looked at the trailer, but it took a moment for the discrepancy to register. The trailer, all 19 feet, was rocking unsteadily from side to side. *Christ, are they going at it again?* Justin thought. He didn't think his parents would start making out in the time he went to take a shower. No, the swaying seemed unnatural — somehow violent.

As he drew nearer, more details became clear. Both the screen and interior door were standing open. *Mom wouldn't leave them open — she can't stand the bugs getting inside.* Something was wrong — very wrong.

Then the screams began — and faded.

Justin dropped his towel and bolted for the trailer.

Something emerged from the camper door. At first Justin's eyes couldn't take it in. It was so far removed from anything he had ever seen before that his mind could not assimilate it, could not make it part of the gestalt. There was a broad, gleaming black carapace from which jutted multijointed limbs, insectlike legs that skittered and scrambled. Growing from the top of the carapace was the torso and head of a man — but a man stunted and deformed. The creature's mouth was circular and filled with needlelike fangs pointing back into the maw. The eyes were lidless and multifaceted, like a fly's.

In its muscular arms it held the limp form of Kate Crandle, his mother.

Justin's run stuttered to a halt at the sight. *Jesus, God!* he wanted to scream, but couldn't. His knees buckled, dropping him to the ground. Tears welled up in his eyes at this utter violation of everything normal.

The first creature scrambled down into the clearing and another exited the trailer behind it. The second was similar in form and structure to the first but possessed its own malformed features: a two-foot proboscis that grew from the middle of its face, prehensile as an elephant's trunk, and a mouth that opened and shut idiotically in the center of its chest.

This second monster held his father. Justin couldn't tell whether his parents were dead or alive.

There, on his knees, Justin stared at these shambling nightmares that even now were disappearing into the wall of vegetation, and he shouted a loud "*Nooooo!*" His cry echoed among the redwood boles, seemed to make the forest quiver with the force of his defiance.

And then the ground fell away from him as he was swept up into the air.

Later, Justin thought it a wonder he did not immediately faint. He knew many others would have. He was turned to face yet a third horror that held him in crablike claws. "Shit! Oh shit!" he shouted, kicking, punching, and connecting with nothing. His captor's five jet-black eyes, set in a horizontal row across the brow, stared down at him without expression.

Two furry pincers, scissoring open and shut with metallic clicks, descended for his throat.

I'm going to die, Justin realized, feeling his bladder loosen. *I'm going to die and I'll never make love to a girl and I'll never have kids and I'll never know what the hell this fuck-ugly thing is that's killing me!*

The fangs were poised to pierce the soft flesh at the base of Justin's neck when suddenly, the thing's head was yanked back from its intended prey. Someone had leaped on the mutation's back. Thick arms wrapped themselves around the arachnoid head and jerked sharply to the right. There was the stomach-wrenching sound of bones popping loose from each other. A convulsive shudder ran through the spider-thing's form as its legs collapsed, spilling all of them to the earth.

Justin propelled himself backwards, scooting on his rear away from the deformity that had captured him, and caught the first sight of his savior.

He's never gonna finish standing up, Justin thought. It seemed to take forever for the man to unlimber his legs. He looked like a rock outcropping brought to life. Justin wasn't sure how tall he was — seven, eight feet at least. He wore an open, fringed leather vest and tan dungarees, but was barefoot. He had the swarthy complexion of an American Indian. His black hair was cut short to his scalp. His black eyes seemed to look through Justin into his soul. Muscles rippled across his form. His face and arms were marked with numerous scars — many smaller ones and some frighteningly longer ones.

Justin couldn't stop trembling. *He's looking at me as if he's trying to decide what to do with me. Is he gonna help me up — or step on me like some sorta cockroach?*

"Jesus! Thanks!" Justin was virtually spitting out the words. "What the hell is that thing? And who are you?"

The giant's face remained expressionless. He extended a hand that looked like it could have ground stone into powder and pulled Justin to his feet.

"Thanks," said Justin, brushing off his jeans. "Can't you — can't you talk?"

The newcomer put a finger to his mouth, then shook it in the air.

"Oh. You can't talk," Justin interpreted. The giant nodded. "OK, but look," his voice grew more frantic now that the immediate threat was eliminated, "two other. . .

things took my mom and dad. We've got to go get help! Please, can you help me?"

The giant turned toward the trailer and sniffed. *He's picking up signals I'll never be able to sense,* Justin realized. The Indian looked toward the woods in the direction the monstrosities had disappeared. Then he looked back at Justin, holding his hands out, palms forward.

"You — you want me to stay here?" Justin asked. His rescuer nodded. More than anything, Justin wanted to agree. As a matter of fact, he wanted to run howling in the opposite direction from the entire madness. But he had seen his parents abducted — and until he knew whether they lived or not, he knew he couldn't simply run and hide. "No way. I'm coming with you. Those are my parents those bastards have."

The giant made a slashing motion across the teenager's midriff with a forefinger as thick as a branch.

"Yeah, I know it could be dangerous. I don't care. Come on. We're wasting time."

He began running for the woods before the Indian.

The silent stranger easily caught up to Justin. With his left arm, he lifted the boy into the air, to his side. "What're we doing?" Justin shouted. *I'm no more than a sack of groceries to him!* The giant took three long bounds and leaped into the air. Justin swallowed, hard. He could have sworn they were taking flight, so high did they rise. In midleap, the giant spun, making five complete revolutions. A strange feeling washed through Justin's body. It felt as if he had touched electric current, only not as painful. His head seemed to grow five times, then shrink back to normal proportions.

Then they landed, and nothing for Justin was ever the same.

• • •

They were still near the edge of a clearing. But when the stranger put Justin on his feet, he realized things had changed.

For one, his new companion had grown even taller. Now the giant must have been near 12 feet tall. "Oh no," Justin heard himself whisper. "Oh no." His rescuer had undergone an even more profound change. His face had elongated, nose and mouth forming a muzzle. The ears were pointed. Heavy, short black fur covered his face and scalp, with whiskers to the side of the nose. Claws protruded from the tips of his fingers.

"Oh, Jesus, mister, please don't hurt me," Justin pleaded, backing away on wobbly legs.

He cast quick, darting looks left and right. He couldn't see his parents' trailer anywhere. The sky was a rich azure blue — a shade that looked somehow untouched by human pollution. The trees around the edge of the clearing for some reason looked more alive than they had seemed a moment ago. Justin could even make out a glow, or aura, around the trunks of the trees. There was an inner life here, a spark he could sense growing even inside himself.

Justin looked back to the giant. He had gone over to the broadest, tallest redwood and was now kneeling in front of it. Justin sensed he was offering it homage.

Oh man, where am I? What the hell is going on here?

Justin cautiously walked over to the kneeling man who now possessed the features of a wolf. As he did so, he could perceive a change within the redwood itself. The bark was assuming the characteristics of a face. The features were majestic and, in a way, regal. Two protuberances in the trunk that must have served for eyes swung toward Justin.

"Greetings," boomed a reverberant voice. "Welcome to the Penumbra."

Justin shook his head. "The tree is talking to me," he whispered. "Please tell me I'm dreaming."

"Don't fight the evidence of your senses." The voice was more confident, more calm, than any man's he had ever heard. "You already know deep in your spirit you are no longer in your world."

"Who are you? And where did you say we were?"

"I am Truebranch, Eldest Glade Child in this section of the Penumbra. The Penumbra is another world that touches on, overlays, your world. Those with the gift may walk between the two."

"And. . . who is he?" Justin asked, pointing to the still kneeling giant.

"He is Silent Fist-That-Wins. He is a member of the Garou, the race that exists between man and wolf. He is an Uktena Ahroun — a noble Indian warrior. He can talk his thoughts to me, and I may pass them on to you. He is angered at the audacity of the Bane. The ferectoi must have wanted your parents desperately to be willing to risk entering the Realm so near to his caern."

"I — I don't know what you're talking about."

"It doesn't matter now. Silent Fist wishes to know: your parents — who were they? Why would the Wyrm want to abduct them?"

"Nathan and Kate Crandle. My dad's a state senator. But I don't know why anyone would want to hurt him."

"Is your father involved in any dealings with Mount Tamilpais State Park?"

"Dad was saying something about some company. . . the Developer Forestry Group, I think . . . that wants to come into Muir Woods for limited logging. He's opposing them in the Senate. He's here to gather notes to take back with him to Sacramento. But what does that have to do with those monsters?"

"Those monsters are ferectoi. They serve Pentex — the true owners of Developer Forestry Group — and the Wyrm. I know you don't understand me. Simply put, they are forces which wish to destroy all that is good in the universe you know. Your father's leadership is vital to defeating the invasion of our bawn."

"But why didn't the ferec — whatever — just kill my parents instead of kidnapping them?"

"Your parents are temporarily paralyzed. They are on their way to the nearest Pit. The ferectoi will hand them over to the Black Spiral Dancers. These are Garou who have turned to the Wyrm. They will expose your parents to the Black Spiral Labyrinth. It will shatter their minds — drive them insane. They will then be escorted back to the Realm. If your parents disappeared, or were found dead, no doubt a sympathy vote would carry your father's veto in the Senate. But if your parents are found wandering around as mad lunatics, no one will want to be associated with them. No one will rally to your father's position, and Pentex will have a legal right to rape the woods."

"There's no fuckin' way I'm gonna let them do that to my parents!" Justin said, surprising even himself at the ferocity in his voice. He ran up to Silent Fist, who now stood looking down at him. "Come on! They've got too much of a headstart now as it is!"

Truebranch spoke behind him. "The journey through the Umbra can be perilous. Freeing your parents will not be easy. Silent Fist can move much more quickly by himself."

Justin looked up at the towering figure. *I'm scared*, he admitted to himself, *but I've got to convince him to let me come, too.* "I won't stay here. If you leave, I'm going to try to follow you. If I do, I'm sure to get lost and maybe killed by whatever else lives in this place. So, the best thing to do is take me with you."

Silent Fist glared down at Justin. *I know he could run away so fast I'd never see which way he went,* the boy realized. The Garou seemed to be weighing something in his mind.

"Silent Fist says he admires your determination. He says he will call you 'Little Flea,' because he cannot shake you off. He will treat you as his own whelp. This means you must fight, and, if necessary, die."

Justin frowned at the massive Garou. "I'll show you that this 'flea' can sting."

Silent Fist jerked his head to the left.

"I know," said Justin. "Let's get going."

● ● ●

They entered the Penumbral forest and began running. Events had been happening so rapidly that Justin really had no chance to take in the unreality of it all. He now saw there were vast, limitless forces all around him he could not begin to comprehend. All the things he had held sacred as true had been stood on their heads inside of an hour. And yet, at the same time, he now felt like he was part of something huge and important. Retrieving his parents, proving himself in the eyes of this massive fighter, gave him something to strive for. Nothing had managed to do that before — not school, not his parents, not his friends.

The Uktena Ahroun led the way through this near-world, leading them by some sense Justin was not privy to. Justin wasn't exactly sure what was happening. He knew that Silent Fist was making all speed to catch up with his parents' captors. He also realized that back on the earth he knew Silent Fist could easily outstrip him. Yet Justin was somehow able to keep up with the wolf-warrior. Perhaps the Penumbra itself lent him part of its energy.

Justin tried to take in as much of his surroundings as he could. He was aware that even back in his world the forest was alive, a delicate eco-system balanced and working together. But here in the Penumbra, he could see bands of energy coursing back and forth between branches and roots, between plants and tiny living creatures. Justin knew he was blessed to see this aura-filled pattern of life. He knew he would never be able to walk through the woods again and see them in the same way.

If I live to walk through any more woods, he added bitterly.

But even as he took in the Penumbra's beauty, he began to see that not all was unscathed in this spirit world. The woods darkened as night approached. Branches began to sag. Trees became more sparse. Roots clawed at the very air for sustenance. The energy emanating from within the ground looked tainted. In the distance, Justin saw large, jagged forms rising against the rapidly dimming sky. At this range, he could not tell whether they were natural or man-made.

Can there be anything in this weird world that's man-made? Justin wondered.

He understood that their only hope to free his parents was to overtake the ferectoi before they reached the Black Spiral Pit. Once there, the spider-things would have the might of the deranged clan at their defense. Looking ahead, Justin caught sight of two many-legged, malformed creatures scrabbling between the twisted forms ahead, forms that looked more and more like crumbling, pitted edifices. He pointed them out, and Silent Fist nodded, having seen them too.

Silent Fist paused, his muzzle curling in a noiseless snarl. Justin thought he knew the meaning. The ferectoi had almost reached the safety of the Pit.

The Ahroun knelt at Justin's side. He held out his left hand flat, palm up. With the fingers of his right hand, he mimicked walking across a landscape. "Us or them?" Justin asked. Silent Fist indicated the two of them.

"Okay, that's us walking." The Garou nodded.

Then Silent Fist put his right fingers at the base of his left hand. He curled his left fingers up and back, touching his wrist. He moved his right fingers to the tips of the left fingers. He uncurled his fist, and his right fingers sprang forward.

Justin fought to understand what it all meant. "There is. . . some sort of shortcut. . . not across the landscape. . . but somehow through it?"

Silent Fist allowed a slight grin and nodded.

The mute warrior stood and raised his arms to the sky. Over their heads, the full moon shone down its glory. Silent Fist opened his mouth. *He can't say anything*, Justin thought, *but his prayers are still being heard.* Justin added his prayers to those of Silent Fist, although he was not sure to whom he was praying, nor exactly what he was praying for. The Garou leaped into the air, waving his arms in a mystic, fluid pattern. As he did, it seemed that the rays of the moon descended and wrapped themselves around the two of them, playfully tickling and caressing them.

A moment later, a shimmering, white path stretched out beneath their feet. It glowed softly, opalescent. *It's — it's pieces of moonlight, making a path and guiding us on!* Silent Fist began running along the glimmering trail. Justin drove himself after.

Sure as hell doesn't seem like a shortcut, Justin thought as the path twisted and curved maddeningly. Whenever he tried to see what was passing to either side of them, his vision blurred, forcing him to concentrate on following the trail.

After what might have been an hour, or only a few minutes, Silent Fist again made Justin slow down. He drew forth a silver knife from a sheath on his back. He reached down and gave it to Justin. In the boy's hand, it looked more like a sword than a knife.

"But what about you?" Justin asked.

Silent Fist curled his fingers upward. The razor-edged talons shone in the lunar glow. "These will be all I need," was the message.

The moonpath came to an end only a few feet ahead. Silent Fist looked down at Justin. He snarled soundlessly, then raised his fist to the sky. It was the universal call to battle. Justin hefted the silver klaive into the air. He understood only battle awaited them. Together they hurled themselves from the moonpath.

Justin had a great deal to take in in only a split second. A light fog had arisen, blanketing their surroundings in an eerie, weblike shroud. Ahead and to the right were shadowy ruins. He had no idea who had made these walls, but none survived intact. It was not as if the structures had been bombed or burned out — it looked more as if they had succumbed to an architectural malaise, the stones themselves somehow decaying from within. To their left ran a deep culvert filled with brackish, stagnant water. Scuttling around a mound of fallen masonry were the two ferectoi, still gripping Justin's limp, unconscious parents.

Justin couldn't hold it in any longer. A savage, primitive war cry erupted from his throat. It echoed among the remaining upright walls, a more lupine sound than Silent Fist himself could emit. Justin felt everything innocent and civilized had been stripped away from him.

There was little of the awkward, gawky 14 year old left. *Goddamn, I feel alive!* Justin wanted to scream. *And I'm so alive, I don't even care if I die!*

Silent Fist was already launching himself at the nearest ferectoi, the one who held Kate Crandle. The startled Bane, caught by surprise, didn't know what to do with its burden. That moment's hesitation was fatal. The Ahroun's claws tore through the spider-thing's throat. Black blood and gore spilled over fur, carapace, and Justin's mother.

Justin hurled himself at the remaining ferectoi. Forewarned, the monster had heedlessly dropped his father to the littered earth. Inhuman cries belched from the creature's chest-mouth. Justin checked his charge and swung at one of the forelegs. The silver blade sliced through the chitinous appendage. The ferectoi nearly toppled before recovering its balance.

Got you now, you bug-bastard! Justin wanted to shout. *You are one fucked spider!*

The lips of the chest-mouth smacked wetly. Justin closed in for another slash with the klaive. Unpracticed as he was at close combat, he couldn't keep track of all of the monster's limbs. The servant of the Wyrm brought a rear leg up between those in front and cut Justin's feet out from under him. He went down, nearly losing his grip on his weapon. The monstrosity reared up. Justin tried to scramble backwards, but knew he couldn't get out of the way before being pinned by a spearlike leg.

Out of the mists flew Silent Fist, jaws open in a noiseless battle cry. He grappled with the skittering spider-thing, huge fists pounding at the mouthless head. The ferectoi worked its chest-mouth and tried to spit venom at the Garou, but the warrior must have been expecting it. He turned his face away just in time to avoid being blinded. Even so, the burning saliva fell on his shoulder.

Justin saw smoke rise as the acid ate into Silent Fist's flesh.

Fighting for balance on the debris-strewn ground, Justin got to his feet and tightened his grip on the Ahroun fetish. The Garou slammed his fist into the creature's chest-mouth. Justin heard splintering bones, saw loosened teeth flying. He ran forward, blade extended. The point sank in the ferectoi's abdomen. The ferectoi's limbs stiffened as news of its death ran along its nerves — and then it fell in on itself like some poorly made toy.

I'm only a flea, thought Justin, *but you don't wanna mess with me.*

At that point, wild howls started up all around them. Both Justin and Silent Fist snapped their heads up. The Garou held up a forefinger and drew a circle in midair, a circle that spiraled in on itself.

"Shit!" cursed the teenager. "Black Spiral Dancers!" He brought up his blade, now dripping Bane ichor. "They've got us surrounded. What are we going to do?"

Silent Fist's only reply was a 10-foot bound. He easily picked up Nathan and Kate Crandle each in a hand and loped over to the culvert. Justin had no idea what he was doing, and there was no time to ask. The Garou dumped the unresisting bodies into the water.

"What the hell are you—?" Justin began, but then found himself relieved of his weapon and hefted aloft. "Would you kill us, rather than let the Dancers get us?"

Then Justin was pivoting in midair, tumbling head over rear, the black surface of the water nearing—

— and he had just enough time to see Silent Fist bring himself to his full height, meeting the charge of a score of twisted, misshapen men-wolves emerging from the mists, all eager to taste Uktena blood.

Then the waters closed over his head.

• • •

Justin kicked his way to the surface. He shook his head, clearing water from his eyes, tossing wet locks back against his scalp. *Gotta help Silent Fist*, he thought. *Gotta help kill Spiral Dancers.* No matter what the odds, he knew he would go down fighting. But although he knelt waist-deep in the stale, rank water of a drainage ditch, the Garou was nowhere to be seen.

His mother was on one side, his father on the other. They were dragging themselves up out of the water, coughing and hacking. They tugged at their damp clothes and looked at him questioningly.

We're back in the Realm, Justin realized. *Silent Fist tossed us out of the Umbra at the last moment. He stayed behind to give us time to escape. He sacrificed himself for my life, and my parents.*

"What in holy hell is going on?" Nathan Crandle shouted incredulously. He recognized their surroundings as one of San Francisco's outlying boroughs — but had no recollection of coming here — or of falling in a ditch!

Justin opened his mouth, wondering just how he would reply.

• • •

Even though he could have sat in on the debate, Justin didn't want to. He didn't think he could sit still for that long. Instead, he paced the Senate halls, nervously awaiting the outcome of the vote. He thought of Silent Fist and felt guilty because he walked in this world that, even though it had problems, was still so beautiful and full of promise.

His father had been surprised when he said he wanted to attend this particular session. "You've never shown an interest in my concerns before," he said. "Why the sudden change of heart?"

Justin had shrugged. "I guess I'm just beginning to grow up," he said weakly, and they had both laughed.

After what seemed like an entire legislative session, the door opened and senators began filing out, ready to break for the day. Justin bounced on the balls of his feet until he caught sight of his father. "How'd it go?" he couldn't help shouting as he ran. "How'd it go?"

His father was grinning like a Little Leaguer who had just scored his first homerun. "We did it! We held enough votes to block the development of the park!" Both of them whooped and slapped each other's arms, heedless of the quizzical stares of passers-by.

Nathan put an arm around his son's shoulders. "Come on. Let's pick up Mom and find ourselves a nice place to go for dinner."

Justin nodded and turned with his father toward the Capitol doors. As he did, he caught sight of someone watching them in the midst of the milling throng. The watcher was tall, standing a good two feet above the heads of everyone else in the broad foyer. There were a few new scars underneath the closely cropped black hair, but otherwise the Garou looked as fit as when Justin had first seen him.

Justin held an arm out and gave Silent Fist the "thumbs-up" sign.

But the watcher had already turned and disappeared into the crowd. ///

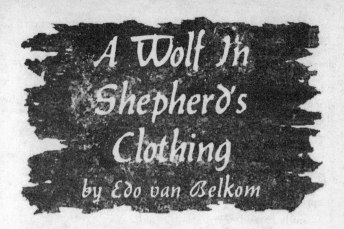

A Wolf In Shepherd's Clothing

by Edo van Belkom

The city streets were bathed in moonlight.

Steam rose from sewer grates.

Rats toppled garbage cans.

And while the citizens of San Francisco slept in the comfort of their homes and apartments, others less fortunate slept in the gutters and alleys cloaked in shadows, waiting for the sun to shed light on their misery.

Or for the night to end it.

In a darkened alley between a department store and bank, Randall E. "Sully" Sullivan III, rolled over in his cardboard box. He reached out with a dirty, blackened hand and peeled the soggy brown paper from the neck of the bottle. Then with a shaky hand he raised the bottle to his lips and upended it. The cheap red wine ran down his throat like ice-water, then burned in his stomach like fire.

He was about to take another swig when his eyes opened wide.

And the bottle fell from his hand.

Something was coming toward him — something big.

He rubbed his fists into his eyes, blinked and looked again.

It was a creature of some sort, more wolf than man.

The sight of it made Sully feel lightheaded, giddy. He shut his eyes, curled up tight in his box, and waited for the two hind legs of the creature to pad on by him. But as he heard the thing approach, he couldn't resist opening his eyes and taking a peak.

It had to be over seven feet tall, topped by a thick shock of almost white hair. Then from the muzzle on down, it was covered in a thick bristly coat of salt and pepper fur.

Sully gasped.

The beast stopped less than a foot from cardboard box.

Sully held his breath, turned his eyes skyward.

There was a man cradled in the beast's arms.

Maybe dead, maybe not.

The beast firmed its hold on the man, then padded quickly out of the alley and into the street.

Sully came out of his delirium slowly, unsure about what he'd seen, but knowing that he'd been terrified of whatever it had been. A while later when things were finally back to normal and he'd all but forgotten about what he'd seen, he realized that something had wet his clothes. Then he remembered the bottle he'd dropped and hoped to god he'd pissed in his pants.

• • •

The werewolf moved quickly through the moonlit back streets of the Tenderloin, staying close to the shadows and the safety of their darkness.

The man in its arms breathed shallowly, the rhythm of his breath interrupted every so often by a weak cough. His clothes had been shredded. There were angry red slashes across his face and chest and a bite had been taken from his thigh, but fortunately he was not mortally wounded.

It would take time, but he would heal.

He would have another chance at life.

A better life.

The white-haired werewolf darted out from the darkened storefront and bounded across Eddy Street.

With three, four, five strides it bounded up the steps to the entrance of the Scott Mission.

There, shrouded in the darkness of the blacked-out porch, the werewolf eased its burden onto the concrete. When the man's head touched the concrete, his eyes opened. He looked up at the werewolf, a brief pulse of fear widening his eyes. He tried to remain awake, but his eyelids became too heavy to keep open any longer. Slowly, they fell.

Before his eyes were closed, the werewolf was gone.

• • •

The sky burned orange, then turned blue, chasing the moon away.

The sun peaked over the horizon, a blazing white ball, chasing the night's shadows from the day.

A light came on outside the Scott Mission. A moment later the front door opened and Father Wendel Oldman stepped onto the porch. He ran a thickly boned hand through his thick shock of ragged white hair, but did not look surprised to see the man lying at his feet.

"Parker!"

His assistant appeared in the doorway. "Not another one?"

Father Oldman knelt over the body and made a token examination of the prone form. "Yes. He's hurt, but not too badly. Take his feet."

Parker grabbed hold of the man's legs, making sure he had a firm grip before lifting.

Father Oldman placed his hands under the man's arms and lifted. He stood up with what seemed like no effort, then waited for the young deacon to lift the man's legs off the ground.

"We'll bring him into my den."

They carried the man down the hall, then into a small room on the right. There was a floor-to-ceiling bookshelf against the outside wall and a great wooden desk in front of it. Pictures of presidents and clerics adorned two walls, while a couch was set up against a third. They laid the man down on the couch, making sure his feet were elevated and his head comfortable.

"Shall I call the police," said Parker.

"No!" replied Father Oldman.

"But Father, seven street people have been killed since Halloween. This man appears to have suffered the same wounds as those who've died. When he regains consciousness, perhaps he could give the police a description of his attacker."

Father Oldman grabbed the deacon by the shoulders, his hands gripping the young man like forged-steel clamps. "I said no!" The tone of his voice left no room for argument.

But then, sensing his harsh tone had hurt the younger man's feelings, he sighed. "This is not a matter for the police." His voice was softer now, friendly. "I would like to handle this myself. "

The deacon opened his mouth to speak, but his words died in his throat. He had far too much respect for Father Oldman to contradict him twice. "All right," he nodded.

Father Oldman released his hold on the young man, then slapped him gently on the arm. "Thanks." He escorted the deacon out of the room, then locked the door.

The man on the couch groaned.

The sound stirred Father Oldman into action.

He went to the locked cabinet in the lower right-hand corner of the bookshelf and opened it. From inside the cabinet he selected several white jars from the top shelf, and a roll of gauze and bottle of alcohol from the bottom. Then he took everything over to the table next to the couch.

With a strong and sure hand, Father Oldman tore the man's clothing away from the wounds on his leg and chest, then began cleaning the dark red streaks with a gauze pad soaked in alcohol.

The sting of the liquid made the man cry out.

"Easy. Easy." His voice was low, but still quite powerful. The man on the couch listened to it, and did his best to tolerate the pain in silence.

"That's good," said Father Oldman. He picked up a large white jar from the table and opened it. The jar was filled with an oily white paste. It smelled of pine needles and moss, black earth and freshly cut grass.

He spread it over the man's wounds.

The man sighed in relief. Breathed easier.

When he'd covered all of the man's wounds with salve, Father Oldman wiped the excess off on the back of his neck. It felt pleasantly cool against his skin.

Several minutes later the man opened his eyes. As he looked at Father Oldman's face, the shock of white hair atop his head, the full salt-and-pepper beard and steely gray eyes, a look of recognition crossed his face.

"You," he said in a whisper.

Father Oldman dismissed the man's curiosity with a wave of his hand. "Now," he said calmly. "Tell me exactly what happened to you last night. And don't leave out a thing."

The man took a breath and swallowed.

"I've been living on the streets for about six months now. The last few weeks I've been in Golden Gate Park, sleeping most of the day and scavenging garbage at night." He laughed. It sounded more like a cough. "Not much of a life really, and I was getting pretty tired of it."

The man paused, but Father Oldman said nothing.

"Anyway, I heard about you and this mission. The people on the street, they say things about you — good things. They say you don't just take people off the streets; you take them out of the city, give them a new life someplace else."

Father Oldman did his best not to smile, but couldn't stop his mouth from breaking into a proud little grin.

"That's what I wanted. A new life." He said the words as if they existed somewhere in the realm of fantasy. "So, I was making my way over here to join you, or sign up, or whatever it is you do, when I noticed this guy following me. It was dark out, but I could make out enough of him in the moonlight to recognize him as one of Bongos' people from the park." His voice was suddenly sharp with fear. "Mean sons of bitches, they are."

"We all have our dark side," said Father Oldman. Although many tribes looked down on them, the Bone Gnawers were basically good Garou. Oldman was fond of Bongos and considered him a friend.

"Anyway, as I got a little west of Union Square I didn't see this guy following me anymore so I relaxed a

286 ///////// When Will You Rage? ///////

little. Then, as I stepped in front of an alley, something grabbed my arm and pulled me into the darkness."

Father Oldman sat up in his chair. "What was it? What was it that pulled you in?"

The man was silent as he thought about it.

He shook his head. "The first thing I thought was I was being mugged, or raped, but I felt *claws* on me. Ripping at my clothes, tearing my skin. There was growling too: animal sounds; wild sounds." His breath shortened at the recollection. "Then, I felt teeth, almost like a dog's, biting my leg."

Father Oldman had heard as much as he needed to know. He got up from his chair and headed to the door.

"It all went black then," the man continued. "I must have fallen or hit my head, because all I remember after that was a dream I had where this sort of werewolf creature was carrying me to safety." He looked at the priest on the other side of the room. "Funny thing is, the werewolf looked a lot like you, with white and gray fur, same as your beard."

"You were most likely delirious."

"No I wasn't. I remember it. It was you, wasn't it?"

"You remember that?" asked Father Oldman curiously.

"Yes, quite clearly. In fact, the werewolf also had a head of thick white hair. Just like yours."

"That's enough," said Father Oldman abruptly, trying hard to hide his conceal his joy at the possibility of having discovered a kinfolk. "You've been through quite an ordeal. I suggest you get some rest." He opened the door. "Parker!"

"Yes father." The deacon answered from the office down the hall.

"Take this man down to the kitchen, please. Get him a bite to eat, then give him a cot in the dorm, and let him sleep for as long as he likes."

The deacon entered the room, helped the man off the couch, then led him away by the arm.

The man's gaze was locked on Father Oldman. There was a suspicious squint to his eyes.

The priest did his best to ignore the man's gaze. "I'll be in my room for the rest of the day," he told the deacon. "Could you come get me at nightfall?"

"Sure, father," the deacon nodded. "I'll see that you're not disturbed."

• • •

Father Oldman ran the Scott Mission, a homeless shelter in the heart of the Tenderloin. Although he was Garou, he was also of the Children of Gaia tribe and had genuine compassion for the men and women who came to him for help.

For these were the homeless, the forgotten, the refuse of human society. And in a way, he shared a common bond with them. Their kind didn't fit in with humans, and neither did his.

But unlike the other shelters along Jones and Eddy Streets, Father Oldman and the people of the Scott Mission didn't just give the city's discards a hot meal and a place to sleep; they actually worked to rehabilitate them, to give them an entirely new way of life.

It worked like this:

After a homeless man has been taken in by the shelter, he is given new clothes, regular meals, and put on a program to rid himself of any substance dependencies he might have. When he's deemed a suitable candidate and fit to travel he is moved to the Scott Ranch situated just north of the Muir Woods where he is educated about the wonder of Gaia and how important it is that she be preserved in all her glory.

After several months, when his love of Gaia is assured, he begins his new life on the outskirts of the Mt. Tamilpais State Park where he lives and works to help the Uktena and Kinfolk to protect the Caern from humans and other enemies of the tribe.

It was a system that had worked well for over six years. In that time Father Oldman had moved dozens of San Francisco's homeless to the beautiful redwooded hills overlooking the bay.

The key to the mission's success was its location. The people who came to Father Oldman were filled with sadness and despair. Their spirits had been broken by the so-called "civilized" world, and they were primed and ready to be rejuvenated by the invigorating new spirits and totems offered by Gaia, the Mother Goddess.

The mission's location was also a factor which had helped Father Oldman, enabling him to live and work among the humans for so long. Although he changed form often, the Delirium was strong in The Tenderloin and allowed him to move freely through that part of the city under the thick protective shroud of the veil. As a result, he was able to use his feral strengths to help the mission flourish, either by taking in those too weak to come to him on their own, or by discreetly obtaining operating funds from opulent nearby homes and businesses.

But now there was a wild card loose in the city, tinkering with the delicate balance of his existence. A renegade Garou had wandered into the midst of his flock, killing off the homeless for no apparent reason.

He couldn't allow it to continue. Something had to be done, tonight.

• • •

There was a knock at the door.

"Father Oldman." It was the voice of Deacon Parker. "Night has fallen."

"Thank you, Parker."

Father Oldman listened to the sound of Parker's steps grow faint, then rose from his bed and went to the window. He knew the moon was full, could feel it hanging over the city like a watchful eye, but he pulled aside the curtain to look at it just the same.

As he looked up at the burnished white disk in the blackened night sky, he allowed the change into Crinos form to begin. His bones grew and his flesh crawled with a pleasant sort of itch.

His entire body surged with power.

Father Oldman moved from the window to the door and stripped down to the waist. The hair was already beginning to tuft on his chest.

He opened the door, padded silently down the hall and down the few steps leading to the mission's back door. He stood there a moment listening to the sounds of people having dinner in the kitchen downstairs. Then he was outside, hidden by the hazy black shadows of the alley behind the mission.

Father Oldman found a dark corner behind a dumpster, sat down, and waited for the change to run its course.

His bones hummed and tingled with energy for several long minutes as the hard tissue of his skull, legs, arms, and chest, thickened and lengthened. Then it was his skin that began to stretch and expand to accommodate the roiling muscles beneath it and the thick new coat of salt-and-pepper fur above. Finally, his teeth and fingers grew long, sharp, and deadly — the most pleasant feeling of all.

Father Oldman rose up from the shadows, the shock of hair on his head gleaming white under the light of the moon.

He stepped away from the dumpster and padded down the alley. He leapt over a five-foot fence in a single bound and was suddenly lost in the shadows.

• • •

Father Oldman walked the streets for hours, seeing and hearing nothing.

Then, at one point, he heard the faint sounds of someone screaming.

He tracked the sound to its source and came upon an empty lot behind a burger joint where two men were in the process of mugging an elderly man.

On another night he might have helped the old-timer, jumped into the fray and severely wounded his attackers.

But he had no time for distractions tonight. Tonight, he was on the hunt.

He was out for blood, and he would have it.

Father Oldman turned his back on the crime and resumed the hunt.

Now, hours later, he was once again on Eddy Street wondering if the Garou he was looking for had caught wind of him and been scared off for tonight, maybe even for good.

He began to double back toward the mission when he heard it: the terrible blood-curdling scream of someone looking straight into the jaws of death.

This was it. It had to be.

He turned his ears into the direction the sound was coming from. And then he was off, not even bothering to stay close to the shadows.

He was in the alley seconds later.

At the end of it, a smallish looking Garou was standing over a human male, hands holding the man in place while its maw dug deep into his neck. The human struggled against the Garou, even though his efforts weakened with each passing second.

Oldman bounded down the alley in great strides, then leaped through the air. He landed heavily on the Garou's back, knocking it away from the human.

The two Garou rolled several times, black and gray fur mixing with dirty brown in a ball of snarling, snapping teeth.

Garbage cans toppled, rats skittered, then they were apart.

Oldman was down on all fours, watching his foe with a malicious stare. The Garou was no more than six feet tall, with scrawny arms and legs and rounded ears and muzzle.

It was more dog than wolf: a Bone Gnawer.

"Corrupted by the Wyrm?" said Oldman, his words interspersed with low growls.

"This is a city, old man," the Bone Gnawer said. "We're all corrupted here."

Oldman was silent. This Garou knew his name well enough to make fun of it. He decided to proceed with caution.

"The homeless are the Bone Gnawers' protectorate. Why would you want to kill them off?"

"The fog. It contaminated the caern, infected the pack with the Thrall of the Wyrm."

Oldman had heard of the impenetrable fog that had washed over the Golden Gate Bridge on Halloween night. But it had disappeared by morning, melting away shortly after sunrise.

Oldman looked at the Bone Gnawer skeptically.

"If that's true, why haven't I come upon more *infected* Bone Gnawers? Why haven't there been more killings?" He stepped closer, his claws extending like talons.

"They. . . went elsewhere. To the east. The north."

There, it was in his voice. The uncertainty of one who lies.

"Liar!"

Oldman pounced on the smaller Garou, locking the claw-tipped fingers of his left hand around the Bone Gnawer's scrawny neck.

"Now," Oldman said, "the truth."

"I have been telling—"

Oldman squeezed hard, cutting off the Bone Gnawer before he could lie again. "I said, the truth!" He emphasized his point by slamming the Garou's head down onto the hard alley floor.

"All right." The words sounded like a gurgle. Oldman loosened his grip on the Garou's neck enough to make speech possible.

"I was one of Bongos' followers. lived with the other Bone Gnawers in Golden Gate Park." He took a moment to catch his breath.

"And. . ."

". . . and Bongos found me smoking crack. He hates the shit and anyone who uses it. He kicked me out of the pack, blackballed me."

Oldman looked beneath the Gnawers' muzzle and for the first time saw the black eight-ball fetish hanging there by a thick black cord. "And still you remain?"

"What better way to obtain my revenge against Bongos and the rest of the pack than to kill off members of his flock, one by one?"

His flock — and mine, thought Oldman. "Then you're lucky I found you before he did. He would have had you killed."

The Bone Gnawer smiled, as if he thought he was going to be set free without punishment.

Oldman felt sorry for the mangy, jackal-faced Garou. Being blackballed from a pack of Bone Gnawers was about as low as a Garou could fall. Oldman toyed with the idea of trying to rehabilitate this mutt as he'd rehabilitated similarly troubled humans, but he knew it would never work. He'd been blackballed, a lost cause, hardly even worthy of the title of Garou. Still, he looked upon the Bone Gnawer with sympathy rather than contempt.

He squeezed his throat hard, releasing his grip only when several tracheal bones had been crushed.

"Consider this a warning," Oldman said. "The Tenderloin isn't a place for blackballed Bone Gnawers. If Bongos doesn't want you around, then neither do I. I suggest you leave as soon as you can. If I find you here again, you'll wish I had killed you this time around."

Oldman grabbed the Bone Gnawers' right forearm and chomped down on the hand with all his might. With two powerful jerks of his head, he tore the hand from the wrist.

Blood spurted from the fresh, red stump. The Gnawer screamed.

Oldman choked off the scream with his hand and spat the Gnawers' bloody hand from his mouth. It landed on the alley floor with a wet and meaty slap, then lay there twitching in a growing pool of blood.

"To remember me by," Oldman said, getting off the Bone Gnawer. "Now. Get out of here!"

The Bone Gnawer cradled his bleeding stump in his good left hand and ran, hunched over, from the alley.

Oldman rose up on his hind legs and looked down on the human lying amongst the garbage. The man's body was covered with bright red wounds. His breath was shallow. He'd lost too much blood while Oldman had dealt with the Bone Gnawer and was already going into shock.

And his eyes were glazed over, blinded by the Delirium.

He was too far gone. Even for Oldman's special salves and creams to remedy.

"Help me," the human cried weakly.

Oldman looked upon the man with pity.

"I will end your suffering," Oldman whispered.

His lips pulled back and his fangs glistened in the moonlight. ///

For Auld Lang Syne

by James A. Moore

I

Gabriel White stared at the distant island of Alcatraz and found himself wondering what it must have been like to be a prisoner there. He had heard all the stories, even seen most of the movies about how harsh prison was supposed to be, but still he wondered. Gabriel had always been a very curious boy.

Gabriel tore small pieces of sourdough bread from a loaf purchased earlier and tossed them into the waters at the edge of the wharf. In a matter of seconds, the waters seethed with anxious seagulls fighting over the scraps he threw. The gulls started by grabbing what was in the waters, then by hovering around Gabriel, discovering that he was the source of all the food. Stan and Teri were beside him, and he tore off large sections for each of them so that they could feed the birds as well.

The three of them looked as if they belonged on a postcard: shorts, T-shirts, sandals, and all three with hair almost bleached white by the summer sun. A passing tourist decided that they should be a postcard, and snapped a picture of them at the end of the pier. They never noticed; they were busy with the birds.

When the bread ran out, the seagulls let out a raucous protest that would have made Alfred Hitchcock proud, and the youths were forced to leave the vicinity or face the risk of pecked fingers and arms (the gulls could be downright nasty when they didn't get their way). Teri smiled shyly at Gabriel, and Gabriel returned the smile; if Stan noticed, he was kind enough not to say anything. Gabriel wondered what it would be like to kiss her lips.

They started walking along Mason Street, heading back toward the cable cars. It was getting close to dinner time, and none of their respective parents liked people being late for the evening meal. Besides, most of their money had already been spent on bread for the seagulls and prawns for lunch. It added up all too quickly. But there was always enough left for the cable cars. None of them wanted to walk these hills in a hurry; they'd be exhausted by the time they got home.

Stan hopped off the car first, waving a casual goodbye, and tried to suppress a smile. Knowing what the smile was for, Gabriel and Teri pretended not to see it, and wrapped their hands together for the remainder of the trip. They stayed that way until they reached Washington Street, the end of the line.

The kiss they shared was tentative and quick, and both of them blushed horribly. Teri was on her way east, Gabriel on his way west, before either of them could consider repeating the action. Gabriel's mind had done that first kiss no justice, but he felt like the king of the world as he wandered in the general direction of home.

"Gabriel White?" The voice came from his left, and he turned to see who was talking to him.

"Yeah?" The man looking at him was only a few inches taller. Even at only 14, Gabriel was close to six feet in height. Light gray cotton suit, sunglasses with polarized lenses, 5:00 shadow — he looked like an extra from *Miami Vice*, right down to the designer tennis shoes. "Can I help you?" The man just kept staring, at least he thought he was staring, Gabriel couldn't really tell past the mirrored lenses.

"Are you Gabriel White?" The man had a pleasant voice, soothing to hear.

"That's me." The man smiled, nodded. Gabriel felt powerful hands grab him by the arms from behind, and lift him off of the ground. The man walked calmly toward a van parked across the street and opened the door. The hands that held Gabriel were strong and big, the long fingers painted with a lavender nail polish. Gabriel lashed his head backwards in an attempt to knock his captor on the jaw, but whoever the guy was, he was too fast. Panic started in Gabriel's gut, pulled at his bowels and pushed his pulse into overdrive.

The man in front was still smiling even as the other one tossed Gabriel into the back seat of the Aerostar. Before he had recovered from the bouncing, the back door was slammed and locked. Gabriel reached for the handles to let himself out, but there were none to grab. He scurried toward the front of the van, hoping to maybe lock them both out, but it was too late; the *Miami Vice* extra and a petite brunette in her thirties were both climbing in. Gabriel looked at the brunette's hands; they were delicate, model's hands. They bore the same color of lavender polish as the bruiser who could not be seen.

Gabriel tried to attack the woman; he had to get home, back to his mom and dad, back to safety. If he was fast, he could get out the door before she closed it.

The man with the sunglasses hit him in the back of the head, and then the sweetly smiling woman pushed him into the back again. She was saying something, but he couldn't hear her. His ears were ringing too loudly. The man was holding a gun, shaking his head sadly. Gabriel froze. H didn't want to die. The man pulled the trigger, and a few seconds later, Gabriel knew only the darkness.

None of them noticed Maria Alverez watching. They were long gone when she called the police a few moments later to report the kidnapping. Had Gabriel been around to see what his old babysitter was doing, he'd have praised God for the woman's existence.

II

Samuel Haight stared at Robert Crombey's open, friendly face, reading all that he could from his associate. His 43 years of harsh experience focused on the young man, stared past the friendly eyes and the freckles, pried past the unruly blond hair. After a few moments, Haight nodded his head and sighed. "It's a deal. Three different types of vampire blood and meat and blood from all of the Garou tribes." Haight noticed the curiosity in their eyes at the mention of different tribes of werewolves, but didn't volunteer to elaborate.

Crombey smiled in return, slapped Haight's shoulder affectionately "That's great, Sam. Believe me, you're doing the right thing."

Haight looked around the clinic, absorbing every detail, filing the information for any time in the future when it might become necessary. Several other men and women stood around — most, like Crombey, dressed in business suits and wearing lab coats. They, too, seemed pleased with his decision. "Let's take a look at what I'm buying then, shall we?"

"Absolutely. He's right over here, Sam." Crombey led the way, followed by Haight and the gaggle of employees at Developmental Neogenetics Amalgamated's clinic.

Haight smiled to himself, nodding almost imperceptibly. If DNA kept their part of the deal, he would have no real worries about the future.

Past a set of heavy sliding doors, guarded by a voice monitor and a retinal scanner, was the room where all of Samuel Haight's dreams for the future would be realized. Haight, Crombey, and the rest paused long enough to slip into surgical scrub gear before Crombey allowed anyone near the inner room. It only took Robert Crombey a few seconds to get past the security systems and into the room. The laboratories behind the doors were all but his private haven these days. The room was almost painfully sterile; no signs existed to indicate that a living, breathing person had ever walked here before. No personal touches rested anywhere in the room. That was just as well, since personal objects would have simply added to the possibility of contamination in the circulated germ-free air.

With a characteristic sweep of his arm, Crombey pointed to the cylindrical tank occupying a large section of his lab. "Here he is, Sam. Ain't he a thing of beauty?" Within the tank, connected to a placenta growing from a nest of wires, was a young adult male. His eyes were open, but saw nothing. His muscular chest moved with regular motions within the vitamin-rich fluids. His black hair danced on waves that could not be seen by the naked eye. Samuel Haight stepped closer to the tank and stared deeply into the unlined face, soaking up every detail and reveling in the figure's perfection.

"He's perfect. At least at first glance." Haight allowed himself to smile. "Cellular density?"

"Up 25% from the norm, just like you asked. I figure this fella ought to be able to lift somewhere in the neighborhood of 500 pounds without breaking a sweat." The pride in Crombey's voice was evident, and as far as Sam could tell, was well placed.

"Vision?"

"Right at 20/20. Enhanced spectrum into the ultraviolet and infrared. This little guy can probably see colors we never even knew existed." Crombey's Southern drawl became more evident as his chest swelled. "Before you ask, his hearing's a mite better than yours, and his sense of smell is about 150% of your human level. Also, his biological clock's gonna tick at about a third the rate of yours. Hell, Sam, you're talkin' 'bout a 200-year life span, if you're talkin' 'bout a day. Overall, he's five times the man you are physically, and you ain't exactly what I'd call a shabby-looking guy."

Haight looked over at his associate, slowly scanned the rest of the faces in the room, and finally came to rest on Crombey's face again. Crombey's face twitched; he was nervous. That was a normal reaction from anyone who knew Sam's history and the primary reason for the business transaction that was taking place. "Let's see the codes you used, I want to double check everything."

Crombey chuckled softly. "Shit, Sam. If I didn't know better, I'd think you didn't trust me." Despite the words, Crombey went over to his list of clipboards hanging on hooks near the tank and pulled down three of them.

The entire group watched Sam nervously. They had been warned of his rather unique talents by Robert Crombey, a man fortunate enough to have witnessed Haight in action — and from the proper distance. Haight scanned the data on the three files and ignored the nervous fidgeting of those around him. His eyes finally caught what he had expected and he turned to Crombey. "What the hell is this?" he demanded.

Crombey stared at the original genetic patterns they had agreed upon, looked at the second pattern — the one that had actually been used — and noticed the spot where Haight's finger tapped at a subtle discrepancy. "Oh, that. Uh, standard operational procedures, Sam. Just a little genetic command to assure that you won't cause us any grief later." Sam tossed the genetic maps on the floor and walked over to the tank again, staring with more intensity than he had before, seeing beyond what a normal person's sight would allow him to see.

Crombey said, "Look, Sam, it's done to all of them; not just yours. We have to protect ourselves — you of all people can understand that."

"Shit, Robert," Haight mimicked, eyes wide with feigned innocence and voice thick with a southern drawl. "If I didn't know better, I'd think you didn't trust me." Haight turned and grinned at the people around him, laughing. Many nervous chuckles erupted into the air, all but drowning out his own laughter. "You've got a deal, folks. I'll take him."

The exchange of goods was made, and Samuel Haight left with a truck that carried his prize. Within a few hours all of his business in San Francisco was taken care of, save for a little shopping for materials that he would need later and a small bit of research that had to be finished.

He rewarded himself with a dinner fit for a king, and settled in his rented apartment with a satisfied smile — just in time to watch the news, just in time to see a face from his past reach out from the television screen and feel the strings still attached to his heart give a fierce yank. "Oh shit," he groaned sitting up straighter and punching the record button on his VCR. "Diane? What the hell are you doing in San Francisco?"

The television image of Diane White answered his question a few seconds later, with her impassioned plea for the kidnappers to return her son. A smiling clod with perfect teeth and a $400 jacket explained a few seconds later that no ransom note had been issued as yet.

Samuel Haight dressed himself quickly in dark gray clothes, making sure that he was properly armed for an urban hunt; above and beyond all else, Haight was a hunter. Tonight his prey would learn quickly the error of stealing from someone that Samuel Haight cared deeply for.

III

John and Diane White were understandably worried. Less than 10 minutes after the old babysitter had come into the apartment and told them what she had seen, the police had arrived, placing men around the house and doing their best to stop the newshounds from becoming a nuisance. The effort was appreciated, but the press was already a blessing in their eyes. Every station had already run Gabriel's picture, every station had recorded and presented their empassioned plea for the safe return of their son. How could they refuse a few simple questions? John was chain smoking, and Diane wrinkled her nose in annoyance. She had quit over a year ago, and really hated the stench put off by the damned things.

"John, could you please not smoke in here?" She regretted the words as soon as they were out, braced herself mentally for his retaliatory arguments. John had been edgy lately, and he really had cut back on his smoking, but Gabriel's forced disappearance wasn't helping either of them.

John crushed the cigarette out without saying a word. He was too worried to fight, or even to glare. Both of Gabe's little friends had made it home safely, and Teri Johanssen only lived about five blocks away. In two and a half blocks, Gabriel had disappeared. "Where is he, Diane? Who would have done this?" Diane White stepped behind the chair where John had tossed himself, leaned over and hugged his neck and shoulders from behind. He leaned into her comfort.

They stayed that way for several seconds before the knock came at the door. The door was almost never locked, and a man stepped through before they could even say, "Come in." The man closed the door, nodding quickly and smiling tightly. "I just got your message. What's wrong?"

They both started at once, but John deferred to Diane to finish the statements. "Maria Alverez told us that he was taken, kidnapped. Shaun, help us, please."

Shaun Ingram looked at the anxious faces before him, did his ritualistic fast nod, and fired off several questions. "When did you last see him?"

"This morning, around 10."

"Did he say where he was going?"

"To the Wharf with Teri and Stan."

"Have you contacted Teri and Stan, or their parents?"

"Yes, both of them were home by 5:00."

"Where did they last see him?"

"Just over where the cable cars stop, just three blocks away." Diane begged with her eyes. John covered his face with his hands. "Oh, Shaun, you've got to find my little baby. Where could they have taken him?"

Shaun held Diane's hands in his own for a second, and, as always, she was surprised that the blunt and scarred hands could be so gentle. He smiled, and his blue eyes danced with sincere affection behind thick red eyebrows. Diane was again reminded of leprechauns; he always made her think of leprechauns. "Don't you worry. If he can be found, I'll find him." He gave John another quick nod, threw a brief hug around Diane's shoulders. Before another word was spoken, all of Shaun's short, heavy body had bolted through the front door.

Diane hugged her husband again. He leaned against her. Both were still nervous; both still feared for their son, but they were more relaxed now. If Gabriel walked through the doors, they would be there, waiting for him. If he had been taken away, or if he was hurt and could not make the distance home, Shaun would find him. Shaun was a private detective. He was also their friend and their next door neighbor. He had always looked after them, and especially after Gabriel. If anyone could find their son, it was Shaun. John stood up and lit another cigarette, this time stepping out the front door to smoke it. Diane lit one and joined him. She could always quit again tomorrow — after they had their baby back.

IV

Shaun Ingram carried a roll of clothes in his muzzle, too hurried to find a safe place to put them. He couldn't decide if he was angrier with himself, or with the fools that had taken Gabriel. In any city but San Francisco, he would have called the hunt hopeless. But here, there just weren't that many cars to follow. Most people took taxis to wherever they were going. Most people couldn't stand the hills that tore car suspensions into debris at a phenomenal rate. The van was leaking oil, and that made the hunt easy.

A man dressed in blue jeans and nothing else reached out to pet Shaun as he rested for a moment. Apparently thinking that he was just a big and somewhat stupid dog, the man tried for the bundle of clothes in his maw. Shaun stood up and growled a warning. The man called him several words that at another time would have gotten him torn apart. Shaun Ingram trotted on his way.

Shaun Ingram was also Garou, a ronin, a werewolf who ran without a pack. It was necessary that he run alone, for his own tribe hated him, and most others both hated and feared him. Shaun Ingram was one of the Wyrm-corrupted, a Black Spiral Dancer. Once, he had been like the others of his tribe, ready to destroy all that was natural, all that was healthy in the world. Now, he knew that what the others of his tribe desired was insane: destruction for the sake of destruction. The Wyrm, the great corrupter — call it death, entropy, or a hundred other names; none would do it justice — had pushed too far with Shaun. It had shown itself for what it really was, and in the process, had driven Shaun away from its nest of death.

Shaun Ingram intended to see that it never got its fangs into Gabriel. The boy was so rare, so pure, a deviant from another time, before the White Howlers had fallen to the Wyrm. He prayed that he would reach him before the boy's true father did. Shaun's ex-packmate was a beast, a savage killer. He increased his pace, pushing himself to find the boy before it was too late.

V

Samuel Haight stared at the front of the White's house and waited. He ignored the Halloween decorations, the children dressed in costumes and being dragged around the area by their parents — all save the odd child in the Terminator mask, the one who's left eye glowed red. That one had walked right up the sidewalk, just as happy as any of the other kids on the street, had even waved at Samuel where he was perched in the shrubs. No one was supposed to see him, strange eye or not, and Sam took the hint and moved to a better position a few feet away.

Just around the time when he thought all of his waiting would be in vain, the small pack of werewolves made their presence known. Again he studied them, double-checking what he already knew to be accurate; they stank of the Wyrm's touch. Potentially, they were allies, ready to kill all of the foul werewolves in San Francisco. But Samuel Haight was not on his sacred quest that night; he was out simply to help a friend.

Ask a werewolf if Samuel Haight had any friends, and they would like as not reply that his only friend was his reflection. Surely, he could not have friends. Surely, any rational soul would know that what Haight wanted in the world was nothing less than insane. Of course, as the target of Sam's personal passion, the eradication of all werewolves, the Garou were hardly unbiased in their opinions. Not that they could be blamed; no one likes the thought of being killed for the skin on their back.

But Haight did have friends — some from childhood, some from his time in the business world, and some, like Diane Anderson White, from his days in college. It was fair to say that most of Haight's friends did not take priority over his mission, but most were not also his first love.

Diane Anderson was the only person Samuel Haight could remember who had ever made him feel needed. Back in his college days Diane had been the only person he cared about. And even before then, back in high school, she had been one of the few people he would have called a friend.

Samuel had proposed to her, asked if she would marry him when the college days were gone and his sports career had taken off, and she had said, "Yes." Once, he had wanted only to spend his life with her, raising children and being a couple. Then the world had thrown another hardball at Samuel Haight and crippled his knee, destroying his fledgling career before it could begin. He tried to pull away from the memories of her tears as he broke the engagement off. What woman would want a failure as a husband? But the memories were stronger than he could handle with ease. So many years alone; so many years without her. He felt the old familiar ache in his chest again and finally forced it from his mind.

One of the Dancers knocked on the door. Samuel Haight tensed and waited. Soon enough he would know their intentions.

VI

The knock at the door was brisk and overly strong. John White prayed it wasn't the police with the news that his son was dead. He answered the door quickly, closing his eyes for only a second, willing the grim face of a policeman from his mind. Behind him, he could hear Diane letting out the breath that she had held tightly in her lungs.

The man who stood at the threshold was not a policeman. He was tall, lean, and hard, almost gaunt in appearance. His long, gray hair was pulled back haphazardly in a ponytail. His face was warm and friendly, surprisingly wide on so narrow a body, and his eyes glittered with a secret mirth.

"May I help you?" John felt at ease with the man, he had that type of face.

"I hope so. I'm looking for the White residence."

"You found us. I'm John White. This is my wife, Diane." John gestured to Diane, and she smiled faintly. The man nodded back.

"I'm Edward McTyre. I'm looking for Gabriel White. I'm his real father, and it's time for us to meet."

The words shocked John, and for the first time he noticed the resemblance, vague though it was, to Gabriel. "Um, I'm afraid I don't know what you mean."

"Bullshit," Edward said, with the same friendly smile, the same mirth in the eyes. "You adopted your son 14 years ago. I'm the real father, and I want to meet my son."

"Get out of here, before I call the police." John White found himself suddenly very angry. He had no desire to see this man, and even less desire for his son to meet him. They had never told Gabriel, they had no reason for telling him. How the hell had the man found out? "Did you hear me Mister McTyre? I want you gone, now, or I call the police."

Before McTyre could respond, Diane White charged forward. Her voice was faint in comparison to her husband's, but the message came through loud and clear. "What did you do to our son?" Her voice trembled, nerves on edge pulled even tighter.

John White listened to her words with dawning horror. Dear God, had the man. . . ?

Edward McTyre slid into the room, moving with ease past the momentarily stunned John White. He looked down at Diane with a serene smile. "Nothing, yet." He reached behind himself, closed the door, twisted the deadbolt in place. John White reached for him, grabbed hold of his arm, and pulled him away from Diane.

"Where is he!" John screamed, his anger fogging the room in red. The smile on McTyre's face became a smirk. McTyre's body started twitching, small muscle spasms running across his entire form. He seemed somehow heavier than he had a minute before. His face now matched the rest of his body, rather than seeming too large.

"John, John, John." he shook his head as he spoke. The voice was at least two octaves deeper than it had been. "Isn't that what I just asked you?"

John and Diane White watched the change take place, watched a man become a monster. Bat-like features grew on Edward McTyre's face. Gray fur sprouted on his body, and his whole shape changed enough, grew enough, to make them both feel helpless.

The voice that came from the bat-thing was warbled and distorted, but still intelligible. Both of the White's were pulled close in a friendly embrace. The eyes were the worst, despite a pale green fire that burned low within them. They still held that same amused smile. "Wasn't I just asking you where my son could be found? Hmm?" Long, taloned fingers stroked John's cheek, and he shivered, his mind denying what was happening. The other hand of the beast gently teased at Diane's breast, and she slapped frantically to get the hand away. The bat-thing looked her way, and the smiling eyes leered. "Tell me, Diane, which one of you is infertile? Hmm?" Diane's eyes grew wide, and John started to struggle, finally accepting that even nightmares could have serious implications. "Either way, why don't we pretend it's John?"

Gripping Diane by one thick claw, pinning her against the wall, the freakish nightmare grabbed a handful of John White's hair and started pulling, forcing the man's head back and exposing his neck. Corded muscles stood out, arteries pulsed with blood. The beast's cavernous mouth of fangs lowered slowly over John's throat. Diane started to plead. John started to whimper.

Then all hell broke loose.

VII

Haight stared at the Black Spiral Dancers, watching them with narrowed eyes as they surrounded the house. A quick look around confirmed what he already knew: the children were long gone from the streets, and their parents along with them. Moving carefully, Sam slid out from the shrubs, readying himself for action. Despite the danger to Diane, despite the open area, Samuel Haight smiled as he slipped the silencer onto his Desert Eagle .44. Four Garou against his hunting skills. He was almost tempted to give them advanced warning to even the odds.

The Dancers were still in their human forms, waiting for the one inside, when Sam attacked. That was good. If he waited too long, they could change shape; then they would be able to regenerate. Sam decided not to wait. Haight braced himself and stepped into the light. The pistol was aimed almost casually in the small pack's general direction. Samuel heard screams from inside the house.

"Dancers! Look at me!"

The three figures turned, staring at the figure bold enough to confront them. Two started shapeshifting instantly. One stepped forward and called forth a challenge. "Who are you?" The man wore what had to be the typical garb for the Dancers: a dirty pair of jeans and a scruffy leather jacket that was a few sizes too large. Sam watched the man's hand slide into his jacket, no doubt reaching for a weapon.

Haight fired. The two who were changing, growing larger and bulkier, were bathed in viscera from the man's head and chest, and both felt the pain of silver creasing skin as the bullets passed through their companion's body. They looked down at their packmate, then back over at Sam. His smile grew wider. "My name's Samuel Haight."

The one on the left stared at him with eyes grown wide and bolted. The one on the right soon followed, screaming as he went. "Skinner! Skinner!" Sam shot them each once, directly through the backs of their skulls. The front door to the house exploded open. From the opening came the gray form of the one that had stepped inside. He was fully changed, unlike his dead friends. Samuel Haight stared at the demonic thing before him and grinned. The werewolf stared back, eyes burning with hatred, mouth open, and misshapen fangs glistening with moisture.

The last Dancer looked at the dead werewolves and watched as they slowly changed into their natural forms. He threw his head back and howled. The sound was high-pitched, a desperate cry for help. Haight knew the calls of the Garou well enough to know that others would be coming to this one's aid. Either that or the deformed beast was bluffing. The station wagon that came around the corner at high speed, with guns blazing, told him that there was no bluff.

Haight moved, dropping down to the ground and rolling back toward the bushes he had left a few minutes before. Glass, concrete, and pieces of the brick wall behind him left their traditional positions, moved forcibly by the impact of bullets meant to cut him in half. Haight chided himself for getting cocky, pulled into a fetal position, and waited for the sound of the wagon's tires peeling away.

When he finally risked a quick look, he saw the Ford's taillights rounding the corner in the distance. Haight felt fabulous; a good jolt of adrenaline always did that for him. Double checking the area as quickly as he dared, he saw that the Dancers had taken their fallen packmates' bodies with them. "Shit. What a waste of good pelts." He shook his head ruefully as he headed toward the house of Diane White and her husband. One more quick look at the road, at the buildings where lights were coming on, and Sam knew he'd have to move quickly. Already the werewolves knew he was in town. The last thing he needed to add to the equation was a bunch of policemen thinking he was a gun-happy burglar.

Samuel Haight stared through the open front door of the house, stared long and hard at the woman who cradled her husband's bleeding corpse in her arms and cried. Long, jagged gasps were the only sound she seemed capable of. Sam approached slowly, shaking his head. "Oh, Diane. I'm so sorry."

The woman looked up at the sound of his voice. Sam was reminded of the past, one of the fews times in his life when he could remember being happy. Her face was older, softened by gravity and years, but otherwise she was still the same, still beautiful, even past the tears and pain so prevalent. Sam felt his knees weaken a little, felt his heartbeat grow a little faster. Years had passed — over a decade — and still she made him nervous.

"Sam? Sam Haight?"

"Yeah. It's me, Diane. I'm sorry. I was too late to help you." Samuel Haight felt his facial muscles pull in ways he was no longer used to, felt his eyes start to burn as he shared the woman's grief. "I saw on the television that your son's missing. I came to help." He turned away from her, the memories stronger than he wanted, strong enough to fog his ability to think clearly. "It's too late for your husband, but maybe not for your son. Come with me. We'll see if we can find him."

Diane started to protest, started searching for words. "Now, Diane. Please, before it's too late for the boy too."

Without waiting any longer, Samuel Haight stepped from the house, forcing himself to concentrate. The trail was still warm. The air still smelled of blood and cordite. If he worked quickly, he would be able to find the Ford's trail.

VIII

Gabriel White burned with fever, his sweat-soaked body trembled. Lois Penobscott stared back at him from the passenger's seat. Beside her Allen Sothersby stared at the traffic on all sides of them and ignored the two. The traffic was completely unmoving on the Golden Gate

Bridge. A heavy fog cloaked the entire area, and they had been stuck for over an hour. The Muir Woods National Monument was still too far away, and they needed to get the boy there, needed to get him to those who could teach him properly.

"It was stupid of us to stop at the apartment." Lois was scolding herself again. "We should have taken him straight away. We should have thought this through better."

"For the last time, we didn't exactly have a great deal of warning."

Lois started to unbuckle herself, a faint whimper of confusion coming from her throat. She looked at Allen and groaned as the seatbelt slipped into its holding place with a faint sigh. "The fog is thick. No one will see us if we carry him across the bridge." Her tone of voice said she wasn't happy with the idea. Allen wasn't thrilled either, but he nodded his assent anyway.

"We should have tried for the Big Basin sept. Less traffic."

"Like I said before, Allen: the last thing the boy needs is to be in the hands of the Get. They're as bad as the Dancers."

Allen grunted his agreement as he slipped out of his jacket and the van. "It's gonna have to be Crinos. It's the only way I can carry him and still move with any speed."

Lois nodded in the heavy, white mist, sighing as she slipped out of her Gucci blouse. "Let's just get this done. If the fog lifts before we get there, there's going to be a big mess."

Both were changing, reveling in the feelings that flooded into their bodies as they grew larger and far more powerful, when the voice came out of the darkness. The voice was harsh, filled with anger and, to their sensitive ears, did not come out of a normal mouth. "You can go on your way, but the boy stays here. I've got a bead on your pretty little head, Lois. Don't make me pull the trigger."

The fog made the voice hard to find. Allen spoke up quickly, his words coming out as deep and as menacing as a roll of thunder off of the distant hills. "Ingram? Shaun Ingram? Is that you?" Contempt made the words even more threatening.

"Aye, it's me, Sothersby. Step away from the van and keep those paws of yours over your head." Sothersby looked all around, futilely trying to place the area where Ingram was hiding. He moved to his right, bumping into a barely visible Toyota. Inside, the driver pushed angrily at the horn. Several more horns sounded in response. Any chance he had actually had to find the voice by hearing alone was lost in the cacophony. Allen slammed his fist into the car's hood. The driver let out a yelp and locked the doors.

"Sothersby, be smart man. You'll never make the caern — not in this traffic."

"Get raped, Ingram. I'm damned if I need a traitor telling me how to operate. Why don't you step down here and let me explain a few things to you."

"You always were a jackass, Sothersby."

Lois Penobscott opened the back of the van, reached inside, and pulled at the feverish boy inside. Gabriel White moaned in his sleep, but did not awaken. Allen could see that she was nervous, and, trying to keep her calm, he called out another challenge to the ronin. "Why don't you come down here and prove yourself worthy of your title, Dancer?"

In the fog, there was the sound of a bolt being drawn. "I've a better idea. Why don't you have your mate put down the boy and back away before I spill her pretty brains all over the fucking asphalt."

The implied insult, the reference that maybe he and Lois were mates, breaking the laws of Gaia and committing incest, was not lost on Sothersby. Also, he had finally managed to locate the voice, ahead of him, possibly ten yards to his right, and 15 feet off the ground. In three steps and one jump, he could reach his target. "Lois, put the boy down. We could be here for a while."

"Allen, we don't have a while. We have to get moving."

Allen made as if to walk over to her faint silhouette through the wall of mist. Then he pivoted and ran toward the sound of Shaun Ingram's voice. Ingram got a few words out before he fired. "Allen, no! Don't make me do this." Then the bullet slammed into his side, and the silver burned into his stomach. Sothersby howled out his pain for all the world to hear. The people on the bridge heard the sound and cowered in their cars.

IX

As they approached the Golden Gate Bridge, Samuel Haight slowed his rental car substantially. Ahead of them the line of cars was completely stationary. Only a few at the tail end of the long line inched forward, as if their insistence would force whatever catastrophe blocked the bridge to move itself a little quicker. The area around the bridge's site was sheathed in fog, thick and white like cotton balls. The area to the left or right a hundred yards beyond the bridge was clear. The same again above the bridge, the fog just stopped a little past where the edges of the suspension cables would be if they could be seen.

Haight looked at the cars in front of him, scoped with his eyes, and saw at last what he was looking for: not 20 yards ahead of them, a battered Ford station wagon rested in the next lane over. The car was abandoned. "Diane?"

Diane took a few seconds to respond, lost as she was in her grief. "I'm sorry, Sam. What is it?"

"I want you to wait here, OK?"

"Where are you going, Sam?" There was panic in her voice, laced with heavy doses of hysteria and even anger.

"I'm going to get your boy. But I need you to wait here. I need to do this alone."

"Why? Why can't I come with you?" Just the promise that her son would be returned brought her back to the real world, made her more alert and able to think. Haight still wasn't willing to take any risks. Willingly or not, she was staying where she was.

"Diane, there are more of the monsters you saw earlier out there, and I need to stop them. But I can't stop them if I have to look out for you. Do you understand?" Haight heard the slight patronizing tone in his voice, wished he could stop it from being there.

"No monsters, terrorists. They were just terrorists." Diane had succumbed to the Delirium, her mind refused to believe in werewolves. Sam made a note to fix that later, if he ever came back this way again.

"Fine, terrorists. But I need to face them alone, I need to know you're safe, OK?"

Diane looked at him and smiled. God, even after so long she could make him weak. "Alright. But, Sam?"

"Yes?"

"Bring my baby back, OK?" She touched Samuel's hand. He felt the old, electrical current dance across his flesh. Diane was the only one to ever make him feel that way. "Bring me my Gabriel, OK?"

"I'll do my best." Samuel swallowed hard, forcing his heart back where it belonged. He touched her face for a second, then reached into the back of the car to pull out his equipment. "Don't you worry, Diane. I won't let you down again."

Without a backward glance, Haight charged down the slope toward the bridge. Just like always, he could feel himself starting to smile. A quick glance at the station wagon confirmed what he had hoped would be the case: beneath some old drop cloths rested the bodies of the three he had killed earlier. "Good, I hate to waste a good pelt." The words were false bravado; Haight was entering into a situation without having a chance to weigh all of his options. Nothing bothered him more than not knowing what he was about to encounter. Still, he had fought Garou before, and he had won, even when he was only a human. And he did have one edge, one he really hadn't expected. He thought back to the two Dancers trying to run earlier, one calling out in fear, calling out a title that was apparently meant for him: Skinner. He liked the sound of that. He liked the underlying threat in his newly acquired Garou name. "Skinner."

Sam dropped his bag next to the station wagon and pulled his supplies from inside. The assault rifle went across his back, and the sawed-off shotguns went into each hand. All were fully loaded with silver, and easily replaceable. If worse came to worst, he could throw them over the side of the bridge and use the knives.

When he hit the fog, he ignored the unnatural chill that lanced into his skin, and started the change into his full werewolf form. The adjustable band on the rifle pulled on his flesh, but he ignored the binding sensation as he walked onto the bridge proper. In the distance, he could hear the sounds of growls and yips of pain. Damn! They had started without him.

X

Shaun Ingram stared at the figure of his former friend lying in his own blood below him, and could have cried. This wasn't going at all the way he had planned. All he had wanted was to make them understand that the boy wasn't from any of their tribes, make them understand that the boy was a White Howler, a pure one from the days before the Howlers had learned to dance the Black Spiral. He had wanted to warn them. They had wanted no part of his warning, and now Allen Sothersby lay dead at his feet.

Once again the Wyrm had whispered in the recesses of his mind, and the Rage had taken control. Even after all of this time, the Wyrm could still sneak into him and cause him to lose control. From the south, from the direction of San Francisco proper, came the sound of wild howls and shrieks of fear, answers to Allen's cries of pain only a few moments before. The howls were made for communication, and the message was clear. The Black Spiral Dancers had arrived, and they planned to have their pure one. Worse still, the howls were familiar. The hideous sounds that covered the bridge came from his old pack.

Shaun forced his change, dropping from the support beam in the process. Lois Penobscott, blinded by the fog, called out, "Allen? Is that you? We've got serious trouble."

"It's me, Lois. Allen's dead, I had no choice."

"I'll see you dead you bastard." It was a promise, not a threat.

"Yeah, well I think that can wait until we're done saving Gabriel, don't you?"

"Is that your pack coming, traitor?"

"Ex-pack — you know that. Save the insults for later too, OK? Right now we need to protect Gabriel. Put him in the van."

"You don't have the right to tell me what to do. You sacrificed that right."

"Whatever. But if you try to use him as a shield, I'll kill you myself." He counted 10 as the howls came again, much closer than before, echoing unnaturally through the pea-soup fog. "They're almost here, Lois. You trust me or you don't, but be ready either way. Hide the boy. I'll do my best to stop them."

Lois Penobscott made no reply. She simply pushed the fever-stricken boy back into the van and locked the door. Many of the people on the bridge had turned on their lights in an attempt to see what was going on. Through the faint glow, they could see the Dancers approaching. Lois dropped low, crouching in preparation for a leap, Shaun lifted his rifle, aimed at the first shadow, and fired. No howl came to tell him he had hit. Instead, there was the sound of a woman crying in pain. He fired at the shadow again and heard the same voice grunt softly. Still the shadow approached. "What the hell?" he whispered. Suddenly, the form jerked violently, split in two, and flew at him and Lois both. He fired, emptying the load of bullets at the half that flew toward him.

The figure landed before him, riddled with bullet holes. The girl was dressed in blue jeans and a T-shirt, her make-up was smeared, and her body was covered in blood. Six bullet holes riddled the body of a teenage girl. Beside him, Lois went down in a flurry of blurred motion, one of the Dancers atop her. Teeth gnashed and claws tore into fur. Both snarled and roared as they fell.

Before Shaun could assist her, he heard the sound of metal collapsing, saw the figure of another Garou soaring towards him, and felt the claws of his ex-packmate sinking into his shoulders. There were too many, simply too many. Before he could slip from McTyre's grip, another Dancer stomped down hard on his momentarily exposed crotch. Shaun heard a high-pitched yelp explode from his muzzle before he felt the pain that came next — pain too intense and all-consuming to allow him even the liberty of catching his breath.

Next to him, only a few feet away, Lois Penobscott shrieked in pain as the last of the Dancers joined in the fray. He was glad to hear a return howl of pain from one of her opponents. Through partly closed eyes, he saw McTyre leaning in, close enough to smell the foul odor of his breath. "Well, lookee at what we have here. The great betrayer." Shaun felt his enemy's knee drive into his already tender crotch. He gasped weakly and pulled into a fetal position. "How they hangin' bro?"

Shaun felt the strong steel cable go over his arms, felt himself turned over and yiped as his arms were hauled behind his back. The pain was too much; he couldn't even manage to resist. Just to ensure that it stayed that way, one of them kicked him in the balls again. The cable snaked between his legs and around his neck again, and Edward "Oorock" McTyre, showed him the slip knot that assured he would behave. Any shift in form would at the least cause him intense pain, but in all likelihood would strangle him and snap his neck. "This is a bonus. We've been looking for you, Shaun. You've been a bad, bad boy."

Looking over to his right, Shaun saw that Lois was in a similar position. Nothing would save them now. They were as good as dead.

XI

Haight looked on as the two downed Garou were pinned and tied; that would make his life much easier. The less of them that could fight back, the better. Then he moved, quietly sliding through the fog. The four remaining Garou busily stripped their opponents of any weapons they could find, taking liberties with their claws. The female was dead; just as well, her fur was rich and lustrous and would make a fine addition to Haight's growing collection. Part of him longed to join in on the fun, but he knew that time would not permit that. Besides —

one of them might know where the boy was located. Judging by the questions being asked between threats, he could safely assume that the victors in this little skirmish had no idea where Diane's son was hidden.

Sam came closer, and one of the Garou turned to look at him. Surprised by the sight of another Garou, the beast started to cry a warning to his comrades. Sam shoved the closest shotgun against his neck and pulled the trigger. Blood, gore, and bone mixed with silver shot and raced away from the beast's neck, but the body remained where it was, twitching and shuddering. The rest of the head flew into the mist.

The other Garou responded quickly, leaping to their feet and rolling away from the spot where the first of their pack had just died. Sam took aim at the closest one and fired from less than four feet away. Much as it pained him to ruin a fine pelt, he hit the Dancer in the chest, tearing vital organs asunder with the blast. The thing staggered backwards and slammed into a nearby van.

The last two Garou started circling Sam warily. The grin on Sam's face grew even broader. Apparently looking at the ground, Haight aimed at both of them, maintaining a stalemate — well, at least as far as the Dancers were concerned. To the one on his right, he pointed with the barrel of the shotgun. The beast twitched a little. Nervous, Sam noted mentally; a bonus in negotiations. He flashed a quick grin, shook his head. "Now, didn't I let you go earlier? Would you like to leave now and save yourself from a painful death?"

Edward McTyre, Oorock of the Black Spiral Dancers, snarled in response, baring teeth that were as foul as the rest of him. Haight lowered his shotgun and fired into the bastard's knee. The Dancer dropped like a falling tree, landing across a car where a dark figure behind the wheel squeaked in fright. His cries of pain were almost enough to make Sam take mercy on him and finish the job. Almost. Instead, Sam turned and fired the other shotgun at the Dancer that was now running pell mell away from him. He watched with satisfaction as the right hip vaporized under the silver onslaught, but the smile quickly turned to a scowl as the figure spun and fell off of the bridge's side. Damn, he thought. Another good pelt lost.

He turned back to face the last of the Dancers, just in time to get his face opened by its claws. "Damn! Goddamn your hide!" Haight dropped the useless shotguns as he kicked at the damaged knee on his opponent. The Dancer cried out and fell to the ground again, giving Haight a few seconds to deal with his own pain. It wouldn't heal quickly. The damage of a werewolves' claws was as severe as silver, and only time could heal the wound. He felt warmth running from his cheek, dribbling past his jawline, and allowed himself a bestial snarl.

Haight ignored the rifle still strapped across his back, and reached for his silver-plated skinning knives. It only took a few seconds to carve through the Dancer's hamstrings. It took a little longer to get past the arms and sever the tendons that led from back to shoulder. "You cut me you fuck! Goddamn you!" Able to move only its head, the Dancer still attempted to fight back. Sam could admire that, but still he was furious.

Such a fine silvery pelt, remarkably full for a Black Spiral Dancer. Ignoring the screams and the snapping jaws, Sam had him skinned in under two minutes. The one live Garou that still lay tied in place watched on, appalled beyond words. He watched the pelt get pulled free, and he watched the still struggling Dancer get tossed over the side of the bridge. A smile slowly spread across his face, until Sam turned fully his way.

Sam looked down at the hog-tied Garou and smiled congenially. "Hi. I'm going to make you a deal. You tell me where I can find Gabriel White, and I'll let you live. How's that sound to you?"

The werewolf groaned in response, and Sam noticed that the Garou had wet himself. The urine was tinted with red. Sam reached down and yanked hard at the injured Garou's ear. The beast turned and snapped. "Good, still plenty of spirit left in you. Listen, you go ahead and finish healing yourself, and then we can have a talk." He paused, then petted the Garou on the top of his head. "The first thing I want to know, is why you're being hunted by your own pack. Then we can move on to the boy. And if you're really lucky, I'll let you out of those bonds. "

From only a few feet away, the roof of the van screamed in protest as huge white-furred paws ripped the metal into confetti. A thunderous roar erupted from the hole where the roof had been, and a beast soon followed the sound.

Haight looked on as the White Howler pup climbed to the top of the vehicle, roaring defiantly and glaring at him with murderous rage. Haight stared at the beast as it dropped to the ground, felt the bridge beneath him shake from the impact.

Sam smiled, started pulling his skinning knives again. Beside him, still prone on the ground, Shaun Ingram cried out. "No! That's Gabriel White! That's Diane's son!"

Haight looked down at the man, shocked beyond words. Diane's son? A werewolf? Oh, but the irony was bitter.

"Please, I can help him. Don't kill the boy. Just hold him and let me talk to him." Samuel Haight shook his head, refusing to believe what was happening. He'd never meant to save a Garou — never in his life. His hatred of the beasts was legendary; his desire to see them all killed was a force of its own. How could this be happening to him — him, of all people? Oh, the Fates could play dirty when they felt the urge.

"Damn me for a fool." Haight tucked the knives back into their sheaths and prepared himself for the inevitable attack by the pup. Untrained in the ways of the Garou, the boy was likely in a great deal of pain, and in unfamiliar territory, he was likely feeling very confused and angry. Haight had fought many a Garou. Even as a human he had been good enough to win the fights, but this was different. This time he had to stop the damned thing without causing it any harm. And why was he going to so much trouble? Why avoid killing the stupid animal and taking its fine, snow-white pelt? He shook his head wearily as images of Diane Anderson ripped through his soul, and memories of Diane White holding her dear husband strobed through his mind. He would do this because of a woman, because of Diane.

Gabriel White, driven insane by the change that he could not have expected, looked at the man before him and charged, just as Samuel Haight was expecting. Being prepared made all the difference. Sam dropped the boy to the ground in one smooth motion and sank his fangs, hard enough to hurt, but not hard enough to kill, into the back of the White Howler's neck.

XII

Some time later, the ronin Shaun Ingram was released from his bondage. By that time Gabriel White had been subdued and helped through his first transformation back from Garou by, of all people, Samuel Haight. Gabriel was sore and confused, and called weakly for his mother. Samuel promised that he would be with her soon.

The night was almost over, and the fog was starting to thin. The bodies of the Dancers were skinned quickly, and after arguing vehemently for several minutes with

Shaun Ingram, Sam agreed to leave Lois Penobscott's hide intact. She was left in her van, along with the young woman that had been used as a shield and Allen Sothersby. The rest of the bodies went swimming in the bay, weighted down with steel cable and every heavy object that wasn't nailed down in the van. Sam watched them sink, satisfied that he had done well.

When the fog finally lifted, Samuel Haight and Shaun Ingram walked away from the bridge, supporting Gabriel White between them. Sam's new furs, wrapped in steel cable, followed.

Diane and her son were left in Ingram's care. Sam did not look at her, or speak to her. There were too many things that he wanted to say, too many choices that he did not want to make. Best to leave the past alone, he thought. His goals had been established and his sacred mission needed to come before anything else. Diane called out once, but Haight just walked faster, the bundle of furs dragging behind him.

Haight placed his equipment in the battered station wagon, unloading the additional pelts as well. He parked it a few blocks away, in the darkest corner of a parking garage that charged outrageous amounts for overnight parking. Before he left the garage the furs were treated and preserved, prepared for the next Rebirth. Five new skins; not bad for one night of hunting.

Samuel Haight left San Francisco. His shopping and research could be done in other places, at other times. His mind whirred helplessly, an endless stream of images trying to distract him. Maybe he would be back some other time, when the feelings overloading him were under control. Diane and her son would be cared for by the Dancer ronin, their needs provided for and their home defended from werewolves. Maybe he would see Diane and actually apologize for all he had done to her. Perhaps it was best to leave it all alone. Call it a favor done for old times' sake. He just didn't know.

Either way, there was too much to do. So many skins, so little time. ////

A Third World

by Graham Watkins

Halloween wasn't supposed to be like this, Rhetta Arquel told herself as she wiped at her eyes. Halloween was supposed to be fun. The nightmares were supposed to pretend; they weren't supposed to be real.

Huddled in the back of the truck as it streaked along a dark and mist-enshrouded Northern California highway, she stared through the steel mesh separating the compartment where she was from the front cab. She resisted the urge to beg with the two suited and stolid men seated up there; she'd been doing that almost since they'd left the environs of Oakland. They hadn't responded to her at all. They'd treated her exactly as if she was a caged animal.

You even look the part, she told herself ruefully. At 14 Rhetta had given up trick-or-treating as childish, but she'd still managed to find an excuse to dress in costume — the Halloween carnival at her school — and she was still wearing most of that costume, although the latex wolfman-head lay discarded on the floor of the truck some distance away. She glanced at it, then glanced down at her brown leotard. She would've liked to have taken it off but she was acutely aware that she wasn't wearing very much under it — she'd wanted the lines of the leotard to be smooth — and she certainly didn't want to give these men any ideas they didn't already have.

She shook her head. Wishful thinking; she'd known that since the men had kidnapped her almost from under the noses of her teachers and several parent chaperones. Reviewing the incident, she could not have imagined what she might've done to avoid it. The beginning had seemed — indeed was — so very innocent. One of the teachers had, on the spur of the moment, suggested something utterly silly: in keeping with Halloween celebrations (since there was a full moon, she'd noted), all those dressed in dog or wolf costume would participate in a howling contest. Laughing, Rhetta — as the wolfman, or, as she'd persistently reminded everyone, the wolfgirl — had, of course, gone outside with the rest. She had also, with an inspired performance that had startled even herself, won the contest.

From there, things took an unexpected turn, a terrifying turn. A man — an ordinary-looking man, a nice-looking man she'd taken for one of the carnival-goers parents — had approached her asking if she'd seen a boy "about this tall, brown hair, blue eyes, dressed in a vampire costume." She'd said, truthfully, no. The only vampire she'd seen at the carnival had been a much larger boy. The man, looking worried, had asked for help in searching for the boy, and, unafraid, she'd gone with him. The search had ended very abruptly. The man had led her to another man, a man standing beside a truck — the truck she was now in — which was parked out of sight of the school's entrance. Before she could react, before she could scream, she'd been seized, had been shoved into the truck, and the door had been closed behind her.

In one way, it hadn't even been too surprising. For quite a while — the last year or so at least — Rhetta had been constantly bothered by fears that she was being followed, that she was being watched. These fears she had confided to her parents, but they hadn't taken them seriously. She herself hadn't been able to dispel them. There was one man in particular; a slender, middle-aged, piercing-eyed man, who looked as if he might be Mexican or even possibly Indian — a man who, with his very dark eyes, his black hair, and his brown skin, resembled Rhetta herself. This man, it seemed to Rhetta, turned up everywhere; never close to her, always at a distance, but always there. Near her school, outside her home, at the mall when she was shopping with her parents or hanging out with her friends, even at the beach. Besides this man, there was a group of older teenagers, mostly boys. These wore the uniform of the "punk" crowd. Neither she nor any of her friends knew any of them. They were there almost every morning and every afternoon, silently watching her — or so it seemed to Rhetta, at least. But, like the Mexican, they never approached her; they never came close.

Now that she had, actually, been attacked, been kidnapped, Rhetta found herself totally confused. These men bore no resemblance whatever to the dark man or to the teenagers. Winding her fingers into the steel mesh behind the front seats, she pulled herself up close. "Please," she begged again. "Please, please, can't you at least speak to me? At least that? I'm so scared!"

The man in the passenger seat turned and looked at her. He was smiling, but it was a cold smile, an indifferent rather than a hostile smile. "Think we should talk to it, Jay?" he asked the driver, flicking his eyes her direction.

"Don't matter," Jay responded. "Do what you want, Stan. Me, I'm not interested. I'm sure not about to make a pet of it!"

"Stan" studied her face. "You sure do look like a plain, old little girl," he said conversationally. "Sure do. You'd fool most anybody."

Bewildered, Rhetta stared blankly at him for a moment. Through the windshield beyond his shoulder, the huge trees lining both sides of this forest road seemingly rushed toward the truck, dividing at the last moment to allow the vehicle to pass. Wisps of fog swirled in the headlights, bouncing the glare back, making the scene even more surreal. "W—what are you talking about? I don't understand—"

Stan laughed at her. "Oh, come on! Hey, there's no point in that! We all know what's what here, don't we?" He shook his head. "You got nerve, I'll give you that much. That howling contest! You went right out there and showed your stuff, didn't you? Thinking nobody'd know!" Pausing, he lit a cigarette and blew smoke back into her compartment. "You were almost right, though. Most people don't know. Most people got no idea. Most people wouldn't think anything of it. Thing is, we've had our eye on you for awhile. Didn't know that, did you?"

At last, there was something — at least — she could hold onto, however tenuous. "You've had your eye on me? Why?"

Stan chuckled again. "'Cause we suspected you were one of them. Our people are always looking for your kind, or didn't you know that? We were hoping to get a blood sample from you, but—" he made a helpless gesture. "That howl — that told the story. There wasn't a doubt after that."

She stared at him and at the taciturn Jay. Were they crazy? "Why," she asked carefully, "were you trying to get a—a blood sample from me?"

He frowned. "I just told you: to confirm things. We'll take it, up at the lab, soon as we get there. But we know how it's going to turn out. We know what it's going to show."

"What? What's it going to show?"

"Why, what you are, of course!"

She almost broke into tears. "I don't know what you mean! I really don't!"

"Oh, come on!" Stan snorted. "You know; you have to. You're Garou. Like I said, we all know that!"

"Garou? What's that?"

Now Stan looked a little confused. Again, he glanced at Jay. "Hey," he said slowly, "she really doesn't seem to—"

"They're smart," Jay said shortly. "Real smart. Don't forget it, Stan. In our line of work, forgetting that can be fatal."

"But maybe she doesn't—"

"She has to. Maybe she's never heard the word." Now, for the first time, Jay deigned to glance back at the terrified girl. "She is young, younger than any we've come across before. I guess maybe you could be right. Maybe nobody's ever talked to her. Not that it matters, Stan!"

The other man was looking worried. "But what if—?"

Jay grinned now — it was really an unpleasant expression — and tossed another quick look at Rhetta before turning his eyes back toward the road. "If," he said, "if we've made a mistake, well, then, you and me get to have some fun. Hell, we can't let her go, can we?" He glanced back again, his eyebrows hopping up and down. "It'd be all right with me. She's a pretty little thing, isn't she?"

"Yeah, but — but — afterwards, we'd have to—"

"Get rid of her. Sure. What else? Like I said, we can't let her go, no matter what!"

Rhetta gasped, rolled her lips in, fought for control. So cold, so cold! They were talking about raping her, about killing her, she couldn't mistake that! Killing her!

Unless — if she'd understood them correctly — she was a Garou, whatever that was. "Please," she asked, trying to speak in a steady voice and almost succeeding. "Please, I really *don't* know. I've never heard that word before. You can tell me. What will it hurt?"

"What will it hurt, Jay?" Stan asked.

Jay shrugged. "Nothing. Nothing that I can see. You can—" He looked over into the truck's side mirror and squinted; the squint changed to a frown, then deepened. "First things first, though," he observed, watching the mirror and letting the truck slow a little. "Those lights back there; they've been with us a long time. A real long time."

Half turning in his seat, Stan looked past Rhetta, out the back glass behind her. He nodded. "Garou?"

Rhetta looked too, and she started to ask again what these mysterious "Garou" were, but, for the moment, she held her tongue. The men were distracted; interrupting now might well annoy them, and that she did not want to do. Besides, she was not unaware that their distraction might, just possibly, offer her some sort of an opportunity for escape. The surrounding forest might have been intimidating, but she wasn't sure there was anything more dangerous out there than the two men who held her captive.

"Can't rule it out," Jay was saying. "I'm sure enough nobody from that party followed us, but those things, they have their ways — you know that."

"Can't be," Stan argued. "If it was, they'd be trying to stop us. They'd know where we were going."

"Maybe. Maybe not." He grimaced. "And, as to them trying to stop us, you just remember: we don't know what's waiting for us on up the road!" He nodded toward the mirror. "Safe way is to assume, for now, that that's who they are, that they know we've got a cub, and that they know right where we're headed. They'll put a lot into trying to stop us from getting there! I think maybe you ought to call in for some backup, Stan."

"Chopper?"

"Yeah."

Businesslike now, Stan picked up a cellular from the console between the seats and dialed a number. "Yeah," he said when a voice crackled in his ear. "This is Marston, Developmental Neogenics Amalgamated, Spec Op number FG-60692. We have a code 37 Charlie X-Ray. We need a pickup." He paused. "Right. Our route is on file, we've listed it by secure line. We are. . . let's see. . . currently one hundred twelve point eight seven miles from our turn into Area J4." Again, he paused, listened. "Right. We'll set a beacon and we'll start looking for your light, 12 to 16 miles." He glanced at Jay, who nodded. He then hung up the phone. Rhetta, watching and listening, saw him reach under the seat and draw out what looked to her like an Uzi. While she suppressed a gasp, he took a clip of bullets from the glove compartment and examined them. The silvery tips glistened brightly in the subdued light of the truck's cab. After slamming the clip into the gun, Stan extracted another, almost identical, from under the seat and slipped a clip into it as well.

Holding it up, he grinned at Rhetta. "Your friends back there," he told her, "won't be expecting these!"

"I don't think," she answered shakily, "that those are friends of mine back there. I think maybe it's the police!

Maybe you should just stop, give up, then nobody'll get hurt!"

Simultaneously, both of the men exploded into uproarious laughter. "There's no chance," Stan said dryly, "of the police finding us out here! There's no chance of them even being after us without us knowing about it. We—"

"Hey," Jay cut in. "Stop talking to her and keep a sharp eye out, will you? We've got 15 minutes to go before the pickup."

Stan, seemingly a little abashed, fell silent. Jay pushed the accelerator down, and the truck shot on down the road though the thickening fog. Behind them, the trailing lights at first fell back a little, then came gradually moving back up until a certain specific distance separated the two vehicles again. Stan and Jay did not miss it, and neither they nor Rhetta missed the significance of it. That vehicle back there was, indeed, following them. Even though Rhetta could not imagine worse company than her present, she felt her tension beginning to increase. Staring out at the trailing vehicle, she was taken completely by surprise when Jay suddenly hit the brakes.

Stan shouted something unintelligible; the truck began to skid, sliding sideways down the road. Whirling around, Rhetta saw that there was another truck up ahead of them: a big-wheeled pickup. It, too, was sitting sideways, blocking both lanes. Jay, coming around a curve, hadn't been able to see it until he was almost on top of it. Desperately, he fought the wheel. He pumped the brakes as the side of the other truck rushed toward them at a breakneck speed.

Then the wheels of the van caught, spun, slipped again, caught again. The vehicle lurched and headed forward, then began to slow down. Jay didn't quite manage to avoid hitting the other truck, but, in the end, it was only a hard bump, not a grinding collision. Rhetta was tossed forward against the steel mesh. The pickup bounced and slid a few feet. There was a sound of shattering glass. The glare of headlights ahead vanished. The van's engine sputtered and died, and for several seconds there was only darkness. There were no sounds except for the soft hiss of steam escaping from a small radiator leak.

"Shit," Jay muttered softly. "Shit." He leaned forward, turned the key. The engine rotated, but metal clanged noisily out under the hood.

"Radiator's jammed back against the fan," Stan noted. "It isn't gonna go." He looked out each of the front windows, then out the back. The headlights of the following car had vanished as well. By now, the tension among the three inside the van was almost palpable.

"We'll have to walk from here," Jay said flatly.

"We'll never make it! You know what this means!"

"Yeah." He threw Stan a sharp look. "But we *will* make it. We have an advantage, Stan: we know all about them and they know very little about us. We—"

"Some of them know all about us!"

Jay let out a disgusted snort. "Well, what the hell do you want to do then? Sit here and wait for them to come for us?"

Stan looked back at Rhetta. "No. No, you're right. Besides, we've got a hostage, haven't we?"

Jay grinned at her. "That we do. That we do." He plucked the cellular phone off its hook, made a call, reset the pickup point for a clearing, that, if Rhetta understood correctly, was about two miles up the road. Then he glanced around, out the windows. "OK, let's get out. You go first. Go get the cub out of the back." He pointed his gun at Rhetta. She shrank from the cold-looking muzzle. "I'll keep our bargaining chip covered until you can cover her outside."

"Got it," Stan agreed. He opened the door, jumped out. A second later she heard him unlock the back, and that door flew open. "Come on," he snapped, pointing his gun at her. Rhetta obeyed. A moment later they all three stood on the road, the trembling and terrified Rhetta between the two hard-faced men. Forcing her to move with them, they started turning in a slow circle, inspecting the surrounding woods. They'd only gotten halfway around when Rhetta caught a glimpse of a gray shape among the trees, a fleeting image of yellow eyes watching them, an image that was gone as quickly as it had appeared.

The men hadn't missed it either. "No doubt now," Stan muttered. "They're here, all right."

"Yeah," Jay agreed, his voice low. "You'd better keep your distance!" he shouted at the dark woods. With obvious menace, he pointed his gun at Rhetta's head. "I think you can see why!"

Rhetta's teeth chattered as she looked at the gun out of the corner of her eye and tried to make some sense of this. Maybe, she told herself, the men hadn't seen what she had. All she'd seen was, well, a coyote, probably — maybe a dog, maybe even a wolf. But that Jay was talking to it — that just wasn't reasonable. Even if it could understand, why would it care about her? While she was still trying to come up with an answer, one presented itself, from the woods near where she'd seen the animal. A man, a young man with glossy brown hair, stepped into sight. Rhetta stared. Clearly, Jay had seen him, but she hadn't even gotten a glimpse of him!

To her, he looked rather ordinary, and he certainly seemed to represent some possible hope. He looked to be wearing a forest ranger's uniform, or perhaps part of one.

"You must realize," he said in a quiet voice, "that you can't make it to your pickup point. You need to consider, gentlemen. What I'm telling you is in your own self-interest. Leave the girl and go. No one will stop you if you're alone."

Jay snorted. "Sure. What do you take us for…idiots?" He now pushed the gun's muzzle up into Rhetta's hair and hard against her head. "Now, you back off," he barked. "Back off, or—"

The man at the woods' edge remained quite calm. "We would much rather," he continued, "see you shoot her here and now than see you take her away with you. If necessary, we'll—"

"Please!" Rhetta shrieked, no longer able to control herself. "Please, please, help me. I don't want to die, please!"

"Shut up," Stan hissed. "Didn't you hear what he said? They want you dead!"

She looked around at him, wide-eyed. He had a sly grin on his face. "But why? Why? What'd I do? Who is he? Please, please, I don't understand!"

"He's lying to you, Rhetta," the man in the woods called. "Don't listen to him. It's just that we'd rather—"

"Shoot him, Stan," Jay ordered. He kept his own gun pressed firmly against Rhetta's head.

Stan obeyed instantly. The explosive sound of gunfire shattered the quiet of the woods. Rhetta screamed. She saw only a freeze-frame of the young man, dark patches decorating his shirt — which only now did she realize was torn — falling backwards into the brush. As the gun's sound died away, several new ones took its place. There was a soft moan from the brush where the man had fallen; there were sudden rustles among the trees from several sites around them.

And then there were howls: two or three of them, wolflike, in quick succession, dying away in a long harmonic chorus. Rhetta, more terrified than ever, shivered at the sound, but, at the same time, she had the most peculiar urge to answer those mournful calls.

"Jesus," Stan mumbled. "They're all over the place!"

"Yeah," Jay grunted. "Look, let's get moving. Both of you — you want to live? Then let's go!"

Rhetta, not knowing at this point where her interests lay, did not argue with him, did not struggle as they started moving past the pickup truck — which she now noticed had a forest service logo on its door — and on down the road. Ahead of them, the still-thickening mists swirled and surged over the pavement. Above, the full moon was, for the most part, casting enough light for them to see. At the same time it was imparting a silvery, otherworldly, sheen to the nearby trees. Among those trees, some thing or things were moving, paralleling them, tracking them, waiting, it seemed, for an opportunity.

"We won't let you go," a woman's voice called out, apparently from far away. "We won't! We'll see you all dead first! Give us the girl!"

"Jay," Stan quavered, "maybe we should give them—"

"No!" Rhetta shrilled. "No, please!"

Jay laughed harshly. "See? We can't. Wouldn't be the right thing to do, Stan!"

"But—"

"Don't worry. We're going to make it!"

Almost as he spoke, a dark shape shot out of the woods to their right, crossing into the road behind them. Stan spun around. His gun spoke again as the bullets caromed off the pavement. The shape, moving so fast it was hard to see what it was, entered the forest on the other side. As it went, something else erupted in front of them. No longer able to make progress, they were reduced to whirling around in a circle, trying to keep up with the elusive darting shapes, the shapes that were merely glimpsed, but never seen. Again and again Stan fired at them, but now he was hitting nothing.

"Stop shooting," Jay advised. "You're doing just what they want you to do: you're using up all your ammo. Once it's gone, we're sitting ducks."

"There's no way we can do this," Stan panted, whirling yet again to follow, without firing this time, another streaking dark shape. "No way. They'll wear us down before we get to the pickup."

Jay scowled at the dark forest. "No. We can. Maybe if we walk back to back, we—"

As if in argument, a gunshot rang out; a different, much heavier sound. Less than six inches from Stan's toe, a chip of pavement flew up into the air. Rhetta let out a little shriek. The men cursed.

"They're shooting at us!" Stan cried. "I didn't think they were going to be shooting at us! We can't stay out here in the open!"

"No, you're right," Jay agreed hurriedly. "Let's get back to the van!"

"You can't escape us!" the woman's voice, much closer now, called from the woods. "Give us the girl!"

The men didn't answer. With Rhetta between them they rushed headlong back to their truck — which wasn't far — and piled inside, Jay in the front, Stan and Rhetta in the back. Jamming the key into the ignition, Jay started the engine again. Metal still clanged, but the motor ran.

"All right," he said through the mesh. "It isn't going to go far, but it might go far enough!" Slamming it into gear, he backed up, then went forward and hit the forest service pickup again, near its rear. The van's wheels spun and the engine sounded like it was about to explode, but it pushed the other truck far enough that Jay was able to maneuver around it. From the woods, the rifle spoke again. One of the truck's front tires blew with a secondary loud bang. Gritting his teeth and cursing, Jay fought the wheel and plowed on, the truck listing badly as the wheel rolled on its rim. The gun barked out another shot and another tire blew, but Jay pressed on nevertheless.

A moment later, there was a sudden heavy *thump* on the van's roof. Simultaneously, Stan and Rhetta looked up. The man raised his gun, aiming it vaguely upwards.

Then, before he could decide where to shoot or if to shoot, the driver's-side window shattered. Rhetta stared, wide-eyed; a huge hand, covered with coarse gray hair and terrifying claws, came swiping inside. Jay yelled something unintelligible and threw himself toward the passenger side. The van careened towards the trees, out of control again. Stan fired through the van's side in the general direction of the thing on the roof, but whatever it was had already been thrown off the truck. Grabbing at the wheel, Jay swerved the van back into the center of the road. Rhetta caught a glimpse of something dark standing in the road behind them, something standing upright. To Rhetta it looked like a bear.

It dwindled behind them. On the van's left, the trees began to thin, exposing an open grassy area thick with low-lying fog. "There!" Jay yelled. "There, we're going to make it!" He pushed the van a little harder, ignoring the screech from under the hood and the steam that was now pouring out, and an instant later Rhetta started hearing the *whump-whump* of a helicopter's rotors. A searchlight's beam suddenly splattered light across the clearing, eradicating the moonlight. Having almost forgotten by now about the threat from her abductors, Rhetta actually breathed a sigh of relief.

"The cavalry," Jay said triumphantly, "has arrived!"

Pressed against the wire mesh, Rhetta stared at the helicopter as it came down, at the letters "D.N.A." emblazoned on its side. Jay urged the van on a few more feet. The chopper, hovering with its wheels six or eight feet off the ground, began disgorging armed men.

"Let's go!" Jay yelled, stopping the van. "It's our game now!"

Stan threw the back doors open, pushed Rhetta out; a moment later he was beside her, holding her upper arm in a vicelike grip and forcing her toward the helicopter. From the woods behind them, a shot from the rifle they'd heard before rang out. It struck nothing, and one of the men who'd jumped from the chopper answered instantly with some large-barreled weapon that produced a small explosion among the trees. A dirty, yellow mist started spreading atop the fog from that direction, and Rhetta could hear cries of seeming despair from there — cries that became louder as the men from the chopper, moving like a crack army commando unit, headed toward them. Soon, she told herself, this nightmare would end; the helicopter's inviting ladder was just ahead, not more than 20 feet now.

They'd covered just about half that distance when they all heard a sharp cracking sound, a sound of splintering wood, from somewhere behind the helicopter. Looking in that direction, Rhetta saw a good-sized tree falling toward the aircraft. She frowned. She could have sworn that the location where the chopper was hovering was far from any trees; more, she'd been certain the ground here was flat and level — not ridged-up into a little hill the way it now, clearly, was.

And yet the tree was falling. As if it were moving in slow-motion, Rhetta watched it fall. It did not hit the main body of the aircraft, but some of the upper limbs did foul the small tail rotor; there was a crashing sound followed by flying pieces of wood and metal. Rhetta and the men with her ducked down as the helicopter's body began turning around lazily in opposition to the spin of the main rotor.

At the same time, the helicopter started to descend. A moment later, the wheels touched the turf. Since the body was still turning, they chewed up the ground as they were dragged sideways. After only a second or two one of the wheel struts gave way and the chopper started listing to the side, the rotor blades now striking the ground and bending themselves out of shape before stopping.

There was a long moment of silence. Not just from Rhetta and the two men who'd captured her, but from those who'd arrived in the helicopter.

A voice, soft, low, almost musical, broke the stillness. "I am sorry," it said. "We had hoped not to intervene. And yet, it is so that we cannot allow this young woman to be taken away by such as you."

All eyes turned toward the speaker. Shocked and surprised, Rhetta realized that it was the slender dark man, the man who'd been in the periphery of her vision for so long. He was standing right out in the open, not 50 feet away. There were two women with him: one young and the other middle-aged, both of them as dark and black-haired as he was. As the man spoke the women dropped to the ground and out of sight. Rhetta could see the grass wave occasionally, as if they were moving off in opposite directions. She could not catch so much as a glimpse of them, however, once they'd dropped down.

Jay peered at the Mexican. "Who the fuck are you?" he demanded. "Are you—?"

"No, I am not Garou." The dark man smiled slightly and bowed a little. "My name is Juan Esteban. What I am is not, I do not believe, known to you. I trust, gentlemen, that we can settle this matter without further violence? If you will just release the young woman, then—"

"Screw you," Jay muttered darkly. He raised his weapon, and, without a word of warning, fired a burst toward the dark man. Rhetta gave voice to a shriek.

But the dark man who'd called himself Juan Esteban had not been hit. With incredible speed and grace, he'd dropped to the ground as Jay raised his weapon. Jay, whose burst had nothing more than to demolish a small shrub, looked confused. A few seconds passed quietly and without incident.

Then, the grass waved near the spot where Esteban had vanished. Rhetta could see that it had parted, evidently exposing the man to Jay but not to herself or to Stan. Rhetta gasped, expecting Jay to fire again. Instead, his face contorted, showing evidence of some sort of profound shock. Then something — at first Rhetta thought it was Esteban — exploded from the grass.

The girl could do nothing except stare. A creature — that was the only mental identification she could make — came rushing toward Jay. It was a big cat, a black and yellow spotted cat like a jaguar, or a leopard, but it was far more heavily and powerfully built than any lion or tiger Rhetta had ever seen. Its mouth was agape; the fangs it bared looked like those of a prehistoric sabertooth cat. Almost too quickly for Rhetta to follow it with her eye, the large cat batted the gun out of Jay's hands and pounced on him. Before anyone could react, its huge teeth had nearly decapitated him and its unnaturally long hind claws had opened his abdomen. Entrails spilled out and blood geysered as Jay went down; by then, the catlike thing had leaped over him and had again vanished into the grass.

Again, a few seconds slipped by. Then Esteban's seemingly disembodied voice was heard, from somewhere a few yards away. "Now," it said, quietly and calmly. "Would you release the young woman, please? Our patience is not without its limits."

Rhetta looked up at Stan; he looked like he was paralyzed with fear, but he looked doubtful, too. Glancing around, he saw that about half of the dozen or so men from the helicopter had gathered behind him. The remainder divided their attention nervously between whoever or whatever was in the woods, and Juan drew strength from their presence. "I don't know what you are," he said, raising his weapon, "but Dr. Jragghold told us to bring her in — at all costs."

"The cost," Juan's voice advised them, "is your lives. And still you will not succeed."

Stan pointed. "There!" he yelled. "There, fire, get him!"

Gunfire erupted, from several guns this time, the bullets tearing at the blades of grass and at small bushes but not — at least not obviously — hitting anything else. The men, their eyes showing evidence of their terror, kept shooting.

The bursts of gunfire accomplished nothing. The catlike creature reappeared beside one of the gunmen; its claws cut him down. The men to the left and the right of him glimpsed it and turned to fire at it, and one of these went down too, cut down by his comrade's bullets. As he stood staring in horror, something else appeared beside him — something new.

This thing, rising up from the grass just as suddenly as the cat had, caused Rhetta's hair to stand on end. It, too, was yellow and black spotted; it, too, had saberlike fangs and a catlike head. The remainder of its enormous body seemed to be composed of almost an equal blending between the body of a big cat and the body of a woman. With an earsplitting scream, it tore the head off one of the men with a swipe of its claws. At the same time, another creature, a virtual duplicate of the first, rose up in another place and killed another of the armed men. Then, both vanished. Wild and undirected gunfire did not stop all three from erupting again and cutting down three more of the men.

A bit farther away, something else was happening. Whatever was in the woods had taken the opportunity to make an attack on the remainder of the men. Rhetta could see great, dark shapes, dozens of them, streaking out of the forest. A couple of these fell victim to the men's guns, but soon enough those men were going down under flailing clawed hands, and more blood could be seen spouting into the air. In all, it took less than two minutes for the battle — if it could be called that — to be finished, for the sounds of the gunfire and the screams of the dying men to be stilled.

Only Stan remained alive. Following Jay's earlier example, he grabbed Rhetta's arm and pressed the muzzle of his gun against her head; by this time she was so used to the feel of gun-metal there that she hardly reacted at all. "Stay back," Stan cried, his eyes darting around wildly. "Stay back, or I'll kill her!"

From a clump of bushes 10 yards away, Juan Esteban stood up; in his hand was his shirt, which he rather casually put on. "You are alone, amigo," he said, almost purring. His eyes glittered. "Alone. Do you imagine you can prevail, alone, when only a few moments ago you were many?"

"You won't risk her," Stan said, his voice shaking too much to convey any sort of confidence. "I'm gonna take her with me, and we're going to—"

At the same time Rhetta became aware of it, Stan seemed to sense some presence nearby. Distracted, he stopped speaking and glanced up, to his right, away from

Rhetta. One of the giant cat-women, having approached them in absolute silence, was standing there, her fangs mere inches from his head. Gaping, she hissed at him. Stan's eyes started out in his panic, and he started to swing his gun around—

—Only to have it neatly snatched from his hand by the other, who had come up, just as quietly, behind Rhetta. Rhetta glanced at her. This one appeared to have changed; she looked smaller and much more human. Not violently, she laid her hands — which were still clawed — on Rhetta's shoulders and pulled her back away from Stan.

Stan, in shock, didn't notice. Turning her head, Rhetta looked up at her new captor. "Please," she begged, "don't hurt me. I haven't done anything to anyone, I don't know what all this is about."

The woman — who was becoming smaller and more human by the second, revealing herself to an amazed Rhetta as one of the Mexican women who'd accompanied Esteban — started to speak, but she was interrupted by a growl from nearby. She and Rhetta looked up simultaneously. Rhetta gasped. In spite of what she'd already seen, she was unable to believe what she was seeing now: a werewolf, or a man in a werewolf suit. Rhetta couldn't force herself to believe the latter; this looked altogether too real. It was wearing torn blue jeans and part of a leather vest, and its eyes glowed ominously in the moonlight as it advanced slowly on the dark man, mouth open, teeth gleaming.

"I am not your enemy," Juan told it. Then he sighed. "But your Rage is upon you and I suppose you cannot see that." He shook his head. "Your people have never been able to control your Rages as we have. . ." As his words faded, Juan began to change, transforming from human form by stages, mutating into one of the cat creatures that had decimated the armed men.

"Gerald, no!" someone called from behind them. "No, do not attack him!"

Rhetta looked around. A woman — from her voice she thought it might be the same woman who'd called out to them earlier from the forest — was running across the meadow toward them. She was very strong-looking, about 50 years old but running like a gazelle. She, too, looked to be Native American.

Hearing her voice, the werewolf stopped, turned its head. It snarled at her, too, but when she repeated her command it withdrew a step. Then it started to change before Rhetta's eyes, the ears shrinking back, the hair on its arms and legs growing thinner. Rhetta glanced over at the cat-thing, and wasn't too surprised to see that it was gone — that the dark man was again standing there, looking human, looking normal. The werewolf disappeared, too. When its transformation was over, it had changed into a young man: one of the teenagers, Rhetta was certain, who'd been watching her for the past several months.

The woman who'd just arrived on the scene stared at Juan, her gaze neither friendly nor hostile. "You are Bastet?" she demanded, her manner authoritative and her words halfway between a statement and a question. "Bastet! What are you doing here? And, more to the point, what is your interest in this matter?"

Juan smiled and nodded. "It is so," he answered. "We are Bastet. We are Balam." He introduced himself, told them they came from Southern Mexico, and, indicating the two women — who, to Rhetta's surprise, were quite nude — introduced them as Juanita (the younger) and Maria. They were, he went on, Mayan by birth.

The woman regarded him suspiciously for a few more seconds. "I am Aileen Yellow Feather," she said at length. I am Shoshonean by birth. We are of the Children of Gaia, of the Sept of the Western Eye." Even though she'd introduced herself, she still did not look friendly. "I still do not know," she went on, "why you are here, or why you chose to help us against the D.N.A.'s men."

"We did not, though it is true that our sympathies do lie with you in this matter. We intervened only when it seemed that they would succeed in escaping with this young woman."

Aileen nodded. "That was our interest too. It was your car, then, following them?"

"Yes."

She glanced at the wrecked helicopter. "And that — the gift of Gaia's Vengeance. Yours as well?" Juan nodded silently. "A very powerful gift," Aileen muttered, gazing at him with even more respect. "We do appreciate your help," she went on stiffly, "but the girl is ours. We've been watching her for some years now, we're sure that—"

"I'm not yours!" Rhetta cried. "I don't know you! And besides, you wanted to kill me! You said so. I heard you!"

Aileen turned toward Rhetta. "No. What you heard us say is that we'd rather have seen you killed here than to let them take you." She threw a contemptuous look at the quavering Stan. "Do you know what they did with the last Garou they captured?"

"No, I—"

The older woman brought her arm down in an emphatic gesture. "He was vivisected! Vivisected! Do you know what that means?"

Rhetta's eyes were wide. "It means dissected, uh, alive!"

"That wouldn't've happened to her!" Stan protested. "We only wanted her for study, that's all! Study!"

Aileen nodded; her contempt and hatred was almost palpable. "Yes: study. Study in how fast her wounds heal; in the extremes of temperature she can stand; in how to better kill and disable our kind!"

"No, we—!"

"Silence!" Aileen barked. She took a step toward him as if she might attack him, but Rhetta interrupted.

"You say 'Garou.' I don't know what that means. I know I'm not one of them! I'm just ordinary, I—"

"We believe you are," Aileen said. "And we will find out, very soon. Then you will learn. . ."

"She should learn now," Juan cut in. "Because there is more, as well." He turned to Rhetta. "Garou," he told her, "is what they are, and that is werewolves; werewolves as you have no doubt seen in films." He peered at Rhetta closely. It seemed to her his gaze was cutting right through her. "And I am sure, Rhetta, that what these men believed about you is correct. You, too, are Garou."

Rhetta felt a cold chill. She? One of these. . . things? "No!" she cried, waving her hands, trying to dismiss the whole idea. "No! No, I'm not!" She laughed almost hysterically and swept her hands down over her body. "Look. Look. It's just a Halloween costume. It was just a mask, that's all. This is all a big mistake! I—!"

"The masks we wear," Juan observed, "say much about us. This is always so. In your case, it says much indeed!"

"But—!"

This time it was Aileen who cut Rhetta off. "You still," she told Juan, "haven't explained your presence here, your interest in this girl."

Juan smiled. "Perhaps that question can be best answered by another," he said. "You were watching over her the last time she donned a costume, weren't you?"

Aileen scowled at him. "Yes. A year ago, last Halloween."

Juan glanced at the girl. "And what mask did she wear then?"

Rhetta looked blank; so did Aileen — but only for a second, after which her bewildered look was replaced by one of complete astonishment. "I was a cat," Rhetta answered. She glanced at the women who'd accompanied Juan; an idea, horrible to think, occurred to her. "And it was just a costume too!" she almost screamed. "Just because a person wears a costume, it doesn't mean that—!"

"Rhetta," Juan interrupted gently, "it is so. You are Garou. I should know."

"You? How? Why?"

"Exactly for the reason I have been watching over you as you came to your maturity." He smiled. "I am your grandfather, Rhetta. Your grandmother — she who was precious to me, she who was Diana Blue Water of the Shoshone. She was Garou. She was of the Children of Gaia. She was of the Sept of the Western Eye. She—"

"I've heard of her," Aileen said. "I have! It's true. She married a Mexican. She went to Mexico; but—but she died. She was killed."

"Yes. By those known as the Black Spiral Dancers. But that was after she had given birth to a child — a child who would, in time, become your father, Rhetta. He is not Garou; the blood lays dormant in him. It has emerged again in you. He is not Bastet, either," Juan went on, answering the question both Rhetta and Aileen were silently asking. "But you are. You are both. It is said, granddaughter, that the Garou and the Bastet are peoples of two worlds. You, child, are of three. You are Garou; you are of the Children of Gaia; and you are Bastet as well. You are of the Balam. Equally."

Aileen was staring fixedly at the girl. "This," she said softly, "is unheard of." She sniffed at the girl, audibly. "And yet, we have long known that she was no ordinary cub, that there was something. . ."

Rhetta's head was reeling; she couldn't accept what they were telling her, and yet, for some reason, she couldn't deny it either. She tried to speak, but all she could do was protest weakly, to say again that she wanted to go home.

"Regrettably, you cannot," Juan said. "Those men — those men from that place, the D.N.A. — they know of you, they will be looking for you, for quite a while. Eventually, they will cease their searches, but for now, you must remain hidden from them."

Rhetta's eyes were wide again. "Are you saying you're taking me to Mexico with you?"

Juan smiled again, softly, affectionately. "You are very special, Rhetta; you are Garou, and you are Bastet, and in your future you must learn the ways of both. It is true, though, that you grew up here. I believe you will find it easier if you learn of that part of you that belongs to the Garou first. You should, therefore, remain here, with your Garou kin."

"But I don't want to!" she wailed. "I want to go home!"

"For that, I, too, am sorry," Aileen told her. "But he's right. For your own safety you must stay with us, with the Sept. As he says, you have much to learn from us, much to learn about yourself." Aileen looked up at Juan. "There has never been much cooperation among our peoples," she said. "But, perhaps, the time has come for that to change. We are aware that you, too, are sworn enemies of the Wyrm."

"We are," Juan agreed. "And yes, especially now — now that there is a living link between us — we believe that our peoples should perhaps become closer. We will visit you in the near future, at your cairn in Muir Wood." He paused. "If we are welcome there."

Aileen hesitated, but only slightly. "You are. I will bring word of you to the others."

"Excellent." Juan took a step back. "You, too, and your people, are welcome at our den in southern Mexico," he told her, handing her a map. Juan also seemed a little hesitant, as if he was doing something that went against something that ran very deep within him. "It is remote. A time may come when you may find in it a needed refuge." He glanced back at Rhetta. "When you first come," he went on, "bring Rhetta with you. To insure that there are not unfortunate incidents. Our people are—"

Aileen laughed, a little tightly. "We understand. We know how your people are."

Juan smiled again, nodded, and bowed. "Good. We will take our leave of you, then."

"No, wait!" Rhetta protested. "I want to ask you—"

"In the future, granddaughter. In the future. You have my word." He smiled again; then he and the two women moved off across the field. To Rhetta it was eerie. They made no sound — none at all — as if they were walking slightly above the ground instead of on it.

"We have much to learn from them," Aileen said, putting her hand on Rhetta's shoulder as they watched them go. She looked down at the girl and for the first time smiled. "Come, we must go. We have a lot to talk about."

Rhetta glanced over at Stan. Several of the young Garou were standing around him, and a couple of them seemed to be undergoing a transformation: a change reversed to the one she'd witnessed earlier.

"What's going to happen to him?" she asked.

Aileen's expression became serious. She put her arm around Rhetta's shoulder and turned the girl away. "Nothing you want to witness, I don't think," she said. She paused, seemed thoughtful. "Not yet, anyway." ////

A Useless Death

by Don Bassingthwaite

Memphis woke up just after sunset on Monday with the taste of blood in his mouth. He groaned and rolled over onto a bag of Halloween candy from the night before. A beer bottle dug into his side. He shoved it away blindly, but a last dribble of warm beer ran out and soaked into the sheets under him. He groaned again and sat up reluctantly, rubbing at his eyes. The gesture reawoke a stiffness in his shoulder. He vaguely remembered someone stabbing him there last night, some punk looking for fun.

Halloween and a full moon did not mix well for Garou. Either that, or they mixed too well. The night before came back to him as bits and flashes of an endless string of costume parties at one club after another in San Francisco's South of Market district, his pack laughing and dancing and riding the rush that came on the razor-edge of Rage. He smiled and yawned. What a night!

His eyes focused on the wall at the foot of his bed. A silver klaive was stuck up to its hilt into the wall.

Memphis' smile turned bitter as he reached to pull the weapon out of the wall. For a moment he let its deadly weight rest in his hands, the brilliant metal cool against his skin. Then he wiped the plaster dust from it with a corner of the bedsheets and set it carefully in the case where it should have been. After all, it was borrowed. Pulling a threadbare robe around himself, he staggered out of his room and downstairs.

Lady, a Glass Walker of his pack, was in the kitchen, fully dressed and looking as if she had been up all day. Memphis growled at her as she looked up. She growled back, a fine deep snarl that was particularly impressive coming from a Garou standing less than five feet tall in human form.

There didn't seem to be anyone else in the house that the pack shared. "Where is everybody?" he asked as he walked on through the kitchen and into the living room. "And where's the remote?"

"Most of the pack is already in the Presidio, watching the site of the duel to make sure Rakes-the-Sky's pack doesn't try anything funny. Bronwen is hashing out the rules with the referee and Rakes-the-Sky's second. Not that Rakes-the-Sky is likely to stick to the rules. And the remote is probably between the cushions on the couch."

"Thanks." Memphis dipped his hand into the upholstered crevices of the dilapidated couch that sat against one wall of the living room, coming up with the remote and a well-chewed rubber bone. He threw the bone across the room and used the remote to flick on the television.

"Are you sure you really want beer and cold pizza as your last meal?" There was a note of distaste in Lady's voice as she came into the room, a cardboard pizza box resting on one hand and a six-pack of beer in cans dangling from the other.

"It's comfort food," he replied absently, skimming idly past a number of television channels. He took the pizza and beer from her, balancing the pizza on one knee as he pulled a can of beer out of the plastic six-pack rings.

Lady sat down beside him. "You could be doing something to get ready for this duel besides getting plastered the night before, sleeping all day, and having a beer-and-pizza breakfast. Don't you think you're carrying this pessimism a bit far?"

"You ordered sausage and bacon on this pizza, right?" He popped the beer open and took a long drink.

"Pay attention to me!"

"I am!" Memphis scowled at her, beer in one hand, a slice of pizza in the other. "Listen, do you think this is easy on me? I am about to get my goose cooked in a duel because of a stupid disagreement 300 years ago between one of my ancestors and one of Rakes-the-Sky's ancestors!"

"The loss of a powerful fetish is pretty serious."

"It's not the fetish, though. It's the honor of my lineage. Most Garou have forgotten about the fetish altogether. Rakes-the-Sky and his ancestors have remembered it though."

Lady frowned as she watched him take a large bite out of the pizza. "And yours didn't?"

"Mmmph." He swallowed, then snarled emphatically, "It's not my fault. Our ancestors have argued about this off and on for generations, but now I'm the last of my line. If I die, the debate dies with me. If Rakes-the-Sky kills me in a duel, he'll have proved that it was my ancestor who was the traitor — 'truth' by combat. I'm just a pawn for my honored ancestors." He toasted her with his beer. "So I have a right to be pessimistic. Tonight I die."

"Stop that! The duel's only to first blood."

"As if that's going to stop Rakes-the-Sky. The first time he draws blood, it's probably going to be fatal." He leaned his head back and lowered a slice of pizza straight down into his mouth.

Lady smiled at him, her expression a mixture of anger and fondness. "I wish you would at least try. You could beat him, you know. There's always that possibility."

He stared up at the ceiling, refusing to meet her gaze. "You'll apologize to Bronwen for the hole I put in the wall between our rooms with her klaive, won't you?"

Lady's face turned stony. "Bronwen was the one who stuck the klaive in the wall after you passed out." She stood and retreated into the kitchen. "Besides, it matches the new cracks in the walls from the earthquake last Friday. Let me know when you're ready to go."

Memphis grunted, taking another slice of pizza from the box balanced on his knees. He began to surf through the television channels, pausing just long enough on each to confirm that he didn't want to watch it. Abruptly, he sat bolt upright, moving so quickly that the pizza slid to the floor. He flipped back one channel.

The television screen showed an office building from the point of view of a cameraman standing on the ground in the middle of a crowd. Midway up the building, a spotlight picked out a figure standing on a ledge. Sirens and shouts were audible in the background as the voice of the newscaster suddenly filled the room. ". . . of the 18th floor of the Russ Building on Montgomery Street in the city's financial district for almost three-quarters of an hour. Police officers are keeping the crowd and the media at a distance from the building. Emergency rescue crews with airbags are responding but have been hampered by rush hour traffic jams."

"The man is as yet unidentified. He is not believed to be a worker in the Russ Building, but how he gained access to the building exterior is not known at this time." The newscaster paused. "It sounds as if something is happening now. Back to our reporter on the scene. Steve?"

"Thanks, Ken." The picture changed to show a close-up of the man on the ledge and a woman leaning out of a window nearby. "It looks like the police have brought in a trained negotiator and they're going to try to talk to the man. It would be fascinating to find out what they're saying, but as you know, Ken, we're actually watching this incredible scene from a window-washer's platform on the building across the street."

The camera shifted to a tight close-up of the man standing on the ledge. It was clear that he did not belong in any building in the financial district. His hair was long, he had a ring in his nose, and his face was pale, gaunt, and dirty. A bandanna in the pattern of the Confederate flag was tied around his head. His eyes were closed and he seemed to be shaking slightly. His lips were pressed together so tightly they seemed almost bloodless.

Memphis' eyebrows went up when he saw him and he drew in his breath in a little hiss. "Mike!" he whispered.

"Who?" Lady stood in the kitchen doorway, a dish towel in her hands.

"Mike; someone I knew before I Changed. Quiet." He leaned forward, sitting on the edge of his seat.

"The negotiator seems to be asking him something. He's shaking his head. She's — yes, she's stepping out onto the ledge to join him! No sign of the rescue crew with the airbags yet, but the negotiator is wearing a safety line." The camera pulled out slightly to record the full drama of the situation. "She's talking to him — it's amazing how calm she seems, Ken. He's shaking his head again. He's taking a step towards the open window. I think he's crying." Memphis found himself holding his breath as the camera dove back in to catch the flood of tears that were suddenly cascading down Mike's cheeks. "It looks like he's pressing back from the edge — Oh, my God!"

Suddenly, Mike's face disappeared from the camera. For a moment there was nothing on the television screen but a close-up of a wall. Then, with what seemed like excruciating slowness, the camera began to pull back and down, trying to track the falling body. The view switched abruptly back to the camera on the ground, just in time to catch Mike falling the last few floors and hitting the hard surface of the street. Against the horrified silence of the crowd, the sound that his body made as it struck was clearly and unpleasantly audible.

The picture feed returned to the aerial camera, looking down as paramedics first rushed in and then stepped back to allow a white sheet to be drawn over a mercifully indistinct figure. The reporter's voice shook slightly. "Well, Ken, I think you saw what happened," he said awkwardly. "A tragic end to a young life."

Memphis switched the television off as the newscaster reappeared on screen and sank back into the couch. "Apparently, I'm not the only one dying tonight," he observed with a casual despair.

"Memphis," demanded Lady, "who was he?"

"At one point in time, he was my best friend. Now…" He looked at the piece of pizza in his hand, then set it down on the arm of the couch untouched.

Lady pursed her lips. "Get up," she ordered him. "Take a shower and get dressed."

"Why?"

"The duel's not until midnight. We're going down to the financial district. Maybe that will knock some sense into you."

• • •

Before the Garou came to find him and he had Changed for the first time, Memphis had been part of a corporate family, moving every few years as his father was shifted from one branch of the company to another. Although he had lived in many different parts of the United States, he always liked to think of himself as a Southerner. He had been born in Tennessee. Most Garou thought his name referred, in the great Silent Strider tradition, to Memphis, Egypt, but it didn't. His father's job transfers had brought Memphis' family back to the city of his birth for an extended period when he was 10.

He had been 11 when he met Mike Cochrane. The two of them had become best friends, and they had stayed best friends for almost four years. Then one night they had been messing around on a construction site. Mike had climbed up onto some partially erected scaffolding. Memphis had been climbing up to join him when Mike had stumbled and knocked a two-by-four off the scaffolding. Memphis had been lucky that the falling lumber had only struck him a glancing blow.

A month vanished from his life as he lay comatose in a hospital. He came out of the coma with almost no after-effects. Mike was gone, however, banished to a cousin's farm somewhere up in the Tennessee hills. He had come in repeatedly to stand by Memphis' bedside for the first week of his coma, but had never said a word. He never called or wrote after Memphis recovered. Six months later, Memphis' father got another job posting and his family moved away.

"I never saw Mike again," Memphis told Lady as they got off the bus in the financial district. "Seven years later and I watch him commit suicide on the evening news." He sighed and shifted the backpack he carried uncomfortably. Inside it was the case containing Bronwen's klaive. "I used to wonder what became of him."

"At this point, you're not likely to find out.

The sky was overcast now and full darkness had fallen. The base of the Russ Building was brightly lit, however. Searchlights mounted on police cars flooded the scene with harsh, white light as grim-faced officers took a few last pictures. The majority of the crowd had left. A few people with nothing better to do hovered around the yellow police-tape barricades, but most of them only lingered a few minutes before moving on. Mike's body was long gone, of course, taken away to the medical examiner's office. Only a white chalk outline and a dark stain soaking into the pavement showed where he had fallen.

"Are you sure it was him?"

"Dead sure. The nose-ring was new, his hair was longer, and he was a lot thinner, but I would know him anywhere." Memphis circled the barrier slowly, peering at the chalk outline on the ground from all sides. He tilted his head back to look up at the cold facade of the Russ Building. From this angle, the ledge Mike had jumped from was virtually invisible. He shook his head. "He must have died almost instantly."

"I hope so." She paused. "Memphis, you didn't have to challenge Rakes-the-Sky to this duel."

Memphis sighed in resignation and turned to face her. "I didn't have a choice. I told you that. When someone calls your ancestor a traitor in front of a crowd of Garou and you don't do anything about it, you get labeled doubly a traitor yourself: once for being descended from a traitor and once for accepting the claim. And you're branded a coward." He shook his head. "You wouldn't understand. You don't have the kind of lineage I do. There are some things you just have to do. I *had* to challenge him."

He leaned up against a mailbox, staring across the top of it at the police cleaning up the scene of Mike's death. "My family had a story that was one of the first things I learned when I Changed. The handles of the chest, guarded by Thoth-Ashur of the Silent Striders and Thundersinger of the Shadow Lords, that held the lost fetish were sabotaged. When the chest had to be moved to escape a Wyrm attack, the handles broke and fomori chased Thoth-Ashur and Thundersinger away before they could recover the fetish. Only one of the two guards could have sabotaged the handles, and it wasn't Thoth-Ashur." He crossed his arms and put his head down on top of them. "Of course, Rakes-the-Sky and his ancestral memories insist that it couldn't have been Thundersinger. Rakes-the-Sky was smart. I'd be willing to bet that he forced me to challenge him so he would get to choose the weapons. He's much, much better at klaive-duelling than I am."

"Didn't any of your ancestors use a klaive?" Lady tapped his head. "You could call on your ancestral memories, too. Use your ancestors to get you out of the trouble they got you into."

He moved his head away sharply. "Silent Striders can't do that. Our ancestors don't pass on their memories. No one knows why. Real pity, too. My great-grandfather whipped Rakes-the-Sky's great-uncle's butt in a klaive duel."

"Killed him?"

"One more reason for Rakes-the-Sky to want me dead."

Lady turned away, looking up at the Russ building. Suddenly, she pointed up at a flagpole that jutted out from the building's third floor. "Isn't that the headband Mike was wearing?"

Memphis lifted his head and looked up, then glanced around. The last of the police were packing up and preparing to leave. None of them seemed to have noticed the scrap of cloth that was caught in the ropes of the flag pole. "Can you get it down for me?" he asked Lady quietly, "I want something to remember him by."

"The remembering is going to have to be awfully short. I thought you weren't supposed to have that long to live yourself. "

He gave her a sorrowful look. "You don't have to remind me. He was my best friend — please?"

She looked back at him for a moment and then nodded understandingly. She turned her gaze back to the flagpole, studying it. Taking a deep breath and focusing on the pulleys at the base and tip of the pole, she made a sharp hissing sound. A catch let go and the pulleys slowly began to turn, the simple mechanical spirits that inhabited them responding to the diminutive Glass Walker's wishes. The flag hanging from the pole slid down to crumple against the wall at the base of the pole; the motion shook the bandanna loose. Lady changed her hiss to a low, rushing whistle. The wind gusting around the corners of the building caught the bandanna and sent it drifting gently into her hands. She passed it to Memphis.

He accepted it without a word, running the dirty, worn material through his fingers, spreading it out to reveal the pattern of the Confederate flag. "A Southerner to the end," he whispered finally. He looked up at her gloomily. "Why? Why?"

Lady smiled sadly and slipped an arm around his chest, hugging him comfortingly. "Does it matter? He gave in, Memphis. He gave in and died." She squeezed him tightly. "You're giving in, too. Rakes-the-Sky may be good, but as along as you have hope, there's a chance you'll be able to beat him."

"I'm glad somebody feels that way."

"Don't talk like that." Lady clenched her teeth in frustration. "You might be able to do it if you'd only try!"

Memphis sighed and looked up to the ledge halfway up the building again. "I like your choice of words: '*might* be able to,' 'a *chance* I'll be able to.'"

Lady slapped him hard with her free hand. "Damn it, I've had it up to *here* with you!" Memphis stared at her in shock as she pulled away from him. There were tears in her eyes. "Do you even understand what I'm saying?"

"Better than you understand what I'm saying! Lady, the only hope in Hell I have of living to see sunrise is that Rakes-the-Sky will cut himself shaving and bleed to death before the duel!" He waved a hand at the chalk outline on the ground behind them. "I don't know why Mike killed himself, but I tell you, when I die tonight, it will certainly not be by choice!"

"Fine! You just keep telling yourself that, and when the time comes for the Galliards to sing about this duel, I'll be sure to remind them that Memphis of the Silent Striders, last of his line and the descendant of great heroes, went to his death like a sheep!" She spun on her heel and stalked away. "I'll be waiting for you with the rest of the pack at the site of the duel," she called back. "I hope you can make it that far without just lying down in the street and waiting to die of old age."

"Hey, I'll be there!" he spat after her. "And the Galliards will sing about a Garou who died uselessly, defending his ancestors' damned honor!"

Lady didn't reply. Memphis stared after her rapidly retreating form. When she was completely gone, he cursed, sat down on the curb, and buried his face in his hands, heedless of the humans who stared at him as they hurried down the street.

Why couldn't she understand? Why couldn't any of them understand? There was no way for him to survive the duel. He was going to die tonight, and that was that. Rakes-the-Sky had trapped him perfectly. He looked at the chalk and the bloody stain that were all that was left of his once best friend. "You were lucky, Mike," he muttered softly, "At least you got to choose your own way out."

It was easy.

Memphis almost jumped as the words brushed his ear. He recognized Mike's voice even though he hadn't heard it for seven years. He glanced around, searching for anything that was out of the ordinary. Before he had Changed, he would have thought he had imagined the phantom voice. Since his Change, however, he had seen more things than he could ever have imagined.

It was so easy.

It wasn't very difficult to believe that the voice really was Mike, reaching out to him in death. He looked down at the Confederate flag-patterned bandanna, crumpled in his hand. Actually, it was too easy. It might just as well have been some spirit of the Wyrm, trying to draw him into suicide. Had Mike succumbed to a spirit's urgings?

Will?

His human name. No one had called him that since the Change.

Come with me.

"No," he said aloud, "I have to go somewhere else to die."

It's easy, the voice responded insistently.

For a moment, he almost considered it, then shook his head. No, if he was going to die, he would die at Rakes-the-Sky's hands, proving the honor of his lineage. He desperately wanted to know for sure what manner of spirit was haunting him, though. Was it a Wyrm-spirit or was it Mike's lingering presence? There was only one way to be sure. Unzipping the backpack he carried, he reached in and opened the case containing Bronwen's klaive, pulling the weapon out just far enough for the light of nearby street lamps to glint off its polished surface. Memphis let the reflected light draw him in. . .

. . . and stepped sideways through the Gauntlet into the Umbra. His first reaction, even before he looked around himself, was to sniff at the air, half expecting to smell the taint of the Wyrm. There was no taint, though; only the distant odor of car exhaust seeping into the Umbra from the physical world and, strangely, the strong scent of broken earth, exposed metal, and dry lumber: the scent of a construction site.

"Will!" called Mike from above. "Shit, it *is* you!"

Memphis glanced up. His old friend looked much the same as he had on the news before his death. He was standing atop a construction site scaffolding, just like the scaffolding from that night seven years ago in Tennessee, except that this scaffolding was situated on the shadowy Umbral reflection of the Montgomery Street sidewalk where Mike had died. Erected, in fact, directly over the chalk outline of a body on the pavement.

"Mike?" He tucked the klaive into his belt. Bronwen had allowed him to bond with the weapon so that it would stay with him if he changed forms during his duel. Because it was bound to him, he had been able to bring it into the Umbra. Strangely, he realized that he was also still holding Mike's bandanna.

"It's not Mother Theresa!" Mike sat down on the scaffolding, resting his arms on a crossbar and dangling his legs over the edge. "How are you doing?"

"Not bad. You?"

"I took a flying header off an office building a while ago. They carted me away with a fucking sheet over my face. Other than that, I feel better than I have in years." He grinned an infectious grin as a look of shock washed over Memphis' face. "Hey, you look like you've seen a ghost!"

Memphis managed a weak chuckle in response. "You know you're dead?" Any time he had encountered the spiritual remnants of humans or Garou previously, the spirits had always insisted that they were still alive.

"Know it?" Mike scowled and lifted a hand as if to scratch at his head. He paused in mid-motion, looked at it in surprise, and let it drop again. "I've been looking forward to it. I never expected to see you in the Afterlife, though. How did you bite it?"

"I'm not. . ." He smiled ruefully. Mike thought he was dead? Well, he was as good as dead. "Killed in a duel." He held up a hand to stop Mike's next question. "Don't ask why."

Mike shrugged. "Okay. How long you been dead, then?"

"A week." A week ago, Rakes-the-Sky had called his ancestor a traitor and Memphis had challenged him to a duel.

"Here in San Francisco?"

"Yeah."

He stood silently, looking up at his friend. A question hovered on the edge of his lips, a question that he had wanted answered for seven years. "How come I never saw you again after the accident?" he asked after a moment.

Mike closed his eyes and leaned his head against the crossbar. "You don't want to know, man."

"No, I do. What have you done for the last seven years? What are you doing here?"

"Working." He sighed and lifted his head. A smile spread across his face, though, as he opened his eyes. "Okay. If you really want to know." He stood. "Come on up."

"That's more like my Mikey!" Memphis laughed. He stepped up to the scaffolding and put his hand on the ladder.

Come on up, Will! It's fun! Really! There's nothing to worry about!

Mike's words from seven years ago, enticing him up the scaffolding that near-fatal night. The Umbra played strange tricks sometimes. Memphis could have sworn he had heard the words spoken aloud. But they had come from behind him. He twisted around. A chest sat where he had stood moments before, an ornate chest heavily encrusted with gold and crowned with a cluster of pearls. Memphis sucked in his breath sharply.

He knew that chest, just as surely as he knew the scaffolding on which Mike stood. He had never actually seen it, of course, but his ancestors had been telling stories about it for centuries. Three hundred years ago, before his ancestor had lost it, it had held a potent fetish. He hesitated for a second, then took a step towards it.

That step was probably all that saved him as a two-by-four came whistling down from above. He threw himself sideways, and the two-by-four missed him by inches. He stared at it in shock.

"What's wrong, Will?" Mike's voice pulled his attention back up to the top of the scaffolding. His friend had changed. He seemed like an exaggerated version of himself, hollow-cheeked and emaciated. His hair was longer than ever and almost seemed to twitch of its own accord. No — there were things crawling through it. Big black beetles, some kind of spirit. He held another two-by-four easily in one hand. "Is this bringing back old memories, or what?" he asked caustically as Memphis scrambled to his feet.

A chill ran up Memphis' spine. Warily, he shifted into Crinos form. The two-by-four that Mike held changed as well, from wood to what looked like pure silver. Mike grinned down at him, his teeth sharp and his smile predatory. Memphis let himself return to human form. There was still no sense of the Wyrm's influence about Mike, although there was obviously something wrong. The Crinos' brute strength wouldn't be of any help here. He needed his wits about him.

He took a step back, brushing his heels against the chest. Memphis spared it a brief glance. Sometimes your imagination could bring shadows of long-lost things out of the Umbra. The duel, and the chest that had started it all, had been foremost in thoughts lately, but the chest looked so real. . . No! This wasn't the time to try and figure out where the chest had come from.

He licked his lips with a tongue that had suddenly gone dry. "Why are you doing this, Mike? If you don't want to talk about the accident, that's fine. But things have changed. You're dead." He held up Mike's bandanna, waving it like a flag of truce as he stepped forward again. "This is yours, isn't it?"

"Don't change the subject!" The two-by-four, still silver, sliced down at him. Memphis barely danced out of the way in time. "You hated me!"

"Hated you? Why? For putting me in a coma? Mike, that was an accident! An *accident*!"

Mike laughed. The sound was more like a fox's bark. "You think so?"

"What do you mean?"

"What do you think I mean?" Mike stepped forward to stand on the very edge of the platform, another two-by-four in his hands. "I guess I should be lucky I was just sent out to the boondocks instead of to jail."

Memphis stiffened. "You tried to kill me? Why?"

"I loved you!" Mike's eyes were bright. The movement of the beetles in his hair made it whip about as if there were a high wind. "Dammit, Will, I'm gay! You were the first guy I ever had a crush on. I didn't understand it."

"So you tried to kill me?" Memphis couldn't keep the incredulity out of his voice.

"You knew about me — I knew you did! What if you told somebody? The wood was there that night. All I had to do was knock it over. It was easy. It was so easy. And no one would ever have to know about me." He laughed crazily and pushed a hand through his hair, dislodging some of the beetles. Most climbed right back in again. "It didn't work. I ran away from my cousin's farm after a while. I became a hustler, worked my way west to San Francisco. I met people. Friends. I thought I was dealing with everything, until the voices started reminding me about it again."

"Voices?" Memphis sidled back a little bit closer to the scaffolding.

"Here." Mike pounded at his head with one hand. Black spirit-beetles went flying. One fell to the ground by Memphis' feet. Carefully, he picked it up. There was a touch of the Wyrm in it, but only a touch. He couldn't have felt a Wyrm-taint on Mike unless he had been much closer to him. The beetle was whispering in a woman's voice, quiet accusations of guilt, worthlessness, and perversion. A spirit of madness. He wished Lady had been there. She was a Theurge and understood spirits better than he did. Memphis simply crushed the beetle in his fist (it gave a little shriek as it died) and looked up at Mike.

Mike nodded. "I know what you must think. The voices told me what everybody would think. That I'm crazy. But if I tried to tell people about the voices, I'd have to tell them about you and I couldn't do that. I had to get away from everybody. Death seemed like it would be peaceful." He hung his head.

"It's. . ." Memphis hesitated. His best friend had tried to kill him. Could he really forgive him for that? He swallowed. "It's okay, Mike."

"No, it's not okay. Death isn't peaceful. Killing myself was useless. The voices were right. I'm a murderer. I'm a betrayer of friends." Mike's body seemed to shift again slowly, stretching until his features were distorted by skin pulled tight over muscle and bone. His eyes were ice white and cold when he looked at Memphis, and the chorus of the beetles rose to a hum even Memphis could hear. "I know now I can't change that. I'm sorry, Will." He hurled the two-by-four he had been holding downward with such force that the scaffolding swayed.

Memphis dodged back, tripping over the chest and sprawling on his rear. The two-by-four actually splintered and broke as it hit the ground. Part of it fell to crack painfully across one of his shins. Memphis winced as he climbed back to his feet. "No! You're not like that, Mike. I know you're not!"

"I am." The scaffolding creaked as Mike began to climb down, one hand clutching yet another two-by-four. "You didn't hear the voices, Will. They were right. Everything they said was right. I'm a traitor and a murderer, and I always will be. Forever and ever." He climbed a little further, then paused, looking over his shoulder at Memphis with dead, hopeless eyes. "You couldn't understand."

Do you even understand what I'm saying? Memphis whirled. It was Lady's voice. But Lady wasn't there. She couldn't be. After their argument she had gone to the Presidio to wait for the duel. He turned back to Mike. "You have a choice!" he shouted at him "You always had a choice!"

I didn't have any choice. I told you that. His own voice this time. And he recognized the words — he had spoken them to Lady earlier that evening. *You don't have the kind of lineage I do. There wasn't anything I could do but challenge him.* The chest, he realized. His voice, Lady's voice, Mike's voice earlier. The voices were coming from the chest. The fetish it had held and that had been lost so many centuries had brought voices out of the past. Not taking his eyes off Mike, he flipped open the lid of the chest.

It was empty. The chest was as richly decorated inside as out, with pearls and thick sheets of gold on every surface, but there was nothing in it. Voices, however, continued to whisper out of that golden interior.

"There was no choice," Mike said flatly. "I had to do what I had to do. I had to die."

"No!" Memphis responded desperately, torn between his friend and the words from the chest, "The voices in your head were lying, Mike!"

You lie. His voice again, spoken in a hiss a week ago. *You lie now and your ancestors have lied in the past. You question the honor and devotion of my forebears when you should question the honor and devotion of your own. If the honor of my ancestors must be proven, let it be proven once and for all. Rakes-the-Sky, I challenge you to a duel.*

"You were confused! That doesn't make you a traitor!"

We both know your ancestor was a traitor to Gaia. He sabotaged that chest to allow the Wyrm a chance to capture the fetish. Why, I wouldn't be surprised if he had secretly gone over to the Black Spiral Dancers! Rakes-the-Sky's voice and the words that had prompted his challenge.

"I have to kill you. What will people think of me otherwise?"

"You're dead, Mike! All of this is useless!"

This offspring of a jackal obviously altered the handles so that they would break! Ancient words. Memphis twisted to stare at the chest. The words were spoken in another language, but Memphis understood them somehow. The words of Thoth-Ashur and Thundersinger after the loss of the fetish, almost identical to the words spoken in the story he had learned so well.

Me? We're the only two who could have done that and it certainly wasn't me. You, on the other hand. . .

"No!" Memphis screamed "Enough!" He slammed the chest closed and pointed at it accusingly, as if he were pointing at his ancestors themselves. "You're already dead! You don't have to worry about dishonor and shame. You don't have to worry about dying again. I'm the one whose life is going to be snuffed out uselessly tonight! Not you — and not you!" He glared up at Mike. "But I don't want to die! *I don't want to die!*" He grabbed at the handles of the chest, anger pouring through him and transforming him into Crinos form. He wrenched at the chest, great muscles straining at the weight, lifting it up to hurl it away.

He got it no higher than waist-height before the handles broke. The chest fell to the ground with a crash, gold crumpling and wood shattering at the impact. Memphis was left with nothing but the handles in his hands. He stared at them stupidly. One thought forced its way into his Rage-maddened brain. "It was too heavy," he growled slowly.

"It was." Mike stepped down onto the ground. Memphis found himself back in human form, his anger at his ancestors finally released. Mike's body was still warped, beetles still twitched and crawled in his hair, but he was leaning on the two-by-four instead of carrying it like a weapon. "Keeping the secret — it was just too heavy. Can you understand that?"

"It was too heavy," Memphis repeated in wonder, almost ignoring his friend. "The handles just weren't strong enough to support all that gold." No one had sabotaged the chest, not his ancestor, not Rakes-the-Sky's ancestors. He fell to his knees and examined the chest. The handles had mostly been for decoration, he saw, added at the same time as the gold and pearls. The chest had probably never been intended to be moved. The Garou had been betrayed by ornamentation!

His ancestors and Rakes-the-Sky's had been wrong for 300 years.

But that only made the duel even more pointless than ever. He grinned sharply and inhaled as if he were taking his first breath. No, it didn't make the duel pointless. It gave it meaning. The fight wasn't against Rakes-the-Sky for the honor of his ancestors now. His ancestors were dead, even though the demands of their honor continued to manipulate his life. The fight was against his ancestors, for his own honor and the freedom to make his own life.

He wanted to live, if only to thumb his nose at his ancestors. He might still die, of course, since it was too late to back out of the duel. He laughed. He *might* die, but then again, he might not. Lady would be proud of him.

A foot came down on the ground beside the chest. Memphis looked up to find Mike standing over him, two-by-four raised in shaking hands. "It was heavy, Will. I'm sorry."

Memphis stood up. "Let it go, Mike."

"But you'll tell everybody my secret." Mike's voice was very small. "And the voices said I don't have a choice. I have to kill you, Will." He didn't sound as if he really believed himself, though.

"The voices already killed you. Isn't that enough?" He stood. "And I've got a few secrets to keep myself, so I can keep one more if you want. Call me Memphis, Mike. That's my name now."

Mike looked at him closely, then nodded. The two-by-four bounced as it hit the ground. He glanced down at it. "I was so worried about what people would think." He shook his head, scratching at the beetles in his hair. "And the voices said—"

Memphis took him by the shoulders abruptly and turned him around. He began to pick the spirit-beetles out of Mike's hair. Each one gave a thin little scream as he crushed it. "What people think can be heavy sometimes. Too heavy. Like gold."

As the madness spirits died, Mike sighed as if a great weight was being lifted off of him. His spirit body began to grow more and more insubstantial, becoming increasingly human at the same time. Memphis smiled. Legends said that Silent Striders had guided the spirits of the ancient Egyptian dead to a peaceful rest long, long ago. He was willing to follow the example of his ancestors as long as they kept their place in the past. "I still have your bandanna, Mike. Do you want it?"

"Keep it. Remember me." Mike smiled, too, and turned to face him, pulling the last beetles out of his hair himself. He was almost transparent. "We probably won't be going to the same places. I'm sorry, Wi — Memphis."

"It's all right. Good-bye, Mike." He watched his friend fade away completely, released, then set off through the Umbra for the Presidio. He had a duel to fight.

• • •

The two combatants stood face to face in an open part of the Presidio, shifted into Crinos form, klaives bared, the light of a great fire painting their bodies. The signal to begin was given. Its echoes had barely died out before Rakes-the-Sky had reared back, then lunged forward with his full weight behind his weapon. The audience of Garou that had gathered to watch the duel gasped as one. It was a killing blow, intended to run Memphis through.

Memphis, however, simply slipped to the side, moving with all the speed and grace of a Silent Strider. His klaive flicked out. Rakes-the-Sky snarled and whirled around, raising his klaive for a second blow. For a moment, Memphis saw his death written on the sharp silver.

But the blow never fell. A big, clawed hand closed around Rakes-the-Sky's wrist. Rakes-the-Sky turned to find himself staring into the powerful, hairy chest of the referee, Silent Fist-that-Wins, a huge, mute Uktena Ahroun standing 12 feet tall in Crinos form. The snarl died on his lips. Silent Fist-that-Wins turned him towards the fire and pointed at his side.

Blood soaking into Rakes-the-Sky's black fur marked a shallow but substantial gash between two of his ribs. Silent Fist-that-Wins released him and pointed at Memphis with a smile. The crowd broke into howls and cheers and surged forward to surround the victor.

Lady stepped up beside Memphis, once again in human form, some time later, just as Rakes-the-Sky spat in the grass at his feet and strode off stiffly. "What was that all about?"

"I told him that I didn't think either of our ancestors was responsible for the loss of the fetish, that the chest just broke." He looked after the retreating Garou in surprise. "I thought he would want this to be over as much as I do."

"I don't think he'll ever accept that either he or his ancestors could ever have been wrong about anything. And no matter what you may say, he's always going to remember that you beat him. I doubt that will sit well in his stomach. Congratulations."

"It was mostly luck. I knew he would probably want to finish me off quickly to make himself look good, so I was ready for him." He hesitated, shifting nervously. "Um, Lady? I — I just wanted to say I'm sorry for not listening to you. Thanks for trying to talk some sense into me."

She growled at him in disgust. "You were acting like an idiot. Somebody had to do it."

He hung his head in shame before her rebuke, looking so pitiful that she broke out laughing. "You gangly dog! I knew you could win if you tried!" Lady reached out and touched the Confederate flag-patterned bandanna tied around his head. "Isn't this Mike's?"

"Yes."

"I'm sorry he died." She put her arms around him and gave him a hug.

"It was a useless death."

"I wonder why he did it."

Memphis smiled and hugged her back. "Sometimes gold is just too heavy to carry." ⦀

Calley's Story

by Alara Rogers

I sat in evening rush hour traffic on Friday night, trying to make my way to the art gallery, and wondered for about the 400th time why I lived in the city at all.

It was the kind of thing I wondered about often. I'd long thought that perhaps my real parents were Glass Walkers, but that didn't really explain my need for the city. My packmates were Glass Walkers. They could see Gaia in San Francisco, in the teeming millions of humans that populated the place. To me, San Francisco was a Blight. I grew up out at the sept, surrounded by Children of Gaia and nature and wilderness and all that stuff. The wilderness was a far superior place to the city, in my opinion; in the abstract, I loved wildernesses. In reality I couldn't live there. I couldn't escape the pull the city had on my soul.

Maybe it was because I was a metis, and a hermaphrodite, and the only place I could fit in at all was in a large population of humans. The Children of Gaia who'd adopted me all pitied me and went out of their way to be nice to me because I was a poor little mule, and most humans treated me like a freak. In a city as big as San Francisco, though, you could find people who'd accept anything. Maybe especially San Francisco, where I could make my human friends among the gay community, where few people disapproved of my weird anatomy. On the other hand, I didn't have many human friends, and my Glass Walker packmates didn't bat much of an eye at me either. They thought I was weirder for being a Child of Gaia who liked living in a city than for being a metis.

In fact, I *didn't* like living in the city; I despised it. But something in this huge, Wyrm-infested Blight called to me, chained me here, to seek out and expose all the worst darknesses in human souls. I was a pessimist, and a cynic, and maybe I'd just have been miserable living any place I could be happy.

That was the sort of statement I could never have explained to anyone but Lee. He was my packmate, probably my best friend, and the reason I was slowly pushing my way through Friday night gridlock, wishing fervently that I had some heavy firepower on my car. Lee, like all my packmates, was at least six years younger than me. He was a college student and a pseudo-intellectual, the kind who thought he knew everything and analyzed everything to death. He was also a Theurge with a tendency to see visions in everything. Lee thought that all modern human culture was a prophecy of the Apocalypse. Gabriel Garcia Marquéz was a prophet. So was Francis Ford Coppola. He'd told me that this new young artist was really a prophet of the Apocalypse, probably Kinfolk or maybe even Garou herself, and that I had to come see for myself. You would think I'd have learned better by now.

But I had nothing better to do that night than sit in my apartment and fume. There'd recently been a bill in the California Senate to lower the environmental regulations for new buildings being constructed, to "expedite rebuilding" after the L.A. disasters. I had done a bit of nosing around, and found some very interesting connections between construction companies' campaign contributions and the identities of the senators behind the bill. Then my bosses at the *Tribune* killed the article, claiming I was making mountains out of molehills. I didn't know whether they were being pressured in purely mundane fashion — money's a pretty powerful force all its own — or if the forces of the Wyrm were behind their sudden cowardice, or both.

I planned to try to get the story published elsewhere — maybe a paper in L.A. would take it, since it directly affected LA a lot more than San Francisco — and in the meantime, I was preparing a version of the story to be told in Garou storytelling format, for the next moot. But I'd always found the *Tribune* to have some guts in the past, and this sudden attempt to hush me up made me furious. It was just as well I had something to get me out of the house. Two days from now, Sunday, Halloween, would be the moon of Rage. Not a good time for me to get mad at my bosses, not unless they really *were* being corrupted by the Wyrm.

The sun was almost gone beneath the line of the bay by the time I reached the art gallery. Lee was there, dressed in black, the-world-is-such-an-awful-place, art-fag clothes. "Calley! Glad you could make it!"

"Far be it for me to miss a moment of this no-doubt thrilling display," I said, and pushed my way into the gallery. It was a small, cozy place, hardly the sort of place you'd expect to see prophecies of the Apocalypse unveiled.

"No, Calley. I'm serious. You have to take a look at this stuff."

He led me past some sweetly pastoral pictures, including a painting of gamboling wolves that might have killed a diabetic. I pointed it out. "*That's* a prophecy of the Apocalypse?"

"That's her early work. You have to see the Persephone Suite."

He led me into the center of the room, where the artist's latest work was showcased. This was the Persephone Suite, a series of four-foot high panels with three or four paintings on each, telling the story of the rape of Persephone. I stood still and stared. The work was beautiful and hideously disturbing, describing the story in nightmarish detail. I studied images of Demeter as a woman half-wolf, half-human, and had to wonder. Maybe the artist *was* Garou.

"You see, Persephone in this symbolically represents humanity, the victim of the Wyrm, corrupted by her defiler and cast out by Gaia, who's obviously represented by Demeter, shown here as a Garou—"

"Lee." I turned on him. A bit of my Rage must have shown in my face, as he backed up a bit as if by instinct, even though Lee's a head taller than me and weighs a lot more. "I want to look at them by myself, if you don't mind."

"What's gotten into you, Calley?" He looked at me hard. "You believe me, don't you. You know what these are."

"I know these paintings have power. What they mean, I don't know. They look more like a personal Apocalypse than the general one to me. And I'd like to figure out what it is they're doing to my head, which I can't do with you standing and prattling at me, OK?"

"Sure." He backed up again. "Sorry. The others are supposed to be coming — I'll tell them to leave you alone."

I turned back to the paintings, momentarily angry at myself. Lee and his friends had taken me in and befriended me, without pity or condescension, without any acknowledgment that I was a freak and not of their tribe, and all I could do was snap at him because I wanted to look at some pictures. Gaia, I was a moody bitch. I didn't deserve friends like Lee. But before my half-formed resolve to apologize had crystallized, I was caught by the spell of the paintings again.

The story they told was straightforward, horrific. Persephone, daughter of the Earth goddess Demeter, lived in her mother's pure and natural domain, at harmony with all living things. Hades, the skeletal god of the Underworld, came in a chariot of corruption to kidnap her. He brought her down to Hell, where he raped and corrupted her, forcing her to eat a pomegranate that resembled a human heart. Demeter, who looked like a stunningly beautiful Garou in a wolf-woman form, rather like an idealized Crinos, came to Hades to reclaim her daughter. At that point the paintings stopped, but I knew the rest of the story. Because Persephone had eaten of the pomegranate, she could never truly return to her mother's domain. Persephone, the innocent daughter of Earth, was doomed to become the cold queen of the dead.

The myth of Persephone had never pulled at me before. Few human myths had. No storyteller, no good one, can live without myths, and so I'd surrounded myself with the Uktena tales I'd heard at the sept, and the Child of Gaia stories, and the urban myths of the vanishing hitchhiker and the Halloween apple with a razor blade inside. I'd made much of my personal myth, that my parents had died in a battle with the Wyrm and my aunt had taken me, a mewling pup with my eyes barely open, and raised me for her own. Occasionally I had wondered if this was one of those little white lies that get told to metis, and if in fact my aunt was my mother, but I was too unlike the Children of Gaia to believe I belonged there by blood.

Unless my attraction to the darkness of the city came from metis madness and was nothing of my parents' at all, I felt certain I came from Glass Walker or Bone Gnawer stock.

This disrupted that. Staring at the paintings, I felt a sudden horrible sense that Persephone was my mother, not Demeter, not Gaia, and that my place was the artist's vision of Hades, not the pastoral greenery of Demeter's world at all.

I shook my head to free myself of the sudden unwelcome sensation, wondering if this was a vision, or if it was just a new form of the uncertainties that had always plagued me, or if perhaps the paintings had a corruptive influence. Things of the Wyrm could have an obscene beauty the way these paintings did. But I sensed no corruption in these, no Wyrm-scent at all.

"You like my work?"

I hadn't expected a voice right then, and I nearly jumped out of my skin. I turned, and there was a young woman, not much older than Lee, with extremely pale skin. There was something seriously wrong with her, and for a moment I couldn't put my finger on what, exactly. "Um — you did this?"

"I'm the artist fêted here," she said in a kind of sing-song voice. "My soul, on canvas. I have ripped out my heart all bloody and invited throngs to walk through its caverns."

She seemed like a lunatic. I wondered if she was a Garou after all or just a human nut. And then I looked more carefully, because she was far too pale, and I realized that, except when she spoke, she wasn't breathing.

I stepped back from her, fear and rage congealing in me. She was a leech! Out of the corner of my eye I saw my packmates. Where there was one leech, there were sure to be more. I considered howling to warn them, but the vampire stepped forward. "Oh, don't turn from me, cousin," she said sadly. "You see whose maw has swallowed me, but do you see the jaws now opening under your own feet?"

"You're crazy," I said, starting to back away. There was an art gallery full of innocent people here. I had to control my Rage, not start a fight with the leech. I wondered why I hadn't sensed her when I'd probed her paintings for Wyrm-taint.

She laughed. "Of course I'm crazy!" she said. "But that doesn't alter what I see. Far more, it validates, it gives depth to my vision. Though Weaver's child I was, I was born under a crescent moon. We your Kin can see through veils and shadows."

"You're not any Kin of mine!"

"No, I am not," she said, "and yet I was. For I was Demeter's daughter and granddaughter of Gaia, as you are Gaia's son and daughter. But my Grandmother turned Her eyes from me when Hades tainted my soul." She stepped forward and put her hand on mine. It was terribly cold, but I couldn't pull away. Her voice, her words, were mesmerizing. "My blood was tainted with darkness and madness, and with madness comes sight. I can see the darkness around you, cousin, moving to claim you. For my blood was infected with the taint of the Wyrm, but yours comes from birth. Generations stretch behind you in the abyss."

I could barely control the Rage. How dare a leech accuse me of being a Wyrm-creature? How did she know so much about the Garou, anyway?

"Give me one good reason why I shouldn't rip your head off," I growled at her.

She was either very brave, very stupid, or completely insane. She held her ground and merely looked at me. "Because you don't really want to," she said. "You seek the truth. You are not one to kill the bearer of warnings. And I am warning you, for I have been down in the pits of Hades, and I see them yawning open beneath you, to claim their long-lost cub. Beware, dancing cousin."

Then she turned away from me blithely, completely unconcerned that there was a furious werewolf behind her fighting to keep from tearing off her head. Maybe she didn't know as much about the Garou as she claimed.

Or maybe she knew us too well. I couldn't kill someone for giving me a warning, even a warning as obscure and obscene as that one. She was right; I sought the truth. And if there was any chance whatsoever that there was a single grain of truth to what she'd said, my own honor wouldn't let me strike. On the other hand, I couldn't stay here and shake with Rage, fighting to restrain myself in an art gallery full of fragile objects, living and otherwise. So I turned tail like a fox and fled out the door, letting the rage become something else — the need to get away, to run and let my shaking limbs transform. I heard Lee yelling my name, but it didn't matter. As I hit the streets outside in Lupus form, the human world melted in a kaleidoscope of sound and smell.

• • •

I could have pinpointed the length of time I was running later, if I'd cared to. I dimly recall that Friday's earthquake happened while I was still running, and that I kept running through it. Since I never cared enough to work out the math, I never did figure out quite how long it was before I slowed down to a trot and became aware of where I was. There was an unbelievable stench in the air. I was over in the industrial district, walking along the road outside a gate to a plastics factory.

It figured I'd have ended up here. Whenever I got mad and ran away from my anger, or even walked away, I ended up hovering around some place that I thought was completely disgusting. It was part of the same instinct that made me roam around turning over metaphorical rocks and watching what squirmed out. And this place was more disgusting than my usual haunts. There was some kind of indefinable foulness in the air — something that was neither a scent nor a sight, but seemed to partake of both. It was like an oil slick on my brain, the sense of the Wyrm, vile and powerful.

A mangy Garou stepped out of the shadows in Glabro form, and my gorge rose as the sense became overpowering. She was obviously metis, but much worse off than me, with a misshapen head and her hair and fur in patches. In Crinos form she probably looked even worse. Scars drew intricate and hideous patterns all over her: bloody tattoos that had to have been inflicted quite deliberately. Ritual scarring, or torture. . . or self-inflicted injuries. Her fur and hair were black, as were her eyes, but her skin was the fish-belly color of something that had never seen the sun, paler and sicklier even than the bloodsucker I'd met earlier.

She reeked of the Wyrm, and I knew immediately what she had to be, though I'd never met one of her foul tribe before.

"Shadow Eyes," the Black Spiral Dancer said. "I've been waiting for you."

My name was Calley. I had no Garou name as of yet — the Children of Gaia got their Garou names from visions, and I'd never had one worth naming myself for. Shadow Eyes wasn't an inappropriate name; when I was a child, the fur around my eyes was darker than the rest of me, and while my fur had since darkened to catch up it could be argued that my eyes peered through and into shadow far too often. Not an inappropriate name at all, but it wasn't mine. No one had ever called me that before.

So why did it sound familiar?

I figured there had to be more than the one Spiral, though I couldn't sense the others. My pack wasn't with me, and I would far rather have given my life in a battle that could make some difference. Letting the Spirals slaughter me was not my idea of a noble way to die for Gaia. For the second time that night, I ran.

I didn't get far. Two Crinos came out of nowhere and grabbed me. Terror turned to rage, and I shifted to Crinos myself, tearing free of them as I threw one against the nearby fence. The barbs at the top caught him and cut him, but they were neither silver nor electrified, unfortunately. He healed in moments as the second one, a huge and bulky creature, pinned me.

"Don't hurt her," the female growled. Her? Was she talking about me? I was a hermaphrodite, yes, and unwilling to undergo unnatural surgeries to make me one or the other, but I dressed and behaved as a man. Not since I was a child, when I looked far more like a girl than a boy, had anyone called me `her.'

The other Crinos, the one I'd thrown, grabbed me, and the two of them pulled me onto my knees. I struggled frantically, but the other two held me as if I were a small child. The stories and songs had let me down. In tales, one Garou hero was more than a match for 10 Black Spirals. The tales lied. Or maybe I wasn't a Garou hero. I was more frightened than I'd ever been in my life. Was this what the vampire had meant when she said the Wyrm was reaching out to claim me? Was I going to be a sacrifice at one of the Spirals' evil rites? *Mother Gaia, give me strength*, I prayed. *Let me at least have a clean death. Please.*

"Don't be afraid, Shadow Eyes," the woman said. "We're only taking you to your true Rite of Passage."

"What're you talking about?" I choked out. "Why're you calling me Shadow Eyes?"

"Because that's your name," the Spiral said. "Or it was, before your parents were slaughtered and you were stolen from us. I am your aunt, Naal'tin. And you are my niece, Shadow Eyes. Now stop fighting us. You need to be awakened to your true heritage."

A surge of Rage overwhelmed me. Mother Gaia had answered my prayer, it seemed. For a moment only, I had the strength to pull free of my captors. In Hispo, I lunged at the lying bitch who called herself my aunt and buried my teeth in her belly, knocking her to the ground. She took the Crinos and tore me free, her intestines still in my teeth, and threw me toward the other two. But I wasn't a metis for nothing — I'd spent my entire life shifting, unlike these two, who were obviously human and had to have spent most of their lives so far without their powers. I took Lupus and twisted in midair, arrowing over their heads. They weren't expecting the move, and didn't counter it. As I hit the ground, I took Hispo again and ran, flat-out, as if the hounds of hell were at my heels. Which, of course, they were.

Again the stories let me down. I thought I knew this city intimately, could lose myself in it and evade any kind of pursuit. Apparently, however, this was a human real-life crime drama and not a Garou tale of heroes. Or maybe this was a human horror film, and I was the victim. Maybe as I'd approached the plastics factory, people in the audience had been shouting, "Don't go in there, you idiot!" — the way I always shouted at the idiots in movies. Maybe people were passing popcorn to one another, or chanting, "We want blood!" as the Spirals caught me again and held me down.

Certainly it *felt* like I was in a horror movie, the kind that people go to in order to see gruesome dismemberments and lots and lots of blood. The Spirals used their claws to cut patterns into me — I thought they were patterns, anyway, but I was in too much pain to figure out patterns of what. I kept begging for the camera to do a tactful fade-out on my pain, but it wouldn't. Hadn't Naal'tin said not to hurt me? Maybe she'd rescinded the order after I'd carried off a mouthful of her internal organs. Or maybe, by Black Spiral standards, they *weren't* hurting me. Maybe this was a Spiral's idea of affectionate play.

At some point, I heard a howling. It sounded vaguely like my packmate Jason. But it was difficult to hear with the blood roaring in my ears and the snarls of my tormentors around me. Snarls? Where had the snarls gone? I heard howling, and screams, and then Alyssa's voice beside me, murmuring, "Don't move, Calley. You're going to be all right."

Calley. Not Shadow Eyes. The horror film was over. It was hard for me to see —some sort of sticky substance was holding my eyes shut. But I could feel gentle human hands on my ravaged body.

Lee's voice came next. "Is he going to live?"

Alyssa, spoke again. "We should get him to his tribemates. A sept full of Children of Gaia has got to have someone who can heal."

I heard Jeannine calling for a taxi — only a Glass Walker would dedicate her cellular phone so it would stay with her through all her transformations — and I heard Jason complaining that the Spirals got away before he could kill any, and Lee should have let Jason go after them. Lee started to say something about how saving my life was more important, but at that point the movie faded to black.

• • •

When I woke up, I was naked and back in my old
bed at the sept.

My injuries were gone. There weren't even any scars.
Someone had gotten carried away, though I wasn't sure
I'd have wanted to keep the battle scars from such a sin-
gularly one-sided battle. Scars were so you could tell the
pups you uncled, "Yes, and I got that in a brave battle
against 20 fomori, all of which fell to my claws!" rather
than, "And this is from where the Black Spirals held me
down and carved their names in my stomach." Always
assuming I ever had a pup to uncle — I didn't know my
Kinfolk, and tribes very rarely awarded custody of pups
with no Garou Kin to metis.

On the other hand, maybe I did know my Kin — or
at least, know *of* them. I remembered what Naal'tin had
said last night, and felt nausea welling up. It couldn't be
true. It *wasn't* true. I wasn't a Black Spiral and that was
all there was to it. The subject was closed.

Only, of course, it couldn't be. My curiosity had always been my greatest strength — and my greatest weakness. I got out of bed and threw on a robe, padding out to
find Aunt-to-Strays, the Child of Gaia who'd raised me.

It turned out that she'd been sitting vigil outside my
door, so I didn't have to go far. "Calley! You shouldn't be
up!"

"I'm fine," I said, and gestured to my body.

"Lay down, Calley," Aunt said, backing me into the
room.

Obediently, I got into the bed, then said, "Aunt, I
need to talk to you."

She nodded and shut the door. One thing about my
aunt: she wasn't slow. Thirty years or so of raising pups
had taught her to follow requests like that without ques-

tioning. From her face, I suspected she knew what I was going to ask, anyway.

I swallowed as Aunt faced me. "Last night, when the Spirals captured me. . ." I saw her trying to keep a reaction off her face, and failing. She knew perfectly well what I was going to ask. "The one in charge, Naal'tin, she said my parents were Black Spirals." From the pain in Aunt's eyes, I had my answer — but I had to ask anyway. "Is it true?"

She hesitated, then nodded, turning her face away. "I've dreaded you asking that for so many years, Calley," she said. "So many times I've played this meeting over in my head, imagining your question, my response. So many times I've thought of lying to you. But I can't arm you against them if you have only lies for weapons. You need to know the truth."

I'd had fantasies about my real parents; every adopted kid does, and maybe especially metis. Being a Galliard, it was easy for me to make up stories about them. Noble Garou heroes, betrayed and enslaved by a secret passion for one another, sacrificing their lives in battle to atone for their sins. That was one of them — not original, admittedly, but my favorite. I had others as well, less cliché and therefore more believable. Some were even downright unpleasant. These were my first stories, and I'd honed my craft around them.

Never in my most bitter fantasies had I envisioned this.

"I'm a Black Spiral," I whispered, tasting the horror of the words. The horror movie wasn't over, after all. The Black Spiral attack had just been the first reel. I'd never seen a Black Spiral before last night, but I knew what everyone else did about them: they were abominations, traitors who served the dark forces of the Wyrm. This was what the leech had been trying to tell me, the secret that her mad vision had shown her. "I'm a creature of the Wyrm!"

"You are *not!*" Aunt snarled, her face twisted with anger and fear. "Never say that, Calley! You're Garou like any other Garou, as untainted and pure as any metis can be. You're not one of them!"

"But I am!" I whispered. "You just said—"

"—I said your *parents* were Black Spirals. And it's true, they were. They were a pair of humans, living apart from the other Spirals, posing as a married couple in an ordinary suburban house. One had a job at the local water purification plant; the other was an enforcer for Pentex. I believe their real purpose would have involved dumping psychoactive chemicals into the water supply, driving an entire suburb insane, and making the whole area vulnerable to spirits of corruption. We'll never know because I killed them both before they had a chance to complete their plan."

"You killed two Black Spirals?" My aunt is a small, thin woman; I couldn't imagine her holding her own against any two of the three Spirals I'd fought last night.

Aunt smiled. "I'm a Ragabash, Calley. I didn't do it face-to-face." Her eyes unfocused as she remembered. "They had two cars. One was kept in the garage, and one in the driveway. I snuck into the garage and wired a car bomb to the ignition. Then I broke into the other and left its headlights on. The next day, after a fistfight over who left the headlights on and drained the battery, they both decided to take the car in the garage to work, with one driving the other. They were both in the car when the bomb went off. It took out the entire garage and part of the house as well."

My aunt was famous for using underhanded tricks to get things done. This story didn't surprise me. Though she didn't tell the story well — her delivery was flat and her word choice lacked punch — I was fascinated. It was easy to get caught up in the tale and ignore the fact that those two dead Spirals were my parents.

"When I was sure they were dead, I went into the house to see if there was anything worth taking. I found you in the basement, chained to one of the house's support beams. You were in Crinos form, howling, covered with debris. A human or lupus pup would have died when the bomb went off, crushed under falling plaster; only the fact that you were a metis, and had access to your shapeshifting powers already, saved you. As if chaining you hadn't been enough, you were also in a straitjacket, and there were claw scars all over your body. But I knew immediately that you were their child. When you sensed my presence, you took human form, and I could see that you looked just like your mother."

"You probably thought of killing me," I said, my mouth dry. "You must have looked at me and seen a Black Spiral abomination."

She shook her head. "Don't put words in my head," Aunt said. "This isn't one of your stories. I saw a terrified, abused child, about two years old, crying hysterically. I knew you were metis, but I couldn't see any signs of your deformity with your diaper on; you looked like a perfect little Garou pup. The only freakish thing about you the fact that you'd been in Crinos when I found you. And even if you had been a mangy, one-eyed, snaggle-toothed child with three legs and a human face on a Crinos head, I would still have seen a terrified, abused child, and I would still have broken the chain around your leg and healed your wounds."

The thing was, I knew she would have. Aunt-to-Strays came by her name honestly; my "cousins" included three other metis, all of whom looked a lot worse than I did. "And you told the tribe I was a Child of Gaia?"

"Of course not. I told them your parents had died at the hands of the Wyrm, and that I would preserve their anonymity completely, because I wanted you to be raised completely as a Child of Gaia. And you have been. I've never done or said anything to make you think you were less than any other Garou." Aunt began to pace the room. "I would have told you after you'd completed your Rite of Passage, if I'd thought there was any chance the Spirals would find you. But I was quite sure you'd been born after your parents had begun their undercover assignment. Records I found in the remains of the house indicated they'd been there for three and a half years. Whatever their assignment was, it was definitely long-term. I never thought there was any chance the Spirals even knew you'd existed, much less that you'd lived through the blast and your parents' assassin had taken you in."

"But. . . blood means something," I said. "Everyone knows it. When you adopt someone into a tribe, they can learn all the tribe's Rites and Gifts, they can be trained to behave like a member of that tribe. But there's something in them that always belongs to the tribe they were born in. Everyone knows that. And I—"

"—Come from the White Howler tribe," Aunt interrupted. "When the leaders of the White Howlers were corrupted, they killed all the members of their tribe that were unwilling to go over to the Wyrm. But that's what the Black Spirals really are, by blood. A Black Spiral Dancer is a Garou who's danced the Black Spiral, that's all."

"What's the Black Spiral?"

"I don't know, but if you dance it you see the Wyrm and it drives you insane. Members of other tribes are frequently impressed into the Black Spirals by being kidnapped and forced to dance the Black Spiral. So if a Garou who dances is a Black Spiral Dancer, a child who hasn't yet danced isn't one. He's a White Howler. He becomes a Black Spiral only when he dances, and you haven't. And as long as there's blood in my body, you won't."

I shook my head. There were things I still didn't understand about all this. "Why now?" I asked. "I'm 27. I've lived in the Bay Area for my entire life. Wouldn't you think they'd have found me before now?"

"Perhaps they did," Aunt said. "Don't forget: it's Halloween tomorrow, and a full moon to boot."

"What does that have to do with anything?"

Aunt rapped me on the head with her knuckles. "Think. The Gauntlet is lowered on Halloween, in many places, and after humans have so long thought of Halloween as a night for darkness and evil, it is especially low for Wyrm-spirits. They intended to make you dance the Black Spiral tomorrow night, I'm sure of it. They're hoping that blood will win out over love and loyalty. I'm positive they intended to capture you in time for Halloween, but as to why Halloween *this* year. . . who knows? Perhaps it simply took them a long time to find you. Perhaps it wasn't a priority with anyone but Naal'tin, and she's only recently gotten to a position of any kind of power among the Spirals.

"In any case," Aunt-to-Strays said as she walked to the door, "you're not going to that Halloween party with those Glass Walker packmates of yours. I don't want you leaving the sept until Monday morning. Your friends are here, waiting for you to recover, so you can talk to them if you want, but don't leave the grounds."

A minute ago, part of me had wanted to crawl into Aunt's arms and beg for her to save me from the Spirals, as she had saved me from those who would torment me all throughout my childhood. But as soon as she told me to stay in, I resented it. I was an adult Garou, dammit — a respected member of my pack, with a certain amount of renown to my name. And if Naal'tin was the one that wanted me, it seemed to me the ideal solution to my problem was to kill her. She was the one who'd called herself my aunt, after all. Probably none of the other Spirals would want me badly enough to try for me.

"Right," I said. "Send them in."

• • •

The Young Urban Werewolves, my pack, milled into my bedroom with the self-conscious movements of people who had no idea what they were doing. I was surprised they'd brought me here, and surprised they'd stayed the night —they weren't very comfortable at my sept, any more than I was at the Silicon Valley Glass Walker sept.

"You feeling all right?" Alyssa asked.

"Sure. Fine. Never better."

There was an awkward silence, and Jeannine could never stand awkward silences. "All right, talky time, Calley," she said abruptly, pulling up a chair and sitting down next to my bed. "What the hell happened back there?"

"I got ambushed by a group of Black Spiral Dancers with burning ambitions to decorate a Garou skin with their claws."

Lee shook his head. "First you don't want to talk to me or any of the others when I invite you to Megan Conroy's art show. I think, 'all right, he's finally getting some culture; I can deal with this.' Then you have a talk with Conroy herself and go shrieking out the door. We chase after you, but you keep running. By the time we catch your scent again—"

"—Keep in mind we chased you through a goddamn earthquake," Jason interrupted.

"Jason, my true love. I knew you'd come through for me," I said. Jason snorted.

"By the time we catch your scent again," Lee repeated in a tone of long-suffering patience, "a group of Black Spirals are attacking you. Now are you going to tell me these three things are completely unrelated?"

I didn't like Lee's tone of voice. My own voice utterly cold, I asked, "Exactly what are you accusing me of?"

"No one's accusing you of *anything*, Calley." Alyssa sounded shocked. She came over and sat on the bed, holding my hand. "We just want to help. It seemed to Lee like there might be some connection between what Ms. Conroy said to you and the Black Spiral attack."

"Especially," Jason put in, "since Conroy's a leech." He glared at Lee. "After you ran, I checked her out. I thought she'd done some kind of vampire trick to you, and I wanted to rip off her head, but Lee said no."

Lee looked embarrassed. "I couldn't let you kill someone who paints like that. I don't care if she's the Wyrm incarnate."

"I worry about you sometimes, Lee," Jeannine said, looking at him askance.

"She warned me," I said quietly. "She warned me about the Black Spiral attack. She told me why, but I didn't understand what she was saying. I ran because I wanted to kill her, and I couldn't kill someone for giving me a warning, even if I didn't understand it, even if she was a bloodsucker."

"What did she say?" Alyssa asked.

I stared at the door for a few minutes, wondering what on Earth I was going to say. These were my best friends. They were the last people in the world I wanted to know the truth about me.

But I was far too addicted to the truth, and to stories, to keep hiding it. So I summoned up all my Galliard talents, and began the tale with the story of my aunt, a packless Ragabash barely past her Rite of Passage, searching for some deed that would bring her renown and make some older pack accept her. I lied in the cause of truth, filling in the gaps my aunt had left in the tale with inventions of my own. I told of her passionate desire for a child to adopt, and how the little Black Spiral metis pup had seemed like a gift from Gaia to her — a baby to love and care for, whose only deformity was a certain ambiguity of gender.

Then I switched back to first person, telling how I had always felt a compulsion toward darkness, an attraction to the things that most repulsed me. I lived in the city I hated, unable to bear the wilderness I loved. I sought out the darkest truths — about humanity, about the Garou — and exposed them for others to see, though the task made me disgusted, cynical, and bitter. Until I saw the mad vampire's paintings, I knew these only as personality quirks. Then I saw the pits of hell, the depths of corruption, painted by someone who had been there and gone mad from it, and recognized some kinship between me and the denizens of those places.

And when I finished, taking the story up to my aunt's discussion with me, I fell silent for a moment, unwilling to tell the last part. But I had no choice.

"My aunt was wrong," I said softly. "There is something in my blood that's tainted. Too many of my ancestor generations have been the Wyrm's slaves for me to escape entirely. I don't serve the Wyrm — I never want to serve the Wyrm, I hate it with all my heart and soul. But something in me draws me to it, despite the hate... I..."

"So what?" Jason asked.

I looked up at him, shocked. "So you've got a dark side," Jason said harshly. "Don't we all? The important thing's what you've *done*, not what you feel."

"He's right," Alyssa said. "For once." She grinned. "You've used your affinity for corruption to seek it out and expose or destroy it, haven't you? You've gotten good at doing so, haven't you? There isn't any other consideration. It's what you've done that matters, like Jason said, and you've done nothing but good."

"But suppose the Black Spirals take me?" I asked. "Suppose they make me go over to them?"

"They *can't*," Jason said. "You can always choose to die instead."

Lee coughed. "In the first place," he said, "you're one of us. We're not just going to let the Spirals take you. And even if they do. . . I think you've got a stronger will than most Garou, Calley. They can't *make* you corrupt. Part of you has to want it."

"Maybe part of me does."

That stopped the conversation dead. Finally, Jeannine stood up. "That's nonsense. You're going on and on about your blood being tainted and whatnot, and *I* think your problem is just that you're a pessimist. You and Lee both. I mean, he goes on and on about darkness and the Apocalypse and how everything is doomed, and no one's accusing *him* of being descended from Black Spirals. I think you're just using that as an excuse."

"An *excuse?*" I said hotly.

"Yeah, Calley, an excuse. You're so overdramatic; you want to make everything into a big tragic story. The Tragic Life of Calley the Werewolf, Metis and Hermaphrodite, Descended from Black Spirals, Abused As a Child. Next you're going to tell us you have multiple personalities because you were used in Spiral rituals or some such."

I lunged out of bed, intent on strangling Jeannine. Alyssa grabbed me. "Jeannine!" she shouted. "That was *way* out of line!"

"Maybe you can't see it," I hissed, "locked up in your little world with your cellular phones and your six VCRs and your daddy's Jaguar. Maybe you can't tell the difference between what's a story and what's real anymore. But this is my life, Jeannine. This is not a recreation for dramatic purposes. This is really happening. And there are really a bunch of Black Spiral Dancers out there who want to make me one of them."

Lee grabbed the back of Jeannine's neck and dug his fingers in. "Jeannine. Apologize."

She had the grace to look embarrassed, at least. "Sorry. I. . . uh. . . was being a little insensitive."

I could have disputed the "little," but I let it go. "My aunt thinks she can keep me safe if she keeps me at the sept until Halloween's over. All that'll mean is that the Spirals will wait until I'm not expecting it. I'm reasonably sure they'll come after me before moonrise tomorrow, and I'm reasonably sure that if I can kill Naal'tin, I won't have to worry about the Spirals coming after me in the future. So I am leaving the sept and setting myself up as bait for Naal'tin. I would very much like it if I could depend on my packmates to back me up in this so I don't actually end up having to dance the Black Spiral like they want me to — or end up with a fancifully decorated hide, for that matter. But if you all think this is some kind of overdramatization on my part, I'll do it alone if I have to."

Alyssa sighed. "Calley, Jeannine didn't mean you were making the threat up. She just meant she thought you were being melodramatic about it, and she did apologize. Of course we'll all back you up."

"Who'd want to miss a chance to kick some Spiral ass, anyway?" Jason said.

• • •

At midnight, we were waiting in a baseball field in a distinctly 'burby section of town. It was a place we tended to hang out when we wanted someplace big to run around; no one ever came to this particular field after sundown. Before us, a pack of Bone Gnawers used to use the field for parties, so it was hard to say which came first, humans abandoning the field, or Garou staking it out.

We were here for a number of reasons. As I said, it was a place we hung out occasionally, and if the Black Spirals had done any research on me, they'd know it. It was some distance from human habitation, so there was less chance innocent people would get caught in the crossfire. And since it was the midnight before Halloween, it made a certain amount of sense that we would have ourselves a party. We'd got some raw steaks, chips, soda and beer — though we weren't actually drinking the beer, just splashing some of it on our faces so we'd smell like we were drunk — and were doing a reasonably good imitation of being carefree Garou partygoers on the night before the full moon.

Of course, we had traps set. Black Spirals might like the toys the Wyrm provided them with, but they were hardly experts on tech. Jason had wired microphones around the place and had them routed to the boom box we were using. We figured we'd hear the Spirals long before we saw them. And just in case they decided to try to go around our traps sideways, Lee had gone into the Umbra, carrying one of Jeannine's phone fetishes. So we were as well prepared as we figured we could be, without tipping them off.

A crunching sound came over the music on the boom box. Jason howled, taking the Crinos and running for the far side of the field. I followed him. Behind me I heard Jeannine call Lee on her phone; it was a Glass Walker fetish that could call its companion in the Umbra. I ran across the field, Alyssa right behind me, to where Jason had already engaged the enemy in battle.

If I was sitting at a moot right now, telling this story around the fire, I'd describe the fight. I would embellish and embroider it to make the five of us sound like heroes, gloriously battling twice as many Black Spirals. I would describe each blow, each rake, each bite in intricate detail. In other words, I'd lie through my teeth. Actually, I remember very few details about the fight — I was too busy being terrified, and lashing out in my fear. Naal'tin was there, all right, but I couldn't get at her. There were 10 or 11 Black Spirals — enough for them to doubleteam all of us, and we hadn't arranged for backup. We'd never imagined I would be important enough that 10 Black Spirals would come for me. Maybe I wasn't. Maybe they'd come to wipe out a Garou pack, and I was a side dish.

Gentle Alyssa went down with her throat torn out. Lee, my best friend, died screaming as two Crinos tore him limb from limb. I didn't see how the others died; I didn't know if they took out any of the Spirals. When I saw Lee die, my vision went red with rage, and I tore into the two I was fighting. It wasn't enough.

Somebody sprayed something noxious in my face, and the rage drained out of me. I felt myself shifting to human, falling over. I thought I was dying, and right then, with my packmates dead and dying around me, I wasn't at all unhappy at the prospect.

• • •

When I awakened, I knew exactly where I was.

It was a dark, smelly cave, reeking of chemicals and evil vapors. I knew better than to try to sense Wyrm here; that Gift might well blind me, in this place. The noxious smells brought back formless vague memories — this place was familiar to me, as familiar as the smell of my aunt's fur. If I had ever doubted my heritage, I did so no longer.

Physically, I was puppy-weak, naked and chained by the arms to what felt like a rough stone wall. I was in human form, which seriously scared me. Metis didn't default to human form; when knocked out, we usually took Crinos. We could be shifted into human if we unconsciously sensed people in human form around us, but we couldn't be prevented from shifting back, once we were conscious enough to know we were in danger. And I couldn't shift. I'd heard of Gifts that kept Garou in their birth-form, but I was a metis, not a human! Crinos was my birth form! How could the Spirals possibly be preventing me from shifting?

A bright and sickly green luminescence approached. I turned my head from it, looking away from the mangy Black Spiral that held it. A hand that might have been misshapen, or Glabro, or both, took my chin and dragged my head around to face my captor.

Naal'tin stood in front of me, an obviously radioactive chunk of rock hanging from a chain around her neck, providing the light. For a second I cringed in fear of the radiation. Then I realized I wouldn't live long enough for it to matter, and met her stare challengingly.

"Good, Shadow Eyes," she said approvingly. "Good. Don't show fear. If you do, I may have to fall on you and tear out your belly. And after I've gone to so much trouble to get you back I'd really rather not."

"You shouldn't have bothered," I said. "You're just going to have to kill me anyway."

Naal'tin laughed. "I don't think so," she said. "Blood calls to blood. You are descended from some of the strongest lines of Black Spiral Dancers; the blood of our heroes runs in your veins from father and mother both. Don't you hear your ancestors whispering to you, calling you to serve your true master? Can those whelps of Gaia truly have deluded you so much?"

"Why can't I Change?" I demanded.

"Because I don't want you to," Naal'tin said, as if it were the most reasonable answer in the world.

"You dosed me with something, last night. I lost the Rage and passed out; otherwise I'd have killed two of your goons at least. What did you do?"

"A little potion some scientist allies and I have been cooking up," she said, shrugging. "It doesn't always work. In fact, it doesn't usually work. But I thought it might on you — a creature at war with her own nature. It must have been so hard for you, denying the truth of what you are." She ran a hairy Glabro finger down my body, coming to rest at the place of my deformity, my duality. I squirmed. "This tells you are no insipid Gaia-creature, nothing dull and normal. This is the mark the Wyrm has given you, to claim you for His own." She leaned close against me, foul breath blowing in my face, as her fingers invaded and explored my private places. "Do they both work?"

I couldn't pull away — I was chained and pressed against a wall, with nowhere to go. So I held completely, rigidly still, and said, "Not for you they wouldn't."

Naal'tin laughed again, and released me. "Perhaps after you Dance, you'll see fit to share the gifts the Wyrm has given you," she said. "There are many less fortunate."

"I'm not going to Dance."

"No?" Naal'tin smiled indulgently, disbelievingly. "Tonight is Samhain, when the barriers between this world and the other crumble. Tonight you will look upon the face of the Wyrm, and take your rightful place among us."

She turned to walk away. I called after her. "Naal'tin!"

"Yes?"

She moved like a character in a horror movie, I thought; a languid, boneless grace that seemed entirely appropriate for a monster. "Why is it so important that I come back? I know about my parents — but surely one lost pup isn't so important to the Black Spirals that you have to risk fighting a pack of five Garou for him!"

"What risk? Your packmates were puppies. They were no match for us."

I felt the beginnings of Rage. But before the emotion could fully manifest, it became a grief and a deep despair, sapping my strength rather than adding to it. "Why am I so important?" I asked again, harshly, hiding the grief as best I could.

"You're not," she said casually. "But *I* want you back. You're all that's left of my beloved sister — *dear* beloved sister, who left me for that human male!" Her voice became a snarl. "She should have stayed with me. I could have given her anything he could. Even a baby, if that was what she wanted — science moves in mysterious ways. She was *mine*. I knew he would kill her. She should have stayed with me." Her face softened slightly, and she came up to me again, her fingers stroking my face in a parody of gentleness. "You look just like her, Shadow Eyes," she said. "When you have Danced, you'll be my proper little niece, and I will take care of you as I took care of your mother. And I'll make you so very happy. You're a metis, and those Gaia-whelps care nothing for love if it can't bring brats. You've probably never been loved, have you?"

I was now very sorry I'd asked. What Naal'tin wanted from me was considerably less horrifying than the prospect of going mad and turning to the side of the Wyrm, but it was still sickening, and when added to all else I was being forced to endure it seemed like it would be the straw that broke me. It didn't surprise me that Black Spirals should practice incest, but it disgusted me that Naal'tin could even imagine that I would reciprocate her desires. Black Spirals *were* crazy. "I'd rather have my lungs ripped out," I said.

Naal'tin released me again. She looked angry. "Oh, well, perhaps we'll arrange that instead," she said. She leaned her head back and let out a howl in a corrupted Garou tongue that I couldn't entirely follow. My two Crinos playmates from the other night stepped into the light from her radioactive rock.

"Shadow Eyes would like to learn what the alternative to Dancing is," she said. "Explain it to her — in detail. Take your time."

There was no cavalry here to rescue me. My packmates were dead and my aunt didn't know where I was. I prayed for death to come quickly.

Gaia ignored my prayers.

● ● ●

To my great surprise, they used instruments in my education, not teeth and claws. The instruments weren't silver, either. In the long run, I was grateful for this, since I regenerated all of the damage. In the short run, however, it meant they could do anything they liked and I wouldn't die of it, and that was a major disappointment. I looked forward to dying. It seemed like a lot more fun than I was having at the moment.

Finally, they left me alone to heal and reconsider the error of my ways. The idea was that if I refused to Dance, they'd come play with me again, and again, until I gave in. I got the impression that this was not normal Spiral behavior — my tormentors didn't speak much, but what they did say implied that ordinarily, Garou prisoners were given only one chance to offer loyalty to the Wyrm. If they refused that one chance, they were killed, horribly. I was an exception only because Naal'tin was obsessed with me, and Naal'tin had risen to be some sort of leader in Spiral society. I imagined that if I had the strength to refuse often enough, I would eventually be killed — Spirals didn't have the resources to hold a prisoner indefinitely. I could die a hero, not that anyone would know it.

But I wasn't at all sure I had the strength.

Spirits whispered to me, offering me all sorts of rewards for giving in. *No one really cares about you. You're a metis, an outcast. This is your true heritage. No one could truly blame you for coming back to your own people.* They showed me visions of my friends laughing at me behind my back, of humans I found attractive ridiculing me, of the Garou at the sept speaking cruelly of me. In defense, I replayed my friends' deaths in my mind, over and over. Perhaps they *had* laughed at me, but they'd died for me. And it was the creatures that now held me who had killed them.

I didn't want to be tortured again. As Garou went, I was far from the bravest. And under other circumstances, the call of the Wyrm might have seduced me through the dark places in my soul. But the Black Spirals had made a fatal mistake when they'd killed my friends. I knew that people I'd loved had loved me enough to die for me, and I couldn't betray them.

When Naal'tin came to take me to the chamber where I would have to dance, I refused her.

She drew away. "You don't hear your ancestors, accusing you? Begging you to come back to us? You should be on your knees, thanking the Wyrm for this opportunity to serve Him!"

"I am a Child of Gaia," I whispered. I was too weak to speak any louder. "My blood may be tainted, but my soul is not. And you might as well kill me because I will never give in to you."

Naal'tin stared into my eyes. I matched her gaze, letting her see the strength of my will, until she turned away. "You're right," she said finally, a devastating grief in her raspy voice. "Even if you agreed to Dance the Black Spiral, your will is to die. You would never come back out again. All that's left of my sister is lost to me forever."

She turned to the other Black Spirals — there were a number of them, I wasn't sure how many, gathered behind her in the darkness. "Help me kill her. Slowly. Very slowly."

At that point there was a commotion. In the dimness I couldn't see past Naal'tin's glowing rock, but I heard claws running on rock, and a frightened, whiny adolescent voice howl something in the Black Spiral tongue. It sounded like something about intruders. Naal'tin hissed.

"*Inside* the shaft? How did they—" She broke off and stared at me. "You have a Fetch on you," she finally whispered, harshly. I couldn't tell if she were frightened, furious, or both.

"This is *your* fault!" one of the Black Spirals snarled at Naal'tin. "Your obsession with the traitor pup is going to destroy—" Naal'tin hit him on the side of the face, raking her claws across his skin. He yelped and went silent.

"All of you except for Thargon and He'heel, go deal with the intruders. He'heel, get me a toy; Thargon, you'll stay here and help me. This should take only a minute."

"Naal'tin, what are you doing?" one of the other Black Spirals growled. "You should kill the bitch-pup! We don't have time!"

"Are you challenging me, too? I'm baiting a trap. Go!"

They went, howling mad songs of war.

I watched carefully as Naal'tin and her assistant booby-trapped the cavern I was in. Most of Naal'tin's orders were in the incomprehensible Spiral tongue, but her technical words were borrowed directly from Glass Walker jargon, with only a bad accent corrupting them. Apparently this cave was wired for electricity. From that I suspected I knew where we were: probably an abandoned mine shaft. They set up a motion detector in the middle of the cavern, an array of multiple infrared beams that even the smallest lupus couldn't get through, and wired it to explosives set under the cavern floor. Most Garou would check for Banes and other Umbral sentries, and trust in their heightened senses to detect any sort of mundane trap. From Naal'tin's words, I gathered that the beams were dim enough that even a lupus or Hispo wouldn't see them. If the intruders turned out to be the cavalry come to rescue me, they would come in to free me, probably without checking for electronic defenses. Who would expect an infrared detector in a Black Spiral cave? The bombs would go off, and all of us would be blown to bits.

It somehow seemed just that my friends would die in a bomb blast just as my parents apparently had years ago.

I pretended to be too close to death to notice what they were doing. If Naal'tin didn't realize I knew her plan, she might simply leave me here as living bait, and I could warn whoever came in. But then the Spiral she'd sent off to "get a toy" came back with a neon yellow plastic egg. Naal'tin took it from her and strode back up to me.

"I've brought you a lovely toy, Shadow Eyes," she said, opening the egg. It had some slimy stuff in it, like an Ick, or a Gooshy Gooze. "Never say I am not a good aunt to you."

Naal'tin dumped the stuff out on her hand and quickly splatted it onto my face.

The stuff was alive, and hungry. It oozed over my face, blocking my eyes, trying to force its way through my lips. I couldn't quite keep myself from whimpering, but I didn't scream, mostly because nothing in the universe could have induced me to open my mouth right then. I shook my head, trying to knock the slime off, but it wouldn't go. It blocked my nostrils and covered my lips, waiting patiently for me to open my mouth to take a breath.

Naal'tin laughed hysterically. "Don't worry, dear niece. If you're fortunate, your brave rescuers will come before the slime invades your body, and then you can die in a nice clean explosion instead."

If it weren't for the fact that I didn't want any more Garou to die for my sake, that actually might have been a comforting thought. I'd seen Alien, and The Blob, and several hundred other movies involving living things that crawled down people's throats, and it seemed like one of the most disgusting possible ways to die that I could imagine. I struggled to hold my breath, to suffocate rather than let the slime get inside me, but my body betrayed me, its will to live too great. My lips parted. I had one chance to suck in wondrous cool air through clenched teeth. Then the slime flowed between my lips, probing for tiny gaps between my teeth. Little bits made their way onto my tongue, carrying a taste so foul it took all my remaining willpower not to retch. At the same time it was crawling up my nose. I thrashed desperately, trying to pull my hands down to reach it, to knock it off my face, to do *something*.

A voice shouted, "Calley!" It was my aunt. Horri-fied, I realized what was about to happen. If I didn't warn her, she would die, and probably other Garou with her.

With no choice, I opened my mouth and screamed, "Trap! Don't—"

Then the slime rushed in, choking me, and I could no longer even scream.

• • •

Someone was pressing on my chest. "Breathe, damn you, *breathe!*"

I coughed, choking.

"Thank Gaia," someone else said. That sounded like my aunt. "He's alive! Let's get him out of here."

It occurred to me that it was very strange that I was alive, but I hadn't the strength even to open my eyes. Someone was carrying me, I didn't know where, or who, or why. I faded in and out of consciousness throughout what seemed like an interminably long journey. Then someone set me on my feet, holding me up, and someone else shook me.

"Wake up, Calley," Aunt said. She was standing in front of me, shaking me. "Wake up and look. Look at it."

I opened my eyes. Something was exploding. I could hear the thundering booms, feel the ground shake. Ahead of me, in what seemed like the very great distance, some-thing was producing bright plumes of yellow and orange light.

"It's the Black Spiral hideout, in the mine shafts," Aunt said. "We think it may actually be one of their Hives. We were able to destroy it because of you."

That's nice, I wanted to say, but my throat wouldn't work. I nodded, and fell back down into the darkness again.

• • •

Later I found out what really happened — how my aunt had had a Fetch on me, and had learned when I was kidnapped and my friends slaughtered. She had managed to recruit a huge party of Garou — not to save me, not even to avenge me and my friends, though most of the Glass Walkers who showed up probably had revenge in mind — but simply because they now knew the location of a major Black Spiral base, possibly one of their Hives. No one had truly expected to find me alive. They assumed that if I still lived when they began their attack, I would be killed to prevent my rescue as soon as the Black Spirals knew they were threatened. Only Aunt had held any hope, knowing how Naal'tin had been obsessed with me. She and a Glass Walker Theurge, kin of Jeannine's, had snuck into the cavern where I was held, and, after I gave my warning, the Theurge was able to disarm the motion detector. They'd managed to get the Wyrm-slime out of me and had carried me to the surface.

So even though I'd gotten my best friends killed, even though I had come within a hair of turning to the Wyrm myself, somehow the story got garbled and I was made a hero. Brave Calley, who engineered his own capture by the Black Spirals so that the Garou community of San Francisco could root out their Hive and destroy it. The fact that I had only been trying to protect myself and had failed miserably and gotten my packmates killed, got lost in the translation. My packmates gave their lives nobly for a daring plan to destroy the Black Spirals, and

I faced down a fate worse than death with a defiant snarl on my lips.

Stories always sound so much better than real life, don't they? They don't cover how the hero felt afterward, when the battle was done. They usually imply that there was a "happily ever after," or at least happily until the next battle. They are, in short, egregious lies.

I never recovered, really. I couldn't bear to go back to the city, now that I knew where my attraction to it came from. Over and over, I kept reliving my mistakes, the stupidity of the plan that had killed my friends. I should have gone out to meet Naal'tin alone. The end result would have been the same, but Lee, Alyssa, Jeannine, and Jason wouldn't have died — except that then, I might have succumbed to the Wyrm's call. For awhile I wanted to kill myself — or rather, to hunt down something bigger and stronger than me and go out in a blaze of glory fighting it, which amounts to the same thing. Maybe then I'd feel like the hero everyone seemed to think I was.

Only that would be stupid. And it would invalidate my friends' sacrifice. I happened to know that they didn't die to destroy a Black Spiral Hive — they died for *me*. If I got myself killed, that would be spitting on their ghosts.

I started losing my tolerance for staying at the sept. Every time I heard a tale of my supposed heroism, it made me sick. I wasn't a hero, I didn't deserve the glory I got, and I couldn't stand to hear the lies they told. When I said so, other Galliards challenged me to tell the story myself. . . but I couldn't, and I couldn't understand how they expected me to. Should I stand up at a moot and rip my heart out for everyone to see? I'd never had stagefright before, but to stand up and tell the world how my stupidity got my closest friends killed, how I would have turned

to the Wyrm if not for their deaths — How was I supposed to tell them that? ////

Trickster Moon

by J. S. Banks

"Leeches!"

Peter Rivard raced out of his apartment into the foyer at the shouted warning, transforming from human to Wolfman before he'd even cleared the door. There were five of them there, all hideous creatures of the Wyrm, advancing on Anson who stood facing them with a bag of groceries in each arm. Fear and primal hatred writhed in Rivard's chest, at these first Leeches he'd ever seen, the first vampires; and they were everything he'd imagined — and worse. He could tell by the look of them, the smell of them — rich, thick and deathly. The Wyrm was more twisted than he could have imagined to have created these.

With a growl, Rivard moved forward. Anson hurled his bags at the lead vampire, who beat them aside. Groceries soared, jars and bottles shattered against the floor and walls, and the vampires and Rivard flinched away from the debris. Anson drew his silver klaive and leaped, transforming to the Wolfman Crinos form. His arm snapped out, and the lead vampire's neck erupted in blood. Another of the Leeches brought Anson down with an elbow in the back.

Rivard's three other packmates raced down the stairs from their apartments and took positions around him. "Leave or die," Rivard said imperiously. "We have made a start. We can certainly finish." Rivard wasn't the largest of the Garou, and he was the youngest, but his attitude and the sheen of his silver fur seemed to give him presence despite his young age — one that even the Leeches could sense. He hoped they couldn't sense his fear.

The tension held for a moment, until one of the Leeches vaulted over his fellows to face Rivard in the clear. Ketchup dripped down the wall behind him, over the mirrored coat rack there, over Rivard's hat and jacket hanging on it, and over Mr. Polokowski's green umbrella leaning against it. It was a perfect pose. Rivard caught just his own reflection in the mirror and had time to realize that the myths were true, that this vampire, at least, didn't cast a reflection; then the world

lurched

and he was elsewhere.

The Umbra. The mystical dimension that contained the Realm known as Earth, and countless other Realms, too. Travel to it was by magic, concentration and looking into a reflective surface, like — a mirror.

"Good Gaia, no! They need me!" Panicked, Rivard looked around for something reflective so he could "step back." There was nothing but the Bay, too far in both worlds. He ran, looking for a shiny stone, a pool, a bit of unearthed metal. Once he thought he'd found it, but it was just the Umbral afterglow of the dead caern in the apartment building's basement. His fear and rage moved further up into his throat with each failure, and soon he could taste it, hot and acidic in the back of his throat. He looked for the moon in the Umbra's ever-twilight, and when he found it, all he could do was howl curses.

• • •

"Pete?" a woman's voice called.

Peter Rivard pulled his attention away from his reflection in the mirrored coat rack to the woman standing in the doorway of the apartment marked "Manager." The coat rack was festooned with stickers of ghosts, witches, and jack-o-lanterns for the season and, like everything else in the apartment building, still carried a light sheen of dust from last night's earthquake, so seeing his reflection wasn't easy. Still, he wasn't entirely checking just to make sure it was still there. "Hmm? Yes, Ms. Polo?"

"Can you come in for a minute? We have a guest who wants to talk to you."

"On a Saturday morning? Can't it wait until I've cleaned up a bit?" He tugged at his sweat-dampened warm-up jacket, and there was a tinkle of glass at his left wrist.

He's been here half an hour already, she mouthed.

Rivard sighed. "All right, Ms. Polo." Rivard cast one last glance into the mirror, and still nothing happened. It rarely did. He shook his head briefly, then followed the woman into her apartment. There was a man in a business suit sitting on the sofa who rose to his feet as Rivard shut the apartment door. "Ms. Polo?"

She smiled ruefully. "Pete, this is Alfred Mahalik. He's a lawyer for a company called — Quintana, was it?" Mahalik nodded. "They want to buy the building."

Rivard shook his head, silver hair flurrying around his face. "I'm sorry, it's not for sale."

"I'm very pleased to meet you, Mr. Rivard," Mahalik said smoothly, holding his hand out for shaking. Rivard reluctantly left the door and took the attorney's hand. Up close, he could see the man was 50 going on 29. He could smell the coloring that kept his hair so very black and the multitude of products to keep it "healthy and shiny." Something in there was Wyrm-tainted, and Rivard hurried to let go of Mahalik's hand so he could surreptitiously wipe his own on his sweatsuit. "I have to say it," Mahalik went on, "you're older than I thought you'd be."

"I'm only 43," Rivard said. "My hair silvered early."

"No, I'm sorry, that's not at all what I meant! The gray looks good on you, makes you look distinguished. What I meant was, when we tracked it down, the owner of this place showed as the Anson Company. In a case where the property this age doesn't show the same signatures but is the same company, the new signer's generally a little younger than yourself, and family of the guy who named the company."

"Mr. Anson was a close friend," Rivard said tightly. "I inherited the Anson from him when he was killed, 25 years ago. I was 18. And the Anson's not for sale, not at any price, nor for any reason."

Mahalik chuckled. "Now, Mr. Rivard — Pete — can I call you Pete? Pete, I represent a corporation which is fully prepared to offer you quite a sum of money for this place. More, I'm willing to admit, than this place is worth. You won't find another deal like this coming along. Quintana will even take care of the details. In fact, your responsibility would end as soon as you sign the papers. A few flips of the pen and we're talking vacation time and set-for-life. Sound good?"

Rivard watched a moment as a spider lowered itself from the ceiling to a point a few inches above Mahalik's head. He wondered if she would drop into the lawyer's healthy and shiny black hair. Not if she had any taste. "No. No it doesn't, Mr. Mahalik," he said finally. "This place means a good deal to me, and I'd hate to see it become a mall or a parking garage. And couldn't all of this have waited until Monday? Shouldn't you be at home watching cartoons?"

Mahalik tossed back his head in laughter, and Rivard saw the spider scuttle up its strand of silk to avoid being swept into his hair. He found himself wishing she would be: Mahalik's forced jocularity was rapidly becoming annoying.

The lawyer recovered his composure. "No, I'd intended to come by yesterday, but we had that quake instead, and traffic was so screwy I figured I'd save it for today, be sure to catch you at home and all that. I didn't know you were a jogger at the time or I might have swung by a little later. I commend you; that's a lot of dedication to health, to be jogging by yourself in a neighborhood like this."

"I consider it doing my share for local crime prevention. I have people's lives and happiness in the balance, after all."

"Yes, there's nothing quite like the comfort of security, eh? That's what Quintana would like to offer you, Pete, and your tenants. For you, the comfort and security of knowing these people are being well cared for; and for your tenants, knowing that there's a corporation in here with the resources to take care of them. This place is kind of security light, Pete. Don't you owe more to your tenants? To Ms. Polokowski? All you have to do is sign."

It was an effort of will for Rivard to remain calm. "Mr. Mahalik, what I do or do not owe Ms. Polokowski or any of my tenants is hardly your business. I am not signing any papers, and in fact, I think if I listen to you any more I'm going to have to tear your throat out in huge red gobbets and do my best to swallow them down while you can still see me. I wouldn't make it, and it wouldn't make my tenants any more secure, but it would be a *lot* of fun."

Mahalik blinked, but that was all. "That sounds like a pretty firm no, there, Pete. Tell you what: I'm going to leave now, but I'm sure Quintana and the company it represents will have a counteroffer that involves a lot less throat-ripping." He reached into his jacket for a business card. "Here's my card, and I'll be in touch later. I'll see myself out. Good day, Mr. Rivard, Ms. Polokowski; Happy Halloween to both of you!"

Neither spoke until they heard the outer door close, then Polokowski asked Rivard, "Did you mean that?"

"Mean what?"

"About ripping his throat out? Or was that another 'scene?'"

"I haven't put pen to paper in a while, so I guess I must have. It seemed the thing to say. They can't have the building, Jana."

"Because of the caern."

"Yes, because of the caern!"

"Pete, is there *really* something in the basement? I mean, I've been working for you for more than a year now, and—"

"Jana Polokowski, there are *lots* of things downstairs, and some of them will eat you and some of them won't. You couldn't see the caern anyway — not here, not really. It's hard enough to spot in the Umbra. It's been dormant a long time. Anson thought it could be reawakened. Most Garou thought he was insane. But he was right about a lot of things, and I think that's one of them. Of course, I seem to be the only one with that opinion. It's all a matter of perspective: impossible vs. possible, insane thinking vs. nontraditional thinking."

He extended his hand underneath the hanging spider. The spider slowly dropped into his palm. "But you believe in him, don't you?" he asked the spider, pulling his hand close to his face. "It's just a caern with a callous, right? And once you pumice away the hard spot, well, anything is possible, true?"

"Pete?"

"Yes, Jana?"

"Go shower, and take your spider with you."

"She'd wash down the drain if I did that. I'll put her on the sink." And he walked out of her apartment, singing "Itsy Bitsy Spider" to the spider in his hand.

• • •

Rivard went to the services. There were no humans there who were not Kinfolk. None of the four dead had birth family there. It was what he'd expected, it was typical of the Garou, but now it hurt. Most fallen Garou had the rest of their pack to sing of them, and the living outnumbered the dead.

They had been two Silver Fangs, two Fianna, and a Stargazer. Fingol, one of the Fianna, had always said that meant they gave a lot of speeches about the enlightenment of drunkenness. The varied pack had gotten along well, so Rivard had never noticed how unusual that was until now, when many tribes were gathered not just for a moot, but for a farewell. He could see the lines drawn between them as plainly as he could see the four bodies. How had the saving of Gaia become such a power game? Even now one of the Glass Walkers was beginning to argue with Tim Rowantree, the new Child of Gaia Arm of the Goddess of this sept, the Western Eye, over the acceptability of computers to track the Wyrm.

Celeste Snowtop, the sept leader, noticed also. She didn't say a word to them. She just began to howl the Dirge for the Dead. When it was done the service was over and it was just another monthly moot. When that came to a close, Celeste Snowtop approached him. She wasn't that old yet, maybe her mid-thirties, but her hair was already well on its way to being white, hence the name she'd been given. She radiated calm and strength, and Rivard realized for the first time since the murders how much he needed them. "You're welcome to stay here," she told him.

But he shook his head. "There's too much to do, yet. The apartments have to be cleaned out and the hallway needs to be washed again, and I'd really much rather sleep in my own bed tonight. And there's the caern. Kinfolk can't guard it. Something bad's already happened. We don't need to court it."

She looked upset when he mentioned the caern. "I've told Anson; now I'll tell you: That was a Visions caern, and it's dead now. It's already showed its Gift to somebody and it's moved on. I think it's time for you to do the same."

"If it's dead, then why does it still show up in the Umbra?"

"It was a powerful caern, Peter. That's leftover energy you're seein' — like the dot on a TV screen when you turn the set off. You may see that dot, but the television's off. Don't believe it's anything more just 'cause Anson told you to. You're a Silver Fang, just like he was, so sometimes you get an idea into your head; but you're a Ragabash too, the Trickster, the Questioner of the Ways, and there's a lot of power in that. Believe in your moon, 'cause it lets you look at things a little off-skew from the rest of us. You can see things lots of us can't, and that's a good thing.

"So go on for now. If you want to come back, come back, and if you want to stay, stay. But don't stay there alone. I can see Harano in your eyes, Peter, like you were ready to put it all down and walk away. You could be startin' a spiral dance of your own right now and not know and not care. I don't want you goin' that way." And she hugged him, then walked away.

• • •

Rivard sat at the computer at the foot of his bed, mostly dry by now, his hair only sending occasional trickles of water down his body. Mahalik and his hair had burst into full-blown allegory in the shower, and Act One was nearly complete, a fact that would make Rivard's agent ecstatic. But the drive was wearing off now, the pauses getting longer, the spasms of typing getting shorter. The bracelet of mirrors on his left wrist was no longer bouncing light onto the walls quite so crazily. He was starting to realize he was chilly. And he was finally noticing that there was an odd sound in the room, like too many people trying to keep quiet. He turned in his chair.

The bed was alive with spiders. More were coming in: from the windows, the heating vents, the ceiling light. Fairy tendrils hung from the ceiling from which so many of them had lowered themselves. Dozens more were dropping. It was a vision from a nightmare. Rivard turned back to the computer and finished Act One.

When he finally sighed and stretched, a woman said from the bed, "I wouldn't eat Jana, Peter. You know that."

"Yes, but it made for a good scene." He turned to her, a tall, slim-limbed woman with skin a rich, deep brown.

She smiled. "Yes, Peter, you are always writing, even when you are not. Perhaps especially when you are not."

"Well, what do you think?"

"About the play? You know I don't read over your shoulder." She smiled again, and it seemed to contain secrets.

"Mahalik. Quintana."

"That he is serious in his desire to purchase this building? Need you ask? That he is an agent of the All-Slayer? Perhaps. That he would taste delicious? Assuredly."

"Zakiya, you have a way of cutting to the heart of a thing."

"Of course. That's the best part."

"I can't let him do it."

"Of course you can." He looked up at her sharply. "Do not confuse choice with ability. You can't fly. You choose not to leap from tall buildings."

"Are you suggesting I jump?"

"I only suggest that a precipice is to be either crossed or turned away from."

"Yes or no would be fine, just this once."

She smiled. "And what else have you found to be so simple? Explaining to Ms. Polokowski, or even your brother, who lives with you, the nature of the caern in the basement and the werespider who lives there? Explaining to yourself why you are still here in this apartment house 25 years later? What would your dead say, Peter? Would they say, well done?" Rivard just stared at her. "Happy Halloween, Peter." And she stood up and walked out. Rivard looked after her for a few moments longer, then turned back to the screen and began typing, "Act Two."

• • •

"Did you know the Golden Gate was fogbound?" Rivard asked.

"That's not the subject at hand, Peter," Tim Rowantree, still the Arm of the Goddess through these years after Anson's death, said uncompromisingly. "If you weren't the best I've ever seen you. . . but what were you thinking? An Ananasi?! Here?"

Another Garou, in Crinos form, stood shaking his head and looking at Zakiya, who sat quietly on a stump, her hands in her lap, trying not to appear threatening to any of the five guardians around her. "You know, Rivard," he said, "whether they believe you or not, you've set this place humming. They won't forget this. Two Kinfolk, a metis and a Wyrm-serving werespider, and you call it a pack. Damn, you're outrageous. I don't know if you're getting out of this one alive." His hands kept moving toward the silver Klaive in its scabbard at his back, and Rivard saw him keep from drawing it with an effort. Able Heart was Warder of the Sept of the Western Eye, and his duty was to protect it from any threat. Kinfolk were hard enough to judge, but the Ananasi had served the Wyrm long and faithfully. That they did this only under threat of the death of their queen meant little to the Garou. Noble intentions were all well and good, but one's actions spoke far more loudly. The Ananasi had quite a bit to answer for.

Now, so did Rivard.

At home, one of his tenants was passing out the Wyrm-free Halloween candy he'd asked her to once he realized he wouldn't be able to do it himself. He hadn't told his brother Thom until long after Mahalik's visit, but it seemed so easy, so right when he did. He'd told what he could of Anson and his notebooks, the caern, of Zakiya and how she had earned his trust — helping him hunt down the Leeches who had killed his pack. Of course, Thom had wanted to see her shapeshift, but she hadn't taken more than her Lilian form, gaunt and over seven feet tall, with true black skin, four arms, and yellow eyes that seemed to cover half her face, before he said, "Okay, maybe not all at once." That prompted him to tell Jana a bit more gently, but she'd merely said, "Thanks for telling me, Pete," and hugged him, then disappeared back into her apartment and, he'd thought, to bed. But he'd found out from Zakiya only that afternoon that she'd gone into the basement then, to see the caern, which to her looked like an old firepit, a ring of stones scarred and blackened with use. It wasn't until she'd knelt close that she'd been able to see the scars were patterns and symbols. Then she'd searched out Zakiya. They talked, and it was a few minutes before Zakiya realized that everything the other woman was saying came down to what Zakiya intended for Rivard.

"If that was ill, what could you do? I am of the Changing Breed, Ms. Polokowski."

"I'd do whatever I have to. He's hurt enough."

"You would die."

"Looks like I'm not, right now. To me, that says a lot."

Zakiya had smiled. "Peter chooses his friends well, doesn't he?" They talked most of the night, and by the time they went to bed with the sunrise, Jana Polokowski had ridden the back of a spider the size of a small car and Zakiya had found a second true friend.

Rivard had felt the weight of Anson's legacy slipping from him as Zakiya told him this as he stood in the foyer holding two plastic grocery bags full of Halloween candy. Just then he'd seen Stephanie coming down the stairs from the apartment she shared and asked her if she could take Halloween duty as he'd just realized he'd have to leave. She said yes, he told Zakiya to stay put, and rounded up Jana, Bent Claw, and Thom. He'd told them, "We don't have enough Garou here, or enough power in the caern to actually form this pack. I want to go to the Sept of the Western Eye and be recognized."

Bent Claw had panicked. "Let's think about this, Mr. Rivard. If we go into that sept with an Ananasi, you and I'll be Shunned for sure, maybe even killed, and she sure will be."

"We'll convince them," Rivard had said. "Celeste will understand; and we can talk to Able Heart. He of all people knows that sometimes a person is worth a little more care and patience." He'd turned to Jana and Thom. "In cases where a human has been possessed by a Bane of the Wyrm, the Garou usually kill the victim. Able Heart has driven the Bane away with herbs and compassion. It's time for all Garou to use a little wisdom and compassion — something a little outside the scribed circle of their ways." They had gone.

And that was the argument he'd presented to the elders of the sept when they'd eventually arrived, standing under the redwoods in the light of the full moon, the Trickster moon, on Halloween, the celebration of tricks and the dead. The panic and anger caused by the pack's arrival transformed into confusion, caution, and annoyance, and the elders went off to deliberate. Having had their says and canceling each other out, Rowantree and Able Heart had returned to watch the group personally. Rivard didn't doubt the outcome and so spoke of the unusual fog on the bridge, Rowantree's ponytail, the fact that his least favorite play to write had been the popular favorite. He tried to ease Polokowski and Bent Claw's minds and save his brother's from boredom. And he was just beginning to talk to Zakiya when he realized Celeste Snowtop was standing behind him. He straightened and faced her. They all did.

She looked into Rivard's eyes for a moment longer. "You finally seem happy. I hope it lasts. Respect the Unicorn; she respects you. I have to admit, this isn't what I expected from you. But I guess that's the point. Trickster moon, huh." She fell silent then, and the guardians moved away from Zakiya, who moved to one side of Rivard as Polokowski moved to the other. Bent Claw and Thom bracketed them. Able Heart, not quite smiling, crossed his arms over his broad chest, while Rowantree stared sullenly. "Thank you, Celeste," Rivard said.

"Probably not for long. There's a lot of Garou out there. Most of 'em won't be too happy to see the bunch of you comin'. Even the ones here are calling you 'Wyrm-tempter.' But maybe you've got a thing or two to show 'em." She smiled. "Maybe.

"Now get on home." ///

Lexicon

The following is a brief lexicon of terms in broad use among the Garou. Garou have taken words from many different sources, and an etymological study of their language would unearth a veritable babel of tongues. However, any attempt to understand Garou and their culture must begin with the peculiar language they have created and with which they define themselves.

Besides their own language, Garou can also communicate with wolves or speak any human language they know.

Common Parlance

These words are in common use among the Garou.

Anchorhead: A spirit gate between the Near and Deep Umbras. (See *Membrane*.)

Apocalypse: The age of destruction, the final cycle, the birth of death, the everlasting corruption, the end of Gaia — a word used in Garou mythology to describe the time of the final battle with the Wyrm. Many consider this time to be the present.

Auspice: The phase of the moon under which a particular Garou was born; commonly thought to determine personality and tendencies. The auspices are: Ragabash (New Moon; Trickster), Theurge (Crescent Moon; Seer), Philodox (Half Moon; Judge), Galliard (Gibbous Moon; Moon Dancer), Ahroun (Full Moon; Warrior).

Bane: Evil spirits that follow the Wyrm. There are many different kinds of Banes: Scrag, Kalus, Psychomachiae and more.

Bawn: A boundary area around a caern, where mortals are watched.

Blight: Any corrupted area in either the spirit world or physical reality.

Breed: The ancestry of a Garou, be it wolf, human or other Garou.

Caern: A sacred place; a meeting spot where the Garou can contact the spirit world.

Celestine: The greatest spirits; the closest things the Garou have to gods. Examples are Luna (the Moon) and Helios (the Sun).

Concolation: A great moot, wherein many tribes gather to discuss matters that concern the Nation of Garou.

Concord, The: The agreement all the tribes reached nearly 9,000 years ago, after which the Impergium was ended. The traditions thereof are still obeyed today.

Corruption: The act of destroying, devolving or debasing life; also, the often overwhelming effects of the Wyrm's actions. In the present age, it often specifically refers to the ecological ruin humans wreak upon the environment.

Crinos: The half-wolf, half-human form of the Garou.

Deep Umbra: The aspects of the Umbra that lie outside the Membrane. Reality becomes more and more fragmentary the farther one travels from the Realm.

Delirium: The madness suffered by humans who look upon a Garou in Crinos form.

Domain: A mini-Realm in the Umbra, usually connected to a larger Realm in the Deep Umbra.

Feral: Slang term for Lupus.

Gaffling: A simple spirit servant of a Jaggling, Incarna or Celestine. Gafflings are rarely sentient.

Gaia: The Earth and related Realms, in both a physical and a spiritual sense; the Mother Goddess.

Garou: The term werewolves use for themselves.

Gauntlet: The barrier between the physical world of Earth and the spirit world of the Umbra. It is strongest around technological (Weaver) places, weakest around caerns.

Hispo: The near-wolf form of the Garou.

Homid: A Garou of human ancestry. Occasionally used disdainfully by ferals (e.g., "That boy fights like a homid.").

Impergium: The 3,000 years immediately following the birth of agriculture, during which strict population quotas were maintained on all human villages.

Incarna: A class of spirits; weaker than the Celestines, but still greater spirits by any measure.

Jaggling: A spirit servant of an Incarna or Celestine.

Kenning: The empathic calling some Garou perform when howling.

Klaive: A fetish dagger or sword, usually of great spiritual potency and nearly always made of silver.

Litany: The code of laws kept by the Garou.

Lupus: A Garou of wolf origin.

Membrane, The: The barrier between the Near and Deep Umbras. To breach it, an Anchorhead must be found. Alternatively, the Garou can travel through the Dream Zone.

Metis: The sterile and often deformed offspring of two Garou. Generally reviled by Garou society.

Moon Bridge: A gate between two caerns; it most often appears during moots.

Moon-Calf: Idiot, simpleton.

Moot: A sept or tribal conclave that takes place at a caern.

Mule: Slang for metis.

Near Umbra: The spirit world surrounding the Gaia Realm.

Pack: A small group of Garou bound to each other by ties of friendship and mission as opposed to culture.

Penumbra: "Earth's Shadow"; the spirit world directly surrounding the physical world; many, but not all, terrain features will be the same.

Protectorate: The territory claimed and patrolled by a pack or sept.

Reaching: Traveling into the spirit world.

Realms: The worlds of "solid" reality within the Tellurian. Earth is referred to as the Realm.

Ronin: A Garou who has chosen or been forced to leave Garou society. It is a harsh fate to become a "lone wolf."

Sept: The group of Garou who live near and tend an individual caern.

Tellurian: The whole of reality.

Totem: A spirit joined to a pack or tribe and representative of its inner nature. A tribal totem is an Incarna, while a pack totem is an Incarna avatar (a Jaggling equivalent).

Triat, The: The Weaver, the Wyld and the Wyrm. The trinity of primal cosmic forces.

Tribe: The larger community of Garou. Tribe members are often bound by similar totems and lifestyles.

Umbra: The spirit world.

Veil, The: See *Delirium*.

Ways, The: The traditions of the Garou.

Weaver, The: Manifestation and symbol of order and pattern. Computers, science, logic and mathematics are examples of the Weaver's influence on the material plane.

Wyld, The: Manifestation and symbol of pure change. The chaos of transmutation and elemental force.

Wyrm, The: Manifestation and symbol of evil, entropy and decay in Garou belief. Vampires are often manifestations of the Wyrm, as are toxic waste and pollution.

Wyrmhole: A place that has been spiritually defiled by the Wyrm; invariably a location of great corruption.

Vulgar Argot

The younger Garou use these words to help distinguish themselves from their elders.

Ape: Slang for human or homid. If the speaker wishes to indicate true contempt for her subject, she may use the word "monkey" instead.

Cadaver: A derogatory term for a vampire.

Flock, The: All of humanity, particularly those humans from whom the Garou recruit their members.

Gremlin: A malevolent spirit.

Leech: See *Cadaver*.

Run: A ritual hunt or revel that takes place at the conclusion of a moot.

Sheep: Humans.

Stepping Sideways: Entering the spirit world. Most elders consider this term flippant and disrespectful.

Throat: To best another in ritual combat. Used as a verb (e.g., "I throated his sorry butt!").

Old Form

These words hail from the distant past of the Garou and display their Fianna origins. They are no longer used frequently. However, all Garou know these terms.

Adren: A pupil or a student who learns from a Mentor.

Airts: The magical paths within the spirit world (e.g., Spirit Tracks, Moon Paths, etc.).

Aisling: A journey into the spirit world.

Anamae: "Soul-friend"; most often a bond with a pack totem.

Anruth: A Garou who travels from caern to caern but is bound to none of them.

Athro: Teacher, Mentor.

Awen: The sacred Muse, the creative impulse. Some say she is a spirit, but she has never been found. Moon Dancers periodically go on quests for her.

Brugh: Any sort of mystic place, whether a Garou caern or a Wyrmhole. Often a glade or cave located somewhere in the wilderness.

Charach: A Garou who sleeps with another Garou or has done so in the past. Often used as a word of anger.

Chiminage: Traditionally, a sept can make a request of any Garou who uses its caern; "chiminage" is the term for the request.

Cliath: A young Garou, not yet of any standing rank.

Fomori: Humans who have turned to the Wyrm and draw their power from it. They are the enemies of the Garou.

Fostern: Your pack brothers and sisters; those who are your family by choice.

Gallain: The Kinfolk of the Garou — those humans and wolves who are related to the People and are not prone to Delirium, but who are not actual werewolves.

Harano: Inexplicable gloom, inexpressible longing for unnamable things, weeping for that which is not yet lost. Some say it is depression caused by contemplation of Gaia's suffering.

-ikthya: "Of the Wyrm"; a suffix appended to a name.

Inceptor: A Garou who guides another through a rite. An inceptor is also called a ritemaster.

Kinain: The relationship among Garou who are related by blood through an ancestor. This term of endearment and pride is never used when referring to metis.

Pericarp: The Near Umbra around each Realm.

Phoebe: An Incarna of Luna, representing the Moon.

Praenomen: The guardian spirit of a pack.

-rhya: "Greater in station"; a suffix appended to a name.

Urrah: Garou who live in the city; also, the tainted ones.

-yuf: "Honored equal"; a suffix appended to a name.

Tales from the Pack

Due to popular demand, White Wolf is releasing a line of fiction novels set in the desperate and dangerous World of Darkness. Not only do these tales of terror and tragedy offer new insight into a different world, but they may be integrated into your Chronicle, adding color and depth to the stories you tell.

These first three anthologies introduce characters both within and around the city of San Francisco. The first, devoted to VAMPIRE, includes stories by recognized vampire authors such as S.P. Somtow (author of *Vampire Junction* and *Valentine*). The second book is a collection of WEREWOLF tales that will explore the Bay Area beyond the urban setting of San Francisco. The third in the series is one of the first forays into the world of MAGE, exploring that game's strange realm of wizards and modern magick.
Look for these anthologies in game and book stores near you.

THE BEAST WITHIN (11001) $4.99 1-56504-086-4
No place in the world of vampires is quite like San Francisco. It's a melting pot set outside the always arcane and dangerous dynamics of Kindred politics. But because of San Francisco's position as a neutral territory, countless plots and mad plans are dreamt in and executed from The City. Herein are the beginnings and players for some of those unspeakable schemes.

TRUTH UNTIL PARADOX (11003) $4.99 1-56504-088-0
Dire portents loom for San Francisco. The recent earthquake (in *The Beast Within*) may not have been an entirely natural phenomena. Mages, the subject of MAGE: THE ASCENSION, who know what's going on have gathered to take advantage of the situation. Those who don't comprehend arrive to investigate.

MORE ANTHOLOGIES
Beginning in March 1994, White Wolf will also release anthologies of high quality fiction not related to the World of Darkness. The first such anthologies are titled *Borderlands*, a series *Locus* has said is "very much the dark fantasy series to follow." *Borderlands 3* will be printed for the first time as a mass market paperback in

March. Edited by Tom Monteleone, it includes stories by Andrew Vachss, Poppy Z. Brite, Kathe Koja, Whitley Strieber, and others.

New paperback editions of *Borderlands* and *Borderlands 2* appear in May. These anthologies feature stories by Harlan Ellison, Karl Edward Wagner, Joe R. Lansdale, F. Paul Wilson and many other notable authors.

Borderlands 4 is scheduled for publication in September.

BORDERLANDS (11801) $4.99 1-56504-107-0
BORDERLANDS 2 (11802) $4.99 1-56504-108-9
BORDERLANDS 3 (11803) $4.99 1-56504-109-7
BORDERLANDS 4 (11804) $4.99 1-56504-110-0

All edited by Tom Monteleone.

White Wolf Signs Michael Moorcock

White Wolf has signed a deal with Michael Moorcock to become his premier North American publisher. Staple products such as the Elric saga, the Chronicles of Corum, and the Hawkmoon Runestaff series will be reprinted. This particular fiction deal will be published and distributed by White Wolf.

White Wolf will also release an Elric anthology of original stories in late fall of this year, including works by Moorcock himself and Neil Gaiman.